Anytime

Sarah Sprinz was born in 1996. After studying medicine in Aachen, she returned to her hometown by Lake Constance in southern Germany. When she's not writing, Sarah finds inspiration for new stories during long walks along the lake shore and enjoys planning her next trips to Canada and Scotland.

ALSO BY SARAH SPRINZ

Anywhere
Anyone

Dunbridge Academy: Book 3

Anytime

SARAH SPRINZ

Translated by Rachel Ward

QUERCUS

First published in Germany in 2022 by LYX, an imprint of Bastei Lübbe
First published in Great Britain in 2025 by

QUERCUS

Quercus Editions Limited
Carmelite House
50 Victoria Embankment
London EC4Y 0DZ

An Hachette UK company

The authorized representative in the EEA is Hachette Ireland, 8 Castlecourt Centre,
Castleknock Road, Castleknock, Dublin 15, D15 YF6A, Ireland (email: info@hbgi.ie)

A CIP catalogue record for this book is available
from the British Library

PB ISBN 978 1 52943 165 0
EBOOK ISBN 978 1 52943 166 7

1

Typeset in 10.5/16pt Swift Neue LT Pro Regular by Jouve (UK), Milton Keynes
Printed and bound in Great Britain by Clays Ltd, Elcograf S.p.A.

Papers used by Quercus are from well-managed forests and other responsible sources.

Dear Readers,

Because this book contains elements that could be triggering, you will find a trigger warning on page 465. We hope that you will enjoy the book!

Happy reading, from
Sarah and the team at Quercus

For everyone who feels
as though they're in flames.

*Hell is empty
and all the devils are here.*

William Shakespeare

Playlist

all for us – labrinth feat. zendaya
bang! – ajr
after dark – mr kitty
sick boy – the chainsmokers
colors – halsey
two nights – javailin
the hills – the weekend
animals – maroon 5
war – brandeus feat. shiloh dynasty
she looks so perfect – 5 seconds of summer
pretty venom (interlude) – all time low
beside you – 5 seconds of summer
when i don't have you – idarose
new americana – halsey
ever since new york – harry styles
mum – luke hemmings
the beach – the neighbourhood
you broke me first – tate mcrae
angel by the wings – sia
complete mess – 5 seconds of summer
home – one direction
to build a home – the cinematic orchestra & patrick watson

Anytime

COLIN

It's a tiny flame but it eats into my skin.

Heat. Pain. Relief. Don't flinch.

Fuck.

Don't.

Flinch.

I shut my eyes, lean my head back against the cold tiles behind me and don't pull the lighter away.

If you walk out that door now, Colin Fantino, don't bother coming back. My mom's voice echoes in my head.

Fuck you. Fuck all of you. Seriously.

It's fucking Homecoming. No way am I staying home just because of a crappy party last night that got a bit out of hand. I mean, I'm seventeen, for God's sake. I'm *supposed* to be pulling crazy shit at this age, aren't I? I didn't get to pick my last

1

name, and don't give a damn what impact my behaviour might have on my mom's fucking reputation.

I don't want you spending another second with the Carnegie crowd. They're a bad influence on you.

I pull back for a moment as the flame gets too hot.

Loser. Letting your parents push you around, tell you what to do.

So what if they threaten me with boarding school in Europe and cutting off my trust fund. I don't give a shit.

I inhale sharply as the pain becomes unbearable.

Hang in there, you fuck. C'mon, you wuss. Better to feel this than wallow in self-pity.

I pull up my pants leg a little to get to the inside of my ankle. It's a risky spot because you can get a better view of the thin, striped burns than when they're on the inside of my thigh. But I used up that whole space the day before yesterday. Stupid of me, I should've pulled myself together, but Mom was being un-fucking-bearable. Everything was unbearable. Standing beside her at that event, smiling like I'm supposed to. The only times when Ava Fantino can spare me more than a contemptuous glare because the whole world is watching and she has to keep up appearances. I always thought I could improve our relationship if I tried harder. At school, at home, with Cleo, my kid sister who doesn't get the same treatment as me, but things didn't get any better. I'm not the son that Ava and Eric Fantino wanted, so I've stopped even trying to live up to their expectations.

I jump as the door flies open and I hear voices.

Fuck.

I thought there was no way anyone would come over to the gym bathrooms right now, at the glittering height of the Homecoming Ball in the auditorium. Guess I was wrong.

I jump up. The lighter slips through my fingers and clatters to the floor. Right next to a couple sheets of toilet paper that are stuck to the dirty tiles near the trash. I stifle a curse as they catch fire.

'Hey, I think there's someone here.'

Shit. I pick up the lighter and stamp out the flames. Just in time, before Trent Barlow and his buddies come around the corner. Totally wasted, obviously. Trent's eyes narrow to slits as he spots me.

'Beat it, Fantino,' he says.

I'd love to punch the fat blunt right out of his lips, then smack him in the mouth. Nobody tells me where to go, or orders me around. But Trent Barlow doesn't get that, and I'm dying to teach him another lesson. Even so, one last glimmer of sense within me says it'd be better to get out of here before Trent starts asking what I've been doing. I kick the charred tissue under the sinks and pray they don't smell burning.

I stroll past Trent. 'Fuck you,' I say, keeping my voice bored. In the mirror, I see them glance at each other, then Trent leans against the tiled wall. He frowns slightly as he pats his pants pockets.

'Shit, got a light?' He looks up, and my blood runs cold.

Like there's some law against carrying a lighter. *God, Fantino, chill. You did nothing wrong.*

I say, 'No,' all the same, though.

'Ah, c'mon, man, I can smell it on you.' Trent's eyes are mocking.

Fine, he noticed. So I guess it's now the lesser evil to act like I've been smoking here too. I reach into my jacket pocket and feel the warm metal of the lighter. Trent nods briefly as I give him a light and he takes his first drag.

'And tell your bitch of a mother that I'll fuck her up if she says another bad word about Nadia.'

I freeze. It's rare for me to stick up for Ava Fantino, but whether or not we're fighting, nobody talks about my family like that. *Nobody.* Even though I loathe the way my mom's been slut-shaming Nadia Barlow and her influencer friends on her show for the way they've gotten their claws into one eligible New York bachelor after another. Pointless to discuss it with Mom, though, seeing that even after the social media shit-storm her words kicked up, she didn't show the one ounce of regret or sympathy that anyone with even basic media training ought to possess. Not my mother, though. She's Ava Fantino, the queen of light TV, and she can do whatever the hell she likes, on or off camera. *People out there switch on to forget the world for a moment and have something to laugh at, not a lecture from me on wokeness, Colin.* Maybe, but if Ava Fantino keeps up this way, she's in serious danger of getting cancelled by our *sissy* generation.

4

I take a step towards him, hating myself for the fact that, despite everything, I feel I have to defend my family's honour against him. 'Seriously, man, was that a threat?'

'I dunno,' he says, blowing smoke in my face. I clench my fist around my lighter and have to stop myself throwing a punch. 'Was it?'

'Talk shit about my family one more time and you'll regret it.'

'Tell your mom the same from me.'

'I can't help it if your sister will sleep with anyone.' *Wow, way to go, Colin.* So I'm no better than my mom. The disconnect between my ideals, words and actions is making me sick. I walk through life that way. And then I'm surprised when it kicks me in the balls, but it's all I know. I don't even flinch as Trent takes a threatening step towards me. 'But, hey, you know she doesn't mean the stuff she says on her show,' I add. His loser friends hold him back as he goes to lunge at me like the Neanderthal he is. I lift my hand and salute him. 'Enjoy the party, Trent.'

'He's not worth it, man,' I hear, as I step out of the bathroom into the corridor, and I have to agree with his buddies. I'm not worth it, I'm worthless, no need to tell me that. I've internalized it. My pulse is racing with fury. And because they almost caught me self-harming. I've gotta be more careful. No more lighter shit in public places. I've gotten careless lately. Probably cos I'm doing it nearly every day now. Whenever the pressure gets to be too much. Which is more or less all the time. But if my mom hears about it, I'll be on some shrink's couch sooner than you can blink and, God, I don't need anyone telling me I need to quit it. Like I don't know that myself.

My footsteps echo in the dark corridor. As I head outside, I pass couples making out and groups smoking. Same old, same old at Ainslee. Parents blow fortunes on this fancy private school so their kids can get beat up same as in any public high school in the country. The only difference between my school days here and my friends' at Carnegie is the small class sizes. The rest of the bullshit is the same. It is what it is. You're just a cog in the machine, and if you don't function, it gets painful.

Nobody notices me as I cross the yard. Then I meet Lexie, from my Spanish class, who gets me chatting with her friends. Once she's glanced three times at my mouth and bitten her own lips, I know she wants to go home with me. But I'm not in the mood. Besides, I'm hoping that Pax will finally get back to me and bring Maresa along. I hate that I'm thinking about her. And I hate that the one-time thing with her turned into a three-time thing, and that I'm fantasizing about number four. And about whether it could turn into something more. Shit, I'm seriously screwed. And I'm sick of always being the one who gets feelings first. All down to my messed-up childhood – I don't need a therapist to tell me that. So I don't let myself feel them. The emotions. Anyway, we talked about it, Maresa and me. No commitments. Just a bit of fun. We're handling this like adults. My cell phone buzzes.

P: Still at your lame party? Can we come get you yet?

I glance around. Fellow students everywhere, chatting, laughing. Seriously, what is there for me here?

I only hesitate a moment before I type.

'You leaving?' Lexie asks, with that mind-numbing singsong in her cotton-candy voice.

'Maybe,' I mumble, not looking at her.

'Can I come?'

Seriously? I'm not one to talk, but how desperate can you get? Luckily, I don't have to answer her because the voices around us get louder. Actually, not luckily. Now I see it.

The flames and the smoke rising into the night sky.

'Where's that coming from?' someone yells.

My blood runs ice-cold.

Shit.

I can't stop thinking about the burning toilet tissue. Was it definitely out? I should have looked again before I left. It was right next to the trash can. Which was full. Fuck.

The others are paralysed, staring at the building. I turn away. My legs and hand move automatically. I dial a number I've never dialled before. It takes seconds for someone at the other end to answer.

'Nine one one, what's your emergency?'

Breathe.

Shit. Shit . . .

'Fire,' I gasp. 'On the corner of 90th and Columbus. Ainslee School, I think.'

'OK,' says the man. He's calm, they probably get special

training. I'm not calm. I feel like the world's stopped turning. 'The fire department is on the way. Please stay on the line and keep away from the building. Can you tell if anyone is hurt?'

My heart is hammering in my ribs, and there's a crackling in my ears as I turn. Silhouettes in long ballgowns and perfectly fitted suits. Students with something to celebrate. 'No, I . . . I dunno.'

'What's your name, sir?'

Oh, God . . . Tell him. You can't deny it. Just do the right thing. Just for once, do the right thing.

'Sir? Are you still . . .?'

Panic breaks over me like a wave of icy water.

I hang up, take three steps backwards. I turn away and start to run.

1

OLIVE

'Take it slowly, pet.'

I bite back the snappy answer that's on the tip of my tongue and force myself to take a deep breath. It's costing every last scrap of my self-control to ignore the sharp stabbing in my right shoulder. It brings the tears to my eyes – annoyingly, I only took my last painkillers a couple of minutes ago. They don't kick in right away and I had no way of knowing that Mum and Dad would get here so soon, be standing in my room ready to take me home from hospital. I've been here weeks, which seems like a lifetime, and now everything's going too fast.

'Let me take that,' says Mum, reaching for my bag. There are a few clothes, some wash stuff, books and cushions, mostly brand new because I couldn't stand the smell of smoke ingrained in the things they were able to save from my room after the fire at Dunbridge Academy in early July. The flames didn't reach the girls' bedrooms on the third floor of the west wing, but the fire raged in the stairwell and almost completely destroyed the lower half of the building. Nobody could tell how bad the damage was for several days. Not till the police and insurance experts combed through the charred remains and collapsed beams – by which time I was in intensive care. It's not like I knew anything about it. Why would I? Almost two weeks intubated on a ventilator, because if I'd been awake, the pain from the burns would have driven me insane. It was still unbearable when they eventually brought me round. It still is, especially around my right shoulder where they had to do a graft, covering it with skin from my thigh so that the wounds could heal. Expressions like 'autologous', 'split-thickness' and 'mesh graft' are part of my everyday vocabulary, because this is my life now. And I hate it.

'I'll help you, pet,' says Dad, the moment we're outside and I'm reaching for the handle on the back door of his car. He opens it for me, like I hadn't spent weeks in physio, relearning every stupid movement, and continually failing at the easiest tasks. Standing up for a while. Putting on a T-shirt. Doing my hair in a ponytail, for fuck's sake, like I did every time I walked from the school to the pool, but I won't be doing that again any time soon, won't be training again in the near future. I'm not being pathetic or melodramatic. The doctors said so, repeatedly, when I couldn't take it in, and, yeah, they're just as insensitive as people say. Dad's the exception, maybe.

I can do it myself. I don't need your help. It's hard not to say the words. But it's more than I can manage to say 'Thank you' to him instead, as I slip onto the back seat. I avoid his eyes, and after a moment, he shuts the door. Our gaze meets again in the rear-view mirror as he glances at me once he's sat in the driver's seat, next to Mum.

My parents don't deserve my rage. What happened isn't their fault. It's nobody's fault. Except for the bastards who were smoking in the Dungeon on that July night. During their investigations, the police found a cigarette stub in what remained of the upper sixth's party cellar. Dozens of people were there but apparently nobody saw a thing. They've closed the case now. Accident, not arson. A tragedy, a misfortune. But the good luck amid the bad is that nobody died. Apart from my dreams but, hey, I'm supposed to be grateful.

You were seriously lucky. If that burning beam had fallen just a tiny bit differently, it wouldn't just have caught my shoulder: it would most probably have killed me. And maybe I'd have been better off if it had, but saying that out loud would just make Mum and Dad do a U-turn and deliver me straight back to the hospital. So I sit in silence in our car, with my silent parents, who are getting a divorce. It's just a matter of time: Mum with her guilty conscience over the affair I caught her out in months ago in Ebrington, Dad still with no clue. I want to cry but I can't. I'm here, I survived.

I will keep on surviving. It's not even that hard if you just get a fucking grip.

Come on, Olive. Keep it cold, live up to your reputation. Be your old self. Except I'm not my old self. Everything's changed.

Don't forget your friends. Don't forget that you finally get to see them again tomorrow. At school, not in hospital, where they all came to visit as soon as I was well enough. They couldn't come so often once term started, though, and I get that. They're in the upper sixth now. Without me.

Damn tears. I blink.

'Are you OK, darling?'

'Yes.' I gulp and lean back on the headrest. Dad's heading for Stockbridge, our part of Edinburgh. I feel it every single time he glances at me in the mirror. He doesn't believe me. Because he knows me.

Nothing is OK. I'm tired, knackered actually, I'm in pain, and there's so much rage inside me that I want to scream. The anger was there even before the summer, but for different reasons. It's been almost a year now. Since everything's been going downhill and I've been feeling like I've lost control of my life.

Why did it happen to me? Why did I have to be the one who headed back to school early on that shitty July night? Why didn't I say, 'Fuck getting eight hours' sleep,' ahead of the swimming meet the next day and spend the evening with my friends at the summer festival in Ebrington? All for a bloody competition I didn't even take part in because I was in a coma, hooked up to the machines in intensive care.

That was nine weeks ago, and at first nobody was certain that I'd ever wake up again. It wasn't just my lungs that were damaged by the heat of the fire and the toxic soot, a burning beam fell on me on the stairs, long after I'd blacked out. The biting smoke, my racing heart as I ran for my life down the west-wing stairs. I can't remember exactly where I lost consciousness. I only remember how incredibly loud the flames were. And how dark it was. Black, hot, panic, panic, panic. And then, what felt like just seconds later, white, beeping, pain. Hospital. Still panic, panic, panic. The same fucking panic even now, like my brain can't grasp that I'm safe. That it was bad but I'm apparently made to survive bad stuff. What choice do I have?

Lucky. I was lucky. I have to tell myself so again and again. What an incredible stroke of luck that I was the only person to get so seriously injured in the fire. Not that I'd wish it on anyone else. Not even my worst enemies. Not, incidentally, that I have any. Not even my mother and the man who decided to smash up our family with her. I wouldn't wish a thing like this even on them. Not on anybody. But I wouldn't wish it on myself either.

Unfortunately, what you wish for and what you get are two very different things. Everyone on my floor had gone down to the festival in Ebrington. It wasn't so far for the younger kids on the ground floor and the first floor to get out, away from the flames. The stairs were empty as I ran down towards the flames, through the smoke, which was already so thick

I couldn't breathe, even holding my pyjama sleeve over my mouth.

I jump as Dad brakes sharply, swearing under his breath. The seatbelt cuts into my shoulder. I grit my teeth with pain but don't make a sound. Dad has to believe I'm fine. Otherwise I can forget our deal. It took hours of arguing and tears of desperation before he and Mum finally agreed that I can do the rest of my physio as an outpatient and go back to school next week.

It's bad enough that Dad can hardly look at me. He's really trying to hide it behind his professionalism, but whenever he's with me, it's totally obvious. My own father, a doctor, can't bear to see me like this. Even though it's his vocation to help the sick. That clearly doesn't apply to his daughter, and I'm not naïve enough to think it's because I don't matter to him. Quite the contrary, and that's the whole problem. Mum and I are everything to him. My dad's a loving man and the fear of losing me almost destroyed him. I know that. Mum knows that.

Livy, sweetie, promise me. Her piercing eyes, her hands on my arms when she caught up with me in Ebrington that time, months before the fire, back when I didn't know what real problems were. Looking around frantically, low voice, still speaking. *Promise me that you won't tell your father. It would break his heart, Olive.*

We're approaching our house. Mum glances over her shoulder to me. I immediately look away. The sight of our drive and the façade of the three-storey townhouse in dark stone doesn't exactly help. I've never spent less time here than in the last few months. And that's saying something, given that I'm at boarding school and only home for occasional weekends in term-time.

I feel like an intruder into the marriage of convenience that used to be my family. Dad's carrying my stuff; Mum's eyes are just as laden with expectation. *You won't say anything, will you, my darling?* I can see it on her face. Every single time I've looked at her since that evening over a year ago. But I can't worry about it now.

I step into the porch. It smells the same as ever. Coffee, old leather and the citrussy air fresheners Mum puts everywhere. I stand on the step to take my shoes off and feel like a failure because my body's telling me it's going to keel over in the next forty-five seconds if I don't sit down. I, Olive Mary Henderson, can't even manage to take off my shoes standing up. I didn't know it was possible to despise yourself this much, but it really is.

Later, eating dinner with Mum and Dad, I feel like I'm on the outside looking in. I still hardly have any appetite, but I've got just about enough sense to finish up my plate of rice and vegetables. I'll never regain my old fitness if I don't eat enough. I didn't have many reserves to start with and my time in intensive care has used them all up. The muscles built up from swimming and regular weight training – gone without a trace. My body's like jelly, and even the bloody bowl is cracked. Everything's so knackering.

'Is it OK to go straight up to my room?' I ask after dinner, because the fatigue is suddenly pulling at me. I long ago gave up being angry about going to bed when primary-school kids are still watching TV. I have to give myself time. Isn't that what everyone keeps telling me?

I stand up. Dad hesitates. I should have known earlier, when he glanced at Mum. I sit down again.

'We'd like to talk to you about something,' he says slowly.

I don't move. I manage to say, 'OK,' but it sounds more like a question.

'We understand that you're longing to get back to school, Olive.'

'Back to normal life,' I correct him. Normality. Everyday life, far from cheerless hospital rooms and constantly stressed-out doctors, who look at my shoulder, ask if I've had a bowel movement, as if I wasn't a seventeen-year-old girl – i.e. someone embarrassed by their entire life at the best of times – then hurry on to the next room without even looking me in the face.

'We know that, love,' says Mum, glancing briefly at Dad. 'And we want to make that possible for you.'

'We spoke to Mrs Sinclair last week,' he goes on. Hold on. Why didn't I know about this? 'She's happy that you want to go back so soon, but she's also very concerned about you and your health. As we all are.'

I nod, holding on to my self-control. 'But you'll be there to keep an eye on me,' I say. Two mornings a week, at least. And any time Dad isn't scheduled to be at Dunbridge as the school doctor, Nurse Petra will be there in the sick bay. It's virtually the same as the hospital. I don't need twenty-four/seven care: I need a glimmer of hope.

'Yes, I will,' he agrees seriously. He folds his hands over his lips. 'Olive, your mum and I agree with Mrs Sinclair that it will be better for you to repeat the lower sixth.'

'What?' I laugh. I really laugh. Then my face freezes. Mum and Dad are looking at me in silence. 'That . . . You can't mean that.'

'It's the only way you can—'

'The lower sixth?' I interrupt Mum. 'But they can't just leave me behind! What about my friends?'

'We know you found last year a struggle, Olive. It's a big step up to A levels and you only just scraped through your exams.'

We may be in Scotland, but at Dunbridge we do A levels, four or five courses in the lower sixth, dropping to three for our final year. So she's got a point. Not that I'm admitting to it. No way.

'Yes, but Mrs Sinclair and all my teachers had faith that I could do it. She said so!' My heart is starting to race, I'm raising my voice, starting to shout as I realize that Mum and Dad aren't here for a discussion. They're informing me of a decision they've made for me, as if I'd asked them to.

'We know that, Olive,' Dad says calmly. 'And we're not making this decision lightly. But that was before the fire. The new term has already started, and you know you've got to switch from A-level PE to Spanish – there's a lot of catching up to do there. The upper sixth is stressful enough as it is, and you can't just cram in a whole year's worth of Spanish on top of that. It's just not feasible.'

Not in the state you're in.

Not while you're still so weak, still having nightmares.

'You can't do this,' I yell. 'Mrs Sinclair said—'

'Olive, we're your parents. Until you're eighteen, we have to take responsibility for you.'

I jump up. My shoulder throbs, but I hardly notice the pain. It's nothing compared to the despair rising inside me.

'You can't do this,' I repeat, because my mind's a blank. Mum and Dad just sit there. The tears well up. 'But what about my friends?' My voice cracks. My friends in the upper sixth. Having this one last year with them before we're scattered to the winds was the only thing driving me on to make quick progress.

'They'll still be there, pet,' says Dad.

Mum says nothing, won't meet my eyes.

I shake my head and turn away. I can't let them see me cry. Not again. I bite my bottom lip; I straighten and walk tall. I don't cry until I get to my room.

2

OLIVE

'I want to be alone,' I snarl, as my bedroom door opens. My voice sounds gruff. I roll over to face the wall, not wanting Dad to see me like this. I'd have sworn he'd be the one to follow me upstairs. But just the firmness with which she shuts the door tells me that it's my mother sitting on the edge of my bed.

'Olive,' she says.

I wriggle when I feel her hand on my back. 'I'm tired.'

'Darling, please. I want to talk to you about something.'

I stare at the wall and don't move.

'I wanted to tell you that the business between Alexis and me is over.'

The realization that she didn't come up here to comfort me hits home with unexpected weight. She's here to reassure herself that I won't give her away. I could boak.

'You haven't said anything to your dad, have you?'

I shake my head automatically, then hate myself for it. The upside of fighting for your life in intensive care is that every problem you had before seems less important. But, sadly, they don't disappear by themselves just because you ignore them for a while. On the contrary. Afterwards, they seem bigger than ever.

'Dad deserves to know the truth, Mum,' I mutter.

'You don't understand, pet.'

'Stop that.' I turn to face her, to look at her. 'Stop saying that. You made a mistake, there's nothing to understand. You're cheating on him. And you know it.'

Panic fills my mother's face as I raise my voice with every sentence. She looks as though she wishes she could clamp a hand over my mouth.

'Olive,' she repeats, fighting to keep calm, 'you're right. It was a mistake, and one I regret bitterly. Listen, pet. You can't want this to break up our family.'

'No, leave me out of this! You did it. It's nothing to do with me. It's bad enough that you keep trying to guilt-trip me, make me cover for you.'

'I've never tried to make you cover for me.'

'Oh, no? So what was that when you ran after me to beg me not to say anything to Dad? What is this now? How am I meant to react when he looks at me like he does because he knows there's something I'm keeping from him?'

Mum eyes me coolly. 'I would very much appreciate it if

you didn't say anything to your father while I'm trying to rescue this family.'

The tears sting my eyes. 'We haven't been a family for ages, Mum,' I whisper.

She flinches. I'm not sorry. It's her fault. She and that stranger who doesn't give a fuck that he's destroying families. 'How can you say that?' she asks sharply.

'How could you do that?'

'Olive, when you're an adult, you'll understand that things aren't always as simple as you think now.'

'When I'm an adult, I hope I'll be a loyal woman, not someone who'd betray the people she means something to, just for a bit of fun,' I spit.

Mum looks at me and, in that moment, I understand she doesn't love Dad any more. Otherwise, there's no way she could stay this calm. 'I'm very sure you'll succeed in that, Olive.'

She stands up. I'm struggling to breathe.

They'll split up. I just know it. It feels like there's no other option. It's just a matter of time and I haven't the least idea how I'm meant to cope with it.

'Get some rest. It's been a long day,' Mum says, as she leaves my room.

Hate is a very strong word, in my opinion, but there's no better one to express what I'm feeling for my mother.

My chest is tight, and my heart is racing. I can't just lie there. I have to do something. But there's nothing I *can* do.

It's an unbearable feeling, but it's true. There's no way of resolving this situation and that's driving me crazy.

I don't know why I go to the door and open it. Downstairs, I hear Mum's footsteps followed by a quiet 'And?' from Dad.

'It was a big shock to her, but I've spoken to her.' Mum sighs. I clench my fists. 'I hoped she'd take it better.'

'She's seventeen, Meredith. Of course it's the end of the world.'

'Do you think we're doing the right thing, Neil?'

Silence.

'I think we are, love.'

3

COLIN

There's only one thing worse than sitting on a plane that's sending you directly into exile in Scotland, and that's sitting next to your mother on a plane that's sending you directly into exile in Scotland. But I guess I should be grateful that Ava Fantino didn't put me in shackles before having me transported across the Atlantic, and is only *accompanying* me. God knows what she's scared of. That I'll skip the flight to Heathrow and get a charter to the Bahamas instead? I consider myself pretty clever but even I would have a hard time doing that after my parents froze all my cards. But, fine, it is what it is. First stop London, then we get the next plane to the middle of nowhere.

There are hardly any direct flights from New York to Edinburgh and that tells you everything you need to know. Looks like Mom and Dad deliberately hunted out the most remote boarding school in the world.

We think a reset, some time away from home, would help you to redefine your goals and to get a grip on what really matters in life.

A reset. Seriously. I'm still laughing.

At least until things have blown over. I'll take care of the whole business. And you'll use this time, finally, to learn the meaning of respect.

I don't know what I expected. That it would be just talk, same as ever. That we'd fight it out around the kitchen table in our zillion-dollar penthouse because I've *crossed the line* and I'm digging my own grave, et cetera, et cetera. But this time they were dead serious. Froze my accounts, informed me that if I carry on like this, I could forget about accessing my trust fund when I turn twenty-one. I still feel like this isn't real life, just some stupid movie. Less than seventy-two hours after the gym at Ainslee Manhattan burned to the ground, Mom had gotten a place for me at Dunbridge Academy. Scotland. Europe. Thousands of miles from my whole life to this point. Still, I guess I can be glad that it's this school. The people there will speak something like my language. Or I assume so. The alternative would have been this mountain school up in the Swiss Alps or somewhere. The promo video on their website alone was enough – students in fancy uniforms, speaking French and German with the sun setting in the background.

So, Scotland. Crappy weather, even crappier food, ruined castles, sheep, total wilderness. But you can drink when you're sixteen so, hey, Europe has its advantages. Though

I doubt there are many parties at this school. I zoned out when they got to the ten p.m. curfew and the alcohol ban on the school premises. Sounds like hell, but I guess I deserve that. Not that I care. I'll be out of there sooner than Mom can turn around. If she's lucky, I'll be able to open the door to our Upper East Side apartment for her in person when she gets back from her business trip to London.

God, I'm bitter. No way I'm the kind of son Ava Fantino wished for. But, hey, she's not the kind of mother I'd wish for either. I didn't wish for any of this. I just want an easy life, back in New York, at another school, whatever. No way am I staying in Scotland. Just a few weeks and I'll be back. Fuck it, I promised Cleo. And now I have to think about something else: if I remember my kid sister in tears at the airport as I went through security, my own fucking eyes start watering. I've hardly slept for days. It was bad. I dreamed about buildings in flames, sirens, ambulances, flashing lights. About getting into Paxton's car and *partying* with them because I'm a goddamn monster. Yeah, I called the fire department, but I was too scared to wait for the cops and answer questions.

I turn up my music and stare motionless out the airplane window at the suburbs we're already descending over as 'All for Us' by Labrinth and Zendaya pounds in my ears. Until a couple weeks ago, I didn't even know where Edinburgh was. Why would I care? It's not the kind of city I think about when I think about Europe. London would have been slightly better but I'd have had too many distractions there, as Mom put it.

I glance over at her. She's sitting upright in the business-class seat beside me, not deigning to look at me. Her entire attention is focused on her iPhone, no doubt answering emails of earth-shattering importance, or cancelling vital meetings. I seriously wonder how she survived transatlantic flights back when there was no Wi-Fi on planes. I can't talk, though. The new season of *Euphoria* was all that got me through the last few hours. Sleep was impossible. My mind was circling too much. Has been since last week. Since I read the headlines. Since there's been no denying that I'm the worst person in the world, too chicken-shit even to take responsibility for my own actions. I don't know why I didn't go to the police but to Mom, who looked at me and nodded. She said she'd make a few calls and I shouldn't speak to anyone. How was I supposed to know that she'd also be getting me a place at boarding school to keep me out of the line of fire? I should have gone to the cops and confessed. Simple. I wanted to, once I realized what Mom and Dad were doing. Calling in every favour to clear my – and therefore their – name. Because that's all that ever matters. No way the press can ever hear that Ava Fantino's son is in the shit. For real this time. But I didn't even have to give evidence, unlike my classmates who were questioned by the police as witnesses after Homecoming. I've never felt as sick as I did when I saw their panicked messages in our group chat.

Since then, everything went so fast that I felt like I was watching from outside as I packed my suitcase and said good-bye to Dad and Cleo at the airport.

I couldn't read Mom's face as I gave my little sister one last hug. She clung to my hoodie, wouldn't let go. Not even when I whispered again and again that I'd be back soon. I'm sure of that. Mom and Dad can send me to a goddamn boarding school across the Atlantic to stop the truth coming out but I'm a world champion at breaking the rules. It's only a matter of time before I'm back in New York. And then . . . no clue. No way I can go back to Ainslee. But there are other private schools in Manhattan: Worthington, Burton, Atkinson . . . I'd have no problem with Carnegie or some public high school either. At least then I'd be with the people I call my friends, even if Mom and Dad see them as second-class citizens. My friends who thought I was kidding when I messaged them to say my parents were serious this time.

Mom looks up, so I quickly turn away. Can't let her think this fazes me. It was damn hard to hold my poker face the whole flight, though. Earlier, when we transferred in Heathrow, and I suddenly saw prices in pounds on the signs and heard unfamiliar British accents as people hurried past us, it was a shock, made it clear that this was really happening. That my dad wasn't making empty threats and that my mom is here in person to guarantee that I really get to this boarding school and don't take some shortcut right back to the States. To be honest, she's only doing it because she can combine it with a business trip to London. I think she's filming an ad for Tag Heuer and then with Chris Marchant, a colleague who had a talk show in LA for years. He was never as successful as my mother, or not until he came home to Britain recently to start over. But in the States, *Late Night with Ava Fantino* has been the number-one talk show for at least ten years now. There's not one A-lister that Mom hasn't had on as her guest. Musicians, actors, politicians, influencers – everyone seems to be just waiting for the accolade of an invitation from her.

A humourless smile plays around my lips: nobody has a clue what this woman's like off camera. The whole world admires Ava Fantino. A career woman with a quirky sense of humour, a beaming smile and a perfect family. But I see my mom on screen more often than I do at home. Dad's not much different, even though he has no taste for the media spotlight. He's just as busy as legal eagle to Mom and the rest of New York high society, covering their asses. And now mine. It's as gross as it sounds. Every time I heard the doorbell in the last few days my pulse shot up because I was expecting it to be the cops, coming to take me away, like I deserve. But I didn't speak to anyone, just got on the plane to England. I only read online articles and screaming headlines. Investigations. Potential arson. Electrical fault, accident, we'd know more soon.

I shut my eyes because I feel as nauseous as I did that night.

I stomped out the toilet tissue. It wasn't burning when I left the bathroom, I know it wasn't . . . But the fact is, the gym was on fire just a few moments later when I got outside and turned around. Flames lighting up the New York night sky, fire-engine sirens, people screaming. And I just ran away like a fucking coward.

I clench my fists and silently curse the airport security guy who confiscated my lighter back in New York. Obviously I know you can't have open flames on a plane but I thought you were allowed a lighter. The officer wasn't interested in a discussion about it, though, maybe because it's one of those windproof ones that can make a pretty big flame, and I didn't want to risk Mom hearing about it.

It's not so bad. Of course there's another in my checked baggage – and that really is against the rules. So I have to pray they haven't removed it, in which case I'll have to find some alternative. I guess I should be grateful I don't have anything on me. Scratching and cutting and all that shit really isn't my thing. But I don't know whether I'd control myself if I could take a lighter to the bathroom right now. Fuck, I've got a real problem, I know that, but I can't tell a soul. I haven't self-harmed since the Homecoming Ball. God knows how I've managed that. Maybe because I was too scared of getting caught. All I know is that the pressure is building and I've spent days feeling like a vent with someone's finger over it. It's only a matter of time until the next explosion.

The fresh air as we step out of Arrivals in Edinburgh helps a little, but as soon as I sit down next to Mom in this car that's taking us to the school, I feel like a caged animal. Then I almost have a heart attack as the driver turns into the oncoming traffic at the first intersection. I open my mouth but can't speak. I stare in shock at Mom. She's totally unfazed and it takes me three more seconds to get it. United Kingdom. Drive on the left. God, anyone would think I'd never been out of the States before. Let's put it down to lack of sleep. Mom just raises her eyebrows scornfully as I sink down again. My heart is still pounding, my palms are clammy, and it's only when I start to feel a bit dizzy too that I catch on: there might be some other reason for my edginess and horrible feeling of panic.

Mom's eyes drift over me as I bring up the app where my current blood-sugar levels are transmitted from the sensor on my arm. She glances at the display as I reach for the croissant we were given on the plane and I'd kept for later. It's gone stale and I hardly manage a mouthful. Lack of sleep is doing its shit. I don't have to look to know that I'm low.

'Everything OK, Colin?' Mom's voice is reproachful and cool. Almost like I did this deliberately. But I didn't choose to get this diagnosis at the age of eleven, since when my entire survival depends on injecting the insulin that my crappy pancreas ought to be producing for itself.

'Yeah.' I try not to sound grouchy, which she'd just blame on low blood sugar. 'Everything's *fine.*'

'You have an appointment to introduce yourself to the school doctor this week,' says Mom, eyes front again. 'He's been informed. You seem to be the only diabetic at the school, by the way.'

I hold back any reply and start eating. The plane croissant

is vile but I don't have much choice – the only alternative is a sandwich that doesn't look any more appetizing.

'It's important for you to know who to contact in an emergency.'

'No kidding.' I stare out of the window again and force myself to focus on the landscape flitting past and not the shakes, which won't stop. We left the city behind ages ago and we're in the total wilderness. Hills, sad-looking bushes and nothing but sheep everywhere. After a few minutes without spotting a single house, I give Mom a quick sideways glance.

She points up ahead and then I see it too. I hate to admit it, but for a moment there, I'm almost impressed. Dunbridge Academy looks like a castle. It sits high above a bend in a river, with fields and trees in the background. The dark brick building looks more imposing than it does in the photos I saw online. But also more weathered.

And there's nothing else. A small lake, the river that snakes through the landscape. I read somewhere that there were stores within walking distance, but it doesn't look as though they actually exist.

'I thought there was a town nearby?'

Mom looks over for a second. 'Yes, Ebrington.' She points to the houses on the other side of the school. 'The village.'

'The village?' I repeat in disbelief. I guess I didn't read the brochure carefully enough because I thought it was in Edinburgh. I was wondering why we'd been on the road so long. Now I get it. We're not in Edinburgh any more. And

Edinburgh may not be New York, but it was something I could have worked with. But this . . . It's an insult.

'You won't want for anything at the school,' Mom says. 'Besides which, you're here to concentrate on your studies.'

For God's sake, she can't leave me here.

I was born at New York Presbyterian; I've lived my whole life in Manhattan. I knew it was a privilege to have the whole big city on your doorstep, and I knew it wasn't the same everywhere. But how can people live like this? There's nothing here. Nothing! It might be kind of nice for a two-week vacation, but not in the long term. I won't even have a fucking car.

And no signal either, I realize, as I check my cell phone. Oh, God, let there be Wi-Fi in this jail . . .

I tense as the driver steers the car over the bridge into the cobblestoned inner courtyard. OK, I admit it's kind of cool. It feels like we've crashed some movie set, because everywhere I look, I see teenagers in hoodies or jackets with the school logo on them. Where are the dumb kilts and blazers from the website? I get a bad feeling that I'm going to be acquainted with them by tomorrow morning when classes start, because I had to give the school my measurements in advance so they could order the uniform for me.

'Won't be long,' Mom tells the driver, once he's unloaded my bags. Her words are a stab in the chest. What was I expecting? Her to take me to my room, to hold my hand? Ava Fantino's a busy woman with no time to waste. Least of all on her useless son who causes her nothing but trouble.

The driver doesn't look thrilled, but he nods.

'Where's the principal's office?' Mom asks the first group of kids to come into the courtyard through the gate. They're younger than me and I feel their curious eyes on me. Did I mention how little I like being the new guy? It makes me nauseous. I say nothing. Not 'hi' and not 'thanks' as they actually show us the way. I feel uneasy that we're just leaving my suitcase standing there but, hey, this isn't fucking Times Square.

'Are you new?' a girl asks, stroking back her hair.

I make an effort not to roll my eyes, just chew the gum I found in my pocket. 'Looks like it, huh?'

'Where are you from?'

I sigh deeply. I'm not in the mood to chat. It's not worth it. 'New York City,' I say.

'Wow,' she says. 'That's cool.' Eyes me. Respect. But the two guys drop back a bit, look scornful, start to whisper. What am I doing here?

I stop listening to what they're saying as we walk to the office. The door opens. A guy who's already past his prime invites us in, ushers us to the principal's office. No, the head teacher's office. Dark wood, a huge desk. The head teacher's younger than I expected and she looks friendlier than I imagined.

'Colin, Ms Fantino.' She comes towards us. 'Nice to meet you in person.' She holds her hand out to Mom and then to me. 'Welcome to Dunbridge Academy.'

4

OLIVE

'Olive,' Dad says, after I haven't said a word for the whole drive from Edinburgh to Dunbridge Academy. I didn't speak over breakfast with Mum either. 'I understand that you're peeved, love.' There's sympathy in his voice now.

'I'm not peeved,' I say. Which is true. I'm not peeved, I'm desperate. There's a difference. 'I'm just not in the mood.'

'It's for the best, pet.'

'Stopping me seeing my friends? That's for the best?' I turn to Dad. 'Not that it matters, I guess, after all those weeks in hospital. I'm out of the loop now anyway.'

'You know it's in your best interests to repeat the lower sixth.'

I turn away and look out of the window. 'Whatever.'

'And you'll see each other just as much as before.'

Right. Till they do their A levels at the end of the year and leave Dunbridge. Without me.

I gulp, but don't reply. There's no point. I know when it's not worth arguing with Mum and Dad any more. They made this decision without me. I can't do a thing about it. Not while I'm seventeen, at least. Which is another seven weeks exactly. So the end's in sight. It won't be long before my parents have no say and I can make my own decisions. Seven weeks. Not for ever. I have to tell myself that over and over.

Dad turns into the driveway and through the gate onto the cobbles of the Dunbridge inner courtyard, and my heart is starting to hammer. It just is. I can't stop it. I'm suddenly only too aware that this is the first time I've been here since the summer. The first time since my entire life went up in flames.

My eyes are drawn straight to the west wing. My body goes numb as I catch sight of the scaffolding over the façade. The dark brick walls are covered with a semi-transparent plastic sheet, emblazoned with the name of the company doing the repair work. It's kind of a miracle that the fire brigade got the flames under control before they spread to the other wings. The damage is manageable. The school reopened in time for the start of term, although the tragedy meant that the hundredth-anniversary celebrations didn't go ahead as planned when the new academic year began in August. They've been postponed until next summer. How thoughtful, how extremely tactful to forgo a glittering party seeing that I was only *nearly* killed, and nobody but me was seriously hurt.

A wee bit of smoke inhalation among the few fourth- and fifth-formers who were still in the west wing at the time. The only other damage was to property. And to my heart, now thumping because I can't tear my eyes off this building. I was in there. I could have died. That feels so unbelievable now that I just can't grasp it, and although I spent weeks in hospital thinking about it, it feels like I've had no time to come to terms with anything.

'Olive.' I jump as Dad takes my hand. I immediately snatch it back. I've got nothing to say to him because apparently anything that matters in my life can be decided over my head now. 'Please don't be angry, pet.'

The sympathy in his voice makes it almost impossible for me not to cry. So I have to focus on the rage. Anger is better than helplessness. Anger drives you; helplessness holds you back. And I can't be held back any more. I was paralysed long enough. I can't go back to those seconds I was standing on our corridor, waiting for my flight reflex to kick in. I have to get a grip on life again.

I reach for the door handle and pain shoots down my arm. I still haven't learned that my shoulder is not OK with sudden movements. Everything is still sore – the grafted skin is super sensitive, and the scarring restricts my mobility. But, sure, I was lucky that the burns aren't even bigger. They cover the area from my right collarbone, over my shoulder to my chest. I've often seen myself in the mirror since then. With the bandages at first, and then without them. I wanted to, but

I never cried. I studied my body, but I think part of me still hasn't twigged that that's really me. Still, I've got loads of time to accept that at my leisure now. In the lower sixth, on my own, without my friends.

Dad looks at me as we get out of the car. He opens the boot but doesn't speak again. He takes the only bag I've got. I didn't need much stuff in the hospital and most of my things are still here. By some miracle, the rooms at the far end of the west wing were undamaged. The fire mainly spread through the lower floors and on the stairs. But that means the girls' dorm wing is largely unusable. Mrs Sinclair and the house-parents must have had a job finding places for everyone in the fourth to the upper sixth to sleep in the meantime. Some rooms in the new block have been turned into temporary dorms for the fourth-formers, and people in the south wing have had to budge up to make room for the fifth. And the impossible has happened – the sixth-formers have been moved into the east wing. Yep, with the lads!

There's never been anything like it in the history of Dunbridge. I can hear Tori's excited voice as if it was yesterday. She came to see me in hospital the moment she was allowed, and she and Grace spent more time with me than anyone else. Thanks to them, I know that the boys in the east wing have been moved around so that the whole third floor is now home to girls in the lower and upper sixth. The larger single rooms have been made into twins, and though it's bulging at the seams, nobody's had to be housed outside the school grounds.

Henry's sharing a room with Gideon, and Charlie Sinclair's currently the only boy with one of the new twin rooms to himself, greatly to Tori's joy. She's sharing with Emma.

It feels all kinds of wrong to turn right through the arcades into the east wing instead of the west as I've always done. It's Sunday evening and everyone's already had dinner. The juniors are running around the second courtyard behind the old church, which is now the dining room, as if this school had never been on fire only a few months ago. Is it possible that everyone but me has already forgotten the disaster because the sun's shining and life's good? Am I being melodramatic? Difficult? If so, then I'm sorry, but I think I have a right to be.

Little groups of pupils wander towards us, people say hello and stare at me, then whisper to each other. I can hear them behind us, all the way along the arcade. Dad walks slowly, regularly glancing doubtfully at me.

'What?' I mutter, because I can't deal with his worries. Like I can't deal with not being the same person I was before the fire. My dad's seen me cry, with pain, with despair, after nightmares that were worse than the reality. He's seen me at my absolute lowest. The fear that this image of me is now seared on his mind, replacing the one of the old Olive, is driving me crazy. The old Olive who managed on her own. It's high time to change that.

'I'll text you if I need anything,' I declare, as we reach the foot of the east-wing stairs. I see the disappointment on my father's face as he realizes what I mean by that.

'I thought I'd just bring your bag up to your room, pet.'

I take it from him. 'No need.' It's heavier than I thought, but I don't let that show. It's important for him to see that it's not too soon for me to be back at school, the way he constantly fears. 'Thanks for the lift.'

Dad hesitates. 'Olive, are you sure you . . .?'

'Yeah,' I lie. 'Tori's waiting for me. She'll give me a hand.'

He doesn't need to know that that's not true. I did message Tori while we were on our way to school, but she hasn't answered. She's probably with Sinclair. I'll find out soon enough.

'Don't forget that you're meeting Mrs Sinclair tomorrow morning.'

I bite back a hollow laugh. How could I forget that? I can't sit in the head's office, like a little kid, to discuss how I'm going to manage back in the lower sixth. What would happen if I just joined my pals in class? Would they drag me out and chain me to my desk? Or suspend me if I won't play ball?

Seven weeks, Olive . . . Then this problem will be a thing of the past.

'I won't forget.' I put my foot on the bottom step. 'See you.'

'See you tomorrow, love. Call any time you need us.'

I turn away so that Dad won't see me fighting to stay composed.

Why would I need you? I mean, seriously. Even Dad can't do anything about the nightmares.

I walk up the stairs in silence. I can't remember when I last did anything entirely alone, unaccompanied by nurses, physios, medical students, visiting friends or parents. And now I know why. After just two flights of stairs, my heart is pumping so hard in my chest that there's a moment I'm scared it'll stop. I wish I could sit down. But I can't show weakness. Least of all now that I can hear voices and footsteps at the bottom of the stairwell.

The corridor on the third floor of the east wing looks almost exactly the same as in the west, but it still feels weird to walk into it. Most of the doors are shut and it's quiet, which might be because dinner's only just finished and people like to hang around a wee while before coming up to their rooms to get ready for wing time. Besides, it's Sunday. Anyone who goes home for the weekend generally gets back as late as possible to have as long as they can with their families.

Arriving now isn't the least bit like coming back after the summer holidays when all the corridors are crowded with pupils, their luggage and confused-looking parents. My academic year might only be starting now, but everyone else has been back for yonks. And nobody's here to meet me.

OK, apart from Ms Barnett. She rushes out of her office when she catches sight of me and gives me a big hug. Of course, she'd be here too, moved over from the west wing with everyone else. Mr Acevedo, the lower-sixth boys' houseparent, has moved up a floor to keep an eye on the upper sixth too – Mr Tanner is now needed elsewhere with the younger lads.

Ms Barnett gives me a serious look. 'It's lovely to have you back with us, Olive.'

Maybe the one advantage of being back in the lower sixth is still having her as house-parent. Although it comes to the same thing either way this year. All the sixth-form girls are on this floor, so we all have the same house-parent: Ms Barnett. Ms Kelleher is now looking after the second form.

Ms Barnett asks me how I am and I reel off my pat answers. *I'm getting there, thank you. Aye, it's been tough. I'm glad to be back too.*

None of which is true. I'm not getting there. It wasn't tough, it was hell. And I'm not glad. I'm overwhelmed, furious and powerless, because there's no explanation. No guilty party. Nobody I can blame for my life having been turned upside down. But I don't say that because people can't deal with it if you're honest with them. And I don't need sympathy, and I certainly don't need special treatment. But obviously I get those anyway.

Ms Barnett tells me I've been given the last remaining single room with the rest of the lower sixth. It's the door nearest the stairs. I should probably say thank you for this thoughtfulness, but I'm too angry. Although I'm genuinely relieved to be closest to the exit, and not at the far end of the long corridor like my old room was. It's just so humiliating to be like this now.

Clearly, I don't have to do the morning run. And I don't have to do games or lessons that clash with my physio sessions in

Ebrington. I've been kicked off A-level PE – my favourite subject – and now I'm doing Spanish. Mr Acevedo, who taught me for GCSE, says he's happy to give me extra tuition to help me catch up. Nod, thank you, nod, thank you. Then Ms Barnett finally hands me my key.

'You know where I am if you need anything, Olive,' she says, letting me go at last. 'Anything at all.'

I nod, pressing my lips together, and head for my room. My things have already been brought over from the west wing. I open the door, and nearly die of shock.

'Welcome back!' Tori yells, as Sinclair hoots a party blower. Emma and Henry are throwing confetti, and I'm frozen in the doorway, like a block of ice.

'What are you doing here?' I gasp, once I've recovered from the surprise.

'Waiting for you, of course,' Tori replies, as if it's the most obvious thing in the world. She smiles and Sinclair grins, pointing to a cake on the desk. It's iced with *Welcome Back, Livy*. I'm not sure exactly which part of that makes my eyes well up, but it doesn't matter. Since the fire, I haven't felt like myself. There are still days when I'm so thin-skinned I'm crying constantly, and others when I'm too numb to feel a thing. I don't know which I prefer.

'Don't cry,' whispers Grace, as she hugs me. I nod and wipe away the tears. That's only too easy as I put my arms around her and feel her hard shoulder blades. This isn't the moment to confront Grace with the thing that's been giving me

42

bellyache for a few weeks now. Weeks . . . Months more like. When she visited me in hospital, I saw how much weight she'd lost. The first few times she came, I was too out of it to notice, but once I was recovered enough to take little walks around the ward, Grace could no longer hide it, however massive the jumpers and cardies she was wearing. Even now, the sight of her scares me because her cheeks are so sunken and her eyes so deep in their sockets. Grace stares at the floor like she's read my mind. She pulls her cardigan tighter and steps back a bit so the others can hug me too. Gideon's eyes meet mine, then rest on Grace. Tori flings her arms around me.

My throat constricts again as she hugs me tight. It messes with your head when everyone treats you like you're made of extra-breakable glass. Tori doesn't. The others do, though. I can understand why.

Maybe I should be glad of that. After all the hugging and saying hi to Emma, Sinclair, Henry and Gideon, my shoulder's aching. Standing up is tiring and by the time I sit on my unmade bed, I'm feeling a wee bit dizzy. Everyone else sits as best they can, dotted around the room, on the desk chair, the desk, the chest of drawers, on the floor. A roomful of my friends, yet it feels like there's an eternity between us. I gulp.

'Have you guys heard?' I ask, when nobody speaks.

Grace is sitting next to me and she puts an arm around me. Henry clears his throat and nods. 'Mrs Sinclair told me there would be two new arrivals in the lower sixth on Monday. I'm supposed to greet you in my role as school captain.'

'Two?' I ask in surprise.

Henry nods.

'You and some American guy,' Sinclair replies for him. 'He's going to be sharing my room.'

'Your room? I thought they were keeping the forms together?'

'There was nowhere else for him to go,' says Sinclair. 'The rest of the lower sixth are already sharing and the rooms aren't big enough to squeeze anyone else in. And it wasn't exactly fair for me to be the only guy with a room to himself.'

'I'll gladly swap with you,' Henry murmurs, barely audibly, but Gideon hears and punches him. '*Heeeey!*' Henry rubs his forearm in mock outrage.

'You know I'm the best roommate anyone could wish for,' Gideon says. 'Statement of fact.'

'Everyone has to snuggle up a bit,' says Tori, with a shrug. 'It's kind of cosy.'

'That's one word for it,' Emma mumbles, taking refuge in Henry's arms as Tori kicks out. 'Hey!' She sounds just like Henry did. I smile, rather against my will, then remember what Sinclair was saying.

'So this new lad . . . Is he here already?'

Sinclair shrugs. 'I didn't see him before dinner, but he might have arrived by now. Let's hope he's chilled.'

'If he's starting this far into term, you can bet he's been in some shit,' Gideon remarks.

'Didn't your mum say anything about him?' Tori asks Sinclair curiously.

'No, you know her, the model of discretion.'

'Aye, right, how could I forget?'

'She seems to know his mum, though. Think she must have owed her one. She doesn't normally take anyone part-way through a year. And if she does, as an exception, they'd start after Christmas or at Easter.'

'So I guess I can count myself lucky I'm not the only newbie crashing halfway through term,' I muse sarcastically.

'So that's settled then?' The suppressed hope in Tori's voice nearly tips me over the edge. 'You're repeating the lower sixth.'

I swallow. 'They didn't give me much choice.'

'But surely your parents understand that you'd rather . . .'

'Tori,' says Grace, quietly.

'No, I'm not having it, OK?' Tori looks like she's about to jump up, but Sinclair puts his hand on her knee. 'Livy belongs with us. We need to do our A levels together.'

'Mum and Dad don't see it that way,' I mutter. 'And neither does Mrs Sinclair.'

Tori turns to Sinclair. 'Talk to your mum.'

'I don't think she'd take kindly to me interfering,' he says.

'But it's our last year together.' Tori turns back to me. Her voice is so choked up that I'm fighting back tears myself.

You. Will. Not. Cry.

Not again.

But it's so bloody hard being in a room with your favourite people when you have to face the fact that everything's going to change. Everything. It was finally perfect. I'd patched things up with Tori, she'd got together with Sinclair, Emma had accepted my apology, we'd put on our performance of *Romeo and Juliet*, and we'd fought for greater equality at school. And then Fate came along and battered me over the head.

'We'll all still be here,' Grace says quietly. I'm sure she means well, but it's only making things worse. 'Won't we, Tori?'

She nods cautiously. 'At least we're all on the same floor. I'm just next door.'

I blink. 'Great.'

'We'll see each other here in the wing, at mealtimes, at midnight parties. It'll only be classes where it's different, but that's not the end of the world.'

Don't make me laugh.

'Everything will be the same really,' Tori promises.

I shut my eyes. If the last few months have taught me anything, it's that nothing stays the same. Nothing at all. Especially not if you wish for it with everything you've got.

COLIN

A closet. A tiny hole with shabby furniture and they have the nerve to call it a *room*. I couldn't believe my ears at the meeting with the head when Mr Acevedo, who was introduced as my house-parent, our resident advisor here in the dorm wing, said that I have to share it with somebody else. This has to be a sick joke, but Mom didn't even bat an eyelid when I turned to her.

'Nope, not a chance,' I say, once Mr Acevedo gives us a bit of space. 'No way am I staying here if I don't even get my own room.'

'You'll deal with it.' Mom glances at her smart watch. I know what's coming before she even speaks. Even so, my gut churns as she looks up. 'I can't leave the car waiting any longer. Want to come back down?'

I clear my throat, then shake my head. Maybe I'm being childish but I can't deal with it any more. I guess I should be glad she even came up after we talked to Mrs Sinclair. That she took this detour to Edinburgh instead of staying right there in London, where she's heading back later for dinner at the Shangri La with some industry folks before flying to New York again. Without me.

'No, let's get it over with.' Everything within me tenses as I take a quick step towards her. I hug her for as short a time as possible, hoping that will make her think. But on the contrary. She seems pleased that I'm not showing any uncomfortable emotion. She might even be relieved that I'm not making a big deal of saying goodbye. Hey, it isn't one. 'Have a good flight. Talk soon.'

'I hope you'll make the best of your time here, Colin,' she

says. A chill spreads through my chest as she turns away. 'See you soon.'

I'll miss you. Take care of yourself.

Nothing. *Nothing.*

She's Ava Fantino, funny and friendly, but only on camera. Only on the dark brown Chesterfield in her studio, where she makes her every guest feel so fucking welcome. She's the exact opposite at home, and if that got out, it would be the end of the world. But it won't, any more than the news of what I did will.

Mom leaves the room, shuts the door. I clench my fists, dig my nails into the palms of my hands. Hard, harder. It doesn't help. I notice my pulse racing.

I try to count silently back from fifty, but it's no use. I only get as far as forty-four before I whirl round and pace through the room like a hunted animal.

I heave one of my black aluminium suitcases onto my bed and choke back a curse because I'm not sure which one it's in. I should have marked it somehow. But I didn't. Even though I should've known how quickly I'd need to get at my lighter once I was here.

Please don't let them have gone through my suitcases. My fingers are shaking as I find the combination. There's no slip of paper to say my baggage was checked. OK, that's good. There's hope. I open the suitcase and dig through my T-shirts. Come on. My heart is pounding in my throat. I'm dizzy as I open the second case. Sometimes I'm not sure if it's low blood sugar when I feel like this, or if it's all just in my head. Either way, I want it to stop. Which only happens if I make it stop.

I laugh with relief as I find the lighter and sink to the floor by the bed. I snap back the cover, feel for my belt and then, through the open window, I hear laughter echo up from the courtyard.

Fuck, I should stop. I'm not alone here and I have no idea if these Scottish people consider it necessary to knock before they enter a room. The place on the inside of my thigh might be the safest because nobody can see it, but I can only use it if I'm totally certain nobody will catch me.

I jump up and lock the door, then sit on the floor again and give in. The memories twitch through my head, flooding my mind.

Awful news breaking on the Upper West Side, 91st Street, where part of Ainslee School is apparently on fire. Over to our reporter on the scene for a live update . . .

The CNN presenter's voice was practically shaking with excitement. I'd been in the car with Pax, Maresa and Ash for ages by then. They'd seen the news on their phones, asked me questions, I shook my head, downed shot after shot once we finally got to the club. It's the last thing I remember about that night but the memory's seared on my brain.

The next morning, I woke up in Ash's apartment next to Maresa, because we never learn. But that wasn't what had made me queasy. I had switched off airplane mode on my phone and found countless messages from Mom and Dad.

Where are you?

Call us.

Screenshots. Catastrophe.

Multiple injuries after the fire on 91st Street, including an FDNY firefighter.

Breaking News – female firefighter killed in blaze. Mother of four, aged 42.

I read that and threw up in Ash's bathroom.

Somebody died.

Because of me. *Because of me.*

And it feels like no time has passed since that day. Now I'm here, but the nightmare doesn't end.

Why do you have to go? When are you coming home? Cleo's huge eyes, slowly filling with tears.

Because I'm a bad person. Because *I* ought to be dead, not that firefighter who was only doing her fucking job.

God, this has to stop.

I fire up the lighter.

The relief is instant. I feel the heat, then the pain. I don't pull my hand away. Not even when I can hardly stand it. I shut my eyes and let my head fall back. Count to five. No longer. I can't risk the effect wearing off the way it happens if I do this too often. A couple of times a week instead of a month. A couple of times a day, but how can I help it if the days are going to be so shitty now?

Breathe. Focus on the pain.

Five.

I clamp my teeth together.

Four.

Not long now.

Three.

It's working . . .

T—

Fuck.

My eyes fly open. I'm not imagining the sound of a key turning in the lock. I snap the lighter shut and leap up. I just about manage to close my fly as the door bursts open.

'Oh, hello.'

There's a blond guy standing in the doorway. Why the hell does he have a key to my room?

'Ever heard of knocking?' I snap.

'On my own door?' He frowns, then strolls in and bangs it shut. 'But maybe you're right. Just let me know in future if you want a wank and neither of us will get a shock.'

I flush. I want to correct him but then I realize it's better if he thinks I was jerking off. Anything's better than the truth.

'I was unpacking,' I say instead.

'Aye, I noticed. Good job you packed it away in time too.'

It takes me a moment to grasp what he means. 'What the . . .'

'Only joking, pal.' He comes closer. 'Sinclair,' he says. *Hold on.* Wasn't that the principal's name, or am I going nuts? 'And you're the newbie.'

'Yeah.' I turn away.

'Right, got you. So you're kind of pissed off about this whole thing.' The blond guy drops onto his bed. 'I thought you Americans were fans of small-talk, polite conversation?'

'I'm a New Yorker,' I growl, which should be explanation enough.

'Oh, sorry, my mistake.' He grins. 'Then I won't ask how your flight was, or if you're settling in.'

God, we've barely spent five minutes together, and I can't stand the sound of his voice. 'Yeah, no need.'

'Fine. And I know your name anyway,' he continues, unfazed. 'My mum told me. Colin Fantino, right? Isn't your mum that—'

'Yeah, man.' I whirl round. 'She is, and would you just shut up or do you want me to ask her for an autograph?'

He blinks innocently. 'My girlfriend loves her show.' I glare at him. 'But sorry, don't mind me. Want me to piss off so that you can get back to your *unpacking*?'

'God, how old are you? Twelve?'

'Eighteen,' he says. 'How about you?'

I say nothing.

'Wait, let me guess. You're going into the lower sixth . . . Sixteen?'

I snort.

'Seventeen, then? Had your birthday already?'

'Uh, no. What's it to you?'

'Just asking.'

'Well, do us both a favour and quit it.'

'Not in the mood to chat, got you.' He sighs. 'Looks like this is going to be a long year.'

'Don't worry, I won't be here that long,' I mumble.

'Won't you?'

'No.'

'If you say so.'

I turn back to my luggage and decide just to ignore the guy. Sinclair. Doesn't he have another name? I'm about to face him and ask when I hear him speaking again.

'You've missed dinner.'

'What a shame,' I say, thinking about vinegar-soaked fries and other highlights of British cuisine.

'We can sort something out for you in the kitchen,' he says, and suddenly I know that he knows. I glance over my shoulder. I want to deny it. But I understand my body well enough to know I'd regret that decision in an hour or two at most. The trip was tiring, then there's the jetlag, and I have no wish for a night of low blood sugar.

'My mum told me you're diabetic,' he says.

'How discreet of her.'

'Look, I'm making an effort. Can't you meet me halfway?'

'Don't bother,' I say. 'I'm not here to make friends.'

'The way you're acting, you're not likely to.'

I can't help smiling, with my back to him. Ha, he's pissed. Bite me, Scotland boy. 'Boo-hoo,' I say, bored.

I hear the bed creak as he stands up. He crosses the room and vanishes into the hole that's meant to be a bathroom. He suddenly reappears and goes to the door. I turn around after all.

'Where are you going?'

'What do you care?' He's shut the door before I can speak.

Great. I didn't even get to ask him for the Wi-Fi password. At least then I could have googled this place, see what there is here. What the hell? Looks like it's going to take some good old-fashioned exploration.

I fling some of my clothes into the rank wardrobe beside my bed, then decide I can't stand another minute in this room. Looks more like a camp bed than a bed. I know I'll fall out when I try to turn over. Where do they go to screw here? It's not just the narrow bed, it's the lack of privacy. God, I have to get out of here ASAP.

My insulin pump beeps. Great. I bet the cannula's snapped, after all that time on the plane. I open the second case, which is half full of insulin vials and the kit for changing them. Seeing my irritating roommate has stormed off, I take the chance to remove the pump, which I would have needed to do tomorrow anyway. Luckily the sandwich I bought for lunch at Heathrow is still in my backpack. I felt too nauseous to eat it, which hasn't changed, but I have no choice now. I'll have to make do. I've just thrown the wrapping into the trash can under the lousy desk when my roommate returns. With wet hair.

He seems to spot my confusion: we have a shower in the tiny bathroom.

'There are shared showers on the wing. They're bigger than the one here.'

'On the wing?' I repeat, because I think I must have misheard.

'Yeah, that's what it's called.'

'I thought the wings were the dorm blocks?'

He shrugs. 'And the corridors. Just go with it, OK?'

Hey, he can be quite funny, actually, when he's pissed. This is almost fun.

Only almost, though.

'OK, whatever,' I drawl, picking up my phone, my key and my jacket.

'Er, what are you doing?' he asks.

'What does it look like?'

'It's almost wing time,' he says.

I laugh. This just gets better and better. 'Great.'

'Which means we have to stay in our rooms now or—'

'Know what?' I interrupt. 'I couldn't care less.'

'What would you do if I grassed on you?'

'I'd thank you.' I give him my most engaging look. 'Seriously. Then I might get out of here even sooner than I thought.'

5

OLIVE

Tori, Henry, Grace and the others hung around until just before wing time. They only left when Ms Barnett appeared. Tori and Emma helped me unpack and make the bed, then had to head off too. Now they're just next door, but the loneliness strikes remorselessly as soon as I've brushed my teeth and I'm staring at my face in the mirror.

I wander from the sink to my desk, to the wardrobe and back to the loo. Putting things away, folding clothes, tidying my bathroom shelves. All so that I don't have to lie down in bed.

It's silly, I know. It's totally irrational to be afraid of it because it's not even *the* bed. I'm in a different room in a different wing from last time. But I'm still back at the boarding school where I went to sleep in the summer and only woke up when the floors below me were in flames. What if I hadn't woken? What if I'd suffocated in my sleep? What if the flames had surrounded me? I woke up and saw them out of the window. I was lucky that the fire was only on the ground floor and in the stairwell. I was on my way down when they blocked my path, not far from the exit.

I'm not scared of it happening again. I know that's vanishingly unlikely, but that isn't what this is about. This is about the likelihood of everything playing out over and over again in my mind, the moment I lie down in bed. And that isn't vanishingly unlikely. It's one hundred per cent definite. I've dreamed it every night since. Or every night I can consciously remember anyway. They've always been there. The images, the flames, the biting smoke, the heat of the fire, my pounding heart, my knees, which wanted to give way beneath me. In my dreams, I can't run – I can't move at all. I just stand there and sink to the floor, my only thought that this is it. And a thing like that repeating every night is exhausting. Exhausting, but sadly no less terrifying for that. On the contrary. It gets worse. You start to be afraid of the fear. Fear of the dreams turns into fear of sleep. Fear of being alone. And fear of everything. Plus the rage. God, I'm raging that this is my life now.

I take a step towards my bed.

OK, no bother. It's only a problem if I make it one. It's all in my head. It feels real because my body hasn't twigged that the danger is over. But it's not real. It's over.

I force myself to slow my breathing as I sit on the bed.

I was sitting here earlier, but it was OK then because Tori, Grace, Emma and the others were here.

I let myself sink back. OK, OK. While the light's on, everything's fine. I stare up at the ceiling and try not to think. And I'm tired. If I shut my eyes now and just drop off to sleep, nothing's going to happen. It's not difficult. Slip under my duvet, ignore my throbbing shoulder, switch off the light. Breathe.

Pitch darkness all around me. And quiet.

I feel my heart rate accelerating.

I have to shut my eyes. I have to . . .

OK, no. I sit up again so fast that pain shoots through my shoulder. My fingers are trembling as I can't instantly find the light switch. My bedside lamp comes on. I jump up and pace around the room.

Good grief, why am I like this? Why is my heart racing? Why do I feel like an animal that's been jammed into a cage to waste miserably away?

I run both hands over my face. Nothing does any good so I grab my door key. Ha, now I'm breaching wing time, on my first day back at Dunbridge. At least I'm not doing it for fun. Anything but. I'm just trying to cope. To run away from the panic that's got me in its clutches. I think the teachers will understand if anyone catches me.

I abandon my original plan – to face up to the west wing to prove to my body that the fire is in the past – as I walk through the dark corridors. It's probably more sensible to work up to that project slowly. In daylight. Maybe start by happening to stroll past with my friends. Baby steps. I hate being like this. A weak, delicate version of myself. The old Olive would never have jumped in panic at loud noises or quick movements. But that happens to me now, seriously. Like my body's permanently in flight mode. And however much I hate myself and put myself down for it, it never stops.

Not even here in the hush of the swimming centre. The place, after the classrooms and my bedroom, where I spent most time. It's locked at night but, like every member of the swimming team, I know the access code to the building, which Ms Cox, our trainer, never changes.

The water is dead smooth and has an almost hypnotic effect on me. I sit on the bottom row of the small bank of seats beside the main pool, at a safe distance from my element, because even the thought of getting too close to the water is painful. Not because I'm suddenly afraid of it. Not in the least. After all, water's the opposite of fire. But it's not my home any more. I've lost it, lost my one true talent. Swimming, doing lengths, faster than the rest, just because I *can*. Sorry. Could.

Eventually, I brave the edge. I didn't put on any lights when I came in. The main façade of the swimming centre is all glass, so you'd definitely have seen a light from all the way over in the school buildings. The low night-time lighting and blue light in the pool are enough for me. As I look at the water, the noise starts in my head. My thoughts, chasing while standing still.

It's over. You'll never swim at that level again. Not with this shoulder, which hurts to move. Front crawl? No way. My dreams? Shattered.

I look up at the ceiling, then crouch down. The water runs through my fingers as I dip my hand into the pool and bring it out again. The chlorine would damage the skin graft so I'm not allowed to spend any length of time swimming for the first six months after the operation. After that, a few swims a month will be OK.

A few swims a month. Back in the spring, I was here every day, training for the galas. Twice a day sometimes, after Mum sucked me into covering up her affair. Anything to avoid thinking about what that might mean.

And then, as so often, I think that none of this would have happened if I hadn't gone to bed so early that summer evening. If there hadn't been a comp the next day, or if I'd just gone out with my friends. So many 'what-ifs' and 'hadn'ts', because I can't change a thing, not a thing, about the past.

I didn't spend the evening with my friends. I was conscientious. I wanted to wake up rested and recuperated. But I didn't. I came round knowing what it's like to be frightened to death. When your body senses danger even before your head knows what's going on. That 'fight or flight' isn't some far-fetched theory dreamed up by Mr Ringling in biology, but the fucking truth. Adrenaline, tunnel vision.

I woke up after ten days that felt like a split second, and even now I find it hard to understand what happened in that time. Operations, intensive care, my weeping parents, whose tears sometimes pierced the fog and got through to me. The recovery phase when, or so they explained to me later, the drugs were being reduced. It's unlikely I'll ever remember any of the time before that because while I was on the ventilator my body was pumped full of medication to reduce the pain and keep me unconscious. Great, isn't it? Almost two months in hospital, no summer holiday, and even though I hoped at first that I could be back for the start of term in August, my physio programme was put back because I wasn't well enough, and the doctors insisted on keeping me in. At least now I can go to a therapist from here.

I should have lived on that evening in July. I should have followed my heart. It wanted to be sitting on those uncomfortable wooden benches in Ebrington with Tori, Sinclair and everyone, talking about the holidays ahead, the play, the school year we'd just finished and the one to come. The lower sixth sucked because I was raging and treated my friends like shit. I thought I'd lost everything that mattered to me, but I was wrong. I had it all. And now it's actually gone.

OK, I'm exaggerating, but that's how it feels. I'm alive. It's not the life I used to have but it's better than nothing. I'm on a wing with my friends. I'll sit in the lower sixth for a few weeks and cram the upper-sixth stuff at the same time. That's doable. And as soon as I'm eighteen, I'll rejoin my people and we'll do our A levels together. And everything will be just as I always imagined.

But coming of age won't solve the swimming problem, so I have no choice there but to listen to Dad and the hospital doctors, who told me again and again that I have to give myself time. Do my physio, moisturize my scars, wait, keep the faith. I hate it.

Right now, I wouldn't even be able to lift my arms over my head for a racing dive.

There's a sound. I startle and jump up. Suddenly my chest is too tight to breathe. My heart starts racing, like it keeps doing these days, mostly when I remember the fire, but sometimes out of the blue. I try to slow my breathing. The air in the swimming centre is humid. Although my brain is telling me that it's getting enough oxygen, I don't feel I can breathe in here just now. I fight back the urge to speed up as I walk past the pool. My knees are shaking as I step through the exit. The darkness wraps itself around me. I take deep gulps of the cold night air and force myself to keep walking.

A sound, a smell, a sensation. Focus on those, not your hammering heart. I'm really trying, but it will never be easy to fight back the rising panic. This stupid technique isn't helping. I do it anyway. I can hear . . . my footsteps crunching on the gravel path back to the school. I can smell the grass. I can feel the cool of the night on my skin. And the closer I come to the north wing, the slower I'm walking. I have to be careful here because now I don't want to get caught. If Mum and Dad knew I was breaking the rules, they'd definitely take it as a sign that I'm not ready yet. Like they always do, whatever happens. I can't get anything right just now, yet I hate myself for thinking that way, because I know they only want what's best for me. They want to protect me and help me. Dad does, anyway. I'm not always so sure about Mum. In the end, all she wants is for me to keep quiet and not tell Dad anything about her wee fling.

My body feels heavy as I walk through the gate into the north wing. The cool air has helped me get my thoughts together, but the exhaustion is draining me. It was a long day. Maybe now I'm tired enough to go to bed and get to sleep quickly, without freaking out. Mind you, I can feel this afternoon's painkillers wearing off. A few days ago I thought I could manage without them, but I failed miserably. I didn't want to believe Dad when he said I should reduce the dosage gradually. I'm not the kind of person who takes things slowly. Once I've got an idea in my head, it's all or nothing. And because there's no way I can go 100-per-cent painkiller-free just now, I feel like a total failure.

I walk through the hallways, which I know like the back of my hand. I have to be careful to avoid the sick bay, because if there's anyone I don't want to bump into it's Nurse Petra, who's guaranteed to tell Dad I'm creeping around the place by night and not sleeping. Luckily, it's all quiet so I can slip past unseen and take a right turn back towards the east wing. That's my intention, but then my footsteps start slowing almost unconsciously.

The display cases lining the corridor draw my eye, like magic. I stop by the one for the swimming team. Our school might be most famous for rugby, but the athletics, tennis and volleyball teams are pretty successful too. And so's Dunbridge Swimming. OK, so half the school doesn't turn out to cheer us on, like they do for the rugby matches, but the number of trophies on show is an indication of how good we are. We . . .

I gulp and stare at our achievements, for which I did my bit. The championship cup that Helen Snider brought home to Dunbridge last year. She's left now and is swimming for Cambridge. I'd thought I had a chance of following in her footsteps, but instead of swimming my way to victory for Dunbridge, I was in intensive care. The others did their best. They weren't bad, but a bronze is a bronze. Even so, I'd take that gratefully if I could go back in time and change everything. But I can't.

I step closer and clench my fists as I study the team photos. *Give yourself time. You'll swim again one day, Olive.*

Yeah, old-lady breaststroke maybe, but I'll never be back to my former level. I want to be the best. I want to win. I want my heart to pump strong and fast as my arms split the water and my legs propel me forwards. I want the feeling of flying when, in the water, everything's weightless and my worries and fears float away as I dive. Is that really too much to ask?

Hot rage pounds in my chest and mingles with despair. Why did it happen? Why did it happen to *me*? Is this a punishment for the way I treated my friends? Is it because I'm not telling my dad the truth? Not that I have any fucking choice in that!

I feel the tears stinging my eyes and see myself raise my

right arm. My fist is shaking, my shoulder hurts, but that's a good thing, right, because it means I'm alive. A stroke of luck. I'm *lucky* . . .

I step back a little to give myself room to swing, I really want to do this. I want to break something the way that fucking night broke me. One moment, one spark, everything lost.

I hear something and whirl around. All the blood drains to my legs as I realize someone's watching me.

'You wouldn't dare,' says the person who steps out of the darkness towards me.

COLIN

I'm fucking tired because my body's been awake for about one thousand hours now and can't go on, but it's not so easy to get kicked out of a school like this. You have to put some work in. So I'd better start right away.

Wing time. Could they have found a more ridiculous term for curfew? Fine by me, though, because it's the perfect thing to ignore. But, to my deep personal disappointment, I don't meet anyone in the dark corridors once I've left my room. I have to admit that it's kind of creepy, but obviously that's just because I don't know my way around here yet. My sense of direction gave up on me the moment I walked down the stairs from the dorm wing. Once I got to the bottom, I didn't have a clue which way we'd come from the head's office earlier.

We . . . Mom, who just messaged briefly to tell me she'd landed back in London. Didn't ask how I was doing or if I was settling in. Ava Fantino doesn't have time for that shit.

I look out from the covered walkways on the ground floor – arcades, they call them – and see the cobblestoned courtyard where we got out of that car this afternoon. I dig my hands into my pants pockets and walk past the rounded arches. There are lights on in a few windows around the courtyard. The only wing that's completely dark is the one opposite. Seems like they're renovating – the building's covered with scaffolding. If the rooms in the boys' wing are anything to go by, that's way overdue. Pity I couldn't come here after they were done, though. Then I might have been able to live somewhere with slightly modern levels of comfort. But, hey, it's not like I'm sticking around.

I kick at a stone with the toe of my sneaker. I wish it was bigger so it would make more noise. But I'm sure to get caught eventually. According to Mom and Dad, this boarding school is supposed to be super-strict, which is just what I need. They have proper discipline here. Not like my old school in New York where I walked all over my teachers. Doesn't seem like it right now, though. Beats me why my parents think this place'll be any different. Especially now. I know it's dumb. But what can I do? Negative attention – stress and fighting – is better than none at all. Attention from the people who are supposed to love you is a fundamental human need, or so I've read. Attention, autonomy, safety, intimacy and affection. OK, so I had autonomy – I could arrange my own daily life – but that's it. And now they've even deprived me of that. Psychology was probably the only class at Ainslee that I got anything out of. The main takeaway was that all our parents screwed up at some point in our childhoods. Not necessarily on purpose; it's simply impossible not to give your kids some kind of trauma. But my parents had to do better than everyone else in this respect too. It would be funny if it wasn't so fucking shit.

I run my fingers over the smooth stone of the pillars. If I just keep heading straight, sooner or later I have to get back to where I started. Assuming I can just walk down every corridor. Well, even if I'm not allowed to, I will.

I turn a corner. The hallway is dark but I can see a figure a few yards away. A girl. She's staring at something on the wall. A display case. She's really studying it. I stop.

She takes a little step back and even raises her arm. I hold my breath as I see her clenched fist. No way . . . Is she gonna throw a punch? Her arm's in the air, I can feel her struggle, and in my head I'm rooting for her.

Go on, do it. Do it. Respect if you do. Smashing up a display case at night has to be big trouble, right? Maybe I should do it for her. Not such a bad idea. No way she's going through with it. She's hesitating too long for that.

But I pull my cell phone out of my pocket. Why? Because I'm an asshole. I lift the camera and snap a photo of this girl I don't know. It's good to be able to call the shots, or so they say. If someone gives you blackmail material, take it, especially if they make it this easy. I have all the time in the world to slip my phone away again and stroll over to her.

'You wouldn't dare.'

She whirls around and stares at me like she's been struck by lightning. She immediately drops her fist. She frowns a moment, then shrinks back from the display case.

I notice two things. One, she's mad as hell. And two, she's gorgeous. Her eyes are puffy like she's been crying. But that doesn't fit with the air of determination in the set of her full lips. So now I'm curious.

'What the hell . . .' she hisses. She doesn't seem too amused that somebody was watching her. Rookie error. The thought leaves a bitter taste in my throat.

'True, though.' I stick my hands in my pants pockets and walk around her. She doesn't even look at me. OK, there's just a glance, for a split second, and I feel it arouse something I never knew I had within me. 'You don't have the guts to do that for real.'

Her eyes are huge and it's too dark to see what colour they are, but they glitter dangerously. I find that kind of amusing.

'You don't know me,' she says.

'True.' I give a bored shrug. 'And you don't know me. Great, huh?'

She goes to walk past me so I block her path. I kind of hate myself for that because I'm taller than her and stronger, and I always swore I'd never use those attributes to take advantage of a woman. But she's daring me.

I nod past her to the indirectly lit case. 'That you?' Say what you like about me, but you can't call me unobservant. I notice shit. For instance, that there's a big team photo among all the trophies and certificates, and that she's in the middle of it, holding a medal that hangs around her slim neck on a wide ribbon. She's wearing sports clothes and her dark hair is in one of those messy buns that really do it for me, sadly. Her eyes are sparkling. Not like they were just now. But like she gives a damn. There's life in her eyes, life that I can't see when I look at her now.

She turns away and hunches her shoulders together.

'What's it to you?'

'Impressive,' I remark, stepping closer to the display. So now I'm not in her way, but, to my satisfaction, she doesn't leave. Of course she doesn't. Because she's intrigued by me. I can sense it, and I don't like it. Because I'm intrigued by her too.

'What happened?' I ask, once I've checked out the achievements of the team that she can't be part of any more. Because she wouldn't be this emotional if she was. 'Accident? Got kicked out? Got beat in the heats?' Her face is as white as the moon as I turn back to her. Her eyes narrow to warning slits. 'Drugs? Doping? Some kind of scandal?'

'What the fuck's your problem?' she spits, taking a step towards me. I want to grin in appreciation, but I stop myself.

'You're pissed,' I say, feeling her grow even angrier. 'I'm just trying to help.'

Before she can answer, I pull off my hoodie. As my head

emerges from beneath it, I notice her eyes dart to my belly, then back to my face. The black T-shirt I've got on underneath rode up and she hastily looks away again. 'I don't need anyone's help,' she declares.

'Yeah, you do.' I press my sweater into her hand. 'If you don't do this now, you'll stay mad.'

She lifts her head and the disdain has gone from her eyes. She opens her mouth but I don't let her speak.

'So you don't cut yourself.' I point to the hoodie. 'It's more fun this way, trust me.'

'You're insane,' she says, in a toneless voice.

I shrug and step away from the glass case again. I study her body as I wait to see what she's going to do. She's wearing the fancy school sweater with black leggings and that combination is my downfall. Long legs, slim ankles. She's actually kind of tiny, but she doesn't look like anyone ever told her so. It's her way of standing. Upright posture, chin up, proud gaze. Right now, it's focused on my hoodie in her hands, and she doesn't have the guts. I know it, and try not to sigh.

'Would it give you the same relief to just watch?'

She looks at me. 'What . . . You mean . . .?'

'You can't hesitate.'

She tears her eyes away and wraps the thick fabric around her right hand. When she lifts her arm, she flinches slightly. And then she hesitates again.

I can feel her fighting with herself. Breathing hard, jutting chin. But she does nothing.

'Accident,' she says suddenly.

It takes me a moment but then I realize she's answering my question.

'It was an accident.'

Aha. That old classic. Lose focus for one moment and bang go your dreams. Pity.

'Oh, OK,' I say. 'Yeah, I'd be mad too.'

She gulps and stares back at the case like she could smash the glass just with her eyes. And I'd believe that.

'Were you good?'

She laughs. It's a dry, arrogant laugh and I like it. 'I was the best.'

'Ouch.'

She lowers her arm.

'And now you don't know who you are any more,' I say.

Her shoulders start to shake. 'It's so fucking unfair,' she says, through gritted teeth.

'Yeah.'

'Why did it have to be me?'

My throat constricts slightly. 'Yeah, why you?'

As she turns back to me, I wrench my eyes off her face and reach for the sweater. I can feel the pressure in my chest. I can feel *her* tension. I know it's not going away, but I also know that the first time is the hardest.

'You need to break something or the anger's gonna break you,' I say, and then I do it for her, without a second's hesitation. The girl jumps back as the glass shatters and rains down on the floor. Relief floods through me, along with adrenaline. I can tell by her shocked face that she feels the same way. She stares at the case and then at me. I shake the glass out of my hoodie and reach for her arm with my other hand.

I don't know if it's wise to run back in the direction I came. I only know that we have to be out of here when the lights go on. Of course, I could just wait here to be caught, which might be the quickest way of getting kicked out on the spot, but now it occurs to me that my mom's only an hour and a half away by plane, so she'd pop right back up to smooth everything over with a few dollar bills, then have me straight on a plane to Zürich where the next boarding school would be waiting for me. I need a plan that'll leave her with no choice but to let me come back to New York.

All those thoughts come up as we creep along the dark corridors. We stop on some stairs, the ones I just came down. Her accident can't have been long ago because as we climb them I see that my nameless fellow student is struggling. When I glance over, she's gripping the banister, but her face is like flint. She hesitates as we reach the third floor. She looks at me and my heart races. It's dark. I'm alive.

'Thanks,' she says, then vanishes through the heavy door onto her wing, and downstairs, the light goes on.

6

OLIVE

I made it back to my room without being caught and, although I was churned up after my encounter with that guy, I must have fallen asleep eventually. It wasn't restful sleep, though: I dreamed of breaking glass and screaming, but nobody hearing me over the noise of the flames.

I woke up, dripping with sweat, and was still feeling shaky half an hour later, during the morning assembly; I still am, even now that I'm sitting with the others for breakfast.

Of course, the smashed display case is the hot topic this morning. I felt like a traitor sitting motionless in my row as Mrs Sinclair informed us all very seriously that vandalism would not be tolerated at Dunbridge Academy. She was disappointed that the culprits hadn't owned up to their actions. Maybe it was coincidence that her eyes rested on me as her gaze swept over all our heads. Or maybe she knows me only too well and can put two and two together. But it's not even true. She should have been aiming that reproachful look at the new lad, not me. Because, yeah, I was seriously raging but I'd never have done that. He did it, and I didn't ask him to. But I can't tell her that because I don't want to grass on him. So I sat out the assembly and sneaked a glance around, but I couldn't see display-case boy anyway. I didn't see him afterwards as we went for breakfast either. I followed my friends to the upper-sixth table like I still belong there. I feel like I'm playing a part, yet most of my former classmates don't seem to know that I'm repeating the lower sixth. They wave to me, look genuinely happy that I'm back. My friends' eyes weigh heavily on me, as do Mr Acevedo's. He's on table duty today, but he doesn't order me to join the lower sixth. I guess I should be grateful for this last period of grace, but I'm not. I'm just angry.

And my anger grows as I find I'm scanning the tables for him. The lad from last night. He's not here. Or so I think, but after a while he strolls in, way late, and everyone turns to look at him. Because he's new, and tall. His brown hair is still damp and he's got broad shoulders. He's wearing jeans and a black hoodie, and there's the fiercest scowl I've ever seen across his face. He looks a wee bit bleary and knackered, but there's a remorseless expression in his chestnut brown eyes that kind of goes with his razor-sharp jawline. He really stands out amid all the pleated skirts and dark blazers. We might have managed to overturn the strictly gendered uniform policy before the summer holidays, but we still have to wear full uniform on Mondays and special occasions. It felt weird to put on my pale trousers instead of the skirt this morning, and not to be told off by any of the teachers.

Gender-neutral uniform is one thing, but turning up to class or a meal in ordinary clothes is quite another. We're only allowed to wear them at the weekend or after study hour during the week, which is the official end of the school day.

I don't hear what Mr Acevedo says to display-case boy, but I certainly see his eyes roll before he nods, and then our teacher sends him to join the lower-sixth table.

'Is he the newbie?' Tori asks, beside me, craning her neck.

'Don't do that,' I hiss.

'What?' She doesn't look at me.

'Stare at him like that.'

'Why not? It's interesting.'

Sinclair glares at Tori. 'He was out after wing time and he's not wearing uniform even though I specifically told him this morning that he had to.'

'No way, Charlie,' Tori teases, biting into her toast.

'It's out of order,' he says. 'God knows what he was up to last night.'

I hastily glance down at my plate as display-case boy's eyes meet mine for a moment, even among all these people.

'Your mum will bring him up to speed on the rules later,' says Henry, who's sitting next to Sinclair. He looks at me. 'Mrs Sinclair wants to see you too, Olive.'

I feel the others staring at me. 'I know.'

'I'll take you both over.'

'I know the way,' I reply, more snappily than I intended.

Henry isn't fazed. However hard he tries to hide it, I can see sympathy in his face. But he just says, 'Course you do,' and sips his tea.

An awkward silence is doing my head in, so I shut my eyes. 'Sorry,' I whisper. 'I didn't mean to bite your head off.'

'It's fine, Olive.'

They have to stop this. Looking at me like that. Like part of me died in that fire because, even if that might be true, I can't admit it. I need my friends to give me the feeling that everything's still the way it was before the summer. Even if it isn't.

'You'll join us in the old greenhouse this evening, won't you?' Tori asks, because she's my best friend and can tell how I'm feeling. I could cry.

'If you'll let the lower sixth tag along . . .'

'Olive, please,' Tori retorts.

'Anyway, the real question is,' Henry points out, 'will the lower sixth let us crash their space?'

'They're fine with us sharing the greenhouse,' Gideon says. 'Nobody can use the Dungeon right now anyway.'

'Such a shame,' remarks Tori. 'I was *so* looking forward to hanging out in that rathole.' Her sarcastic tone makes me smile. Or maybe it's just the relief that we'll still have evenings in the old greenhouse together. It's faint comfort, but better than nothing. Even so, it feels wrong not to join Tori,

Sinclair, Emma and Henry on their way to class after break-fast, but to take the south-wing stairs up to the offices.

Mr Harper's face brightens as I knock on his door. He asks me about eight times if I'm OK, then tells me to take a seat outside Mrs Sinclair's offices. It's clear what I'm waiting for or, rather, who. He's still wearing his hoodie and jeans, along with that unbearably arrogant grin.

'Mr Fantino, has your uniform not arrived yet?' Mr Harper asks, when display-case boy walks in.

'Yeah, it has,' he replies.

'Then kindly go and change.'

I would have loved to hear his reply to that direct instruc-tion, but at that moment, the door to Mrs Sinclair's office opens. Her eyes meet mine, but she doesn't look at me like everyone else does, with deep concern, as if I'm suddenly a different person. She didn't do that even when she came to visit me in hospital to see how I was. She looks at me as if I can do anything I set my mind to: this thing hasn't broken me but has made me stronger. For a moment, I'm tempted to believe her.

'Olive.' She nods to me, then looks at display-case boy. Then she steps aside. 'Colin. Please come in.'

Uh-huh. Colin, is it? I follow Mrs Sinclair and feel his eyes burning into the back of my neck. Colin Fantino, the newbie from the USA. The name sounds too soft for him. Too . . . nice. But it kind of fits him too. I noticed his accent last night of course. It's a total turn-off.

'Colin, full uniform is compulsory on Mondays,' Mrs Sinclair says, almost as soon as we've sat down in front of her desk. 'As I told you yesterday.'

Colin leans back provocatively. 'I guess I forgot.'

What the . . .? I stare at him in disbelief. It's one thing to take that silly tone towards me, but speaking to the head like that is bang out of line. Not even Valentine Ward would have dared, and he had zero respect for this school.

Mrs Sinclair pauses in front of her desk and gives Colin a long look. She stays calm, which is exactly what I'd expect of her, but her expression will tolerate no contradiction as she replies. 'Well, such a thing may happen on your first day. After our meeting here, you will go up to your room and change.'

'Yes, ma'am.' He slides back in his chair and crosses his ankle over his knee.

'Kindly sit up straight.'

Colin actually does as she says, but rolls his eyes when Mrs Sinclair looks away for a moment. I've lost all respect for him.

'There's no need for a long chat now,' Mrs Sinclair says. 'We met only yesterday, Colin, and, Olive, you already know how things work here. But I wanted the two of you to get to know each other seeing that you're both starting the lower sixth together now.'

Something in me tenses as she speaks. Her words sound so damn final.

Seven weeks, Olive. Seven weeks until you can make your own decisions.

'You're starting a few weeks into term, but your teachers have drawn up individual plans to help the two of you catch up, so you can both, please, see them all to discuss that in detail. And you can each arrange additional tutoring from them if you like. I would particularly encourage you to take up that offer, Colin, if you find that the level here is higher than at your old school.'

He laughs quietly. 'With all due respect, I was at Ainslee, Manhattan.'

'And with all due respect, Colin,' Mrs Sinclair says, slowly, not looking away from the challenge in his eyes, 'you're now at Dunbridge Academy.' Colin glances at me as a snort of amusement escapes me. I bite my bottom lip and look away. I love Sinclair's mum. But Colin hates her. I can see it in his face. 'And I'm sure you'll soon be feeling at home here. I'm certain that Olive and the others will be only too happy to answer any questions you may have about everyday school life. I am very proud of every pupil at this school, and I'm sure that you'll soon find your place in our community.'

Colin stays defiantly silent, and I wonder how old he is. Twelve? He's acting like it.

Mrs Sinclair doesn't say anything more so I look enquiringly at her. But then he does speak again.

'Is that it?'

'No, there's one more thing, as it happens.' Mrs Sinclair is pacing slowly up and down in front of her desk. A sure sign that a lecture is coming. And I can guess why. 'You might not have had time to read the school rules yet, Colin. And, Olive, I'm very happy to give you an up-to-date copy, as a reminder that malicious damage to school property will not be tolerated.'

I don't dare look at Mrs Sinclair so I stare fixedly at the edge of her desk.

'I will ask the two of you only once. Have you anything to say to me? Now would be the time.'

Colin blinks innocently. 'About what?'

'Last night, a display case was smashed in one of the corridors.' I don't need to raise my head to feel Mrs Sinclair's eyes on me. 'The one for the swimming team.'

I didn't do anything. But I didn't stop Colin smashing that case for me. I might even have been happy that he did it.

'That's terrible,' he says, turning to me. That's when I start feeling scared. Surely he won't ... 'I hope you find the perpetrator.'

When I glance at him, a challenge sparkles in his chestnut eyes.

'I hope so too,' I say, with a threatening undertone, but Colin just twitches the corner of his lips. *Bite me, Fantino.* Seriously. I have no proof that it was him, and if I grassed on him, Mrs Sinclair would ask questions. Like why I was even down there, watching him do something out of bounds. What gave Colin the idea of smashing the swimming-team trophy cabinet? After all, he's not the one raging at being out of the team. Although he *is* angry, I can tell. But it's a different kind of rage. I need to find out what that's all about.

'Well?' Mrs Sinclair asks, and I tear my eyes off him.

'I didn't see anything.' I kept my voice steady.

Colin clicks his tongue quietly. 'Me neither.'

'Fine.' She crosses her arms over her chest as somebody knocks on the door.

'Sorry I'm late,' Henry says, as he comes in. 'I got held up.'

'No problem. We've just finished here,' she says, turning back to Colin.

'Colin, this is Henry Bennington. He's the school captain and the first port of call for you if you have any questions or concerns. Henry will take you back to class now. No, up to your room, Colin, so that you can change.' I'm about to stand up but Mrs Sinclair adds, 'Olive, do you have a minute?'

Oh, no . . . Does she actually know more about the display case? I mean, she's Mrs Sinclair. She's no fool. On the other hand, I also know that she's a big fan of the benefit of the doubt. She proved that in her willingness to listen to Henry and Emma when they got into trouble last year. But I'm inno-cent here. I didn't do anything. Not a thing.

I straighten my shoulders and settle down again. 'Sure.'

Mrs Sinclair waits for Henry and Colin to leave the room. Then she looks at me. 'It's good to have you back, Olive.'

Oh, no. It's going to be this kind of conversation then. Maybe I'd better talk about the trophy cabinet after all, to stop her asking me how I am.

'I'm glad to be back,' I mutter woodenly.

'I'm truly happy you're on the mend. And I appreciate how

motivated you are to get back to class. But I want you to come to me or Ms Barnett if you realize it's getting to be too much for you.'

'I can cope,' I say evasively.

'Olive, this isn't a request, it's an order,' says Mrs Sinclair. 'You've been through a lot in the last couple of months.'

'I'd find it easier if I could go back to my old class. Be with my friends.'

'I know you think so, Olive, but please believe me that your parents have your best interests at heart.'

'So do you agree with them that I don't know what's best for me?'

'I think you're in danger of overdoing things if nobody keeps an eye on you.'

Splitting me up from my friends and dumping me down a year group is going to help fuck-all. OK, maybe it'll be easier to keep up in the lower sixth because I've done the work once already, but I'd manage in the upper sixth too. I'm Olive Henderson. I always cope. Although maybe I'm not the same Olive I was in the summer. Maybe it's time to admit that to myself.

'Clearly you're let off the morning run and games for the time being,' Mrs Sinclair goes on. I guess most people would consider that good news, but A-level PE, the morning runs, and swimming training, of course, were the times of day I felt most myself. And now all of that is gone.

But I nod as if I'm grateful. What else can I do? Insist on being allowed to do games even though every movement is so painful I can't get bloody dressed in the morning without pills? Great idea.

You're young, you have every chance to get back to normal, to get to grips with everyday life again. That's great, but I don't want a normal life. I want my old life back. I want to be able to swim. I want those hours when I can just forget all the bullshit.

'Good, Olive.' Mrs Sinclair looks at me and there's that damn sympathy in her face again. 'If there's nothing else, you can get along to class.'

I thank her and leave the office. The corridors are deserted because the first class of the day has started. On the south-wing stairs, I meet Henry and Colin, who has actually changed. My treacherous mouth dries out at the sight of him in the perfectly fitted blazer and matching trousers. He looks like a completely different person. Which doesn't mean his phoney skater look – baggy jeans, Vans and outsized sweatshirt – didn't suit him too. Entirely objectively speaking. I'm not that shallow. Clothes don't change the fact that he's an arsehole and that I don't want anything to do with him. I hurriedly turn left, praying that Henry will be leading Colin elsewhere. But Fate seems determined to kick me in the teeth, and they follow me.

'What have you got now, Olive?' Henry asks.

'Spanish, with Mr Acevedo,' I mumble.

'Oh, great. Then you're on the same course. And I'm sure Olive can show you the way to maths later.' Henry stops and looks questioningly at me. 'Can't you?'

'Nothing I'd like better,' I mutter, seeing I don't really have a choice. Saying no would just make Henry ask questions. Wonder why I'm so pissed off with Colin. And I'd end up giving myself away and everyone would know that I've got more to do with the broken display case than I'm letting on.

'Perfect.' Henry knocks on the door. 'Sorry for interrupting you, sir, I'm just bringing you your two new class members.'

COLIN

Luckily for me, however irritating this new Spanish teacher is, he only introduces me briefly to the class. No wonder, because he was there yesterday when Mrs Sinclair assured Mom that interesting details like my surname would be dealt with discreetly here. I guess they're good at that stuff at this school because, according to Mom, all kinds of influential businesspeople and celebrities like to send their kids to Dunbridge Academy. She says they have scions of aristocratic families from across the world getting their education here. I can't believe the news won't be all around the school at lightning speed anyway, but maybe they're just used to that kind of thing and nobody will care. Nobody at Ainslee gave a damn who my mom was either, any more than I cared if my fellow students had bankers or actors for parents or anyone else equally out of touch with reality. I was just Colin, and here I'm just Colin from New York.

And once he's done with me, Mr Acevedo introduces display-case girl.

'And you know Olive already. Nice to have you joining us from now on, Olive.'

Whoa, hold on. Does that mean she's repeating a year? It's the only explanation I can think of. I was kind of surprised to see her at the conversation with Mrs Sinclair just now. At first I thought she was just being told to look out for me a bit, but apparently that wasn't the case.

She doesn't seem particularly happy that the only free desks are side by side in the second row from the back, which means we soon have to buddy up for a conversation exercise.

I lean back and don't open my textbook. 'Olive, huh?' I link my arms behind my head. 'As in Olive Garden?'

She glares at me. 'What's your problem?'

'C'mon, you have to admit it's kind of funny.'

'What the hell are you on about?'

'Olive Garden?' I repeat, and pause as she still doesn't get it. 'Wait, don't you have that here?'

'Is it a shop?'

'Man.' I laugh quietly. 'I need to get kicked out of this place ASAP. Could you give me a hand with that?'

She looks at me as if I'm totally out of my mind. 'I'm not helping you with anything,' she says.

'OK, then we can get kicked out together.' I shrug and reach for my phone.

Her eyes widen slightly at the sight of it. 'You have to hand

85

your phone in before class,' she whispers, pointing to the shelf full of cell phones by the door.

'Uh-huh,' I say, unimpressed. Obviously, I'm aware of the rule. But Olive Garden doesn't need to know that. She stares at me in disbelief. Her eyes dart over to Mr Acevedo, who's walking around the room, and I'm really very interested to know if she's enough of an asshole to rat on me. I'd like to see her try it because, like all the staff, he's well aware that I have special permission to keep my cell phone on me at all times, seeing that it's also measuring my blood sugar and controlling my insulin pump. But no way is it going to be me who tells her that.

She looks away so I take the chance to glance at the app – I've got the feeling I'm a bit low. Maybe the insulin bolus I took at breakfast was a bit over-optimistic, because I could hardly swallow a mouthful.

'You're not bloody serious, are you?' she hisses, as she turns back to me and I adjust my basal rate before opening my photos.

'Is there a problem, Olive?' Mr Acevedo enquires, suddenly materializing beside her.

Aha, now things could get interesting. She freezes, looks at me. I bestow my most innocent expression upon her. She hesitates.

Go on, rat on me. But she doesn't. Her eyes are daggers, but she shakes her head. 'No, everything's fine.'

OK, so that's how you are, Olive Garden. I couldn't have said for certain that I'd have stayed loyal if it had been me. She stiffens as I slip her my phone under the desk.

'What are you doing?' she whispers, trying to push it away like it's burning her fingers, but I'm already flipping through my book.

'You'll help me get expelled or you can get expelled in my place,' I mutter expressionlessly.

She leans down to take a closer look at the photo. Her breath catches for a moment.

'Yeah, that's you,' I say. It might have been dark, but my phone camera got a great likeness of her. 'I'm sure your head teacher would be delighted to find that on her desk. There's no point trying to delete it. I backed it up long ago.'

She turns her face towards me. 'What the fuck is your problem?'

'Olive, Colin, please.' Mr Acevedo looks sternly at us.

I'm only too pleased to retrieve my phone from Olive and ignore her for the rest of class. With deliberate calm, I unwrap a muesli bar and she freaks out as I start eating in class.

Normally I'd say something at this point. Get under her skin by letting her know I've got a chronic condition so she's the one being fucking insensitive. But for some reason I don't. I just glance sharply at her before I take a bite. She stares at me in disbelief and looks at the teacher. He doesn't say a word. He's up to speed, like they all are. The normal rules don't apply to me. I get to eat in class, use my phone and walk out any time I please. Amazing.

A while later, the bell goes for break and, fortunately, Olive Garden follows me outside with the others. 'So, you're showing me the way to math, apparently?' I ask, but that seems to be the last thing on her mind. With surprising strength, she grabs me by the sleeve and drags me into an alcove along the hallway. 'Or is the nerdy school captain going to do that?'

'Excuse me?' Anger glints in her green eyes. Fuck, he's a friend of hers. I should have known.

'Nothing, forget it.' I straighten my shoulders, but it seems like she's only just warming up.

'I don't care if you hate this school or don't want to be in class, but anyone who insults my friends will have me to deal with, got that?'

'Oh, no, I'm terrified,' I mock. Then I look her over. I take my time about it and I can sense it's working as my eyes roam over her body and her uniform. This ridiculous schoolgirl look. OK, so she's hot, but I'd never let her know I think so.

'Delete that photo,' she insists.

I give a tired smile. 'Sorry, not gonna happen. I need some kind of leverage over you.'

'I'll go to Mrs Sinclair and tell her it was you.'

'Why would she believe you?'

'Why would she believe *you*?'

'She was standing there, in the dark, and I tried to stop her,' I begin, not taking my eyes off Olive. 'But she really laid into it. There was nothing I could do.'

'That doesn't even make sense,' she snaps. 'If you're so keen on getting expelled, go and confess.'

I give a long sigh. 'If only it was that easy, Olive Garden.'

'Don't call me that.'

I'm not reacting to that right now. 'I have to be more subtle about it. And I need something better. Something that will leave this head teacher of yours no choice, if you see what I mean.'

'Well, I've never been expelled so I can't help you there.'

'Oh, come on. I bet you'll think of something. Otherwise this photo will be going around.'

She eyes me, then shakes her head. 'What the hell happened to you to make you this vile?' she mutters. She doesn't seem to be expecting an answer because she spins on her heel and walks off without another word.

'Hey!' I actually lower myself to follow her. 'Wait. I thought you were going to show me the way to math.'

'I didn't think you cared,' she says, not looking at me.

'I don't,' I snap back.

'Right, as I thought. There's a map of the school in your welcome pack, along with your timetable. Knock yourself out.' She marches off, and I'm not going to make an ass of myself by running after her again. I glance furtively around but, sadly, I can't see that Henry guy anywhere either.

'Looking for something?'

I'm about to say no, but for some unknown reason, I take a liking to the guy stopped a yard or two from me. Maybe it's his rolled-up shirtsleeves that show me he hates the uniform just as much as I do.

'You're new, right?' he goes on, when I don't reply.

'Yeah, but you can call me Colin,' I say. It's a test, which he passes by grinning.

'If I must. I'm Kit.' He holds out his hand to me. There's no mistaking his Scottish accent but he doesn't sound as posh as certain other people around here. He strikes me as chilled. 'You've got the guts to mess with Olive – respect.'

I give a quiet laugh. 'Just a minor difference of opinion.'

'Aye, right, pal. Be careful with her, she's gone through enough shite lately.'

OK, maybe he's not so chill. I'm about to ask him what he means by that when a bunch of other students come over. Kit introduces them all to me. I make a note of their names and I won't forget them. You learn that young when you're dragged to public events as a kid with your VIP mom and have to make a good impression.

Kit doesn't mention Olive again, but he gives me a meaningful stare as he drops me off outside the math classroom. Seems like he has a different subject because he heads off again. Luckily for me, Olive Garden's already sitting next to one of the girls. She lifts her chin as I walk past and looks pointedly away.

What's the shit you've gone through, Olive Garden? C'mon, tell me. Or else make sure it doesn't interest me, because that way danger lies.

I sit two rows behind her and spend the rest of class watching her ignore me.

7

OLIVE

He doesn't seem to have grassed because I don't get called to
Mrs Sinclair's office the next day either. I get let off politics
the next morning so that I can go to my first physio session in
Ebrington. And anyone who thinks that's just a bit of massage
and lying around is mistaken. Seriously. It's more like strength
training and mobility exercises, where I fail at even the sim-
plest movements and leave the practice with a throbbing
shoulder. The sessions usually make it worse for a while
before it can get better. Hey, it would be nice if that applied to
my life in general, but that seems miles off just now.

My rage at Colin and his silly threats doesn't fade until
I'm sitting in one of Ms Barnett's art classes – the school is
very keen on 'enrichment' like this. He's not here, but there's
another new girl, although she started in September, of

course. Elain is from Germany and something about her reminds me a bit of Emma, even though her hair is more like mine – long and dark. We're sitting at a table for four with Tori's brother, Will, and Kit, his boyfriend, and they succeed in taking my mind off the irritating encounter with Colin.

It's good to see Kit here after a bust-up with his drunken dad back in the spring that landed him in hospital. A lot has happened since then. He now boards at the school instead of coming in for classes as a day pupil. That seems to have taken a lot of the heat out of the situation with his dad because, according to Grace, Kit's back to helping out with his family's village shop sometimes now. Irvine's is as much a fixture in Ebrington as Sinclair's bakery, the Blue Room Café and Ebrington Tales bookshop. Suddenly I feel an urge to show Colin around the place. I give myself a quick shake to get back in my right mind. Why would I want to show him anything? He's horrible, disrespectful and ungrateful. Anyway, I doubt he'd be interested. He's not even here, but I jut my chin at him before turning my attention back to the basket of fruit we're meant to be drawing. Yet at break time, I can't resist the urge to google the stupid nickname he gave me yesterday.

Olive Garden.

An American restaurant chain. Seriously! He can do one. Who does he think he is, waltzing in here like that, having the fucking arrogance to try to blackmail me? Just because he's tall and moderately attractive. OK, that's not true. He's outrageously attractive and the problem is that he knows it, with his perfect brown hair and dark eyes, but he can take a hike. At least I'll only have to be around that cowboy for a few weeks. Once I'm back with my pals in the upper sixth, he can bite me. OK, so he'll still be sharing a room with Sinclair, but we won't keep bumping into each other every day. Either that or I'll actually help him get expelled – that way I'll be rid of him. Mind you, I'm sure he can achieve that by himself.

After English, I just want to join Tori, Grace and everyone. I spot Colin at the hatch in the dining room. I don't deign to notice him, obviously, but take my tray and join my friends. Yesterday evening, Ms Ventura insisted on me sitting with the lower sixth. It felt like someone had stabbed me in the back with a sword as everyone watched me pick up my tray and move tables. Total humiliation. And then I ended up sitting with Ana and Luke. They're in the swimming team, so listening to them tell me how much they all miss me didn't exactly boost my mood. They mentioned the whole display-case thing but I acted like I didn't have a clue. Colin was sitting across the table and must have been able to hear us because he kept shooting amused glances at me that made me sweat. There's no way I'm voluntarily sharing a table with him at lunch.

It's only compulsory to sit with your year group at breakfast and dinner, but most people stick to it for lunch too, to be with their friends. But my friends are in the upper sixth. Everyone must know that I got put back a year by now, but nobody bats an eyelid when I join them. In fact, Tori immediately gives me a hug. I'm sure she saved a place for me. Inés and Amara smile at me across the table. Sinclair and Omar are here, while Emma and Henry soon join us. Just as it should be. It's only now that I realize how much I've missed mealtimes with my friends.

'So, how's it going?' Tori asks, at some point, dropping her voice. 'Doing any of the same subjects as him?'

'Who?' I ask unnecessarily.

'American Boy, obviously. Colin.' Tori looks around inquisitively.

'Stop it,' I mutter.

'He's hot,' she murmurs dreamily.

'He's an arsehole, OK? He's come up with this minging nickname for me, and he's trying to blackmail me.'

'What?' breathes Tori, eyes wide. She loves gossip, always has. 'Tell me more.'

That's when I realize my mistake. I can't tell her what actually happened to that display case. Tori would never grass on me, but the fewer people who know about it, the better.

'Oh, nothing,' I say, stabbing a bit of pasta with my fork.

'Come on, Olive, spill,' Tori insists.

'I can't,' I mumble.

'Oh, God . . . Was that you?'

'What?'

'Don't give me that, Livy. The swimming cabinet . . .'

'Sssh,' I hiss.

'I knew it!' Tori grins to herself. 'So why's he blackmailing you? Does he know?'

'He's got a bloody photo of me.'

'The fucker. No way.' Tori's captivated. 'This is thrilling stuff . . .'

'He's an arsehole, Tori,' I repeat.

'Maybe he's into you.'

'God, Tori. He's just a bawbag. End of.'

She just smiles and shoves a forkful of pasta into her mouth. 'Charlie says he's really off with him too,' she says, in the end. 'I'll bet he's got some dark secret. You could find it out and then he'll fall madly in love with you.'

'Sheesh,' I say.

'No, seriously. How exciting. Do you know why he switched school?'

'I couldn't care less.'

'Oh, come on. Everyone's dying to know.'

'Dying to know what?' asks Grace, sitting down beside us.

'Why Colin Fantino came to Dunbridge weeks into term,' Tori explains.

'Can't you find out, Livy?' Grace glances conspiratorially at me as she starts to peel a banana. The only other things on her tray are two little mandarins.

Is that all you're eating? The question's on the tip of my tongue but I bite it back at the last second. I have just about enough empathy spare to understand that embarrassing Grace in front of everyone won't make anything better. It's out of order to comment on other people's eating habits. Or their figures. But that doesn't mean I'm not worried about her.

I notice Henry's expression as he glances at us. He doesn't speak but I can tell he's thinking something along the same lines. And I can see that he's concerned. He and Grace were together for a long time, and I spent ages raging at him and especially Emma, his new girlfriend, for hurting Grace so badly. Since then, I've realized you can't judge people for developing (or losing) feelings for someone. Not unless they intentionally harm a person by cheating on them. Which Henry didn't. He split up with Grace first, as kindly as it's possible to split up with someone, but sadly, that doesn't stop the pain. Which has dug deep nicks out of Grace's heart.

'You should ask him,' Tori says, snapping me out of my thoughts.

'Fantino?' I laugh. 'No way. I don't want anything to do with him, OK? I don't have time for that shite. I need you guys to give me your notes after class so I can keep up with you.'

Tori and Grace look up simultaneously.

They exchange glances. 'Why?' Grace asks.

'Isn't it obvious?'

Tori pauses. 'Olive . . .' she begins quietly, but I shake my head.

'No, drop it. I'm going to cram up on your work at the same time as mine so that as soon as I'm eighteen, I can come back up with you.'

My best friend says nothing, and that hits me unexpectedly hard.

'Isn't that what you want?'

'Of course we do.' Grace reaches for my arm. 'But we're worried, Livy. That's a lot to take on.'

Something within me immediately shuts down. 'I'll manage. Can you just send me your stuff?'

They're eyeing me sceptically, but in the end, they nod. Their reaction unsettles me more than it should. Do they think I can't do it? Grace of all people should have a pretty good idea of whether I can cope with the upper sixth, seeing how much she helped me revise for the exams last summer. But I don't care what she thinks. I've set my mind to it, so I'll do it. That's always worked out for me so far.

COLIN

Beats me what VIP status Olive Garden has at this school but, apparently, it's a big deal for her not to mix with the riff-raff from the lower sixth at lunch, and to sit with her cool friends from the year above. I'm surprised that none of the teachers says anything, seeing as she was sent down to our table last night. Pretty embarrassing for her. But it looks like those rules don't apply at lunch. And, to be honest, I'm kind of glad not to have Olive Garden at my table giving me the evil eye as I check my blood sugar on my phone, and set the dosage via the insulin pump. She really didn't get it in class yesterday. And my other new classmates don't seem to have noticed what I'm doing. Lucky for me, the pumps and sensors have gotten less obvious in the last few years. Back when I was first diagnosed, I had to use an old-fashioned glucose meter and do a finger-prick test every single time, which screamed 'Diabetic!' to everyone within a five-mile radius. I can't say how sick I got of the looks. Nobody at Ainslee ever made a big deal out of it, but it still feels kind of nice to have a totally clean slate here at this school.

That's the only good part, though. I'm not in the mood to chat, so I sit on my own. Besides, I hadn't seen any familiar faces as I walked in. It takes a while for Kit and his buddies to come into the dining room and I'm actually glad they join me. I don't say much, but they accept me into their group. Kit asks me if I'm into tennis and want to try out a training session tomorrow. At first I'd rather decline. Not because I can't play. Anyone who's anyone in a certain level of New York society wants to be seen hitting a ball around in a swanky tennis club. So obviously I took tennis lessons. Not to mention private coaching sessions during our vacations in the Hamptons. But then I think it might not be such a bad idea. Thrashing a little yellow ball around might be a better way of easing the pressure, might help me get through at least one day without my lighter. In the end, I remember that I'm meeting the school doc tomorrow, so I tell Kit that I'll come the next time.

After lunch, he shows me the way to the physics classroom. Olive Garden's apparently not in this class and that makes me almost sad. It's boring when I can't bug her. Luckily, I meet her in the hallway after the last class of the day as she comes out of a classroom two doors down the hall. Her eyes meet mine, her steps slow. Then she sticks up her chin and turns away. She doesn't get to leave, though, because that snooty school captain comes towards her. Henry Bennington. He's with a blonde girl who was sitting with him and Olive at the upper-sixth table earlier. Before I can make tracks, they come over.

'Hey, how's it going?' he asks, and I deserve a medal for not rolling my eyes.

'Amaaazing,' I say.

'Are you done for the day?'

I nod.

'If you like, I'll give you a quick tour of the school. Olive will tag along, won't you?' He glances at her. They must have some kind of dirt on her because Olive Garden looks like there's nothing she'd like less. 'Oh, this is Colin,' Henry adds, introducing me to the blonde girl.

She eyes me somewhat sceptically, then smiles. 'Emma. Pleased to meet you.'

I just make a noncommittal grunt.

'See you later,' says the blonde girl, standing on tiptoe to give Henry a quick kiss. Olive turns her head away, but catches my eye and looks away from me too.

'OK, let's go,' says Henry. It's not exactly my idea of a good time, but I decide to follow him. The school grounds are big and it won't do any harm to have a vague idea of what's what.

I'm trying to look bored while filing away everything

Henry shows me. Now and then, Olive Garden adds in some piece of information. On the ground floor, we don't walk along the hallway with the trophy cabinets, but step through the arcades into the cobbled courtyard.

'You know the dining room already so we'll go this way.' Henry points to the left. 'That's the west wing, and behind it are the new buildings with the science labs.'

I nod uninterestedly but my eyes take in the scaffolding on the west wing. The building seems totally empty. 'What's in there?' I ask, heading towards the door.

'We're not allowed in there,' Olive Garden says.

'Why not?' I turn to her, taking a couple of steps back.

'I'm dead serious, Fantino,' she snaps.

'It's out of bounds,' says Henry. 'There's repair work going on in there and pupils aren't allowed in.'

I give a disappointed 'Hmm,' and turn away.

A place we're not allowed to be sounds like the perfect way to get expelled. On the other hand, if I kill myself in the process because the building is falling down, that won't help anyone. So maybe I'd better file this one under 'in case of emergency'. It would certainly fuck with Olive Garden, the way she reacted just now. Being that chicken seems out of character for her. But maybe she's so scared I'll rat on her over the display case that she doesn't dare break any other rules. So much for not giving a damn if she gets kicked out of here. But I won't hold it against her. I know what it's like to have a place you don't want to leave. And she seems genuinely afraid, because once we've spent half a lifetime walking around the grounds, Henry announces that it's time for 'study hour' (ha!) and she sneaks a glance at me.

I learned about this stupid rule yesterday. We have to spend an hour in our rooms every afternoon doing homework (a.k.a. 'prep') or studying. Obviously I did no such thing. I haven't had classes in all my subjects yet, but I paid attention the last couple of days. I had to do tests in English and math to assess my level. They were tough but no problem for me. I feel sure I did well, so there's no need to waste what little free time I get at this school on studying. I've always found school easy, and I've always done my best not to let anyone else know that. It's more fun when people think I'm a lazy punk.

When Henry declares the tour has ended, we head over to the east wing. We climb the stairs together, but when we get to the third floor, instead of disappearing down her corridor, Olive Garden holds me back.

'Fantino, can I ask you a quick question about . . . Spanish?' she says, staring almost pleadingly at me. Henry stops too, then says goodbye and carries on up the stairs.

'About Spanish, sure,' I repeat, once he's out of sight.

Olive Garden glances around briefly, then looks at me.

And somehow she's not looking furious any more, she looks . . . desperate?

'Hey, you won't really say anything . . .' she says. 'Will you?'

Even though I don't really feel it any more, I look at her as arrogantly as I can manage. 'You know the terms,' I say, as

I slowly stroll around her. 'That forbidden building – think it'd be useful for getting thrown out?'

'The west wing is no-go, Fantino, I'm serious,' she says. Her voice is shaking. There must be something up with that building. And I'm going to find out what.

'OK. Well, I can't wait to hear your other suggestions,' I say. 'What's the situation with booze?'

'You get a warning,' she says weakly.

'And after that?'

'If you get into more trouble, it might get you expelled.'

'Great.' I face her again. 'So where do you get it? Is there a liquor store in the city?'

'Liquor store?' she repeats. 'You can just go to Irvine's. It's the village shop.'

'Wait, you can get the hard stuff in the village shop?' I stop. 'Whoa. And you don't have to be twenty-one, right?'

'No, eighteen. Same everywhere here,' she says briefly.

I smile. 'Thanks for the info, Olive Garden.'

'Would you mind?'

'Don't you like the nickname? You're welcome to come up with one for me.'

'Why the fuck would I do that?' she spits.

'Whatever, Olive Garden,' I say, turning away. 'See you around.'

'Not if I see you first,' she calls after me.

I hold back my smile until she can no longer see it.

8

OLIVE

Fantino also spends the whole of the following day reminding me that he's got something over me, partly by his mere presence and partly by these little sidelong glances. My rage at him still hasn't cooled by the afternoon, when I'm sitting at my desk, trying to study. It's not going too well, because my thoughts are everywhere but in this room. Everything within me is crying out to go back to bed and pull the covers over my head, but I won't give in to weakness. If I can't keep up with the lower-sixth prep, there's no way I can fulfil my plan to catch up with the upper sixth on the side.

Mind you, that's also true if Colin means what he says and grasses on me over the broken display case. I don't know him, but I'd believe anything of him. He's one of those people who have absolutely no interest in anybody else. On the other hand, I do know Mrs Sinclair. I'm very sure that she'd be angry or, worse, disappointed if she knew, but I've been at this school long enough to be equally sure that you wouldn't be immediately expelled over something like that. And I've never done anything that bad before. Besides, and however much I hate the idea, I can always play the sympathy card. Her school went on fire and it almost killed me. I wouldn't like to claim that means I can get away with anything, but I'm pretty certain Mrs Sinclair feels guilty. Not that the fire was any more her fault than anyone else's.

I get goosebumps when I remember Colin's questions as we stood outside the west wing yesterday. Luckily, Henry didn't tell him about the fire either. I couldn't have dealt with it if Colin had kept digging. *No way, a fire. Did anyone get hurt?*

Yeah. Me.

Then he'd know and he'd be able to start giving me the same sympathetic looks as everyone else here. Although, no, that's not true. Fantino isn't the kind of guy who'd look at you like that because he has zero empathy. Even so, I don't want him to know. And I don't want to know anything about him either. Such as why he's so desperate to get kicked out of Dunbridge. I don't care. I seriously couldn't give a fuck. Maybe I would if he wasn't such a total arse. It's not like I'd been hoping to make loads of new friends in the lower sixth. A few good friends are enough for me. So I'm fine with knowing some people already in Will and Kit, plus Luke and Ana from the swimming team. And Elain from Enrichment seemed really nice. I'll get through the next few weeks somehow or other. And if Colin's gone by then, all the better. I'm annoyed with myself for thinking about him so much.

I drag my mind back to my maths prep but I'm nowhere near finished by the end of study hour. When the noise level out on the wing rises, I push my books away and go to see Tori. Or, rather, Tori and Emma. The fact that everyone else is sharing rooms again will take some getting used to. In lower years, we were four to a room. I kind of miss that, chattering the nights away with Tori, Inés and Amara. Knowing someone's always there. The memory of us planning to go to St Andrews together is like a dagger in my heart. We were full of ideas for sharing a flat there, still living together. No rules, no wing time, just my friends and me. Even Grace, who lives with her parents in Ebrington and doesn't board, could finally have joined us. Mind you, Tori's plans all revolve around Sinclair these days, and Grace is now hoping to study law at Cambridge.

Sometimes I wonder if there's something wrong with me because, while I used to long for freedom after our A levels, the thought of being cast out into the world now makes me panic. I've always been stressed out by change, but it's worse as I'm getting older. I left home young to board at school, but that was hardly fleeing the nest, given that I see Dad the whole time and can go home to him and Mum any weekend I like. The idea of my familiar life at Dunbridge being a thing of the past gnaws at my belly. I don't want us all to leave here.

I don't want my time at boarding school to be just a memory that fades with every passing year. I don't want to come back some day and find I don't know any of the pupils and even the teachers have forgotten my name. I want something to hold on to. Is that really too much to ask? These days, I'm increasingly scared there's no such thing.

As I'm heading towards my friends' room, the door opens and Emma walks out. She's in her running clothes, so she gives me a wave, holds the door for me, and disappears.

I knock on the door frame when I can't see Tori anywhere. Is she in the bathroom? But then she pops up from under the desk.

'Oh, hi,' she says, clapping the dust off her trousers. 'My bloody plug's not working again.'

I shut the door and drop down onto her bed. It wouldn't occur to me to ask if I can come in, or sit down. This must be what it's like to have a brother or sister. Knocking is as good as it gets.

'Have you asked Ms Barnett to get an electrician?'

'Too lazy,' Tori responds. 'Just as well Emma's still works.' She plumps down beside me. 'What's up?'

'Nothing. Do you have time?'

Tori glances at her watch. 'Theatre club in half an hour.'

'Oh, right,' I say hastily. I learned only recently that Tori joined the theatre club at the start of term. Possibly she was trying to spare my feelings. It was the evening after she and Sinclair starred in last year's play when the fire broke out in the west wing. 'I just wondered if you could fill me in on what you're covering at the moment.'

'English or maths?' asks Tori.

I hesitate. 'Both?'

She looks at me in the way I can't stand. 'Livy . . .'

'No, Tori, seriously. I need to know.'

'It's only your first week back at school.'

'Exactly. I can't allow myself to get any further behind.'

Tori's never been good at hiding her feelings. Even now, I can read her like a book as she wrestles with herself. 'I'm scared you're trying to do too much.'

'Well, don't be,' I insist, but then she says the thing I could see in her and Grace's faces yesterday.

'You know, maybe your parents and Mrs Sinclair have a point. It might actually be better for you –'

Tori falls silent as I stand up: I'm suddenly freezing. 'For me to what?' I repeat. 'Not to be with you all any more? What's better about that?'

'No, not that, Olive. But for you to get back to your old self slowly.'

'I'm back already, in case you hadn't noticed.' I have to force myself to stick to an indoor voice, and I hate myself for snapping at my best friend. Again. Breathe. Cool it.

'Livy, we're just worried about you, don't you see?' Tori says quietly. She's still sitting on the bed and she takes my hand.

'I know,' I whisper, as she pulls me back down to the mattress. 'I'm sorry.'

'Hey, I've known you long enough. You don't have to keep stinging me away, Mrs Scorpio.'

I can't help smiling, despite myself. Tori's obsessed with astrology. I'd love to get her to guess Colin's star sign. If there's anything in her theories at all, he must be a Scorpio too. But then he'd be the same as me, and that's the last thing I want. I have no desire to think about Colin Fantino at all.

So instead I say, 'Huh, according to you and your star-sign shite, I have no choice.'

'Sure you do. And you're learning.' Tori slips back so she can rest against the wall. Suddenly a burning pain stabs through my shoulder. I bite my bottom lip and try not to wince, but of course Tori spotted it.

'Sorry,' she says at once. 'Did I hurt you? I keep forgetting . . .'

'Me too,' I say, instead of answering her question.

Tori doesn't reply, and when I turn to her she meets my eyes.

'Don't make me cry now,' I manage. I know my best friend. If she keeps on looking at me like that, she'll say something very like 'I'm so glad you're here,' and I'm not in the mood for more tears.

'I wouldn't dare,' says Tori, starting to plait my hair. That doesn't make it much better, because she started doing that in the hospital when I couldn't manage any of the hairstyles I used to be famous for. To plait your hair properly, you have to be capable of holding both arms above your head for several minutes, and the sad truth is that I'm not any more.

'So how's the theatre club going?'

'Pretty cool. We've just started planning the auditions. I can't wait to see who'll play the leads this year.'

I think back to the performance in the summer when Tori and Sinclair made the best Romeo and Juliet I've ever seen at this school. 'Like there's anything to decide,' I say. 'Or aren't you and Sinclair auditioning?'

'We are,' Tori answers. 'But Mr Acevedo might want to give somebody else a chance.'

'Would you mind?'

'A wee bit, maybe,' she admits. 'But whatever will be will be. And we were lucky to get the chance to audition a year early last time around . . . So, how have your first nights back been?' she asks.

'Dire,' I say, without hesitation. 'On Sunday night I had a panic attack. I couldn't stay lying in bed, so I got up.'

'I still can't believe that was you with the trophy cabinet.' I stay stubbornly silent. 'And Colin has a photo of you?' Tori persists. 'Why was he even there?'

'No idea,' I say curtly. 'Coincidence.'

'Did he try to stop you?'

I give a dry laugh. 'Not really, no.'

'He didn't? So did he watch you . . .?'

'Tori, he went one better than watching – he did it for me.'

'What?' Tori asks, in disbelief.

'Yes,' is all I say.

'Colin smashed the cabinet?'

I nod.

'Is he actually Ava Fantino's son?'

'Whose son?' I ask, although there's a vague bell ringing in the back of my mind.

'*Late Night with Ava Fantino*,' Tori explains. 'The American talk show. You know.'

'As if.'

'Her son's called Colin,' Tori insists.

'There's probably more than one Colin Fantino in New York.'

'Aye, right.' Tori laughs.

'How d'you even know that?'

'No clue. I must have read it somewhere.' Tori shrugs. 'Wild,' she continues. 'Reckon he's met loads of celebs? I heard that Hayes Chamberlain is going on her show soon. That would be his first public appearance since he left the band. Imagine Colin seeing him there. I'd die.'

'Tori.' I sigh.

'Yeah, sorry. Sorry.' She pulls herself together again, but then bursts out: 'OK, so let me get this straight – Colin Fantino smashed the swimming-team trophy cabinet?'

'Could you speak up a bit?' I suggest warningly. The door might be shut, but everyone knows how thin the walls here are.

'Sorry.' She claps a hand to her mouth. 'Crazy,' she whispers. 'But why did he?'

If Fantino wasn't such an arse, I'd have said he did it to help me. On Sunday night I genuinely thought that. But apparently he was only interested in causing me trouble. 'He's threatening to tell Mrs Sinclair it was me.'

'You? But it was him, wasn't it?'

'Yeah, but he's got a photo. Of me by the display case. And I might have kind of raised my fist, and . . . I'd never have done it, I just wanted to know what it felt like.'

'And then he did it?' Tori asks. 'How romantic, Livy,' she breathes, when I nod. 'He smashed it for you.'

'Aye, *very* romantic. Especially the moment he showed me the photo and blackmailed me.'

'But why would he do that?'

'I don't know,' I say. 'Because he's an arsehole?'

'Is he a Scorpio too?' Tori asks, and now I want to leave. 'Let's google him.'

'God, Tori . . .' I groan.

But she's already pulled out her phone and typed in his name. 'You could always ask him when his birthday is.'

'I'm not speaking another word to him.'

'That could get tricky. Yes, here it is. Scorpio, I knew it. That's funny. His birthday's the day before yours, Livy.'

'And that interests me why?'

'It doesn't, I know. But I could tell right away that he's another misunderstood water sign. And he's hot, right?'

I jump, feeling seen.

'Don't you think so?' Tori goes on. 'Yeah, I knew it. He's just your type.'

'He's not my type at all,' I contradict.

'No?' Tori raises her eyebrows at me. 'He kind of reminds me of Ludwig who used to be on the swimming team.'

'Let's not talk about him,' I mumble. The time when I had a fierce crush on the Swiss boy two classes above me was definitely not my finest hour. I sometimes get the shivers right out of nowhere if I remember the one slippery kiss we had after a training session. And not in a good way. Luckily, that was just before the summer holidays at the end of the fourth form, and by the next term, he was back in the Alps.

'Ludwig,' says Tori, shaking her head slightly. 'Those were the days. But Colin's on another level.'

'Tori, I really don't want to talk about Fantino.'

My best friend sighs. 'Fine. What do you want to talk about, then? We've got about fifteen minutes.'

'You sound like a therapist,' I say, immediately regretting it. Because now I can feel Tori's eyes resting heavily on me.

'Have you ever considered—'

'No,' I shoot back.

'You don't even know what I was going to ask.'

'Yes, I do.'

'Fine.' Tori sits up a little straighter. 'So why not?'

'I'm fine,' I say, and it's amazing how easily some lies slip over your lips. You could think it was the truth.

'You can still see a therapist when you're doing fine.'

'I know, Tori.' I cough. 'And I can chat to Ms Vail any time I feel the need.'

'OK,' she says. But I can tell we haven't finished with the tricky issues. 'How are things with your mum now?'

I remember my last conversation with her. *You haven't said anything to your dad, have you?* Fuck it, I should've told him. Not to give Mum away but because it's the right thing to do. The older I get, though, the more often I'm afraid there's never just one *right thing.* You can only weigh up which is the lesser evil.

'She says she's not seeing the guy any more.' My voice is so flat it makes even me shudder.

'OK,' says Tori, but it sounds more like a question.

I rest my head on her legs and stare at Tori's desk. 'That's good, right?'

'Even so, it was such an arsehole move,' says Tori, and I'm reminded yet again of why she's my best friend. Last term, I forgot that for a while: the business about Mum and her affair was messing with my head so much that I was convinced I couldn't speak to anyone in the whole world. I seriously hurt Tori. I regret that, and that I didn't know whether I was coming or going is no excuse. Maybe it was a learning experience I had to go through. A mistake that almost cost me our friendship: I was raging, yet felt so powerless I just pushed away everyone who was worried about me.

I'm trying to see it as progress that I'm not doing it any more, even though I still feel the same. Raging and powerless, for the same reasons as before, plus a whole set of new ones.

'You're right,' I say.

'Not just cheating on your dad, but pulling you into the whole thing too.'

I just pull a face. There's nothing more to say.

'Are you going to tell him anyway?' she asks in the end.

I gulp. 'I think so. But he'll ask questions and then he'll find out how long I've known and . . . Tori, I can't deal with that. It'll really break him.'

'You don't know that, Livy.'

'I do,' I whisper. After all, I've seen it with my own eyes in Grace. She was more in love with Henry than he was with her, and now she's broken when he didn't even cheat on her like my mum did on my dad.

'But don't you think it'll just make everything even more complicated if you wait any longer?'

Not saying anything won't solve the problem, that's true. But part of me – an incredibly weak, cringeworthy part – still hopes that everything could turn out OK. That my family will survive this. That one day we'll be able to sit down to breakfast together at the weekend and not have to weigh up exactly what is and isn't safe to say.

Tori looks at me. 'Do you think she's really dumped the guy?'

'She said she had.' Even as I say the words, I notice how pathetic they sound.

'Do you believe her?'

I straighten up. 'Tori, she said she wants to rescue our family.'

'Do you think she meant it?'

I can't nod or say yes with any conviction, and that should make me think. Which it does, but I can't change the fact that I'm seventeen and, given everything else is in chaos, I'm wishing hard for my family not to break up too.

'I hope so,' I say quietly.

'I hope so, too, for you all.'

'How's your mum?' I ask, after a while.

Tori gives a weak smile. 'She's got through withdrawal. I think she really wants to kick the booze this time.'

'It's OK for you still to be scared.'

Tori kind of twitches. 'I'm afraid we'll always be scared.'

I nod slowly. 'I'm afraid I will too.'

'OK, but you really don't want to talk about Colin . . .?' Tori's voice fades away as I glare at her.

'I couldn't be less interested in Fantino,' I say.

But Tori just gives that knowing grin of hers.

9

COLIN

They're really serious about this study-hour shit. Every lousy afternoon. To my surprise, I got my English and math tests back by Wednesday. I was less surprised to have gotten everything right. So I don't see any need to use study hour for studying. I've been here half a week now but I'm still feeling jetlagged. It's worst in the morning, though I still fall into a hole of exhaustion in the afternoon. By the start of wing time in the evening, my body's reliably wide awake and there's no point even trying to sleep. So I've spent the past few nights exploring the school under cover of darkness.

But I'm paying for that decision now because I'm dead beat as I head up to my room after the last class of the day and drop onto my bed. From sheer force of habit, I open TikTok and groan as the app won't load. Same thing happened yesterday afternoon, and the day before, at this time, because they turn off the Wi-Fi punctually at the start of study hour and wing time.

My roommate looks up from his books and glares at me. I haven't exactly been a model of friendliness in the last couple of days, and I'm still amused by the way he can't stand me. We speak as little to each other as possible, which is fine by me. Truly. Even though it feels like a stab in the chest to catch sight of him around the school with his buddies when I've got absolutely nobody. Not that I want anybody. It's enough that I can sometimes sit with Kit and his crowd at meals. That's enough social interaction for one day for me. I'd be better off working on not losing contact with Paxton, Ash and Maresa although, now I think about it, they haven't messaged our group since I've been here. I'd text them right now and ask how it's going in New York if I weren't cut off from the rest of the world.

I really need to figure out why my phone won't switch to roaming. I need data, like my roommate – he's constantly on his cell phone during study hour.

'Hey, can I use your hotspot?' I ask, sitting up slightly. Sinclair raises his eyebrows patronizingly, and for the first time, I wish I'd been a bit nicer to him. Shit, it should've occurred to me that I'd need his help in something eventually.

'Aye, right, you've got no internet on that thing,' he says. 'That must be pretty shite.'

I roll my eyes, because somebody really needs to teach him that he isn't funny. 'Yeah. So, can I share your data or not?'

'Sorry, I'm running kind of low myself.'

'Is there a phone repair shop around here?'

'Near here?' he repeats. Is he dumb or what?

'Yeah,' I say, annoyed.

'Loads of places in Edinburgh.'

'But here?' I ask, because I'm not in the mood for trekking through the boondocks for hours by bus.

'In Ebrington, you mean?' Now he's laughing. 'Irvine's might sell you a prepaid SIM, if data's the issue. Ask Kit, he might know. Hey, what are you doing?' he adds, as I stand up.

'Going to find out.'

'It's study hour.'

'So what?' I mutter, as I slip on my shoes.

He keeps staring at me for a while like he's shocked, but then gives a quiet laugh. 'Aye, right, you want to get expelled. Well, have fun.'

'Thanks, I will.' I grab my key, my useless cell phone and some money before leaving the room. Out on the corridor, I dip into the bowl of cookies in the kitchen and walk towards the stairs. Mr Acevedo's door is open, which must mean he's playing watchdog, ready to spot anyone trying to creep out.

'Ah, Colin.' He turns up behind me at that very moment. 'I was about to come and see you. Dr Henderson called – you had an appointment with him?'

Shit, that's right. I was supposed to go and introduce myself to the school doctor before study hour. I totally forgot.

'Yeah, could be,' I mumble, as I turn around.

'Why are you even out here on the wing? Have you finished your prep? In that case you can go and see him now, OK?' Mr Acevedo says, walking past me to his room.

Fine, so I'll pay a visit to this doc, then go into the town. Suits me.

Someone else is coming up the stairs towards me. There's almost a hint of fear in Olive Garden's eyes, but then her expression becomes unreadable.

'It's study hour,' she pants, as she hurries past me.

'Yeah, knock yourself out.' I shove a cookie into my mouth. She stops. 'Where are you going?'

'To see the goddamn school doctor. Can you tell me where he is?'

'I'm sorry?' She takes a step towards me.

'Yeah, or d'you want to come along? After that I thought I'd go see Mrs Sinclair and then you can explain to her what *you did* in person.'

She gives a slightly manic laugh, which secretly makes me grin. 'Do whatever you like.'

I walk over and rest my hand on the wall, level with her face. I notice again how tiny she is as I look down at her. There's a warning glimmer in her green eyes. 'Don't you worry, Olive Garden, I will.'

She juts out her chin provocatively, which sadly I find only too pleasing. 'You really think you can just come here and do whatever the hell you like, don't you?'

I shrug. 'I don't know. Can I?'

'You're not a good person, Colin Fantino,' she says, with disgust.

I smile wearily and eat another cookie. 'You don't say.'

She's still looking up into my face, and comes a little closer, and, oh, God, my body responds. I forget to chew.

She smells nice. Like a flower.

Oh, crap, Fantino. Since when have I been thinking about how Olive Garden smells? I don't give a damn how she smells. And I don't even like the scent of flowers all that much anyway. It's OK, no more. God.

'And *the goddamn school doctor* is my dad,' she says, before she walks away. 'You'll find him in the sick bay on the ground floor, first door on the right, after the trophy cabinets. Say hi to him from me.'

He really is Olive Garden's dad. I spot his dark green eyes right away, which are just like hers. But there's a lot less hatred in his expression, which makes a pleasant change.

I've met a lot of doctors in my life, so I can generally tell within a few seconds if they've got it or not. I don't mean if they know what they're doing, but whether or not their work's turned them into the kind of soulless robot who just reels off standard questions, hammers on their computer keyboard and never looks me in the eye.

Olive Garden's father makes time for me, and he's done his research. He knows my insulin regime, and introduces me to the school nurse who, unlike him, seems to be here round the clock. I hate to admit it, but I feel good around him. Which is obviously nothing to do with whose father he is.

And even that's kind of ridiculous. The school doctor is display-case girl's dad and the head teacher is my clown of a roommate's mom. What next? Should I call Ava Fantino and ask her if she wants a job here too?

Study hour still isn't over as I stroll through the empty corridors towards the south wing after my appointment with Dr Henderson. After what I said to Olive Garden, I don't want to risk missing Mrs Sinclair. I don't know how late she stays at the school, so I pick up the pace a bit. It's been fun to threaten Olive Garden with putting the blame for the display-case thing on her, but I know when it's time to back down. She looked seriously stressed just now, so that's enough.

When I get to the offices, I ignore the school secretary who tries to stop me interrupting Mrs Sinclair, and I knock on her door instead of letting him schedule a meeting.

She looks up from her desk when I walk in, and I can see the resemblance to her son. 'Colin,' she says, like she deserves a medal for remembering my name. 'What can I do for you?'

'It was me,' I say, as I come closer and sit down without waiting to be asked, because I have no respect. I can see from Mrs Sinclair's face that she doesn't know what I'm talking about, so I kindly help her out a bit. 'The display case.'

She doesn't look all that surprised, which ought to make me

think. 'You are responsible for the damage to the swimming-team display case?' she says, looking intently at me.

'Yes, I am.'

She stands up, which is probably meant to be intimidating. I lean back slightly and enjoy the show.

'I'm disappointed that you're getting your time at Dunbridge Academy off to this kind of start, Colin.'

Oh, God, the I'm-not-angry-I'm-disappointed schtick. This woman is a teacher to her bones.

I shrug. 'And it happened after wing time.'

Mrs Sinclair reaches for an expensive-looking leather bag. When I realize she's starting to pack away her things, I feel nervous. What's going on here? Why isn't she giving me a lecture? She isn't letting me provoke her, and that unsettles me.

'For the next four weeks, you can spend an hour a day helping Mr Carpenter, our school caretaker,' she says, not looking at me. 'And that's on top of your other duties.'

'No warning?' I ask in disappointment.

'No, Colin.' Now she does look at me. 'I'm not giving you a formal warning, but if you continue to break the rules, you can expect further additional work, curfews and the confiscation of your technological devices.'

'Why don't you just kick me out?'

'Your mother warned me that you would try to get yourself expelled. So instead of wasting your time and energy on the attempt, you'd be better off making the most of the opportunities that this school offers.'

I feel a deeper chill at her every word.

Mom warned her. She knows me well enough that she persuaded her not to throw me out. She knew I'd have a plan.

'I'll ask Mr Carpenter tomorrow whether you turned up. If not, Mr Acevedo will confiscate your mobile phone.'

'But my phone is my glucose meter,' I point out.

'Dr Henderson will happily issue you with an analogue meter that works just as well.' Mrs Sinclair walks past me to a coat hook by the door and puts on her coat. 'Think carefully about your actions, Colin. And now please go back to your room for the rest of study hour.'

10

OLIVE

I spend the whole of study hour waiting for Ms Barnett to send me over to Mrs Sinclair. Because Colin stuck to his guns and grassed on me. It's his fault that I can't concentrate on anything. Not on my maths prep that's due tomorrow, and not on the upper-sixth stuff I wanted to look at afterwards either.

Why is he so mean? Why did I even go downstairs that night, and why did I let him smash that case up? I didn't even bloody ask him to do it, so does it now give him some sick feeling of power to blackmail me over it? What's wrong with the guy?

My heart thuds nervously as I go down after study hour. Ms Barnett doesn't stop me, which must mean that Fantino didn't rat after all. Or else he's in with Mrs Sinclair this very moment, dishing up his lies.

What the hell? I've been at this school for seven years – it's home to me. I almost lost everything, and now some bawbag comes along from New York and thinks he gets to threaten me? Well, he's very much mistaken, and if he seriously wants trouble, he's got it.

If I'm in luck, Mrs Sinclair will still be in her office. I don't know if I'd be so keen to tell her the truth about the broken trophy cabinet tomorrow morning. I'm not usually the type to tell tales, but Colin has it coming.

Fate seems to be on my side, because as I get to the bottom of the stairs, the head teacher is just stepping out of the south wing and heading for her dark Range Rover that's waiting on the cobbled courtyard. She and her husband have a house in Ebrington. Unlike Sinclair, who boards here, she spends her days at the school and drives home every evening.

I speed up to catch her before she gets in.

'Mrs Sinclair?' She stops, turning to look at me. I try to guess from her face whether or not Fantino's been to see her. I seem to have got in first, because she smiles at me, rather than instantly launching an interrogation into how I dared vandalize school property. 'Do you have a minute?'

'Of course, Olive.' She waits. 'What is it?'

I hate myself for being this weak. For the part of me that's fighting vehemently against sneaking on someone to the head. I'd never normally do anything like this, but I'm not prepared to let Fantino blackmail me any longer. He asked for it.

I gulp. 'Er, about the display case . . .'

Mrs Sinclair raises her eyebrows in surprise. 'That has already been dealt with, Olive.'

My blood runs cold. So has he already spoken to her?

'Did Colin come to see you?' I burst out.

'Yes, he . . .' She stops. 'Wait a moment, how do you know that?'

Rats. That was careless. 'Yeah, I . . . I don't know what he told you, but I didn't do anything. Honestly. The sight of the trophies, and knowing I'll never win any more races for the school, made me so angry, but you have to believe me that I'd never have smashed up the cabinet, and when Colin came along, I didn't want him to—'

'You were there with Colin?' the head interrupts me.

'Yes, I . . .' I pause. 'He . . .'

'He just came to see me and admitted that he damaged the display case,' says Mrs Sinclair.

He what? I freeze. He confessed? He didn't go through with his threat?

'Is that true, Olive?'

Suddenly I'm overcome by the need to protect him. It's ridiculous. I'm raging with Fantino because he threatened me. And now I'm trying to save his skin, even though he doesn't deserve it.

'He was only trying to help,' I explain.

'Help?' Mrs Sinclair looks at me like I'm out of my mind. 'By destroying the trophy cabinet?'

'Yes, I . . .' *He was trying to help because I didn't have the guts.* But I don't say that. 'He didn't do it on purpose.'

Oh yes he did.

It would serve him bloody well right if I told Mrs Sinclair exactly that. But I can't.

She eyes me, then shakes her head. 'Well, it doesn't make any difference, either way. It's noble of you to want to defend him, but we can't have that kind of behaviour here. Colin will be given an appropriate punishment. And now we need to discuss what you were doing out of your room after wing time.'

I shiver. OK, I didn't think this through. Because even though I didn't smash the thing up, I was still out of bounds. My pulse quickens as I force myself to meet Mrs Sinclair's eyes. They bore through me.

'I'm listening, Olive.'

Should I lie? Claim that I was on my way to the sick bay for more painkillers? I'd probably get away with that, but I can't face it.

'I couldn't sleep,' I say in the end. 'I was in my room, in bed, but . . . I couldn't. The moment I shut my eyes, I started to panic, and I had to get some air, to . . . I'm sorry.'

When I look up at Mrs Sinclair again, I see surprise in her eyes, followed by pity. And I hate it.

'I see,' she says slowly. 'I'm sorry to hear that, Olive.'

I shouldn't have said anything. What if she tells Dad? 'It's

OK,' I say hastily. 'I should have stayed in my room. It won't happen again, I promise.'

'I know we've already talked about this, but I would encourage you again to speak to Ms Vail. You might find it a relief, Olive.'

'Yes, I know. I'll think about it.' I hesitate. 'Will you give me a warning?'

Mrs Sinclair gives me a hard stare. 'Just promise me that you'll ask for help if you need it.'

I nod and mumble, 'Thank you.' Mrs Sinclair glances at her car and I hastily add: 'Please don't tell my dad what I just told you, Miss.'

Great. Now I sound like my mum. But if Dad hears that I'm not sleeping because of panic attacks, he's sure to conclude that I'm *not ready* after all.

'Very well, Olive,' Mrs Sinclair says, after eyeing me again. 'Have a nice evening.'

'You too,' I say, as she gets into the car.

I shove my hands into my hoodie pockets and turn away. I walk across the courtyard wondering if that conversation really happened. To say I was confused would be a massive understatement. What made him fess up after he threatened me again just now? Was he only teasing and never intended to accuse me? I'd like to find him and ask him, but then another thought distracts me.

Please don't tell my dad.

Mum coming into my room and shutting the door. I don't

want to sound like her. And I don't want to ask other people to do a thing I hate. Because, if I'm honest, I still wish I could go to Dad and tell him everything. It's just that I'm afraid he'd be totally devastated to hear that Mum's been sleeping with another man.

Not that I even know for certain that she has. Maybe they only kissed. She and that guy looked very close when I saw them in Ebrington. They must have slept together. I don't even want to know. It's just minging. The way she is at home, so natural, acting like nothing's happened. Like she wasn't the one who destroyed our family, which she did the minute she decided to cheat on her husband. I can hardly find words for how angry that makes me. The only thing I know about the man is his name: Alexis. Does he have a family? Is he going behind their backs too? Does he hope Mum will leave Dad for him?

Almost without noticing, I'm walking through the main school gate and onto the road that leads to Ebrington. There's still a while till dinner and I feel too churned up just to sit in my room. All this free time is unsettling. I'm not used to it. In the old days, I barely had a spare minute between classes, study hour, meals and swimming. And I loved it. Being busy. The rewarding ache after a particularly tough training session, rather than the pain of the skin graft and my shoulder.

But that's all in the past. I straighten my back as I get closer to Ebrington. I ignore the wee high street and turn off into the estate where Grace and her family live. I was here on one of my rare free afternoons, totally unsuspecting, when I saw the sight that changed my life.

Sometimes I really wish I hadn't been in the village that day. Then I'd have as little idea as Dad about what my mother gets up to when she claims to be doing home visits. OK, so most of the time that will have been what she was doing, but the idea that she uses her job as a midwife to cover up her assignations with her lover makes me want to boak. My heart sinks as I come closer to the semi-detached house outside which I saw her car. There's nobody on the narrow street, but I can't shake off the images. The dark front door opening, the expectation of seeing her in the company of either a pregnant woman or a new mother. And then the numbness that spread through me as she kissed a stranger goodbye.

Back then, I ran away as fast as I could, but this time, I stop outside the house. Dark bricks, two storeys high, lattice windows, a neat, simple front garden. I don't know what good I think it'll do me to find out who lives here. I saw the man. About as tall as Mum, thin, dark jeans, pale shirt. Ebrington might be small, but I've never seen him before or since, not that that proves anything – a lot of people who live here work in Edinburgh.

I feel like I'm breaking some rule as I get closer to the garden gate. But just as I'm about to push it open and venture up to the front door, a car turns into the road.

Hastily, I turn away, dig my hands into my jacket pockets and walk down the pavement. My heart beats faster as I half turn at the end of the road and watch out of the corner of my eye as the car stops beside the neighbouring house.

Why, for God's sake? What's the use of knowing who the man is? Leave it – it won't make anything un-happen. On the contrary. The more I know about him, the more real everything gets. There's no answer to any of this. I'm caught between a rock and a hard place: whatever I do, it'll be wrong. I can go to Dad and tell him, then pray that my parents don't get divorced. Or I can say nothing and risk Dad finding out anyway – that Mum had an affair and that I didn't tell him.

My head aches and so does my heart. I'm sick of all this. I just want a bit of peace. I didn't want anything to change, but apparently you don't get to wish that because *everything* has changed.

I walk aimlessly around the village because I don't want to go back to school, but my mind is whirling. I head for the castle loch because the way the sky reflects in its smooth surface has an almost meditative effect on me. It's a wee bit of peace amid all the chaos that's my life now. It always has been. Water is my element. Liquid serenity, especially when I can swim lengths, dive, be weightless.

There's nobody here but me, or so I think as I let my eyes roam across the loch. To the far bank.

And then I see him.

COLIN

I put my shoulders back and try not to start running as I leave the office and step into the corridor. It's never been so hard. I don't go up to my room because I'm so not in the mood to set eyes on anybody else.

Ava Fantino and Mrs Sinclair agreed that I'd be punished but not expelled. So everything's lost. I won't be able to stroll out of here in a few days and fly back to New York, like I promised Cleo and my friends. I have to stay here. In Scotland. All fucking year.

I'm surprised by how hard it hits me. I feel so dumb for believing I could get the better of my mother. She knows me. She's more cunning than me. After all, I have to inherit it from somewhere. And she always gets what she wants.

My stupid heart just won't stop racing. Not even after I've explored this godforsaken hole and bought a prepaid SIM card in the tiny supermarket. Not even after I've messaged my friends and been ignored by them in return. And not even after I've left the rows of houses and followed a well-trodden path to a little lake. Luckily, I don't see anyone by the water or on the narrow boardwalk. I follow the path to the water's edge, pass little bushes and curved weeping willows, whose spreading branches reach down to the water. It's peaceful here, little ducks swimming on the lake, which is fringed by tall grass that bends with the wind. But that's no use to me so

I walk on. Halfway around the lake, I look around me again, then sit down on a weathered bench. For a moment, I let my head fall back and stare up into the clear sky. Then I pull my lighter out of my pocket.

You were going to stop. You promised yourself.

But, shit, what can I do? I've just discovered that my mom's still calling the shots, same as ever. That I can't get away from here, or at least not as fast as I thought. I feel naïve and ignored. I'm angry, I'm scared. Fuck it. I don't want to feel this way.

Why can't you just suck it up?

Why, why, why?

But why am I supposed to suck up so much in my life? Why is my mom so cold and emotionless towards me, and why did I even let them send me away? Why do I still care? Why does the thought of New York and home make my throat tighten? I'm seventeen, for God's sake, and almost crying with home-sickness. And because I'm finding it harder and harder to suppress what happened in New York. What I did. Someone died and it's my fault . . .

I flip open my lighter and push up the sleeve of my hoodie. The spot on my wrist is always risky, but nobody knows me here. Nobody will get suspicious if I say I burned myself some-how, in that tiny wing kitchen, on the hob, whatever the hell.

I hold my breath as the flame hits my skin, then bite my bottom lip. The pain is sheer relief and I deserve it. It twinges through my body and, for a moment, it drives out all my thoughts. Because I'm focused on breathing and holding it. Because I can feel it. Because I can feel *myself.*

I've just shut my eyes when I hear a crack.

Fuck.

I pull back my hand, pull my sleeve over my wrist. I just have time to slip my lighter into the front pocket on my hoodie before I see someone walking down the path towards me, between the trees.

'Fantino.'

I jump. Great. Act normal. There's no way she can find out what you were just doing.

'What's up, Olive Garden?' I cross my right ankle over my left knee.

'Spare me your pointless wisecracks and tell me what the fuck your problem is.' She looms over me, and it's irritating that I have to look up at her.

'What do you want?'

'Mrs Sinclair,' she snaps, crossing her arms angrily over her chest. I forget the dumb remark I was about to make as I see her wince at the movement. Pain crosses her face. Then her expression is blank again. 'She says you told her it was you.'

'Yuu-uup,' I say slowly. 'You must be pleased.'

'What's wrong with you? What makes you think you can just mess with people's heads and then go and confess anyway?'

I have to grin. 'So you really thought I'd snitch?'

'God, I don't know. I don't know you.'

She should count herself lucky. 'I'm devastated that you had such a low opinion of me.'

'Your own fault.'

'True. And your dad sends his love back. He's way nicer than you.'

Olive laughs. For a moment, the enmity fades from her face, giving way to an almost painful expression. But then she seems to decide not to follow up on that. 'So, get yourself expelled, then?' The tinge of hope in her voice is a punch in the guts, which I deserve.

'You'd like that, wouldn't you?' I pluck an imaginary bit of fluff off my pants leg and wish she'd sit down next to me instead of standing over me like that. 'But I'm sorry to disappoint you. She didn't even give me a warning.'

'What?' She's startled. 'No warning?'

'No.' I shrug. 'You just need the right surname.'

She gasps, then gives me a scornful look. Guess she didn't pick up the sarcasm in that last line. Whatever. She probably thinks I'm genuinely proud to be Ava Fantino's son.

'I wish you no harm, Colin Fantino,' she says coolly. I would reconsider that statement if I were her. 'Just that one day someone will treat you the way you treat others.'

I give a tired smile. 'Ouch. That hit home, Olive Garden.'

She turns away. I fight back the urge to ask her to stay. What's up with me? She clearly doesn't like my company and I'm not exactly trying to change that, but something inside me enjoyed the battle of words with her. It's weird, but I feel more alive. Olive Garden standing in front of me, trying to test whether looks can kill, also helps me forget everything else, at least for a moment. All my miserable problems, for example.

Which all catch up with me as she stomps away.

I don't follow her.

11

COLIN

I spend the whole next day winding her up. I feel it every time I eat in class, don't follow the rules, or say something rude. It's a game and I'm kind of enjoying it. And I need the entertainment because the rest of my day is mostly crap. Later on, I go to tennis training with Kit, though, and that's moderately fun. It helps me to let off a little steam after my first time serving my punishment by dusting shelves and scrubbing floors for Mr Carpenter, the school caretaker. I have to report to him again on Friday, after study hour, when everyone but me will be starting their weekend. I don't know whether or not Mrs Sinclair has told my mom about my behaviour – Ava Fantino hasn't been in touch. Not that that proves anything. Hey, it looks like she'd been expecting to hear that I was in trouble, so news of that sort wouldn't be any reason for her to contact me. After all, she's a busy woman.

I gather from her socials that she's back in New York. Some wannabe actor's on her show tonight, not that I give a shit about that. But it was surprisingly painful when I realized that she's not even on the same continent as me any more.

I'm in Scotland, constantly thinking about how I can get out of here. At first I thought there was no point in breaking the rules again because that would just land me with more punishment, but then it occurred to me that I'd have to do something so serious that the head teacher would have to put her foot down. And of course I've considered simply running away and to hell with Mom and Dad's attempt at blackmailing me over the trust fund. It's a load of money, but I'm prepared to work hard if it means I can do my own thing. Though that would be majoring in psychology, and no part-time job in the world would pay enough to get me through college without the help of my parents. Not in New York anyway, and the one thing my heart is set on is to study at Columbia and finally live my life my way. A life with Maresa, Paxton and Ash, even though they've practically ghosted me the last few days. They're probably just busy, but I can't deny the toxic stab of pain I feel, which worsens with every snap I see of them and how much fucking fun they're having without me.

Mr Carpenter is outside waxing the floor, but he hasn't bothered to look in to make sure I'm putting in a good graft, as he puts it, so I let myself drop onto one of the wooden chairs with a groan. Then I send a snap to my friends and go on Maresa's chat because I like tormenting myself. I'm about to message her when a new photo comes in. I click on the picture and an icy cold spreads through my body as I take in what it shows.

Interlinked hands. Maresa's long, slender fingers and the back of a clearly male hand, belonging to my nemesis.

Suddenly, every sound fades into the background. The noise of Mr Carpenter's floor polisher out in the hall, the ticking of the wall clock. All I can hear is my own heartbeat pulsing in my ears as I stare at the white heart that Maresa's adorned her chat with.

It's an unmistakable message that I never saw coming. She's with somebody else. But can you be ditched when you were never really together? We were never exclusive – not because I didn't want to be but because she's a self-confident, independent woman, who likes her fun and didn't want to commit. I don't even know why I'm so shocked. Did I actually have a bit more than a crush on her, or is it just a blow, however shitty, to my male ego that she's replaced me so fast?

My head is empty. My heart's taken a hard knock and, rather than deal with that, I get mad. Because the woman I was sharing a bed with not so long ago doesn't see the need to unfriend me before sending out cute snaps of her and her new lover. I hate being the one who had feelings and is now hurting, even though Maresa never promised me any more than a couple of nights. I thought I could live with that, but apparently I was wrong. And maybe it's not just my crappy emotions, but the realization that my friends' lives are still going on in New York. Even without me. And I won't be back any time soon, the way I originally planned.

I feel a sudden sense of despair and nausea. I close Snapchat and suppress the urge to hurl my iPhone against the wall. Just then, I get a FaceTime call. At first, I don't want to speak to anyone, but I see that it's Cleo. I can pull myself together for my kid sister if for nobody else. I eye the door cautiously, jump up and close it, then take the call.

'Hey, Peanut,' I greet the pixellated image of my sister, which gradually sharpens. 'No school today?'

'I just got back,' Cleo explains, and her little voice makes my heart clench. Fuck, I miss her and the afternoons when we both finished early and I could take her home. Mom and Dad were never there at that time of day. Our nanny Kirsten was in charge in the afternoons. It must be about two p.m. in New York, because it's early evening here. I never thought that anything as meaningless as a five-hour time difference would make me feel a million miles from my family. It's like I'm existing in a different reality from them, because whatever I do – brushing my teeth, having breakfast, lunch or going to bed – I'm never doing it at the same time as them.

'Great,' I say, trying to sound natural. It's kind of ridiculous how well I succeed. 'So, what's up?'

'I'm bored.'

'No homework?'

I grin as Cleo glances over her shoulder. She's sitting at her desk and I know that Kirsten pops in regularly to check that she's not getting distracted. 'Sure.'

'Don't let Kirsten hear that.'

Cleo ignores that remark and brings her face closer to the screen. 'Where even are you?'

I sigh. 'Some storeroom.' I lift my phone so that Cleo can see. 'I'm cleaning.'

'Why?' she asks, baffled. I'd like to say, *Because I have to, Peanut*, but I'm a good big brother who wants to be a role model, so instead of telling her that it's a punishment for vandalism, I explain that this boarding school has all these annoying duties, and that I have to *do my bit* like everyone else.

'So, what's boarding school like?' Cleo asks, and I could cry. 'Is it like in *Wild Child*?'

'Way cooler,' I lie, my soul leaving my body.

'I want to go to boarding school too,' Cleo murmurs, resting her chin in both hands. 'Do you miss us?'

God, stop that, Peanut . . . It's never been harder to smile. 'Of course.'

She doesn't smile back. 'Can you play for me, Col?'

My stomach knots. Cleo always used to play me her favourite songs, so that I could listen to them once and play them back to her on the piano. It was like a ritual between us, one that now seems like a lifetime ago.

'I haven't found a piano here yet, Peanut.' Apart from the grand in the hall where the morning assembly took place on

Monday. I'm pretty sure you're not allowed to play that without permission.

'Ask someone.'

Sometimes I'm amazed how simple the world is in the eyes of a thirteen-year-old. And I usually see then that my kid sister is right and I'm making things way more complicated than I need to. I really could just ask. I'm absolutely sure there's more than one piano at a fancy school like this. It's just that I hate asking anyone here for anything.

'I'll find out,' I promise. 'And you can save up your song requests.'

Cleo's face brightens a little. 'Deal.'

'So, what are Mom and Dad up to?' I ask, because a small, pathetic part of me wants to hear that they miss me. Not that they do. I know that even before Cleo shrugs.

'They're busy.'

Same as ever. And maybe the thing I hate most about this whole deal is that my kid sister is now sitting at home alone, apart from our nanny, and my parents don't see any need to spend time with her and show her that she matters to them.

'It's so boring without you, Col,' she adds, sounding so sad that it breaks my heart.

'It's boring here too,' I say.

'When are you coming back?'

I swallow hard. 'Soon,' I promise, despising myself for it. I was truly certain of that when I told Cleo so just before my flight, but I'm not any more. And I don't want to be the guy who makes her promises he can't keep and lets her down. So I've got to find a solution. It's that damn simple.

Cleo whirls around as her door opens.

'How are you getting on?' I hear Kirsten say. 'Don't forget you have gymnastics in half an hour.'

'Almost done,' says Cleo.

'What are you doing?' Kirsten comes over. 'Oh, Colin. It's you. How are you doing?'

'Amazing,' I lie.

'Do you like boarding school?'

I almost laugh at that. 'Yeah, it's great.'

'That's nice. Cleo, get changed now, or we'll be late.'

'I will,' she says, turning back to me. 'Got to go, Col.'

'No problem,' I say. 'See you soon.'

'Yeah, soon, OK?'

'Miss you, Peanut,' I say, but the video's already disconnected. It feels so wrong sitting here, imagining my little sister running around our apartment packing her sports bag. I ought to be the one taking her to training, like I always did. I ought to be there, even though I know I don't deserve to be. If Cleo knew what I did, she'd be shocked. The thought of her hearing rumours at school about me and the fire makes me sick. Mom will have assured her that I had nothing to do with it. And Cleo will have believed it because she always believes Mom. And because she sees me as the kind of role model I'm not.

Maybe this is all part of the punishment I deserve because,

to be honest, I don't deserve to be with her. Maybe it has to be this way. Because Cleo Fantino needs better company than her no-good brother, who has a person's death on his conscience.

OLIVE

I never realized how much I missed the midnight parties with my pals. This Saturday evening, the old greenhouse is fuller than normal, because it now has to serve as the party location for two year groups not one.

'Olive!' I'm barely through the door when Theresa O'Malley and a few other girls from my lower-sixth English group pounce on me. 'We were just talking about you.'

'Oh, really?' I ask, like I should be pleased about that.

'Yeah, we were wondering if you'd be involved in the school newspaper. You know the centenary celebrations got postponed, so we're planning a special edition for the party in the spring and we're looking for someone who'll do the sport and hobbies section. Would you be up for it?'

Theresa sounds euphoric, and even though I'm sure she genuinely doesn't mean any harm, her offer makes my stomach clench. 'Why me in particular?'

'Well, you know everyone in the upper sixth, you were on the swimming team and doing A-level PE. So we thought . . .' Theresa trails off.

'That I've got loads of time on my hands now that I can't swim or do PE any more?' I suggest.

She glances down. 'No – oh, man, I'm sorry if it came across that way. We just thought it would be nice now that you're in our form.'

I feel like saying, *Not for long*, but I don't.

'Think about it, yeah?' Theresa suggests. 'But it's totally OK if you don't want to. I just thought I'd ask.'

I nod mechanically. 'I'll think about it.'

She smiles and I should probably chat to her and the others for a bit to settle into my new form, but everything within me wants to join Emma, Henry, Tori and Sinclair. I link arms with Grace, who's just come in with Gideon.

'The school newspaper?' Grace asks, when I tell her about Theresa's idea. 'That might be cool, though? You really do know someone on pretty much all the teams. I'd be your woman for athletics.'

'And me for rugby,' Gideon adds. 'Your man, that is. You know what I mean.'

'Or don't you want to?' Grace persists, as Gideon goes over to a few of the rugby lads and we join Tori and the others.

'I don't know,' I say. It would mean talking to more people on the swimming team, which I've been avoiding up to now. They sent me flowers and get-well cards in hospital, but I haven't said thank you because I can't bear the thought of even setting foot in the swimming centre while they're training. However much I miss my team and Ms Cox.

145

'Because of the swimming?' Grace asks, like she's read my mind.

I shrug. 'I'm not part of the team any more.'

'You'll always be part of the team,' she insists. 'I can seriously imagine you as the Dunbridge sports reporter, armed with a camera, asking insightful interview questions.'

'I've got enough on my plate with my schoolwork and keeping up with you all. And stop looking at me like that.'

'Looking at you like what?'

'So . . . knowing.'

'Sorry.' Grace stands up. 'What do you want to drink?'

'Don't mind,' I mumble, watching her back as she disappears into the crowd.

Tori immediately draws me into her conversation and for a brief moment I manage to forget that I'm not in the upper sixth with them all. She fills me in on all the gossip and suddenly it's just like the old days.

Except that, every now and then, my eyes wander to the door as people come into the greenhouse. Colin is never among them, and I'm annoyed with myself for even noticing that. Can I really be surprised that he considers himself too cool for a midnight party?

Even so, when Henry asks Sinclair about him, I prick my ears.

'Obviously I invited him,' he says hastily. 'But do you seriously think he'd come?'

'Is he still being an arse?' Tori asks.

146

'He laughed and told me to enjoy our kiddies' tea party.'

'I hate him.' I only realize I said that aloud when the others turn to look at me. 'No, really,' I add. 'He's such a bawbag.'

Tori laughs. 'He's a total Scorpio.'

'Tori, I'm going to start taking that personally in a minute.'

'No need, you can't help it.'

'Give it a rest. I'm nothing like Fantino.'

Nobody replies, and I cross my arms in outrage. 'Whoa, you don't mean it?'

'You can seem kind of prickly until someone gets to know you,' Emma says, with an apologetic shrug.

'Even if I am, Fantino's next level. He has no respect for anyone.'

'She's not wrong . . .' murmurs Sinclair.

'You see? How do you manage, sharing a room with him?'

'We try to keep out of each other's way. And talk as little as possible.'

'That's so sad,' Henry remarks. 'For you both. He doesn't seem to want to settle in here.'

'He doesn't,' I agree. 'He just wants to be provocative. I've never met anyone who speaks to the teachers like he does. Not even Valentine Ward.'

'And that's saying something,' mutters Gideon, who's joined us now.

'Colin really thinks he can do whatever he likes. And he eats the whole bloody time! I mean, constantly, and everywhere. Even in class, and no teacher says a word.'

'Olive . . .' Sinclair tries to get a word in, but I don't let him.

'No, you guys don't get it. I'm going to flip if I have to spend even one more day—'

'Olive, he's got diabetes,' Henry interrupts.

'What?' I laugh.

And then it goes quiet. I must have misheard, but Henry's face is serious. Sinclair meets my eyes. And suddenly I feel like a total idiot. 'He has? Seriously?'

Henry nods.

'Did you all know that?' My friends look embarrassed, which tells me everything. 'You're kidding?'

'I didn't,' says Grace, but that doesn't help much.

'My mum told me,' says Sinclair.

'She told me too,' Henry says. 'As school captain.'

'But why didn't anyone say anything in class?' I ask. 'The teachers must know if—'

'They do,' says Henry. 'They all know. But Colin didn't want a big fuss about it.'

'And none of you thought to mention that to me?'

Tori looks kind of guilty. 'You didn't want to talk about him.'

'I don't,' I say at once.

Tori and Henry exchange glances.

'But this is important! I need to know what to do if he—'

'I think Colin's perfectly capable of telling people what he needs,' Sinclair replies.

I stand up.

'What are you doing?'

'I don't know,' I say, although I know perfectly well. 'I need to go and do some research. I mean, don't people with diabetes have to avoid too much sugar? He eats the whole time.'

'Sit down, Olive,' Henry orders, taking a quick breath. 'There are different kinds of diabetes. Colin has type one. It's genetic and mostly appears when you're young. His body has stopped producing insulin so he has to take it externally. And if his blood sugar is too low, he has to eat.'

I can't speak. I had a go at Colin for eating in class, but he only did it because he had to. God, I'm stupid. I'm a total idiot.

And then my blood runs cold as I follow my friends' eyes over to the door.

12

COLIN

She knows. I'm absolutely certain of that when her eyes meet mine as I set foot in this stupid greenhouse. Admittedly it's quite a nice venue with all the threadbare armchairs and sofas they've got here. Olive's expression has changed. I see concern instead of disdain.

Word that I'm diabetic is gradually getting out, so it was only a matter of time before that fact reached her too. I was kind of surprised that her dad hadn't mentioned it to her, but apparently he takes doctor–patient confidentiality seriously.

I immediately look away and bury my hands in my hoodie pockets. I'm already regretting having come. I didn't even want to, but after first Sinclair and then Kit invited me, I thought I could at least give it a try. Besides, I couldn't stand the idea of spending the whole weekend holed up in my room, wallowing in self-pity because Maresa's snaps keep popping up in my head.

I stroll over to a bunch of guys from my English course, where I spot Kit too, give them a nod, and then glance aside. Suddenly, Olive Garden is standing in front of me.

'Hi,' she says curtly, her green catlike eyes boring through me. Her long dark hair falls over her shoulders, the skin pale and soft-looking. Yeah, soft. I can't think of another word for it.

'What's up?' I say, forcing myself to look away again. Don't want her thinking I'm pleased to see her because I'm not. Not one bit.

'We need to talk.' It sounds like a threat. Is she pissed with me again? What have I done now?

'At a party?' I laugh. 'Crazy idea, Olive Garden.'

Before I have time to react, she's grabbed my arm and is pulling me away. Past the others, to the door and outside. The night is fresh and I can't help noticing how she shivers and hunches her shoulders. Briefly I consider lending her my sweater. But I'm not doing that. This isn't some crappy teen romance. Quite apart from which, she'd be way too proud to accept anything from me.

'So . . .' I cross my arms and lean back against the wall behind us. 'Talk to me.'

She doesn't talk. She looks at me and swallows. My mouth kind of dries out. And then she does speak.

'I heard that you – ' she pauses – '. . . you're diabetic?'

'Don't worry, it's not catching,' I snap, but she's not being scared off by that.

'I know it's none of my business, but you're going to tell me what to do in an emergency.'

I narrow my eyes to thin slits.

'I mean it, Fantino,' she insists.

I can see that, Olive Garden. 'Why do you even care?'

'I don't care.'

'You're contradicting yourself every other sentence.'

'Yeah,' she says stubbornly. 'Well?'

'So you want me to explain it to you even though you don't care?'

Her glare could kill. 'I haven't got all day.'

I sigh, but common sense wins out. If things ever do get complicated, it probably wouldn't be a bad idea for someone to know what to do.

'OK,' I say coolly, pushing myself away from the wall. 'It's basically very simple. It's about sugar, i.e. carbs, and insulin. When I eat, I need insulin so that the sugar reaches my cells and can be turned into energy. Your body can produce its own insulin and does that automatically. Mine can't any more.'

She gives a controlled nod. 'So you have to inject it?'

'I have a pump,' I say, but I can tell she has no idea what I'm talking about. So I lift my T-shirt to show her the round pod above my left hip that combines my pump and a measuring system. I'm surprised she hadn't spotted it on Sunday night by the display cases, but hey, it was dark. Now, I can't help noticing the way Olive's gaze flits over the waistband of my jeans, and my belly. I suppress a grin. *Oh, Olive Garden, are you really that easily impressed?*

Then she seems to remind herself of who she is, because she looks away from my belly and back up to my face. 'That's it?' she asks calmly.

I nod.

'I always thought . . .' She stops. 'No, doesn't matter. Forget it.'

'That it would be more noticeable?' I ask. She stares at the ground, like she's been caught out. 'It used to be, until a couple of years ago. Back then I had a tethered pump with a tube and a separate sensor for the glucose meter. The technology's improving all the time. So are the meters. Now everything works through this pod and I can control it on an app.'

'But how does it work? That's only a plaster.'

'The pump system's in there, with a needle to supply the insulin and measure my blood sugar.'

'A needle?' She's taken aback. 'You mean, it's in there? The whole time?'

'It's really small and fine,' I explain. 'But, yeah, the whole time. Of course I have to change it regularly. About every three days.'

Great, she's got a phobia of needles. Her face has gone even paler – I can see that even in the dim light out here.

'It doesn't hurt or anything.' No idea why I say that. She'd probably be glad if it did. Most of the time she looks at me as if she isn't exactly averse to the idea of hurting me. But now she's looking at me differently. With that fucking worry in her face. Suddenly I wish we hadn't had this conversation.

'OK . . . How do you know how much insulin you need?'

My smile is tired. 'I've had diabetes since I was eleven. After a while you can just kind of tell.'

Such a long time now. I can see from her eyes that she's thinking the same thing. 'The pump releases small amounts of insulin all the time, which covers what I need for the day,' I continue. 'At mealtimes I can give myself a bolus dose. So that's fast-acting insulin for when I eat. I don't really think about it any more – after a while, it's just routine.'

Olive nods but doesn't speak.

'I used to have to actively check on my levels, but now I can look at my daily profile in the app at any time, which also shows me if there's a trend up or down. But most of the time I can tell anyway if I'm having a hypo or a hyper. So then, depending which it is, I either eat something or adjust my blood-sugar level with insulin.'

'How do you feel it?' she asks.

'I just do,' I say. 'The important thing is to be around one hundred most of the time. That's the baseline.'

'So, your blood-sugar level has to be a hundred?' she repeats.

'Yes, wait.' I pull out my phone and open the app. When I hold it out to her, her eyes widen slightly.

'Colin, that's too low.' She lifts her head. 'Isn't it?'

Colin . . . Not Fantino. I think it's the first time she's ever called me that.

I turn the screen back towards me and, oh, she's right. I don't actually feel that low. I remember what Dr Calder, my doctor in New York, said before I left, when we were talking about my levels over the last few months, which get sent directly to her by the app. Too many hypos that I didn't notice, or didn't notice in time, and were reflected in my HbA1c level being too low – that's the long-term blood-sugar level that she calculates at every check-up. In the long run, that tends to be better than being permanently too high, which can damage your blood vessels and lead to problems with your eyes or kidneys, or pretty much any other organ.

But all the hypos are more annoying because they sometimes catch me by surprise and they can get serious pretty quickly. They call it impaired awareness of hypoglycaemia, which means that my body's gotten used to the warning signals and doesn't bother sounding the alarm until things are critically low. So low that I don't have much time to act. Dr Calder wanted to sign me up for a special class that would teach me to be better at paying attention to the warnings, but then I was suddenly in Scotland, not New York, so I never had the chance.

I reach into my pants pocket. 'Yeah, so what are we gonna do, Olive Garden?'

She looks at me and I can see this slight panic in her eyes. God, she needs to chill.

This early in a hypo, I can still help myself and I've got at least fifteen minutes before my body switches off the lights.

'Eat,' I say, shortly, holding an individually wrapped candy under her nose. 'Anything sugary. Cola, juice, candy, they're all great. Followed by carbs, which you metabolize more slowly.'

'Muesli bars or bananas,' she says tonelessly.

Sure, the swimmer who can't swim would know that stuff. I unwrap the candy. 'You were pretty pissed off at me for being allowed to eat anytime, weren't you?'

She blinks, caught out. 'I thought you were being rude,' she explains, crossing her arms over her chest.

'I think passing out in class would be kind of rude too.'

Olive freezes. 'That can happen?'

'If I didn't do anything about it.'

'So . . . if you didn't eat?'

I nod.

'So you always have to have something on you?'

'Generally a good idea.' I'm trying to sound sarcastic so that she won't notice the slight tremor in my voice that always sets in if I start to get shivery and a cold sweat breaks out.

But she spots it. Her eyes flit from me to the benches a few yards away. 'Want to sit down?'

'No,' I say immediately. If she hadn't been standing there, I might have considered it. But there's no need. I'll be better soon.

'What happens if you forget?' she asks.

'Forget what?'

'To bring something to eat.'

'I don't forget. It's just habit now. Like the way you always have your phone with you, don't you?'

'What if you can't respond any more?' I don't like how serious she sounds. 'Tell me what I should do.'

'Nothing,' I snap.

'Colin . . .'

'Call an ambulance,' I say curtly. 'Or get your dad. They have a glucagon pen in the sick bay for emergencies. They know what to do.' When Olive doesn't reply, I turn away slightly. 'Right, so that's everything you need to know. See you, Olive Garden.'

'No, wait.'

'What?'

'I don't think it's a good idea for you to be alone just now.'

There's a treacherous tingle in my belly. 'I'm not.' My voice is hoarse as I point to the greenhouse with my chin. She doesn't speak as I head for the door. Then I stop and turn back to her.

'What?' I ask again. 'Planning on putting down roots out here?'

Her eyes rest heavily on me and I feel weird. She's looking at me differently. Less hatred in her expression. Gentler. Almost like she cares. Something stirs within me and it takes me all my strength to push it down. Not an option. I can't develop feelings and be the rejected one again. I've had enough of that. The thing with Maresa should've taught me a lesson.

'No.' She shakes her head and the defiance comes back to her eyes. I repress a grin. 'No, that's sorted now.'

But, apparently, I never learn.

OLIVE

I left the midnight party early, shortly after Colin went. I'm still surprised he was even there. After our chat, we avoided each other as far as possible, which wasn't hard because he hung out with Kit, Will and some other lower-sixth lads, while I was with my friends. Even so, I spent the whole time thinking about our conversation.

Now I'm lying in bed and, for a change, I'm not panicking about going to sleep. Instead, my head is whirling with thoughts that won't let me rest. I can't stop thinking about Colin and the insulin pump that's permanently attached to his body. I spent long enough in hospital to imagine what that must feel like. But for Colin, it's not just a few weeks. It's for ever.

I've had diabetes since I was eleven.

Eleven. That's so young. How do you teach an eleven-year-old kid to inject themselves with insulin every day, and to check what they're eating? Or wasn't it so bad then? How did he get diagnosed? Why didn't I ask?

Because I was overwhelmed. Because I only had eyes for the two-digit number on Colin's phone when he was trying to show me how he checks his blood sugar.

I automatically reach for my own phone. The room is dark and the screen is bright. I pinch my eyes together as I start googling.

Low-blood-sugar symptoms.

I click the link to the most serious-looking website and start reading. About the shivers and sweats, pallor, dizziness and nausea that indicate hypoglycaemia.

Colin's shaking fingers as he unwrapped the sweet.

Aggression. Aha. Perhaps he's permanently hypo. That would explain a few things.

I shiver as I keep reading. Anxiety, fidgetiness, difficulty concentrating, hallucinations. Heart palpitations, weak knees, headaches, confusion through to loss of consciousness, cramps. Stopping breathing. Potentially fatal if nothing is done.

How could he not tell anyone? OK, apparently, he did. Apparently everyone knew but me. But how could he not tell *me*? I had no idea and now I feel a total idiot for going on at him about eating in class. That was out of order. And now I understand why no teacher ever told him off. They all know.

So does Dad. Colin had that appointment with him on Wednesday. Why didn't *he* tell me? We've only seen each other a few times since then, but it's an important piece of information. Didn't Colin want me to find out? I saw how uncomfortable he was when we were standing outside the old greenhouse. Obviously, he was trying to sound distant and pissed off, but that couldn't hide how serious this is.

I put my phone down and stare at the half-drawn curtains that are letting a little moonlight into my room.

I don't know why this new detail has changed my view of

Colin. Previously, the thought of him just made me angry but now there's something else too.

Worry. I'm worried about him. About Fantino.

Damn it. That's got to stop.

I couldn't give a fuck. I really couldn't give a flying fuck.

I roll onto my left side and stare into the darkness.

I could. There's no point in denying it. Colin Fantino has burst into my life, seriously wound me up, and done something to me.

And now I'm thinking about him. At night.

Oh, shite.

13

COLIN

Olive Garden treats me differently now. More aware, some-how. Which is exactly what I didn't want, so I try to be extra cold and aloof around her. Seems to be working, because we don't bump into each other much for the next few days. I hate to admit it, but my schedule at this school is so full that I drop into bed exhausted in the evenings and sleep like a log all night. Last week, I got to know another highlight of boarding-school life: the morning run, which takes place before breakfast, Tuesday through Friday. Because I get special treatment, I'm allowed into the dining room for something to eat before the run, but I don't take up the offer. Even though I often have a hypo overnight, by the time I wake up I'm gen-erally hyper. That's just as confusing as it sounds, and has to do with hormones, like cortisone, which your body releases more of at night, and which raise your blood-sugar levels. Hey, don't want things getting too simple.

Obviously, this morning-run thing came as a bit of a shock at first, especially because my charming roommate wakes up cheerful and bursting with energy. But, to my surprise, I've discovered that it does me good to start the day by running my ass off, breathing fresh air and forgetting everything for a few minutes. And there's something else I've noticed. Olive Garden doesn't run with us. It would be easy to blend into the crowd as the entire school is forced to do one lap of the perimeter wall every morning, but in the last few days, I've seen her buddies in the upper sixth running together often enough. And she's never there.

This morning, I met her on my way back to my room and she wasn't wearing athletic gear, so now I'm certain she's getting special treatment too. Which must have to do with her accident. I want to know what happened, why Olive Garden doesn't do the morning run or gym class. I don't reckon she's sitting out just because she has her period.

When I shut my eyes, I can picture her standing by that display case, with all that rage and despair in those green eyes of hers. The way she tried to sound unfazed as she told me her sports career was over. I really wish I didn't care but, annoyingly, I have to find out exactly what's going on.

Ask someone.

Cleo's voice in my head, and although she wasn't talking about Olive Garden, I find myself remembering the simplicity of her words. But it's not that simple. It's none of my business. Besides, there's no way Olive wants me to look at her like she looked at me. So concerned. That still bugs me.

I clench my fist around the rag in my hand as I walk down the corridor, looking for the room I've been ordered to clean today. I can't put into words how pissed I am about this whole thing. My original plan was just to sit out my time, but that's no good because the caretaker actually checks to make sure I do the job properly.

I find the right room with a groan. There's no escape now. I open the door, and there in the centre of the room, I see not stacks of tables or chairs, but a covered object suspiciously like a grand piano. My heart leaps with hope.

I glance over my shoulder, then step inside and shut the door. Mr Carpenter is nowhere in sight, so I walk over to the thing and lift the cloth cover slightly. Yes. The piano is a little elderly, and can't compete with the gleaming instrument I've seen standing in the hall. I cautiously press a few keys and wince at how out of tune it is. But, hey, it'll be fine for the dumb boy-band songs Cleo always wants. And I miss playing. I really miss it.

It's not like I wouldn't have the chance at this school. They offer piano lessons here, obviously. But there's nothing I enjoy less than the kind of classical shit I'd have to practise and then repeat to some grim music teacher.

I don't like sheet music. It hems me in. When I sit at a piano, I just let the music flow. Obviously, I can read music, but anyone can learn that. Not everyone can play by ear. It's like a mini competition with myself every time Cleo plays me a song, and I memorize the chords and the tune. There's nothing to compare with the gleam in her brown eyes when I get the song right away. Or the feeling of satisfaction it gives me.

Everything disappears when I play, and I'm certain that nothing else can move people like music. The first time I heard about music therapy, I knew that was what I wanted to do. Bringing psychology and music together seems like the only logical conclusion to the way I feel. So, for the moment, I just brush aside the fact that, with so many problems of my own, I'd be better off having therapy myself. I do actually want to. Some day, in peace. Without my parents getting involved because that would mean it wouldn't be worth shit.

Reluctantly, I close the lid over the keys again and turn my back on the piano. My fingers are itching, but I need to play undisturbed. There are too many people around this part of school by day who might hear me. Quite apart from Mr Carpenter, who'd be sure to notice something. And I really don't want to get slammed with even more punishment duties because I'm making music rather than cleaning. But, then, what are the nights for? It makes sense to come later anyway. Midnight in Scotland is seven p.m. in New York. That's a time when I'll definitely be able to catch Cleo and surprise her with a song. And if that's the only meaningful thing I can achieve at Dunbridge Academy today, that'll be enough.

I spend the rest of the time actually doing what I'm supposed to be doing. Dusting and clearing the crap off the shelves. Eventually Mr Carpenter is satisfied and says I can go. My idea of heaven right now would be dropping into bed and not moving an inch, but I bump into Kit, who insists on dragging me off to tennis. I'm embarrassed to admit that my muscles still ache from last time, but it does me good to feel my body like this.

It's not exactly warm, but the sun's shining so we make our way to the outdoor courts near the rugby pitch. My backhand's been better, but I still manage to win the last match. Adam, who's in my math class, is a tough opponent, but I focus on the rage in my gut. I channel it into every stroke, even when my arms are burning and I feel like I can't catch my breath. Serve. The firefighter didn't have a choice when she died in the flames. Forehand. She wanted to help. Backhand. And I partied. Volley. With my no-good friends and Maresa, who doesn't give a crap about me.

'Set point!' shouts Mr Scheff, the trainer, after I smack a ball deep into the corner and Adam can't get to it. I feel nothing as I take up position on the line and get ready to serve.

My heart is pounding, I'm starting to panic. I'm playing fucking tennis at a boarding school in Scotland instead of owning up to what I did. Nobody here knows. And neither does anybody at home. Because my fucking parents made sure I didn't have to face any consequences. I clench my jaw and toss the ball up. I know it's going to be a good serve even before I hit it, packed with all my rage and despair.

Adam has no chance, and that's putting it mildly. I take the set with an ace, but I don't care. I feel numb as I hit with him for a bit, then help collect the balls.

The others have finished their games too. Kit glances over to me. I look away, but it doesn't help. 'You OK?' he asks, as I hand back my racquet.

I can't guarantee that any reply would be friendly, so I say nothing. And something tells me Kit gets that. He seems like a guy who knows what it's like to be carrying so much rage inside. He just seems to have found less destructive ways of letting it out.

'Out of breath, or up for more?' He slips his jacket on.

'Fuck off,' I mumble, bending down to my bag.

He grins. 'Aye. Thought as much. C'mon, then.'

God knows why I go with him, but in the end I'm glad I do. I follow him from the tennis courts back into the gymnasium, then through a maze of corridors into an amazingly well-equipped fitness centre. There are a few guys on the treadmills and girls on the squat racks, but Kit leads me into a side room. And then I know what he has in mind.

'There, now you can properly punch something,' he says, putting his racquet bag down on the floor by the bench, slipping off his shoes, taking a pair of boxing gloves off a rack and throwing them to me, before grabbing a pair of pads for his hands.

I hesitate, but Kit gives me an encouraging nod, so I kick my shoes off too, pull on the gloves and take a stance on the mats. I've boxed before, but I feel kind of shy as I face Kit. Then I just give it a go.

Kit laughs and doesn't move. 'All you got?'

Shut your face . . .

I don't say it, I show him. Not in a bad way. Kit's a good guy, and this proves it. But I'm *angry*. I'm so fucking angry, and scared. It's a dangerous mixture that tends to build within me and generally ends up with me messing around with the lighter. This isn't as good as burning myself, but it's not nothing.

Kit's stronger than I expect. He absorbs my punches effortlessly. My muscles are burning, I feel alive.

'One more, come on!' He drives me on when I ease up for a second.

A repressed growl finds its way out of my throat as I box out my last ounce of self-control, then turn away and crouch down.

'Feels good, huh?' Kit gives me an approving punch on the shoulder then takes off the pads and hands me his water bottle. And a cereal bar. Like he knows my body needs carbs after a hard workout like this.

I pull the Velcro on the gloves with my teeth, take them off and briefly nod my thanks – it's all I can manage right now because I'm still seething. But I get the feeling it's under control.

'Want a turn?' I ask, once I've eaten and drunk something, gesturing at the gloves.

Kit shakes his head. 'I'm all right today, thanks.' His tone is light, but his expression is serious.

'But you have other days?'

He shrugs. 'The days that are total shite? Aye.'

'Want to talk about it?' I ask. It's always better to offer than to open up yourself. And most people are only too happy to fall for that trick.

'Just my old man, who's always on my case. He and Mum live in Ebrington. In the spring, he got drunk and hospital-ized me.'

'Fuck, I'm sorry, man,' I say.

Kit just grunts. 'It's been better since I've boarded at school. But I spend a lot of time in here, pounding the punchbag.'

'To be ready for next time?'

Kit doesn't say anything, but his jaw muscles tense. 'Violence doesn't solve anything,' he says, and I nod lamely. 'How about you?' he asks, looking back at me. 'Just raging?'

'Just raging,' I confirm, silently thanking him for accepting that.

'You're into her,' Kit says out of nowhere.

'No way, man,' I reply at once, but he just grins.

'Interesting that you instantly knew who we're talking

about.' He puts the boxing equipment away, gets his things together and throws his bag over his shoulder.

For a moment I'm tempted to hate him, but I just give the lousy floor mats a good kick before following him out.

OLIVE

'That's looking pretty good,' says Dad, and I nod, with gritted teeth. Not because having the bandages changed is all that painful, but because I can see myself in the process. In the mirror over the sink. I'm sitting on the treatment couch in the sick bay and the scars on my right shoulder are plain to see. Gnarly skin alongside the fine grid pattern of the skin graft. I sometimes think I look un-human these days, and although it feels weak, I'm incredibly glad that in the daytime I can hide the memories of the fire under high-necked blouses, T-shirts and jumpers. Even though the way people stare at me so blatantly since I've been back at Dunbridge sometimes makes me scared that they can see through the protective cloak of my clothes.

'If it carries on healing so well, we'll be able to leave the bandages off from next week,' he continues. He smiles at me, but I can see how hard it is for him to do so. He's not my dad while he cares for my burns. He's Dr Henderson, doing his job. Friendly and caring, but nothing more. And I die inside a wee bit every time I force myself to smile and, at all costs, not to cry.

'Fab,' I manage, turning my face away as he puts a fresh dressing on. It's only a light gauze, totally different from the sticky dressings that covered the burns during my first weeks in hospital.

Dad takes another glance at the place on my thigh where they took the skin for the graft – that's healing well too – and then I can get dressed. He's just packing away the rest of the bandages and stuff when there's a knock on the door. Nurse Petra sticks her head in. 'Neil, we've got a sprained ankle waiting out here.'

'Be right with you,' Dad promises.

My pulse quickens slightly. 'Dad?' I say, as he turns back to me.

He looks at me. 'What is it, pet?'

'Why didn't you tell me that Colin has diabetes?'

Sometimes the best way is just to come straight out and ask the question that's on your heart.

Dad raises his eyebrows in surprise. 'I'm his doctor.'

'And you're my father,' I say. 'You should have told me.'

'Even if I could, I had no way of knowing it mattered that much to you.' Dad leans against the sink.

I want to say, *It doesn't*, but that wouldn't be true.

'Are you two friends, you and Colin?'

'No,' I say firmly. I try to underline my words by raising my chin slightly. 'He's . . . unfriendly.'

'Hmm.' Dad eyes me. 'He's sure to settle in soon. Did you want to ask anything about his condition?'

170

'No, I . . . He told me about it.' I pause. And I spent half the night on the internet looking it up, informing myself. But Dad doesn't need to know that.

'That's good. Well, if you want to know anything more, you can always ask me. The teachers are all aware, Olive. I didn't tell you because it's up to Colin who he wants to know about it. Not to keep secrets from you.'

Almost the moment he's said that last bit, my stomach lurches. 'I know, Dad.' And I don't want to have secrets from you.

He only glances at the door for a second but I know he needs to go to his next patient. How am I meant to find the guts to tell him I've been keeping something so big from him for months?

Mum cheated on you. She had an affair.

Simple phrases. But it's plain impossible for me to say them when Dad looks back to me again. 'Anything else, love?'

Tell him. Do the right thing.

Aye, right. Hurt him. Rip his heart out and make absolutely certain that your family will be smashed up.

'No, I . . . It's fine.' Smile. 'Thanks, Dad.'

'Love you, kiddo.'

He's said that all the time since the fire.

'Love you too, Dad.'

My heart feels heavy because I just couldn't tell him what I wanted to tell him. I just follow Dad out of the treatment room in silence. He heads for the tiny waiting area where there's a sobbing first-former and her friends.

'So, which of you is the unlucky patient?' I hear Dad ask, as I leave the sick bay.

Mum would be glad to know I kept my mouth shut. I clench my fists and shut my eyes, then immediately open them wide.

'Olive, hi!' Theresa's coming this way. 'I've been looking for you. Have you had a chance to think about the school newspaper?'

I give a deep sigh because that's the last thing I want to focus on just now. But ever since she asked me at the midnight party, I've kept thinking about which members of which teams would be the best to profile in the centenary edition.

'Please say yes,' Theresa begs. 'We need you.'

And I need something to do. Something meaningful that will take my mind off things, stop me freaking out day or night about my family or feeling sorry for myself.

'OK,' I say, before I quite know that I've made up my mind.

'You'll do it?' Theresa beams. I flinch as she impulsively hugs me. She takes no notice. 'I knew we could rely on you. This is going to be way cool, Olive. We've got our first editorial meeting at the end of next week. See you there!'

14

OLIVE

'You're making great progress, Olive,' says Andrea, the physio I've been seeing in Ebrington since I've been back at Dunbridge. 'Are you noticing the improvement in your everyday life?'

'Yeah, totally,' I say, as I pull my jumper back on, because I think that's what she wants to hear. In reality, I discover at every opportunity just how many things I still can't do. It's hard to register the little successes because they don't feel like success. Just like the bare minimum. Like finally being able to put a top on with a moderate degree of grace and no pain. Just now, after three-quarters of an hour doing physio exercises, it's not quite as smooth as it is in the mornings, when my shoulder's rested. But I'm getting through the nights without painkillers now.

'If you keep up this level of progress, we'll think about whether you can get back to joining in with games at school next month.'

I'm surprised. 'Isn't that too early?' I ask, although I've been longing to hear those words.

'No, I don't think so,' she replies. 'You can start gently, and only join in when you feel up to it. Believe in yourself, Olive. You really are doing excellently.'

My smile feels forced. 'If you say so.'

'I'll see you again on Friday,' she says, after a glance at her table. 'And don't forget your exercises.'

'I'll try.'

She smiles. 'I know, Olive. Be proud of yourself. You've come so far already.'

She means well, I know that, but her words don't improve my mood. That doesn't change until I've left her practice and see Emma and Tori, who promised to come and meet me so we can hang out in the village a wee while.

They bombard me with questions about the session and how things are going in class. To my relief, I found it pretty easy to get back up to speed with A-level Spanish. After class this morning, Mr Acevedo told me he's happy with me. I could try harder in the oral, he says, but that's difficult because I'm sat next to Fantino and, compared to his, my Spanish is abysmal. To be honest, I hadn't expected him to be so academic. He'd probably find it way easier in the upper sixth than I would, and I don't like that thought at all. Still, I guess it wouldn't make sense for him to join halfway through the A-level courses, same as with Emma when she came here from Germany last year.

'So, what are you doing in maths just now?' I ask. We're in Irvine's and Tori's just grabbed a bag of crisps to join the chocolate and teabags in her shopping basket.

'God knows, I don't,' she mutters, continuing to scan the shelves. The shop's too small to have much of a range, but somehow we always manage to spend hours here.

'We're doing mechanics at the moment,' Emma replies, lobbing a packet of tampons into Tori's basket.

'Yeah,' Tori says. 'I'm really lost with all that.'

'Henry will be able to help you for sure,' Emma tells her.

'Can I tag along?'

They give me that look, the one that drives me insane.

'It's my birthday in six weeks,' I say curtly.

'Do you think you'll really be able to move up?' Emma asks. 'Is that even possible this far into the year?'

I give an exasperated shrug. 'It has to be.'

'Is it that bad in the lower sixth? Will and Kit are there too,' says Tori.

'And I thought you'd made friends with that new girl from Germany,' Emma adds. 'Elain. We got talking the other day and she's really nice.'

'No, yeah, but I have to come back to you guys.' I gulp. 'You don't know how crap it is suddenly not to be part of things.'

'You're just as much part of things as ever.'

I gaze at Tori with everything I can't put into words. 'You don't even believe that yourself.'

'Yes, I do, Livy. We all believe it. It's only you who doesn't.'

'I just miss you.' I dig my hands into my jacket pockets as I stroll down the aisle.

'We miss you too, Olive.'

I have to bite my bottom lip and focus on the pain to take my mind off how shite Emma's words make me feel.

'Everyone got everything?' asks Tori, who followed me.

I just nod because I only came into the little supermarket to be with the others. I don't need anything, but after this, we're taking a detour to Ebrington Tales and then we'll wind up in the Blue Room Café. Like the old days. I hate how little we see of each other now that we're not in classes together. Sometimes I wonder what it will be like when my friends leave the school after their A levels and we're all scattered to the winds. I don't feel ready for that, but I'm afraid nobody ever will be. So it's all the more important to pull off my plan to get to the upper sixth ASAP.

My eyes wander over the sweets and chewing gum beside the till, while Tori and Emma look at magazines. Then I catch sight of a row of little packets. Scottish tablet is almost pure sugar and way too sweet for me – I didn't even eat it for energy just before a swimming gala – but, given my recent discoveries, it suddenly seems vitally important to have a little stash.

I remember what Fantino said when I asked him if he always has sugar on him in case of emergency. I believe him, but still better safe than sorry. It might come in useful some-time. And if not, he never has to know. It doesn't mean anything. I just like to be prepared, that's all.

Tori gives me a quick sideways glance but says nothing as I put my purchase on the counter.

'Be right with you,' a voice says, and I tense up.

Crap, it's Kit. I didn't know he was working in his parents' shop today.

He emerges from between the shelves and comes up to the till. 'How are you?' he asks, glancing at my shopping. 'That all?'

'Yeah,' I say cautiously, not even sure why I'm so nervous. It's just tablet – there's nothing wrong with that. But I've noticed lately that Kit and Colin seem to be making friends with each other. They spend their breaks together and usu-ally sit together at mealtimes too.

Kit scans the little packet with a somewhat knowing expression.

'Cut that out,' I snarl at him, holding out a fiver.

He grins. 'What?'

'Don't know. Just cut it out.'

'No worries, Olive,' he says soothingly. 'Need a bag?'

'No, thanks,' I mutter.

'Great.' His lips twitch as he digs my change out of the till. 'Here you are, your change and your receipt.' I take it from Kit and wait for him to scan Tori's and Emma's shopping through too. He's still looking at me in that amused way as they take their bags and head for the exit.

'See you,' I mumble.

'Byeee,' calls Kit.

'So, want to talk about Colin now?' Tori asks, once we've left the shop.

I slip the tablet into my jacket pocket and don't look at Tori. 'No. Why?'

'Well, I thought, now you know that he . . .'

'That he has diabetes?' I laugh softly. 'That sadly doesn't alter the fact that he's an arsehole.'

'But you were talking at the party the other night?'

'We were arguing,' I lie. It's not like my friends didn't see through me long ago, but I don't feel any need to let them know I had something approaching a proper conversation with Fantino for the first time.

'You'd make such great enemies to lovers,' Tori remarks, giggling as I glare at her.

Emma sighs. 'You read too many of those books, Tori.'

'And you don't read enough. Besides, you're not one to talk. You and Henry were classic insta-love.'

'Explain, please.' Emma raises her eyebrows.

'Love at first sight.'

'It was not love at first sight.'

'You had a crush on him before you even got here last year,' Tori says. 'I saw it when you were standing in the courtyard looking so lost and trying to spot him.'

'I wasn't looking for him,' Emma contradicts, but the flush in her cheeks gives her away.

I can't help smiling, and I don't know whether to be pleased or shocked at myself when I grasp that. Emma joined the school at about the same time that I saw Mum kiss the other man. Nobody could miss the serious chemistry between Emma and Henry, but he was with Grace then. It made me so angry, because suddenly they were everywhere – people hurting the people who loved them. Although I know now that I can't accuse Henry of cheating.

God, we're so grown up now, but we don't know who we are or what we want from life. Maybe this is just a painful phase when you have to learn that nothing in this world lasts for ever. Especially not if you try to cling to it with all your strength. But there's no changing how worried I am about Grace, who hasn't been herself since she and Henry split up. And even Gideon doesn't seem able to change that, however much time they've been spending together since last year's play rehearsals.

I only hope she can trust him. And that he won't hurt her like Henry did last year.

I don't know much, but if there's one thing I'm sure of, it's that I don't have time for that crap. Falling in love, opening up to someone, and them letting you down.

Fantino's name is the one that springs to mind, and that ought to make me think. After all, I hate him. And I really have no desire to speak about him. I get the feeling that Tori's not buying that, but at least she doesn't mention him again, even once we're walking back up to the school in time for study hour.

I work my way through a mountain of prep, then read the notes I've borrowed from my friends in the last couple of days. After two and a half hours of calculations, my brain is smoking and I have to admit that I might be lacking some background knowledge that would help me understand the upper-sixth work. I feel no better in the dining room at dinner. Luckily, I'm nowhere near Colin. All the voices and chatter seem too loud. I'm knackered when I finally drop into bed at wing time.

I can already tell that this is one of those days when, however tired I am, my head is just going to love replaying a bunch of panic scenarios as I try to fall asleep. I make an effort to put the thoughts aside, but it's tough. I must have nodded off eventually, though, because I smell fire and dream my stupid I-want-to-run-but-my-legs-won't-carry-me dream. I sit up with a start, heart pounding. For a few seconds, I can't move. Then the paralysis breaks. My eyes fill with tears, and rage rises inside me. I punch my pillow because I'm fucking sick of this, then grind my teeth as the pain twinges through my shoulder. So much for the amazing progress Andrea was on about this afternoon.

But the physical pain is the least of my problems just now. I'd take it gladly if it would get rid of the horrors in my head.

God, will this ever stop? And why is it still just as bad as ever? Even though part of my consciousness knows perfectly well that they're only dreams, my body doesn't care – it switched into flight mode ages ago. And that's knackering. It's just so knackering.

I rub my face with both hands, then rest my head on them and force myself to breathe evenly.

This evening, telling myself over and over again that everything is fine is just not going to work. I realize that when I'm still shaking even after several minutes. My eyes are burning, my head aches, but I get up anyway, because the only things that will really help now are fresh air and movement.

Tonight I'm desperate enough that I'd actually consider going to see Ms Vail. But the school psychologist is only available in her office in the south wing in the daytime. And by daylight, my problems seem way more manageable than they do at night. The flashbacks only start after dark when I'm trying to get some rest. Almost like my sneaky brain is waiting until I've stopped bothering it with trivial everyday thoughts so that it can start taking things out on me.

My feet carry me out into the dark corridors, and today it takes me ages to start feeling better. I go up and down staircases, wander aimlessly around corners. I must be somewhere in the north wing when I hear something.

I stop and listen to the darkness. Maybe I'm actually going out of my mind. But then I hear it again. Quiet notes, a tune that seems vaguely familiar. It's drawing me like magic down the corridor towards the theatre. At first I think the music must be coming from there, but then I stop outside a door a few yards further on. I've no idea what's in this room. The props and costumes are stored behind the stage, but apparently there are musical instruments here. I pause outside the room that the sound is coming from, and listen. Then I notice that the door isn't quite shut. It's open a wee crack.

I hold my breath as I push it to peek in. I don't know what I expected, but it wasn't the sight of Colin Fantino playing a grand piano.

The melody comes to an end and I'm about to creep away when I spot his phone on the music stand in front of him.

'That was perfect, Col,' says a bright voice.

'Got another?' he asks hastily, because he's clearly as bad at accepting compliments as I am. He's got his back to me, but I can hear that he's smiling. I don't think I've ever heard him sound so gentle, and part of me is genuinely surprised that he's even capable of it.

'Yeah, wait.'

I stand slightly on tiptoe so that I can squint at the screen over his shoulder, and see a wee girl's face. She looks like a younger version of Colin and her accent is the same as his too. He has a sister? Must suck for him that she isn't here at the school too.

She plays a song I recognize, and it makes me smile. I don't know what it's called, but I'm pretty sure it's on Tori's boak-worthy *Hot Guy Shit* playlist.

'Seriously, Cleo?' Colin groans. 'You need to find bands that still exist.'

'One Direction are getting back together,' the lassie says, dead serious. 'Some day.'

'You were in kindergarten when they split up. I don't get it – why are kids your age all into them again?'

'TikTok,' she says, putting her finger to her lips so that Colin will shut up and listen to the music.

His sweatshirt strains slightly over his broad shoulders, his left knee bobs up and down in time with the beat. His fingers flicker over the keys, but don't press them. After a few seconds, he nods. 'Yeah, OK. I reckon I've got it.'

'Oh, my God, I can't wait.' She stops the track.

Colin lowers his head and I get goosebumps as he starts to play. He's good. I know right away it's the same song, and he's playing with such ease. Can he really do that, just out of his head? I'm impressed.

I don't seem to be the only one. The wee lassie beams, and when Colin's finished, she applauds enthusiastically.

'That was way cool,' she says. 'And I think someone else is listening.'

Colin whirls around. I step back and crash into the door frame. The pain that jars through my shoulder makes my eyes water. Dull throbbing, nausea, right in my throat.

Breathe. Just breathe and stand up straight.

Colin must have noticed, because the hint of panic in his eyes gives way to concern, so I jut my chin slightly.

'It wasn't so touching that you need to cry over it, Olive Garden,' he says slowly, not taking his eyes off me. If only he would, because somehow I get the feeling he can see a part of me I don't want to show anyone. A weak, vulnerable part. A part I wish didn't exist.

'Get tae fuck, Fantino,' I snap.

I hear a laugh and wish I could take my words back. 'Is that Olive, the one you told me about?' the girl on Fantino's phone screen asks, and I feel like I'm on the outside, looking in. But he heard it too, because he goes bright red, right up to his ears, as he whirls around. He must be glaring at his wee sister, but I heard what I heard. He's told her about me. For whatever reason. Probably bitching about me. Which would serve me right, because I moaned about him to my friends. But somehow I'm affected by that information. Because it means Fantino's bothered about me. Like I'm bothered about him, though I'd never admit it. He's just an arrogant, unfairly attractive, spoiled brat from the USA who's never learned any respect for anyone. But, sadly, that doesn't stop me flushing hot every time his dark eyes rest on me. Like now, for instance.

'Cleo, we'll talk later, OK?' he says roughly. Still looking in my direction. I cross my arms challengingly over my chest, ignoring the dull ache in my shoulder.

Fantino looks back to his sister.

Cleo. Pretty name. Cleo and Colin Fantino. He must be a great big brother. Aye, I mean that totally unironically – I can imagine that Fantino's the kind of guy who wouldn't hesitate to beat up anyone who upset his wee sister. He knows how to fight and how to protect, and he can be very intimidating. Not that he intimidates *me*, however fierce he can look. He annoys me, and those are two very different things.

I chew gently on my bottom lip as I wait for Fantino to say goodbye and end the FaceTime call.

'So, you told your wee sister about me,' I say slowly, as he puts his phone away. He doesn't turn immediately, but I can see his shoulders rise and fall slightly.

'Would you like that, Olive Garden?' he asks, turning side on. I notice how handsome his profile is. Not that his face isn't nice from the front. But lots of faces look good from the front. If you look great from the side, you're winning at life. And, yeah, Fantino's the bloody champion.

The phrase pisses me off in books, but his jawline is razor sharp. His nose is almost a wee bit too straight and perfect, in contrast to his full eyebrows. When he frowns – which he does very well – they contract until there's this little ridge over the bridge of his nose. But he's grinning smugly just now, so his brow is smooth.

'Not at all,' I say, bored, strolling towards him. I nicked that move off him, and I hope he doesn't notice. It seems to have the desired effect, because while my eyes roam around the room, I can sense Fantino watching me. My skin-tight sports leggings, which remind me that I used to be an athlete, and the short, baggy sweatshirt I'm wearing with them. It stops just above my waistband, and if I stand up straight, a little flash of skin peeps out. I'm sure that's what Fantino's looking at just now. And I do like that.

'What will you give me if I don't grass on you?' I ask, with a sigh, running my finger over the dusty piano. I didn't even know the school had another, besides the highly polished specimen in the main hall.

Fantino's laugh is nervous and angry. Yeah, that's how it feels, my friend. Suddenly I've got the upper hand.

'How are you going to rat on me when you're out after bedtime yourself?'

Bedtime. Cute the way he refuses to use the school jargon, like admitting he's at Dunbridge now would make him less cool, less individual. He's one of us, whether he likes it or not.

'I was on my way to the sick bay to get some paracetamol when I heard a noise,' I say, radiating innocence. It's winding him up.

'Noise,' he repeats, to my surprise. I'm amazed that that seems to faze him most, because it shows this really means something to him. All this. Playing the piano. I'd have believed anything of him, but not that Fantino's a brilliant pianist. I'm not musical, but I know it takes emotion and passion to coax so much out of the piano keys. And I wouldn't have thought he had that in him.

When he was playing, there was something soft and vulnerable in this room. More than just the constant rage he has to take out on me and everyone else.

'It's not fucking noise, OK?' he says, when I still don't say anything.

'Right, yeah, sure, sorry.' I raise both hands. 'I'd never have guessed you were a secret amateur musician.' He exhales sharply. Ha-ha. 'And I have to admit, it was impressive,' I continue because, unlike him, I'm big enough to give credit where it's due. 'Did you play that all from memory?'

'By ear,' he answers grimly, but I can see that he's a bit unsettled by me asking him questions, being interested, rather than snapping at him. I bet that's what he told his wee sister. Olive Garden, this bitchy drama queen. So *annoying*. That makes me smile.

'Amazing,' I say. 'Do you write your own songs too?'

'No,' he says curtly.

'Uh-huh.' I wait a moment, but he doesn't reply. 'You're a great conversationalist, Fantino, so easy to talk to.'

'I want to study music therapy,' he blurts, and I fall silent. 'It's fascinating. Processing your emotions through music. People underestimate that, but they shouldn't.' His voice has dropped with every phrase, almost like he's already regretting having told me that. 'So, go ahead and laugh at me now.'

'Why would I?' I ask.

He hesitates. 'Beats me,' he admits in the end.

'Only arseholes laugh at stuff that matters to other people.' He swallows hard.

'What? Don't you want to contradict me?'

He glares at me. 'You're impossible, Olive Garden.'

'So are you, Fantino.'

'And stop looking at me like that,' he says, out of the blue. It's an effort not to flinch. 'Like what?'

'So worried. I can see it. I don't need a watchdog, suddenly looking at me with different eyes just because she knows about my condition.'

'I don't see you with different eyes,' I say, not looking away. 'I find you just as much of a shite as I always have done.'

His lips twitch slightly. 'Great. The feeling's mutual.'

We both whirl around as the light goes on out in the corridor.

'Fuck,' I whisper, as Fantino jumps up from the piano stool. I get to the door first and close it, also feeling for the light switch on the wall. I can sense him beside me as the ceiling light goes off and we're standing in the dark. Immediately my heart rate quickens.

'Anyone there?' Fantino asks, but I shush him furiously.

The house-parents are experts at picking up the tiniest sounds if they come out to check up on us at night. And I really don't fancy another grilling from Mrs Sinclair. Especially not in his company.

'Don't move,' I breathe, as one of the old floorboards creaks. I can feel the warmth of his body. My eyes are slowly getting used to the darkness, and I can see the outlines of things now. Fantino's beside me with his back to the closed door. He turns his head towards me and I'm sorry to say that he smells good. Of some cologne, which I'll bet was expensive and that he only bought because TikTok told him it drives the ladies wild. Well, what can I say? They were right. I'm only human. He moves and his arm brushes my shoulder, making me shiver.

'Want me to play something else?' he whispers, even though I can hear muffled footsteps through the door.

I put my finger to my lips and dig my elbow into his ribs. He groans and I hold my breath.

It goes quiet in the corridor. I shut my eyes.

No, no, please, no.

I look up to the heavens and pray to God as somebody rattles the door handle gently. Fantino and I press all our weight against the door, which seems to do the trick and makes them think it's locked.

I only dare breathe again once the footsteps retreat. Fantino exhales almost inaudibly. Neither of us speaks for quite a while. I feel him turn his head and look at me, which is infuriating.

'What?' I hiss angrily.

'If you hurry out now, you've still got time to rat on me,' he whispers.

I laugh very quietly and move away from the door. Fantino has nowhere to go as I stand in front of him. I'm annoyed he's so tall that I have to look up at him. His dark hair flops into his eyes as he looks down at me.

'I'm not the kind of arsehole who goes around blackmailing other people for fun, *Colin*.'

'Oh, my actual name,' he murmurs, bringing his face closer to mine. My core muscles tense slightly. 'Say it again.'

'No way,' I retort.

'Shame, Olive.'

'You think?' I lean forward and feel his thigh against my hip. His firm body beneath layers of clothing. He stops breathing, just for a second, but I notice. Close, he's close. Very close.

I bite my bottom lip – I do it very intentionally. And maybe because I can't help myself. Colin gulps and lowers his chin. God, is that an invitation? If I leaned forward just a wee bit more, I could kiss him. I can barely make out his features in the darkness, but I know them only too well. He's here, he's driving me crazy. I don't like how confused I feel when I'm near him, but at the same time it's all so thrilling, like this thing between us is a game in which nobody really knows the rules. Maybe there aren't any. Maybe that's it. I think I'm ready to find out. And so is he. He comes closer, I draw back. A reflex action, my heart suddenly racing.

'Er, good night, then.' I reach for the door handle. He freezes. My voice croaks. 'And next time, give Cleo my love.'

15

What am I doing here? I'm asking myself, as I take a seat in the empty classroom where the first planning meeting for the school centenary newspaper is taking place. I don't belong here – but, then, I thought the same thing six months ago when, very much against my will, I took up Mr Acevedo's suggestion of helping out with costumes and makeup for the theatre club. In the end, that led to me making up with Tori and genuinely enjoying myself during the rehearsals.

I'm not so sure that will work out this time, but maybe that's because the average age is considerably lower on the newspaper team. The younger kids are eyeing me almost with awe, which is irritating because it reminds me that I belong in the upper sixth, where I ought to be working way too hard on my A levels to have time for the school paper. But it is what it is and, to be honest, I'm impressed by the businesslike way Theresa and her friends are approaching the editorial meeting. They genuinely have thought of everything, and at the end of the session, they even hand me a camera they've borrowed from the tech club.

Straight after study hour, which follows the meeting, I head out to the rugby pitch. Most teams have training now, including the swimmers. I hang around by the running track for a while, where I spot Emma and Grace among the athletics team, while Gideon and Henry are with the rugby lads on the pitch in the centre. I can hear Mr Cormack from miles off, the stands are empty, the floodlights on, and in the distance, the sun is setting. The whole thing makes me weirdly emotional as I stand on the edge, watching them all. My fellow pupils moving, chatting, cheering each other on. Their yells and laughter fill the cool evening air, and the thought that I'm no longer part of all this is painful. But I'm not going to sink back into self-pity. So, I do what I came here to do – watch the teams and make a note of people to interview for the profiles. In the end, I even venture into the swimming centre.

The air is warm and heavy with moisture. It settles on my skin and my hair as I slip off my socks and shoes at the doorway and walk barefoot over the tiles. There's the biting smell of chlorine, which I've missed. Being in here fully dressed reminds me yet again that my time as an active member of the team is over.

The younger kids are in the shallow end, practising their technique, while my team are, as ever, doing lengths of the main pool. Euphoria rises within me as I see Ms Cox and Luke walking up and down the edge, urging on Ana, Imogen and everybody. Luke glances up and a smile spreads over his face as he spots me.

'Olive!' He walks over. 'How cool that you're here.'

'Yeah.' I wave my camera and notebook at him, slightly uncertainly. 'I'm here for the school paper. I'm on the lookout for people to feature in the sports section for the centenary special.'

'You're the new sports reporter?'

I smile despondently. 'Well, I've got to do something.'

'How's your arm?' Luke asks, and I wish he didn't sound so earnest.

'It's getting better, I think.'

'So, will you be back any time soon?'

I swallow, then shrug. 'I'm afraid not, not after the skin graft. I'm not allowed in the water properly for ages.'

'Man, that's so pants. The team keeps losing without you.'

Aye, Luke. I find it *so pants* too, believe me. But I don't want to come over bitter and crabby to my old teammate, so I force myself to smile. 'You'll just have to work harder, then.'

'You heard it, Luke,' says Ms Cox, who joined us without me noticing. She smiles as I turn to her. 'Olive's dead right. Off to the starting block with you now.' She waits till he's gone before she looks back at me. 'How are you, Olive?'

'I'm getting there.' My standard answer, which is sometimes true and sometimes less so.

'It's nice to see you here,' she replies.

I know what she means, because before my accident, I did regular lifeguarding duty during the times that the pool was open to all pupils at the school. When I got back this term, I signed up for library duty instead, in the hope of bumping into as few people as possible I know from swimming. And I'm sure Ms Cox can guess that.

'Yeah, I never really got the chance before,' I say evasively. She doesn't need to know that I've been here by night. 'I've missed it,' I say in the end, and that's the truth.

Ms Cox smiles. 'Well, that's handy. I wanted to ask you if you could see your way to helping me out a bit with the coaching.'

'Me?'

'You know the team better than anyone, Olive. Two pairs of eyes see more than one, when it comes to keeping the squad in check and pointing out sloppy technique.'

I hesitate. 'Wouldn't that be weird? I mean, I used to be on the team with them. Why would they let me boss them around?'

'I wouldn't worry about that if I were you, Olive. You're highly respected on my squad.'

Present tense. She says it like it's still true, and for a moment, it's hard to find the words.

'Just think it over. There's no rush, not if you're busy with

194

the newspaper for the time being. We won't swim away from you, don't worry.'

I had no idea how much I needed to hear those words. And I nod, almost on autopilot, and say, 'That would be great.'

'Wonderful, Olive.' Ms Cox smiles. 'Do you have fifteen minutes? I'll get everyone together at the end so you can fill them in on your request. I heard what you were saying to Luke about the school paper.'

I nod and sit on the edge of the little bank of seats. It still hurts to watch the others swim. I would love to regain the weightlessness I feel in the water. But for the first time in weeks, I can think about it without raging. I wait for the end of the session, explain my plans for the special edition of the school newspaper and arrange to interview Ana, Josephine and Marc in the next few days. Then I make my way back outside.

It's almost dark now and the rugby team have finished their training too. It's only the athletics squad still doing tempo runs. Henry gives me a wave, so I walk over to him and we watch Emma, Grace and two other girls get into position on the starting blocks. The whistle goes and they sprint away. Emma and Grace immediately take the lead, and race it out, head-to-head. Henry and Gideon are staring at them, at least as fascinated as me.

Grace crosses the line a split second ahead of Emma, and I join in with Henry and Gideon as they clap and whoop. Emma looks over and laughs breathlessly as she slows to a jog. Grace has already stopped and jammed her arms against her knees. Then she straightens. Emma comes over and raises her hand to high five, but Grace doesn't respond. My blood runs cold as she staggers back a step and Emma grabs for her. Grace's legs look like matchsticks that buckle beneath her as she collapses to the ground. For a moment, I'm frozen. Then I start to run. So do Henry and Gideon, who reach her and Emma ahead of me.

Every stride jars directly up into my shoulder but I try to ignore the pain. Ms Ventura, the athletics coach, is with Grace now too, and Mr Cormack is jogging over from some distance away.

The first thing I hear when I finally reach them is Gideon's voice: 'No, you can bloody well sit down here for a bit.'

His face is as white as Grace's, and although he sounds astonishingly calm, I see the panic in his eyes.

'I just felt sick,' Grace gasps. 'God, stop making such a fuss . . .' She's clearly hating the attention and I can feel the relief as she starts to complain.

Emma looks startled. Henry pulls her away slightly and gently strokes her shoulders as I approach.

'All the same, I would prefer it if you let Nurse Petra check you over, Grace,' Ms Ventura says.

'There's really no need. I just didn't drink enough,' Grace assures her. It's plausible, but I can hear the suppressed tremor in her voice.

It reminds me of Colin, and at the thought, I reach into my trouser pocket. 'Here.' I hold the bag of tablet out to Grace.

Her eyes dart to the packet, but she doesn't budge, so Gideon reaches for it.

'No, I—'

He cuts her off: 'Yes. Grace, I mean it, this is important.'

Grace looks at Gideon, a warning glittering in her eyes. 'I'm OK now.' She shakes off his hand and gets to her knees. 'Come on, guys, chill out.'

Gideon opens his mouth, but Ms Ventura gets in first. 'Grace, I want you to go to the sick bay.'

She sighs. 'Fine.'

'Olive will go with you, won't you?' Ms Ventura glances at me.

I nod.

'You don't have to,' Grace whispers, as we cross the pitch to pick up her stuff from the stand.

I stop. 'Yes, I do, Grace. What just happened isn't funny.'

She turns away and lapses into a stubborn silence.

'Have you eaten anything at all today?' I ask.

Grace groans. 'Why does that matter to you?'

'Because it *does* matter.'

'It's nobody's business but mine.'

'Grace,' I say. 'Stop it. Seriously. I can see what you're doing, and it scares the shit out of me because you're just fading away.'

Now she looks me full in the face for the first time. 'Olive, I've got it under control,' she says, emphasizing every word. 'Stop turning this into such a big deal.'

197

Talk to Ms Vail. Get some help. That's what I want to say to her, but I have to admit it would be kind of absurd for me of all people to give her that piece of advice.

So I don't say anything as Gideon comes over to us. He ran on ahead of the others and now hands Grace her tracksuit jacket. Their eyes battle it out in silence, then she puts it on. Gideon has slung his sports bag over his shoulder, and as Grace reaches for hers, he moves it away.

'Everything OK?' he asks, and while his voice sounds hard, I can see the worry in his eyes. Grace's face softens as he puts his hand on her back. She nods, and he gives her a nudge. 'Come on then, let's get you to the sick bay. I'll take it from here, Olive.'

'Gideon, I—'

'Stop arguing, Grace. Unless you want me to call your parents.'

She falls silent and Gideon looks triumphantly at me. I fall back, joining Emma and Henry on the way to school.

'I'm worried about Grace,' Emma says, as Grace and Gideon turn off towards the sick bay and the rest of us continue to the east wing.

'Me too.' Henry's voice is flat.

'Maybe it's just a phase,' Emma says, not very convincingly. 'Did she talk to you, Olive?'

'No.' I sigh. 'I hope she will to Gideon.'

'He gives me the impression that she does,' Henry says. It's obvious that he blames himself for Grace still seeming to be doing badly so long after they split up.

'Henry, hang on a mo,' I say, once we reach the third floor. 'Can I ask you something?'

'Sure.' He turns to me. 'What's up?'

'Do you think you could help me with some work?'

Henry raises his eyebrows in surprise. 'What subject?'

'Maths,' I say.

'What are you doing at the moment?'

I hesitate. 'I was thinking more about the upper-sixth stuff.'

'Why do you want to do that now?'

'So that I'm up to date when I get back up to you lot. It's nearly my birthday.'

Henry's face softens. 'Olive . . .'

'No, stop it,' I say at once. 'I've started to have a look at what you're doing. But I can't do it on my own. Will you help me?'

It's mean of me to ask Henry. I know he's too conscientious to say no. He nods with a sigh.

'Thanks, Henry,' I say.

'Just for the record, I don't think it's a good idea to put yourself under this much pressure.'

'It'll get easier once I move back up.'

Henry gives me a long stare. 'I know, Olive.'

16

COLIN

Olive Garden has gotten inside my head. Seriously, she just crept in and took hold like a disease. That sounds negative, but I never claimed to be a nice person. I'm sitting behind her in class today, staring at the back of her neck because I can tell that her skin there is sensitive and soft. Side glances in hallways, eyes darting away, eyes flitting right back. Sometimes, when she stares absently into the middle distance in the dining room or the classroom, there's a hint of pain in her green cat-eyes. It reminds me of the night she stumbled into that door frame and winced in agony. I can never again resent her for looking at me with that annoying anxious expression because, apparently, I'm no better. I don't like the idea that she's not doing well, even though it's really none of my business. However much of a monster I am, there seems to be at least some last scrap of humanity left in me.

Of course I go to great lengths to hide it whenever I meet Olive Garden. Why? I hate to admit it, but Maresa Vega really did a number on my heart and I never want to feel that way again. So dependent on another person's attention. You'd think I ought to have learned that early enough with my fabulous parents. You only get attention when you've seriously screwed up. And that's not positive attention. Sometimes, I'd like to ask Ava and Eric Fantino why they wanted kids. If our relationship was better, I might know. But as that isn't the case, I've come to the conclusion that I was most probably an accident, and Cleo was the planned child later. I'm not into self-pity, so I don't mind. The main thing is for them to treat her better, especially now, when she has to cope without me.

Does Olive Garden have siblings? They'd definitely go to this school if she did, and then I'd have seen them around. I bet she sees her friends here as her sisters and brothers. No, wait, that's way too kitschy for her. I grin to myself as I picture her eyes like daggers if I were to say that to her. Olive Garden trying to stare you down intimidatingly is other level. It freaks her out when she realizes it's not working. But somehow, lately, I feel less and less into trying to make her freak out. I feel very much into other things. And I don't mean making conversation with her. Or not only conversation. I can't stop thinking about her little cherry-red lips. They're so pretty and I think they'd be prettier hot and swollen from kissing. From me kissing them. Only for fun, of course. Furious, lustful kisses where we have to gasp for air and she grabs onto my hair. God, I'm so horny, it's not funny any more. But my last time with Maresa was the night after the fire, and I was so drunk I can't even remember the details. I guess that's for the best, because otherwise I'd be even more heartbroken over her. But I knew what I was getting into. It's not Maresa's fault that I nodded and said, 'No feelings, sure,' but still hoped. Hope is for losers like me, so I'm done with it. But hopelessness feels all kinds of shit, so I picked something more bearable instead. Emptiness, indifference. Maybe that's weak, but I'm really not up for that stuff any more.

Luckily, I manage to work off my punishment by the start of my fourth week at Dunbridge Academy, so now I no longer spend my afternoons helping the caretaker and clearing out storerooms or scrubbing floors. Instead, I'm doing tennis training with Kit twice a week and boxing my guts out in the fitness centre whenever I need to. Sometimes with Kit, other times just me and the punching bag. Although it's kind of better when there are two of us.

Sometimes I creep into the room with the piano in the afternoons and FaceTime Cleo. Today I don't get there until the late evening, not that it's a problem, given the time difference. But Cleo doesn't pick up. I try again, then remember it's Wednesday and she's probably already at her gym class. Shame, but there we are. I play songs at random, out of my head, for a while, but it doesn't bring me the usual relief.

I was thinking about grabbing my lighter earlier, even though I've managed several days without it now. Which is better, because I don't want to risk getting caught. Luckily, I can hide my scarred ankles under my socks when I wear shorts for games, and I don't go into the communal showers if anyone else is there. You do what you can.

All the same, I feel the urge tingling in my fingers as I eventually stroll back towards my room. The halls are dark and everywhere is quiet, except my head, where it's incredibly loud. I know that it'll only get worse if I lie down now and shut my eyes, so I head right past the stairs to the east wing and wander on. Through the arcades and then the gate onto the path to the sports facilities. The air is cool, the gravel crunches under my feet, and my thoughts gradually quieten. I'm not heading anywhere in particular as I pass the windows of the swimming hall. As ever, the pool is lit up at night, and then I see her. Olive Garden is crouching at the edge, knees drawn up, staring at the water. I freeze, even though there's very little chance of her seeing me.

She doesn't move either, just squats there for an eternity. When she eventually leans forward and stretches out her hand, her dark hair cascades over her eyes like a waterfall. For reasons that I can't explain, I shiver as her fingers dip into the pool. I find myself imagining her running them over my body. I just have to. I have no choice. Olive Garden's slender shoulders and elegant neck, she's somehow not a swimmer at all now, yet I picture her athletic body gliding through the water, swimming away, leaving them all in her wake. She's not even my type, but that doesn't stop the blood rushing between my legs at the idea of her touching me.

There are basically only two options now. One, I turn around, go back and leave her in peace. Or two, I carry on from where we left off, back in that dark storeroom. Nobody can tell me there was no attraction between us when Olive Garden switched off the light and stood next to me in the darkness. So close. I heard her breathing hard – just saying. And I want to hear it again. I want to hear it with her standing in front of me while I press her up against a wall.

I stand out here. I watch her as she lifts her hand out of the water again, clenches it into a livid Olive Garden fist. A few droplets fall from her fingers into the pool. She shakes them off. I turn away.

OLIVE

It's been another stressful day. It was packed with classes, physio and an hour's tutoring from Henry, when I nearly cried as I understood how far ahead he and the others in the upper sixth are now. Dragging myself down to the swimming centre to help Ms Cox out at training didn't exactly help either. It was fun to encourage the others and give them tips, but it's just not the same as swimming myself.

After dinner, I was totally knackered but, of course, by wing time there was no chance of sleep. So I came back. To the swimming centre. There's total silence here now, and with nobody else around, it feels like a completely different place.

I remember my first gala, swimming for the Dunbridge team, back in the juniors. Mum and Dad watched from the stands and, maybe, everything really was fine in those days. I remember going up into the senior team even before I got to the sixth form, the only girl of my age. Because I was good. Because I was really good. Some people call you arrogant if you're aware of your strengths, but I don't see it that way. I know what I can do, and I know what I can't. Swimming was always my thing. Training sessions were my favourite part of the day. They were all too often my reason for getting out of bed in the morning.

I never had to ask myself why I was doing it. The discipline, going without, constantly saying no when my friends went into the city, had midnight parties, went off for the weekend, while I was driven with the rest of the team to pools all over the country, to throw heart and soul into the two hundred metres again and again, to stand on podiums, to have medals hung around my neck. I loved winning, but that wasn't really what it was all about for me. The adrenaline that drove my body on to perform when I positioned myself on the starting block and waited for the signal. Pushing off, tensing, flying, diving under, flying again. My arms splitting the water, my body feeling weightless. The burning in my lungs, my heart thumping. You could say I was addicted to that feeling, which would explain why everything's been so shite since none of that has been part of my life. I'm going cold turkey. Although that would mean the first few weeks were the hardest and after a while it should start to get better, but there's no sign of that.

You have to give yourself time, Olive.

Yeah, but how much?

I shut my eyes and take a deep breath, then bend down and dip my hand into the water. I know I could try a few lengths if I really wanted to. *Swimming would be a great form of rehab for you, Olive, as soon as the skin graft is fully healed. Low impact.* But I don't want low impact. I want to be able to give it my all and push my body to its limits, like I used to. There's no point in anything else.

I clench my fist and shake off the water, then dry my hand on my jumper. In a way, I don't want to believe the doctors who told me I'll never be able to swim at that level again. I mean, who do they think they are? God? They don't have a fucking crystal ball to see into the future. But it's hard to convince myself that they're wrong when my own dad is a doctor and tells me at great length that their prognosis is *evidence-based*, not just plucked out of thin air. And that makes me feel like even Dad's given up on me, even though the sensible part of me knows that's rubbish. Emotions are seldom rational – that's the whole problem with them.

I'm so deep in thought that the sound of a voice makes me jump.

'So, what shall we smash today?'

I whirl around, even though there's no need. His voice kind of echoes in here, but I know it right away. I force myself to breathe first, then speak. I have to beat Fantino at his own game. 'Are you following me?' I ask, with the bored tone I learned from him.

He laughs like he knows perfectly well how hard I'm trying to sound unfazed. I'm afraid he knows me well enough by now that that's probably true.

'Would you like that?'

I roll my eyes as he comes closer. 'Can't think of anything else to say?' He's actually grinning. 'How did you even get in here?' I ask, because only the coaching staff and swimming team know the code to the door.

'It wasn't quite shut. Wasn't that meant as an invitation?'

'No, actually.'

I keep sitting there as he comes over. Don't want him thinking I'm intrigued by his presence. Because I'm not. Not in the least.

'So, Olive,' he says, looking at the pool. I fight back the urge to correct him. *That's Olive Garden, thank you.* It isn't but, apparently, I've got used to Fantino calling me that. Without that little extra, my name sounds almost naked from his lips. 'What do we have here, then? The diving board? Could be tricky – everything in a swimming pool is kind of robust.'

I give a derisive snort as he looks at me.

'Or there's the glass here if you're feeling hardcore?'

'Are you nuts?' I yell, as Colin walks from the poolside and knocks his hand on the window. I'm immediately pissed off with myself for giving him the satisfaction of getting a reaction out of me. He grins with smug triumph.

'Oh, Olive Garden, what do you think of me?'

'Can't you just stop being so fucking annoying?'

He turns back to me. 'Fucking annoying?' he repeats.

'Yeah.' I look away. 'Seriously fucking annoying.'

'It breaks my heart that you're not pleased to see me.'

'Like anyone would be,' I mutter, which sounds more unkind than I meant to. Apparently, I'm not the only one to think so. Colin's eyes rest on me as I glance at him. He doesn't look hurt, but then he doesn't look unhurt either. I wish I could take back the words.

'No, you're right.' I hear the bitterness in his voice. 'I can't think of anyone either.'

'Hey, sorry,' I say. 'I didn't mean it like that.'

'Yeah, you did, Olive. C'mon, admit it.'

I gulp as the look in his deep brown eyes bores into me.

'But you have to live with that,' he remarks, more casual again now. I don't like how easily he can hide that my words upset him. I don't have any chance to think about that now, though, because Fantino suddenly slips off his shoes.

'What are you doing?'

He kicks them aside and looks down at me. 'What does it

look like?' he enquires, reaching for the hem of his hoodie. He pulls it over his head in one fluid movement, and his T-shirt rides up slightly with it. I hate men. I hate them for divesting themselves of their clothes without a bloody care in the world, and flaunting their flat bellies. I hate Colin Fantino and his grey joggers sitting low on his hips. And then he takes them off too. Oh, God.

If I look away, he'll think I'm prudish, but it feels wrong to stare. Not that it isn't a pleasant sight. Colin Fantino is tall and athletic, long legs, defined shoulders. Shit, he's seriously hot and he knows it.

My eyes fall on the insulin pump just above the waistline of his black boxers, on his right hip.

'Is that thing waterproof?'

A lock of dark hair falls over his forehead as he looks up. 'Let's find out.'

It's not a bad dive for a beginner, as he hits the water a few seconds later. He's got good body tension and a kind of elegance I'd never have suspected in him. You couldn't see it under his baggy jeans and sloppy hoodies.

I don't budge an inch as he pops up again in front of me, stroking his wet hair out of his face.

'Oh, no,' he says, not taking his eyes off me. 'It wasn't waterproof, Olive. This is an emergency.'

'Ha-ha,' I say.

'Come on,' he says, swimming over to join me at the edge. 'Stop being so fucking boring.'

'Then you stop being so fucking annoying.'

He grabs my ankle and I flinch. 'Colin,' I say threateningly.

'Uh-oh, first-name time – she's deadly serious.'

'Stop it,' I say, keeping my voice cool even as I feel my heart start to quicken.

'What if I don't?'

'You don't want to find out.'

Some kind of challenge flickers in his eyes.

And then he pulls me over to the edge of the pool. Hard, fast, so that my fingers slide over the smooth tiles. He gets hold of my hips, and a second later, I hit the water in front of him.

I'd forgotten how cold the main pool is. But not how good it feels to float weightlessly under the water for a second or two. I hold my breath, and because Fantino's a bastard, I count seconds under the water. My eyes sting slightly as I open them, but now I can make out the shape of his body. I give him ten seconds tops before he panics.

I'm counting down in my head, and I haven't even got to five when he grabs me. I'm pulled upwards, and I only put any effort in myself just before I break the surface.

I can't read Colin's expression as I wipe the water from my face. His eyes look me over, in shock and then pissed off as he realizes I was testing him.

'Oh, no, it's an emergency,' I imitate him, while his hands are still gripping my arms.

'What the hell, Olive?' he snaps. He's never spoken that

seriously to me before. Something stirs in my belly. 'D'you think that's funny?'

'Do *you* think it's funny?' I retort. After all, it was him who just pulled me in.

For a few seconds, we face each other, then seem to become aware that we're only centimetres apart. He's right in front of me, and he's wearing practically nothing. Tanned skin that looks so outrageously smooth I want to touch it to find out how it feels. His muscly arms, his wet chest.

I push myself away, and Colin immediately snatches back his hands.

'It was not funny,' he snarls, as I turn over to float on my back.

'No, it wasn't,' I agree. When he doesn't speak, I glance at him.

'You're unbelievable, Olive Garden,' he murmurs. It doesn't sound as snarky as I'd expected, but perhaps that's just down to the water in my ears.

The graft on my shoulder tenses as I stretch out my arms. I know I'm not meant to be in the water yet, but a few minutes won't kill me. My jumper's sodden and it's pulling me down, but there's no way in hell I'm taking it off. Even if I wasn't ashamed of the way I look, I'm really not in the mood for Colin seeing my scars and starting to ask questions.

I dive under, and when I resurface, Colin's looking at me again. Or else he never stopped.

'What?' I ask, and I'm annoyed at how hoarse my voice

sounds. Anything but detached. But then 'anything but detached' is exactly how I feel about what's going on here. I'm in the water. With Colin.

'Nothing,' he says, not taking his eyes off me. He comes over, slowly. 'Nothing at all, Olive.'

There's chemistry between us. It was obvious from the very first seconds we met. From the moment I was standing by that display case and Colin was there. And then he was everywhere, and even if there are times I could launch him into outer space, I don't want him to leave here now. Because there's something between us that I've never felt with anyone else. It's the certainty that Colin can see through me. And that's what stops me pulling away when he closes the last wee gap between us.

He's right next to me and my heart is beating fast. Very fast.

His mouth, which really is very handsome, is open slightly and his eyes, which really are very handsome, are dark. He's watching my lips, just for a moment, and then he looks me in the eyes again.

'Are you going to kiss me now?' I ask, because the silence is unbearable.

Colin gulps. 'No,' he says.

'OK,' I whisper. So I'll do it for him.

Colin neither moves away nor comes towards me. In fact, he doesn't move at all. He's simply there, a warm body with hot, soft lips. Softer than I thought. He doesn't move until I let go of him again. Before I can pull back, he reaches for me. His hands find my face and then he kisses me. And I mean kisses me. Self-assured and tender, but urgent.

Underwater, my hands touch his skin. Warm, smooth, really smooth. They glide over his chest to his shoulders and the back of his neck as I open my mouth. Colin doesn't hesitate. He keeps kissing me and I can't remember how to breathe at the same time. Everything's gone.

Not that I've got all that much experience. Apart from Ludwig from the swimming team, who was, it should be said, a pretty average first kiss, there's only been Eduardo, on holiday in Andalucía with my parents a few years ago. He was a holiday rep in our hotel and his kisses were pretty uninspiring too. Colin's kissing is better. Better than anything.

He pulls me to him and I wrap my legs around his hips. My pulse quickens, my head stops thinking as I pull him to me with my legs and Colin gives a throaty growl.

Kissing in the water is tiring – I know that from the time with Ludwig. We're in the deepest part of the pool. Colin pushes me back against the edge and pins me there with his arms.

'Now you're kissing me,' I say, as we briefly come up for air.

'Now I'm kissing you,' he repeats. My stomach lurches as he strokes a strand of hair out of my face. His touch is careful. My whole body tingles. 'I bet you didn't enjoy it.'

I have to grin. 'No, I didn't.'

'Thought as much,' he says, and does it again.

I have to shut my eyes. 'Are *you* enjoying it?' I whisper, between two kisses.

'Fuck, I'm *loving* it, Olive,' he says hoarsely, a voice that shoots directly between my legs. Why is he suddenly being honest? I wasn't prepared for that. I thought he'd say, 'Not at all,' dripping with irony, because those are the rules we're playing by. But for the first time, this thing with us doesn't seem like a game. It seems like something real. I can deal with the version of Colin I'm used to. But when it comes to this one, I'm done for. But in a good way.

I'm sure that he feels me shudder when he slips a hand onto the back of my neck. Then he plunges his hands deeper, to my bum. I grab the pool wall behind me, I clamp my teeth together because the movement hurts, but I still push myself up, even as Colin lifts me. I wrap my legs around him again as I sit in front of him on the edge, bending down. Colin puts his hands on my knees, from where they roam up my thighs until he's holding my hips. It's only when I see the goosebumps on his bare forearms that I budge back slightly.

'You realize we've got to walk back to school dripping wet?' I ask.

Colin laughs quietly. 'Well, my clothes are dry.'

I snort. 'I hate you, Fantino. You pulled me in.'

'Like you pulled yourself out again.'

I say nothing because he's right.

'Go and undress. In the changing rooms for all I care, but you have to get those wet clothes off.'

'Then what? Walk back naked?'

'I guess my stuff will fit you,' he says gruffly.

'What about you?'

'There are things in my locker in the sports centre.'

So here it is. The moment Colin Fantino offers me his clothes. Which I obviously find equal parts romantic and ridiculous. Or maybe it's mostly ridiculous. No, romantic. Whatever. Colin Fantino is offering me his clothes.

'OK,' I manage.

'OK?' He laughs. 'How about *thank you*, Olive Garden?'

'Only if you stop calling me that stupid name.'

'You can freely admit that you've started to like it.'

'You seriously think I like being called after an American restaurant chain?'

'Yeah, I do,' he replies, without missing a beat.

Ha, maybe you're right, Fantino . . .

'Stop that now and kiss me again.' I come to sit back on the edge and pull him by the shoulders between my legs, then I lean down to him. Colin is only too happy to oblige. I'm just about to rejoin him in the water, when a voice makes us spin around.

'You can't be serious!'

Fuck.

I stare into the outraged face of Ms Barnett, who is clearly on wing duty tonight. I've generally felt more or less out of danger in the swimming centre at this time of night, but of course I've never been entirely certain that no teacher doing their rounds would come across me.

'Olive? Colin? Get out of the water right now.'

I glance briefly at Colin and hastily stand up, as Ms Barnett comes closer. She shakes her head at the sight of my dripping clothes. Colin rests both hands on the edge of the pool and presses himself up, but then, after a few seconds, he sinks back into the water. For a moment, I'm confused, but then I shiver even more.

'Are you OK?'

'Yes, I . . .' Colin hesitates. 'Maybe I should check my blood sugar.' He lifts his head. 'You really fuck me up, Olive Garden.'

I flush.

'Just get the fuck out of the water,' I mutter, which is fortunately drowned out by Ms Barnett's tirade.

'Can I just cool down a bit first?' he hisses, swimming the few metres to the ladder in slow motion. He doesn't seem to have entirely succeeded, because he's got both hands over his crotch as he walks towards us.

'Unbelievable! This is absolutely unbelievable,' Ms Barnett says, as Colin drips all over the already soaked tiles, and throws me his clothes once he's fished in his hoodie pocket.

'May I go change now, ma'am?' he asks, in his provocative Fantino way, but there's a softness somehow. Or maybe I'm just imagining that because his equally soft mouth was on top of mine only a few minutes ago. 'Or do you have to drag me in chains through the freezing night?'

'That would help you out, right?'

'Olive, Colin, that's enough,' declares Ms Barnett, and I immediately regret my remark. You'd have to have a death wish to provoke her because, however much I like her, she can bawl you out like a sergeant major. Even after seven years and more at this school, I'm still scared of her at times like this, though I know that by the morning, she'll be just as friendly towards me as everyone else. Ms Barnett is anything but vindictive, but she's not to be trifled with when it comes to the school rules – it's not without reason that she's one of the best house-parents in the place. I have to give her that, even when I don't like it. Now, for instance.

'Go and get dressed.' Her eyes narrow to dangerous slits. 'In your respective changing rooms,' she adds warningly, as I follow Colin. 'And in three minutes, you'll both be fully dressed and outside the door, or you'll wish you'd never left your bedrooms.'

17

COLIN

Oh, man, are we in trouble. The next morning, we're summoned to Mrs Sinclair's office for a lecture. I lean back in my chair and count the knotholes in the floorboards at our feet while she chews us out.

Olive Garden's hunched into the chair next to me, shoulders around her ears, looking guilty. I don't know if that's a ploy to get a less harsh punishment or if she's truly overwhelmed. There's no telling with Olive Garden. She's shrewd, but softhearted. That's her weak point, and I like it only too well.

I get two more weeks' caretaker duty, and Olive has to join me this time. I'm almost sorry about that, but then I'm not sorry because it means we can spend time together. If they shut us up in some room together to clean it, we can start up where we were before we were interrupted last night. If she isn't already regretting the kiss, that is. I haven't had the chance to speak to her yet.

Obviously, I'm not regretting it because it was worryingly good. But I don't want all that stuff. I don't want to kiss any more women, kidding myself that it's meaningless. And the thing with Olive Garden definitely doesn't mean a thing. Not for her anyway. Or I don't think it does. I'm just some asshole from the States, who nobody wants to spend time with. She's right about that.

All the same, I want her to like spending time with me. I'd go as far as to bet that she does, to some extent at least. I'm not that bad a judge of people. I might be a jerk, but I can read Olive's body language. And it changes the moment she catches sight of me. She stands a bit straighter, touches her hair more often. Awkward little gestures that she tries to balance out with crossed arms and fierce glares, but she doesn't need to. Somehow she likes me, the way somehow I like her. We're on the same wavelength, even if it's one that consists of being jerkish to each other. God knows why, but I've started to enjoy it and I don't want it to stop. OK, so I don't want to keep on being mean to her for no reason, but that's just part of the deal. A little part at least. It's a friendly meanness, she gets that.

I'm sure of it as she glares sharply at me once she's breathed a humble 'Yes, Mrs Sinclair,' and I've rolled my eyes as we leave the room.

'Very thin ice, Fantino,' she hisses, not looking at me.

'Oh, yeah?' I dig my hands into my pants pockets.

'You know that, once again, it's your fault we're in trouble?'

'Did you expect anything different?'

'No.' She sighs in resignation.

'You see.'

'Off to class with you,' Mr Harper calls after us.

This time it's Olive who rolls her eyes.

'I mean, we could go somewhere else,' I say casually, as we head down the stairs.

'You're not fucking serious, Fantino?'

'Why not?' I ask innocently. 'Didn't you enjoy last night's kiss?'

'It was the heat of the moment,' she says shortly.

'Oh, right, yeah, sure felt that way,' I retort, but it's pointless. My heart plunges. Lousy emotions. Like she believes that. It wasn't just the heat of the moment. And even if it was, even heat-of-the-moment kisses can mean something. Why am I so fucking needy? I could accept that we just had a bit of fun in the pool and that nothing between us has changed. But something *has* changed. There's no point denying that.

Olive scowls at me, but before she can say anything, Mr Acevedo comes around the corner. 'Chop-chop, you two, the bell's gone for class.'

We flit into the room ahead of him. I'm still finding Spanish easy, and I don't have any difficulty in my other subjects either. Not that it interests my parents. I've been here several weeks now, and I can count how often we've been in contact on the fingers of one hand. In my video calls with Cleo, she fills me in on what's going on at home, but without her, I wouldn't have a clue.

I don't like how easily I forget now what's waiting for me at home in New York. My life at high school, tennis practice and all-night parties with my friends are a thing of the past. Even if I went back right now, nothing would be how it used to be. Maresa, Pax and the others can go fuck themselves because they've practically ghosted me. We check out each other's Insta stories and Snapchats, but that's about it. Sometimes the photos and videos of Manhattan make me feel like I was never a real part of their lives at all.

I glance at Olive. She's hunched over her textbook, so I risk a quick search. At first I googled for stories about the fire almost every day. My name never crops up. Obviously. When my mother says she'll take care of something, she takes care of it. I don't even want to know exactly who she bribed, or how, to keep me out of the story.

So, of course, I don't feature in any of the articles this time either.

Ainslee school fire – investigations continue

NYPD calls on witnesses to come forward

Then there's a phone number and the name of the department involved.

'You OK?'

I snap my head up and look straight into Olive Garden's green eyes.

'Yeah,' I snarl, hastily slipping my phone away. Did she see anything? I hope not. I don't want anyone here to know about it, even though it would serve me right if they did.

'So, which are you going to be?'

What's she talking about? I frown and Olive points to the whiteboard, where Mr Acevedo has put up a dialogue to practise.

'Whichever,' I say. 'I'll take B.'

'Fine.' She gives me a suspicious look, then focuses on the task.

18

OLIVE

It wasn't a lie. I kissed Colin Fantino in the heat of the moment. It wasn't planned, but I don't regret it. It felt too good for that.

All the same, I'm pretty confused. This afternoon things were kind of different between us. We still bickered and fought a war with words as we cleaned according to Mr Carpenter's instructions, but Colin doesn't look at me the way he used to. I wish I was even a wee bit less bothered about that, but the truth is that I spent the whole morning sitting in class unable to concentrate on anything. I don't know which is worse: the time I spend sitting in classrooms with him where it feels like the air between us is crackling with tension, or the time without him, when I'm analysing the shit out of last night and our kiss in the swimming pool.

It isn't until I get to my bedroom for study hour this

afternoon, after our first cleaning duty, that I have time to stalk Colin on social media in peace. Not that I hadn't already done that. But it seems that as well as his public Instagram account, he has a private one which he updates way more often. God knows how I missed the fact that he's been following me from that one for a while. I follow him back right away because I'm nosy. Besides, it feels desperately urgent to find out all about Colin Fantino. As if I could find the answer to whether or not the kiss, and everything he showed me of himself yesterday evening, was genuine hidden somewhere among his Insta photos and TikToks.

After twenty minutes' scrolling and careful zooming into pictures to make sure I haven't accidentally missed any chance to give him a hey-I-stalked-you like, I've come to the conclusion that his life in New York was pretty crazy. I've probably experienced less in the last six months than Colin did in a week. And that's got nothing to do with my having spent a good chunk of that time in hospital. Colin knows thousands of people, goes to parties – it looks as if he was having a bloody good time – and now he's here. I'm gradually starting to understand why he considers Dunbridge and Ebrington so lame. There's none of that here. If you've been at the school for seven years, you don't know anything different, but to him, the contrast must be massive.

Once I've gone through his whole feed, I focus on his story highlights, and get goosebumps every time I hear Colin's voice on a video. Re-posts of his friends' stuff, Colin in his slouchy jackets and baseball caps. He looks just the way I imagine New York lads. I find it almost impossible to imagine that this Colin and the one who turns up reluctantly to Monday-morning assemblies in full uniform are the same person. The next story makes me freeze. Colin with a girl, blonde hair tumbling down her back. You get just a glimpse of them before the camera pans away, but Colin's got his arm around her shoulders, pulling her close. I watch it again. And again.

Fourteen weeks ago.

OK, that's quite a long time and, anyway, I don't care. So why do I go through the stories in the accounts he tagged until I find the girl?

Maresa Vega has one of those Instagram accounts that consist only of fuzzy snapshots. I know how time-consuming it is to take that sort of snap, the kind that says: *Hey, my life is so much more exciting than yours that I don't even have time to take posed photos.* Even so, her selfies are elegant and her legs are long. She has no photos with Colin. At least not at first glance, but then I trawl through her latest photo dump and find him on the next to last image. A kiss, and not so long ago. I kind of want to work it out, but my mind has suddenly stood still.

The only thing I know is that that wasn't fourteen weeks ago. It's way less. A week or two longer than Colin's been here at Dunbridge. She must have uploaded the photos just before he left New York. And now he's here, kissing me in the swimming pool.

That's not true. I kissed him. But he didn't do anything to stop me. He let me kiss him and then he kissed me back. Even though there's a Maresa Vega in New York who posts photos with him and is presumably longing for him to come home to her.

I could boak when I understand what that means. I got into something with a guy who's in a relationship, or at least something that was important enough to him and Maresa for there to be photos of them both on the internet. I don't want to, but I look at more of Maresa's stories. Colin's only in them now and again, but when he is, it's very clear that they're more than just friends. You can rarely see their faces, but I recognize Colin Fantino's arms when I see them. His hands around my hips, pulling me towards him.

My heart is thumping in my throat when I eventually close Instagram. I can hardly move. I don't know whether to laugh or cry. All I want to do just now is to confront Colin fucking Fantino, but study hour hasn't finished yet, and after last night, I don't want to bump into Ms Barnett.

My thoughts won't stop whirling.

How could he let that happen? Did he think she'd never find out so it was perfectly fine to kiss women on the other side of the Atlantic? Maresa is so going to find out. I'd love to send her a DM to prove to her that her so-called boyfriend is a cheating bastard, but I'll save that up for later, once I'm done with Fantino. I don't pick up a single book for the rest of study hour, but use the time to keep stoking my rage. Almost the moment the tower clock strikes five, I grab my key and slam the door behind me. Up on the boys' wing, the first of them are out and about. I ignore them all and head right for Fantino's room.

I knock but don't wait for an answer, just open the door.

Fantino's chilling on his bed and Sinclair's across the room pulling on his jodhpurs. They glance up simultaneously as I stand there in the doorway.

'D'you mind? I'm naked here,' protests Sinclair, but I ignore him and walk over to Fantino.

'He's naked,' is all he says.

'Hurry the fuck up, then,' I snap at Sinclair.

'Jeeze, Olive,' he mutters, doing up his fly. 'What's got into you this time?'

'Don't you have to be down at the stables or something?' I ask in irritation.

'Are you seriously chucking me out of my own room?' Sinclair enquires in disbelief.

I say nothing, just wait by Colin's bed while Sinclair grabs his stuff and finally clears off. I give a quick check that the door is shut, then turn back to Colin.

COLIN

She's apeshit. Anyone can see that, but I still don't bother to stand up. I'm way too pissed at the casual way Olive Garden thinks she can just burst into my room and make a scene. What the hell is her problem? Kicking Sinclair out is fine by me, but how long is she planning to stand by my bed and stare at me? Am I supposed to be able to guess what's bothering her?

'What?' I ask, and I can't resist the temptation to link my arms behind my head.

'You've got a fucking girlfriend at home.'

I freeze. What makes her think that? 'No,' I say curtly.

'I saw it,' she spits at me. 'The photos with Maresa.'

Maresa . . . I wait for the stab in the chest, but there isn't one. Even so, I feel kind of exposed. And confused. Why's she stalking me? Because how else would she know about Maresa? And why do I have to justify myself? I never made Olive Garden any promises. Not one.

'She's not my girlfriend,' I growl. 'She's a goddamn bitch.'

'Mind how you speak about women,' Olive snarls, taking a threatening step towards me.

'Mind how you speak to *me*.' I sit up.

'You can't kiss me just because you happen to be a few thousand miles from her!'

'I can kiss whoever I like,' I say, even though I know I can't.

Why's she freaking out like this? I've done nothing wrong. Olive has no clue what there is or isn't between Maresa and me, and I don't have to answer to her. It's none of her business. And I really don't need Olive to remind me how humiliating the thing with Maresa was for me.

'Besides, I didn't kiss you,' I add, standing up so that she has to look up at me. 'You kissed me.'

'Like you didn't want me to.'

'That's a bold assumption, Olive,' I snap at her. 'If I remember rightly, I said that I wasn't going to kiss you. And you went right ahead and did it anyway, and now turn up in my bedroom to chew me out?'

I've stepped closer to her with every sentence, and I hate myself for it, but she winds me up. Who does she think she is? This constant flip-flopping is messing with my head.

Her chest rises and falls, but there's something sparkling in her eyes. It scares me as much as it turns me on. But, no, that's enough. I don't want all this again. I knew it would end in drama if I let her get close to me. It was naïve to think it could be different with Olive. I can't do this: I've got enough other stuff to work on in my life. I can't keep getting into fights with her, so I have to convince her to keep her distance from me.

'For a moment, I thought you weren't as much of an arse-hole as you make out.' Her voice is shaking. 'But I guess I was wrong.'

Yeah, Olive Garden. How nice that you've finally figured that out.

I grit my teeth then wind up for the knock-out punch. 'I'm truly sorry for you that you thought I'd want to kiss someone like you.'

Wow. Still got it.

But it's not funny any more.

She clenches her fists, pain flickers in her green eyes, followed by rage.

There you go.

'Get tae fuck, Fantino.' Eventually she gets the words out.

And then she storms out.

OLIVE

My life was easier before Colin Fantino was part of it. It was really so much easier, and nicer too. No meltdowns, no hot rage in my belly.

'What's he done now?' asks Tori, when I run into her on our corridor. Normally, I'd tease her that she and Sinclair are getting more and more similar, even asking the same questions independently of each other, but I'm really not in the mood for joking just now.

'Olive Mary Henderson, I asked you a question,' she yells, as I walk on.

'He's a bloody bastard,' I say, unlocking my door.

Tori follows me, unasked. 'So nothing new, then?'

'Did you know he's got a girlfriend?'

She raises her eyebrows. 'Has he?'

'Aye.' I want to punch something.

'Why would I know that?'

'Aren't you following him and his celebrity mum on social media the whole time?'

Tori drops onto my bed with a long sigh. 'At the moment, I've really got enough on my plate just keeping an eye on all the clues about Hope MacKenzie and Scott Plymouth. Aven Amenta suddenly appeared in the post-credits scene in *Icarus Rising*, and now there are rumours that Hope's written a new spin-off for the *Aroda* universe. I wouldn't be surprised if there was an official announcement dropping soon. Besides, she posted a selfie with Aven the other day. If she's playing the lead role, I'll scream.'

'Doesn't Aven just do her Disney stuff?' I ask, because that's all I know about the American actress. She was in practically every series I loved as a kid.

'Yeah, but a role in *Aroda* would be a total breakthrough. God, I'd love it. Can't you ask Colin? Maybe his mum knows something that's not public yet.'

'No way am I asking Colin anything,' I say at once.

'OK, sorry, I didn't mean to derail away from your issues. So, he's got a girlfriend?'

I nod grimly.

'Hmm, fine, but that doesn't matter to you, does it?' When I don't answer, Tori raises her eyebrows enquiringly. 'After all, you can't stand the guy, right?'

'I hate him,' I correct her.

'Oh, sorry.'

'And I kissed him.'

Tori's eyes widen. 'Don't mess with me, Olive.'

'Yesterday.'

'What? Why?'

Yeah, why? That's what I'm asking myself now. Why did it seem like a good idea? I wasn't even burning to kiss him. I should have just let it be. But I really thought there was some kind of attraction between us. Apparently I was wrong. Maybe, in America it's nothing special to pull girls into lit-up swimming pools at night and look at them in that intense way. It was special to me, but if I'd known what it really meant to him, there's no way I'd have done it. If I'd had even a hint of a clue that Colin's with somebody and was cheating on her with me, I'd have had a thing or two to say to him. But all I say is 'I don't know.'

'You don't know why you kissed him?'

'Yeah.'

'There's generally a pretty obvious reason,' Tori begins, and I give her a warning look, which she ignores.

'He's a shite and I don't want anything to do with him.'

'Maybe you also find him kind of hot.'

'He's a shite,' I repeat. 'And he's got a girlfriend, Tori. That's a real no-go, and he didn't say a word.'

'Well, what should he have said?'

'*Er, sorry, this isn't OK*, maybe? And not just kiss me back and act like everything's cool.'

'He kissed you back?' Tori sounds excited. 'Was it good?'

'Stop it, Tori.'

'No, I have to know now. Where were you?'

I shut my eyes for a moment. 'At the pool.'

'Oh, God, a water kiss?' Tori squeaks. 'And how did it happen? Why were you even–'

'Tori, he's with someone and I'm the arsehole he's cheating on her with. Don't you get that? It's like . . .' I stop, but I don't have to say it for Tori to know what I mean. I can see it in her face.

'You mean your mum? Livy, it's totally different.'

'It's not.'

'You didn't know. You didn't do anything wrong.'

I laugh mirthlessly.

'What did he say? I bet you confronted him.'

'Of course I confronted him.'

'Aye, you're a Scorpio. So?'

'He said she isn't his girlfriend and then we argued.'

'But that's a good thing, right?' Tori says hesitantly. 'If they're not together?'

'Tori, he said he was sorry if I really thought he'd wanted to kiss anyone like me.'

'I bet he only said that to hurt you.'

I say nothing because I'm scared that my voice will shake.

'So, did he?'

'I don't care about him,' I force myself to say.

'I know, Livy.'

'Stop it.'

'Stop what?'

'You sound like you don't believe me.'

'Why wouldn't I believe you?'

'I don't know. I really don't care about him. He thinks he can just come over here, totally disrespect everybody, and then get involved with me when he's got a girlfriend at home!'

'You two need to talk.'

I laugh out loud. 'I'm not saying another word to him, OK?'

'OK, Livy. How about this? We'll go down to the old greenhouse later on with everyone, forget what's happened today for a couple of hours, and tomorrow the world will look totally different.'

'There's no way I'm going to a midnight party and risk seeing him there.'

Tori raises her eyebrows. 'You don't really think he'll come? Charlie says he thinks the midnight parties are childish.'

I snort. *'He's* childish.'

'Far be it from me to defend him, but I think that Colin Fantino is all fear and façade.'

'He's not a hero in one of your stupid books, Tori,' I snarl.

'And you don't not care about him, Livy.'

I glare warningly at her. Maybe she's right, but that doesn't change the fact that I wish with every fibre of my being that it wasn't so.

19

COLIN

My blood is boiling as Olive Garden slams the door behind her and storms off.

At last. Or then again, maybe not . . .

Fuck.

A pathetic part of me wants to run after her and explain the whole thing with Maresa, but my last remnant of self-respect holds me back. What the fuck business is it of hers what I did in New York, and what makes her think I was even remotely serious about her? I'm Colin Fantino. I don't take anything seriously, least of all someone like her.

I've had it with all this drama. I want to go home. I want to be left in peace. I don't want to think about flames towering into the sky, or the aggressive wail of fire engine and police sirens. I don't want to be the one to blame for a woman's death. I want to get something right just one time, but it seems like I was born to always do the wrong thing.

I don't see Olive anywhere at dinner and I'm fine with that. God, she's making such a fucking drama out of something she knows nothing about. *Nothing*. I can kind of understand her being pissed at seeing photos of Maresa and me, but I really don't find it OK to assume from them that we're together. She could at least have listened to an explanation. And maybe I could have kept calm and resisted the urge to insult Maresa. But, apparently, I can't stay calm when Olive's standing in front of me blowing her top. I don't want her to have this negative image of me but everything I do in her presence confirms it, again and again.

After dinner, I hang around outside, despite the ever-colder temperatures, and don't head back to my room until wing time. But not to sleep. I'm meeting Kit, his boyfriend Will, Adam and some others at the midnight party. Sinclair invites me too, which is surprisingly nice of him, so after a while we stroll down together. I'd been expecting him to take Olive's side and give me the silent treatment, but he starts to chat. I might not find him as irritating as I did to start with, but I'd never admit that.

I've learned that the others are relatively unfazed about being out after wing time so I can totally scratch my original plan to get kicked out that way. Besides, I'd just get some other punishment dumped on me. Even so, I haven't given up hope of finding a crime so heinous that Mrs Sinclair will have no choice but to throw me out of Dunbridge Academy. I can think about the consequences of that later, but the main thing is to get out of here, especially now that Olive hates me. It's bad enough that I've been so distracted in the last few weeks that I dropped the ball on that one. Distracted by Olive, classes, tennis, boxing with Kit, cleaning duties . . . but that's over now. I've got to focus on what matters.

It's not long before I'm regretting having come, and now I'm slumped in one of the armchairs in the old greenhouse. It's seriously lame tonight. But at least these Scots are into their booze. There's some hard stuff, the kind of thing it's difficult to get hold of underage in America. Here, you can buy it in any goddamn supermarket once you're eighteen.

Olive Garden isn't here, but I start drinking as fast as I can. At the same time, I remove every memory of Maresa from my socials, like I should have done long ago, and try not to get sucked into any conversations. Not very successfully because people keep talking to me, and I have to keep reminding myself that I'm not here to make friends. But why do I feel so weird every time I see Sinclair mutter something into Henry's ear, on which the two of them look expressively at each other, then burst out laughing? I wouldn't call it jealousy. It's more disappointment that I've never had that kind of friendship. Things weren't like that at my school. People just hung out together to share the pain. Paxton, Ash and I never asked each other how we really were. It was just about having a good time. I barely ever spoke to anyone about personal shit.

Even the conversations I've had with Kit went deeper than anything with my buddies in New York. They've got something real here at Dunbridge, something that goes deeper and forms real bonds, because of being together twenty-four/seven. That can be super-annoying, but it's kind of nice too. Maybe I should say so to Kit sometime.

Right now, he's preoccupied making out with Will. Which is fine by me, even though it reminds me of kissing Olive. A kiss I obviously do *not* regret. I'd do it again in a heartbeat if I ever got the chance. But I can't because I showed her what a jerk I really am. And this is my reward. The music's shit, everything's shit, so I drink more. And more.

Eventually, Olive Garden shows up with her girlfriends, gives me one of her silly death-glares and grabs a bottle for herself. She's impossible and I hate her. And I wish I didn't keep glancing over to her. Though apparently she's the same. We aren't speaking, we're miles apart from each other, we're not listening to the other conversations – or at least I'm not. I'm way too busy winning the silent staring match we're fighting.

I raise my wine bottle; she raises hers. Maybe this is childish, but she's childish. Everything here is childish. I'm just fitting in. She drinks when I drink. She looks livid.

So, you really want to do this, Olive Garden? No problem.

I drain my bottle in one swig and reach for the next.

But don't say I didn't warn you.

OLIVE

'So much for "No way he'll be coming"!' I hiss, as I slip through the door after Tori, and the first person I see in the old greenhouse is Colin Fantino. To be fair to her, I have to say that Tori seems genuinely surprised, so at least it looks like she really didn't know he'd be here. At *our* midnight party, even though I bet he thinks he's too cool for us.

'Hmm. Charlie said . . .' Tori's pulling her phone from her jacket pocket. Before she even has a chance to look at it, Sinclair's appeared in front of us.

'Hey, sorry, I did text you.' He glances at me and gestures at Fantino. 'For some reason he actually wanted to come when I asked him.'

I must have misheard. 'Seriously, you invited him?'

'Yeah, you've got to be polite.'

'Why would you be polite to him?'

'Olive, he's new, and I'm sharing a room with him,' Sinclair says patiently. 'It would be pretty shitty of me not to ask, wouldn't it?'

'That's a matter of opinion,' I mutter, but he's got a point. Somewhere deep down, I'm in favour of being nice to people. But Fantino's taken the piss once too often.

'Just stick with us.' Tori shoves me past a few lower-sixth people to the back of the greenhouse, where I see Emma and

Henry, and the rest of my friends. Just as well because I'm really not in the mood to chat to Theresa about how the school newspaper is coming along. Although she's with Elain, and I'd like to ask her how she's settling in, but, well, I've got other problems.

I fight down the urge to make a scene by flouncing out. I'm not going to let Colin Fantino mess up this evening with my friends. But I find it harder than I expected to ignore him while the others chat and laugh. Especially once I notice that Colin's not exactly holding back on the drink. I've seen enough Insta stories and TikToks of him with his cool New York pals to be sure that, in the States, he was used to partying at a whole different level from what we can manage here at school, but I still don't like it. He might be used to it, but that doesn't change how much trouble we'll be in if a teacher finds us boozing. It's an open secret that they turn a blind eye to the midnight parties so long as we don't push it too far. And binge-drinking is definitely pushing it.

But if Fantino wants to take his chances, let him. It's not my problem. Quite the opposite – maybe then he'd get himself expelled. Which is what everybody wants.

I notice that Grace isn't here. I text to ask if she's coming, and she says she's too tired. I wouldn't be surprised if there's no sign of Gideon here either. The other day, I asked Grace how she'd got on at the sick bay after training, and she snapped that Nurse Petra said she was in perfect health. I really don't know what to do about Grace. But even if she were here, I probably wouldn't feel any better. I don't fit in any more. Not like I did before the summer. I can't deny that, when Tori, Sinclair and everyone burst out laughing over something I wasn't there for. Stuff in class, new in-jokes – sure, they explain them, but it's not the same. It'll never be the same again, even if I get to rejoin them.

The thought comes like an unexpected blow as I sit, knees drawn up, on the worn-out carpet and listen to their plans for after their A levels in the summer. I can't shut my eyes to it any more. Grace is talking to Gideon, not me. Tori has eyes only for Sinclair, and as for Emma and Henry, well, let's just not go there.

I ignore Tori's brief side eye as I reach for the wine bottle that Sinclair just opened. I never drank alcohol while I was training for a meet, but there's nothing to prepare for now. Apart from the moment when my friends leave Dunbridge and I'm really alone.

The first few swigs taste minging, but after a while I get used to it. When the bottle is half empty, I look up and find Fantino's eyes on me.

I narrow my eyes to slits and lift it to my lips again, and he follows suit with his. Apparently, he thinks drinking constantly makes him extra adult and cool. Surprise: I can do that too. And with a bit of luck, I'll have a couple of hours where I can forget that I'm now just as bad as my mum.

An unpleasant chill spreads through me, and it gets harder to smile as Tori and Sinclair eventually piss off. They're not the only ones – the old greenhouse has emptied out and I don't think it'll be long before the last stragglers want their beds. Henry looks as if he could fall asleep on the spot. He seems relieved when Emma looks enquiringly over to him and points to the door.

'You staying?' Emma asks, as they stand up.

'Think so,' I mutter, forcing myself to smile. 'Sleep well.'

'You too, Olive.'

It's not like I'm not tired. The idea of lying in bed is tempting, but I know it's a long way from reality. And I want to spend a while longer acting like the fear of the nights isn't shaping my everyday life. Maybe I'll be in luck and actually get to sleep tonight if I keep drinking a wee bit longer. Although the slight dizziness and sick feeling are maybe signs that I should stop.

I can't help my eyes automatically looking for Fantino once Emma and Henry have left the greenhouse. I don't see him among the lower sixth. Did he leave without me noticing? What the hell? We didn't even fight. And somehow it doesn't feel so good not to be able to see him any more. Although objectively speaking, it's fabulous. Yes, it's fantastic. Amazing. He's finally gone and that's what I've been wanting all along.

'That's enough.'

I jump as someone takes the almost-empty bottle from me. Turning my head makes me feel kind of sick, but I try not to let that show. Fantino's face comes into focus above me, his expression grim. Ha. He has no right to order me around.

'Who do you think you are?' I snarl, but my tongue won't obey me. I reach for the bottle, but Colin just holds on to it. Bawbag.

'You've had enough.'

'And who are you to decide that?'

He glares warningly at me. 'Go sleep it off, Olive Garden.'

I open my mouth, but before I can reply, the door flies open and a couple of lower-sixth lads burst in.

'House-parents incoming!'

Their voices are drowned by the music, but just seconds later, it breaks off. The others jump up, there are shouts mixed with panicky laughter; someone switches off the light. I go to stand up too, but I stumble sideways.

Shit. Sitting down, I felt reasonably OK but now . . . I don't. Glass clinks on glass as I crash into bottles in the dark, and dizziness seizes me. Then a hand pulls me firmly aside.

20

COLIN

I grab Olive Garden by the sleeve of her jacket and pull her along as the others run out of the old greenhouse, laughing hysterically. This would be my chance to chill here for a while, and serve myself up to the teachers on a silver platter, but what am I doing? Getting Olive Garden out of the line of fire before they find her in her current state.

'What the hell?' Her tongue is heavy with alcohol.

'Shut up,' I warn her, pulling her through the door and shoving her behind one of the bushes near the greenhouse.

'You're such a pain, d'you know th–?'

I press the palm of my hand over her mouth as I hear voices nearby.

Olive actually shuts up. Her face against my palm is warm, and my heart beats faster. I hurriedly take my hand away and stash it safely in my pocket. To stop it getting stupid ideas. Like touching Olive's face, for instance. But why would I want that?

I glance around the corner and see the beam of a flashlight a way off, moving across the greenhouse, which is now dark and deserted. My chance to show up and let the head finally throw me out of her school. But I don't move.

I don't know why I don't run. Instead I glance back over my shoulder. Back to Olive, who's got down on her hands and knees and is no longer looking at me. Her breath is laboured.

'Seriously?' I mutter. 'Need to barf?'

She just makes a grim sound, then drops her head.

'I give up,' I murmur to myself, running through my options.

Abandoning Olive Garden, the way she deserves, and handing myself in to the night watch. They'd be sure to scoop Olive up too, and she'd be in big trouble. What the hell made her think it was a good idea to get this wasted? Was it some kind of pathetic power game that she actually thought she could win? I'm sorry, truly, but she really ought to have known that her tiny body can't hold as much booze as mine.

God, she's so dumb. And my stomach clenches as she starts to retch.

Fuck, Olive Garden . . . I totally don't need this. I know what it feels like when the gall burns in your throat and for a moment you think you can't breathe.

When I hear a muffled sob mixed with her gagging, I find myself automatically kneeling beside her. Before I realize what I'm doing, my hand's on her back. And then I'm holding her hair while she spews into the bushes. 'Hey, it's OK, everything's OK.' What am I saying? I don't want her to think I'm pitying her. But she probably can't even hear my words. Her slim body shakes, the trembling shoulders rise and fall.

Shit, she really can't hold her drink. How embarrassing for her. But, unfortunately for me, I care more than I'd like.

My jaw is tense, and my eyes are fixed on her white face. When it seems to be over, Olive Garden sinks to her knees. I pull her hard to one side before she falls into her own vomit.

'Breathe,' I order, as she wipes her mouth with her sleeve.

'No, really?' she retorts, her voice weak. That she's as impossible as ever is kind of reassuring.

'Shut up and sit down.' I press her down onto the grass and look around in all directions. The light is inside the old greenhouse now. Good luck with that – they're not going to find anyone in there. 'Count yourself lucky you barfed so quietly.'

'Get tae fuck, Fantino.' She groans, burying her face in her hands.

'Have you got the grace to be embarrassed?'

'What for?'

'I had to hold your hair while you threw up.'

She's still resting her face on her hands. 'Nobody asked you to.'

I weigh how risky it would be to go back to the greenhouse to look for water and decide on very. Besides, there's a greater probability of finding a water bottle in her room. And I can put my plan to get caught into action later. Or some other time. Right now, the important thing is to get her safely to her bed.

'Can you stand up?'

She groans quietly.

'Pull yourself together.'

'I'm dizzy . . .'

Goddamnit. I hate caring that she feels bad. 'Don't make such a drama. Or else I'll have to carry you.'

She raises her head and blinks up at me. 'Was that a threat?'

'Depends,' I say grimly.

'Give me two more minutes . . .' She falls silent as we hear voices nearby.

'Come on.' I grab her hand and pull her up. I don't like the way she sways, but I don't want us to get caught now. She'd be in real trouble, especially after the recent incident in the pool. And she's wasted. Yep, big trouble all right.

Throwing up seems to have helped, but I still can't believe how slow she is as we cross the lawn. We have to stop several times because she feels sick, but she doesn't barf again. I breathe a sigh of relief as we get to the east wing without any further incidents.

'What the hell?' she asks, way too loudly, as I open the door to her corridor.

What does she think? 'I'm walking you to your room,' I say calmly.

She props herself against the wooden door frame. 'I don't need to be walked to my room.'

So I let go of the door and it swings back, making her stumble a couple steps backwards. I jam my foot in the doorway again and grab Olive Garden by the arm. 'No, course you don't,' I mutter. 'Give me your key.'

'Why?'

'Because you're gonna make a hell of a noise trying to find the keyhole in your state.'

'Oh, and you're in such great condition, right, got you.'

'You're impossible,' I mumble. 'Shut the fuck up, would you?'

'Shut the fuck up,' she imitates me, laughing as I glare warningly at her. God, that's a beautiful sound. I don't think I've ever heard her laugh before. So . . . light-hearted. I wish she'd do it more often, but if it takes alcohol to get her there, I'll do without.

It takes her half a lifetime to hand over her key. I realize I have no idea which room is hers. After all, I'm not the one who keeps turning up, mad as a hornet, to make a scene. That's her specialty.

She points to a door, and this time she doesn't complain when I unlock it. That she's suddenly gone so quiet unsettles me, so I hurry to get the door open. 'You've got a room to yourself?' I ask, in amazement, as I glance inside.

'Aye, great, huh?' she says, with an ironic undertone, walking past me.

'What's the matter now?'

'I just don't want any more bogging special treatment.' Her voice sounds sluggish and she has to lean against the wall. I don't like that, so rather than turning and getting out of there, I shut the door behind me. God knows why. I've delivered her back to her room. The rest of it is not my problem. In fact, none of this is my problem, so why does it feel like it is? It's fucking me up that I can't just beat it and get some sleep. Not when she's suddenly looking so sad.

So I say, 'Special treatment sucks,' watching as she pulls off her shoes and drops her jacket to the floor in slow motion. Among all the other clothes and stuff lying there. It makes me smile. She's total chaos, and I love it.

'You know how that feels, don't you?' she says drily.

I reach for her as she stumbles over something. 'God, just get to bed before you break every bone in your body.'

She pauses and all at once, our faces are incredibly close. But I don't want to. I don't kiss drunk girls. Besides, she's just thrown up. But Olive Garden makes it so fucking hard. Her green cat-eyes are huge and her lips are slightly parted. She closes her mouth and gulps, without taking her eyes off me. And then she gives me the death blow. 'Can you stay?'

Fuck it, Olive Garden, just fuck it. So now we've sunk to this level. I can see the fear of being alone in her eyes and I know she's been through shit that runs deep. I just know it.

I don't need the details to understand that it can feel overwhelming. So I just nod, even though I know I shouldn't. I want to guide her to her bed, but she won't let me.

'I need to brush my teeth.' She groans.

I laugh quietly. 'Not a bad idea.'

'Hate you,' she murmurs, then walks past me into the bathroom. I follow because I'm scared she'll trip over something and hurt herself. 'You can too,' she says, digging in the drawer under her vanity, and actually coming up with another toothbrush.

'Is that the one you usually clean between the shower tiles with?' I ask.

'No, the toilet.' She's way funnier when she's drunk.

I laugh and make her sit down on the lid. Then I take her toothbrush from her to put toothpaste on it before handing it back. After that, I stand there, leaning against the sink, finding the silence unbearably loud as we brush our teeth. Olive doesn't seem fazed. After a while, she's apparently stared at me long enough because she carries on brushing her teeth with her eyes shut.

After an eternity, she's finished and I can steer her to her bed. Conveniently, she's wearing leggings and a cosy sweater, so I don't have to face the embarrassment of asking her if she wants to undress. She looks too spent for that.

I look around as she curls up under the covers. Desk, chair, dresser and wardrobe. Her room is as Spartan as mine so I'll have to make friends with the floorboards.

'What are you doing?' she asks, as I kick aside some of her clothes.

'Making up my bed,' I say sarcastically.

'Don't be an idiot.' She sniffs. 'You don't really want to sleep on the floor?'

'I don't mind.'

'I do, though.' She scootches over a bit and turns her back to me. When I don't move, she glances over her shoulder. 'Need a special invitation?'

'Yeah,' I say. 'I don't generally get into bed with women unless they've expressly asked me to.'

'Oh, how proper of you,' she murmurs, as I don't budge from the spot.

'It's impossible to do anything right for you, isn't it?'

'No.' I can hear in her voice how tired she is. '*You* can't get anything right for me. There's a difference.'

'At least you're honest when you're drunk.'

'I'm always honest. And now get into bed with me.'

God knows why that makes me shiver, but I hide it under a sigh. 'Don't you generally say the opposite of what you actually mean?'

'You know all about that, don't you?' she says, as I slide in next to her.

I grab the quilt. 'Maybe we're not as different as you'd like to think, Henderson.'

'You and I have nothing in common, Fantino,' she declares. 'Nothing at all.'

I smile wearily. 'If you say so . . .'

'You don't know me,' she murmurs. That old classic. Her back is lying against my shoulder. I can feel the warmth of her body. And I want to put my arm around her, pull her to me and hold her tight. I'm so screwed.

'I know, Olive Garden,' I say quietly. *I know . . .*

She doesn't reply and I wish I could see her face as she shuts her eyes. But I can't. I just lie beside her and listen to her regular breathing. It gets very deep very quickly. Just as quickly as the urge grows within me to stroke the dark strands of her hair that are slanted over her face. But I don't dare.

I'm lying next to her in her bed, wondering what I'm doing there. How we can yell at each other, hurl insults at each other and then, a few hours later, wind up side by side in yet another darkened room. It's like Fate gets a real kick out of forcing us together, just to see what'll happen. If only I knew that. The next step. When Olive Garden is near, I have no idea what I'll do next. Mainly because it makes me do the exact opposite of what I really want. Not a very cheerful fact. Because now I'm here. In her room. She's fallen asleep beside me, and it's doing something to me. Doing a whole number on me, to be honest, because in the sudden silence, I can feel everything more intensely. Every heartbeat thumping in my ears, every dry gulp, which seems way too loud. Don't move. Don't make any weird noises. Don't touch her. But, fuck, this bed is narrow. It would definitely be more comfortable if I turned towards her and put my arm . . .

No. Enough is enough.

I don't care if I wake her, I need distance. I roll onto my other side and pull my phone out of my pants pocket. I dim the screen as much as I can before scrolling through Instagram, not really taking anything in. My eyes are burning – maybe I'm a bit more tired than I thought, or maybe it's just Olive Garden's even, peaceful breathing gradually rubbing off on me.

I must have dropped off, because when I wake up, I've lost all sense of time. I suppress a groan as I remember where I am. My shoulder is numb, and I wish I could roll over. I've been here quite long enough, and upstairs there's a bed where I can sleep in comfort without having to squeeze myself onto a foot-wide strip of bed. But I don't feel I can leave now. Especially not when I suddenly hear something. Beside me, Olive Garden is whimpering quietly, which is probably what woke me.

At first I think it's just one of those noises people make in their sleep, but I freeze as I realize she's shaking. She's dreaming. I turn slightly more onto my side and my phone, which must have been on the mattress beside me, crashes to the floor. I pray to God it'll wake her, but although she jumps, her eyes stay shut.

Her breath is heavy and irregular now.

'Hey . . .' I hesitate, then touch her shoulder. 'Olive.'

My blood runs cold as she makes that whimpering noise again. It makes something switch off in my brain and I start to panic. Because I know how fucking real these dreams can feel. I grab her tighter and shake her slightly. 'Livy . . .' Fuck, since when do I call her that? I guess I've heard her friends say it and this is some pathetic attempt at soothing her. 'You have to wake up, come on.'

When she startles out of her sleep, there's a moment when I'm not sure if she's even breathing. Yes, she is, but the realization doesn't calm me. Because I can see that she's crying. And that's when I give in.

The second I fling my arms around her and hold her tight, her stiffness melts. A hoarse sob sounds from her throat, and then she gasps for air, like she's spent ages underwater. The sound melts something deep within me, so I hug her tighter.

'Hey, it was a dream. It was only a silly dream, OK?' My voice sounds rough and I'm not sure if she hears me. But suddenly her hand is on my arm – and, fuck me, she's gripping hard. On to me. My heart beats faster. 'It wasn't real, everything's OK. It's all good, OK?' I can't stop saying that even though I doubt it helps. And she can't stop crying. It's driving me crazy, but I force myself to sound calm because that's probably the only way I can actually help her now.

'Want me to put the light on?' I ask after a while, ready to let go of her, but she holds on to my hand.

'No.'

My heart skips. 'Fine.' I shut my eyes and try to pull myself together. 'Want to . . . tell me about it?'

She doesn't answer right away. Strictly speaking, she doesn't answer at all. Maybe I'm just imagining the slight shake of her head, but her breath is gradually calming.

'OK,' I say. If she's still crying, she's doing so silently now, but there's no way I'm letting go. Not while her fingers keep gripping my wrist, so icy cold. I rest my brow against her shoulder and don't speak as I slowly stroke my thumb over her arm. It's dark; in reality, I'm really too chicken for these invisible touches, but even through the cloth of my hoodie, I think I can feel her racing heart. Or maybe it's mine.

Her small body grows calmer and fits perfectly with mine. She snuggles into me like we were made for each other and she's close. I'm close. I can feel everything and hear everything. Her swallowing, for example.

'Is this – ' I clear my throat and loosen my hug slightly – '. . . is this OK?'

She just digs her fingers harder into my skin and nods silently. Maybe everything just now was so terrible she can't even speak. I recognize that only too well, so I hold her closer again.

'Sorry,' she whispers, after a while.

'Don't be,' I say, and it sounds harsher than I intended, so I nuzzle her shoulder gently, then move away. 'Nightmares are shit.'

'They really are,' she manages, her voice still like sandpaper.

She said she didn't want to talk about it, but the whole time I'm thinking about what she said when we first met. An accident . . . And even though I still don't know exactly what happened, I'm sure that must be what's tormenting her. I could blame it on the alcohol still in my body, but maybe it's my own deliberate decision when I press my lips into her shoulder. It's the shoulder that makes her wince when she lifts her arm too fast or bumps into door frames. Her vulnerable spot, and when I gently caress it with my lips, she makes a muffled sound.

'Colin.' She has no idea what effect it has on me when she says my first name. I hear the pain in her voice.

'What happened to you?' I ask quietly, and instantly regret it. She tenses.

'Please, I . . . Can we just not talk about it?'

'OK.' I pull away from her slightly. 'But only if you promise me that you have someone else to talk about it with.'

'I don't need to talk to anyone.'

'Yes, you do.' I hesitate as I remember what the head said when I arrived here. 'They have this school shrink here . . . Stop that,' I add, as she snorts derisively. 'Go see her or I'll tell your dad that you're doing shit.' When she tries to pull away from my arms, I hold her tight. 'I fucking mean it.'

'What's your problem?'

You're my problem. And I wish I could solve it.

Of course I don't say that. I let go of her and glare back as she turns to me. Her curtains are open and the moonlight makes the tears glitter on her cheeks. I lift my hand to wipe them away but she doesn't let me.

'Tell me that wasn't a lie.'

'What wasn't?'

'How long ago did you split up?'

Maresa . . . Got you. God knows why she's starting on that now.

I don't want to have this conversation, but there's no getting away from it so we might as well go through with it now. She seems like she's sobered up enough to remember it in the morning.

'We were never together,' I say, and she can't miss the bitterness in my voice.

Olive raises her eyebrows in surprise. 'In those pictures, you're looking at her like she's the only person in the world.'

I clench my jaw. 'We were never a couple,' I growl again. She seems to understand. There's sympathy in her eyes now and that makes everything worse. 'Not that I know what business it is of yours.'

Unfortunately, we seem to have got to a point where she doesn't scare so easily. She watches me attentively.

'It wasn't a lie,' I say. But it's dark, she's lying in her bed in front of me, and just now, during that nightmare, Olive Garden was so vulnerable that I feel the need to give her some vulnerability in return, to keep things fair. I'm afraid otherwise the universe could tip off kilter. With us, you never know. 'I thought it was something more too. Ha. My mistake.'

'Are you in love with her?'

A question like that is mean enough when you're not lying an inch from someone and forced to look into their face. But the answer is clear.

No.

I don't know what love feels like. I only know the desire to be seen by someone, and that has nothing to do with being in love. So there's nothing to think about, but I hesitate all the same.

'She hurt me, so it hurts, but I . . . I'm not in love with her,' I say in the end. 'I never was. I think there's more to being in love. And that's no lie.'

Olive nods. 'My mum had an affair.' I freeze, but I'm not imagining it. Olive is lying beside me, staring into the darkness. 'And she talked me into not telling my dad.'

'Man,' I say. Such wisdom, I know. 'Seriously?'

'Yeah,' Olive answers. 'So now do you understand that I can't just kiss someone, knowing there's someone out there who doesn't have a clue?'

Suddenly I get it. The shit with Maresa and me must have reminded her of that. No wonder she freaked out. Suddenly I feel like a total idiot. 'Olive, I—'

'No, I believe you.' Her voice is quiet. 'I just wanted to explain why I reacted like I did.'

I nod silently. 'It wasn't a lie,' I repeat after a while, when the silence gets too much. 'But something else was.' I see her hold her breath. 'And you know what I mean.'

'No, I don't,' she retorts. Silence. She's a masochist. 'You have to say it.'

'Don't force me to.'

'You have to,' she repeats, not taking her eyes off me.

I close mine. 'The thing about me not wanting to kiss you, that was . . . I've wanted to kiss you this whole fucking time.'

She's not moving now. She lies motionless in front of me, and then everything happens very fast.

'I'd say *kiss me now*, but I'm afraid I just whiteyed . . .'

'We've brushed our teeth since then,' I point out, because she seems not to remember that. 'You insisted on it.' I lean forward. 'Just so you know.'

And then I do it.

It's a hungry kiss, and for a few seconds, she's overwhelmed. Then she wraps her arms around me and presses into me. And, oh, God, this woman will be the death of me. I move against her and press her against the wall behind her bed. She groans in surprise. I take her bottom lip gently between my teeth, and then I let her go before she feels how tight my pants are getting.

She gasps for air. I kiss her quickly on the tip of her nose and roll to one side, even though that's anything but easy. But she's still not entirely sober, she had a nightmare and . . . I want to get this right. Yes, it's out there. I don't want to have a bit of fun with Olive Garden. I want something real and I can't expect to have that without some effort on my part.

I get goosebumps as I feel her hand on my chest. Maybe she can sense what she's doing to me when she runs her fingers over me, or maybe not.

She rests her head on my chest. 'That was a kiss,' she announces in the end.

'Your powers of perception are astonishing.'

'I know, Colin.'

Colin. I have to shut my eyes. Not Fantino. That's what she calls me when I piss her off. And right now I don't want to piss her off. Yeah, plot twist.

Her arm is on my stomach, and her fingers are caressing my body. I don't know how this is possible. Maybe I'm dreaming too. I want to kiss her again. I want to keep holding her, I don't want it to get light outside because, once it does, there's a chance that this is all in my head. Right now, though, I'm very certain this is real.

Her hair is tickling my throat, the taste of her is in my mouth, and her body is warm. I don't know if I've ever fallen asleep like this. There was nothing like this with Maresa. There was fucking, followed by turning away. Didn't faze me, or so I always thought, but maybe I don't know myself as well as I thought I did. Maybe Olive Garden is awakening something inside me that scares me and makes me braver in equal measure. Maybe I am capable of feeling. Real feelings. And of showing them to her.

She puts her arm over me, scootches closer, and then her head grows heavier against my chest. Mine is heavy too. She's warm. And I'm not letting her go. I won't ever let her go.

21

OLIVE

My head aches. Maybe because I had too much to drink, maybe because last night feels like one long fever dream. Colin Fantino holding my hair while I whitey. Colin Fantino in my bed after the nightmare, the memory of which still sends ice-cold shivers down my spine. Colin Fantino kissing me, hungrily yet incredibly gently, and me falling back to sleep in his arms.

We almost got caught because, suddenly, it was getting light outside, and I now know that Fantino is absolutely useless in the mornings. It's just as well Ms Barnett doesn't come to wake me for the morning run like she does the others, or we'd have been so busted. As it is, he managed to slip up to his own room unnoticed, leaving me time to sit motionless on my bed, staring into space.

I don't know what this thing between us means. I just know that my belly feels warm when I think of him. Remember the way he held me tight. He was a different Colin from the one who never misses a chance to show everyone what a monster he is. It was a version of him I want to see more of, yet I'm scared that last night was a one-off. That he only treated me that way because I was drunk and needed his help. At least in his eyes, because of course I didn't really need help. I don't need anybody. But I can't deny that the way he looked after me felt nice. So I'm weak. Great.

I go down to breakfast feeling nervous because I don't know if he'll have pulled the walls back up around himself.

I'm early and he doesn't show up for ages, but then, when he walks through the double doors into the dining room – which is buzzing like a beehive, same as every morning – his eyes rest on me first of all. He seeks me out among everyone else, and I feel warm again.

'If you can face eating, that's some kind of miracle,' he comments, coming to sit next to me. Just like that. Like it's the most natural thing in the world.

I can't help smiling. 'Get tae fuck, Fantino.'

'Language, Olive, really!'

I jump. That was Mr Acevedo, who's just walking behind us.

'Sorry,' I mutter. Colin gloats at me as the teacher moves away again.

'Instant karma,' he says quietly, lowering his gaze to his phone, where he's tapping in assorted numbers. It takes me a while to grasp that it's his insulin dose, which he's setting for his breakfast.

'How do you know what it needs to be?' I ask, without thinking.

Colin looks up wordlessly.

'Sorry for being interested.' He doesn't need to look so pissed off.

'You get an instinct after a while,' he answers.

'But you don't even know how much you're going to eat?'

'Well, I just have to figure that out in advance.'

'What a pain.'

'Very helpful, Olive Garden. Very helpful.'

'Sorry,' I mumble.

He mutters in a decidedly hostile way. Then he glances up again and watches me, like he wants to check how it landed. And his eyes are so brown that I can't even come up with a put-down.

Colin grins, like he knows all of that. And I hate him. But I'm starting to worry that I'm well on the way to falling in love with him.

22

OLIVE

'Is there anything else you want to say before we wrap up?' I ask, holding my pencil ready.

Imogen, from the swimming team, thinks. 'Only that it's an honour to swim for Dunbridge.' She smiles. 'And to be interviewed by you.'

'Thanks for taking the time for me,' I reply.

'I hope you can make some sense of my answers.'

'Definitely. You were way chattier than the hockey lads – talking to them was like getting blood out of a stone.'

Imogen laughs. 'Only the cool kids on our team.'

'You said it.' It takes a few seconds for it to sink in that I'm joking around with our team like I'm still part of it. Imogen glances over to the pool entrance, where the first people are arriving for training. We agreed to meet up half an hour early so that I could take a few photos of her and do the interview. Now it's time for Imogen to get into the water, and for me to put the camera away in my locker to keep it dry while I help Ms Cox run the session. The first few times, I kept right in the background, but I've noticed myself gradually getting more confident. The others are way happier to accept my tips and advice than I thought they'd be. At first, I was scared they'd think I was an imposter, but the genuine way everyone thanked me soon changed my mind.

Today, too, I can forget my anger and bitterness as I praise the juniors, whose flip turns are getting better all the time. Seeing their progress makes me proud. It's a different pride from when I was swimming and getting personal bests, but – and this genuinely surprises me – not in a bad way. It feels a bit like making peace with things when I leave training early to get to Mr Carpenter on time. Colin's already there, listlessly pushing a broom around. This is our last cleaning duty but one as punishment for being out of bounds nearly a fortnight ago, and I'm almost sad about that, because cleaning with Colin is part of my routine now. The only new thing is that we sneak in as much winching as we can, until my stomach tingles and my cheeks are flushed.

I ignore the pain as Colin pushes me up against the thin strip of wall between two lattice windows. Today we're in the biology storeroom, where we're meant to be dusting off the animal and anatomy models. We dropped our dusters ages ago, though. Colin takes my hands and pins them to the wall at my side. Not being able to touch him while we kiss is making me lose my mind.

My knees go soft as he presses his hips against me. God, is he trying to kill me?

He bites gently on my bottom lip, and I never had a clue that, apparently, I'm into that kind of thing. But now I know, and I can't stop a quiet moan escaping me.

A moment later, there's a loud crash and we jump apart.

'Olive, Colin, for heaven's sake!' Mr Ringling is standing in the doorway, staring at us. In one hand he's holding a frame of mounted butterflies and there's another on the floor at his feet. 'It looks as though we've been discussing animal mating behaviour in a little too much detail in class lately.'

'Nothing we didn't know already, sir,' says Colin, wiping his flushed lips with his hand. The thought of what he was just doing with them makes me burn up.

'Lord, children,' Mr Ringling mumbles, bending down to check on the dropped frame. 'Well, luckily nothing's broken. But don't let me catch you in here again, or I'll have to report you to the head. How did you even get in?'

'Mr Carpenter let us in,' I explain.

'Mr Carpenter? No way. He knows how valuable these models are. It's strictly out of bounds to pupils.'

'We're supposed to be cleaning them,' I add.

'With your tongues? Well, good luck with that.' Mr Ringling puts the butterflies up on a shelf. Then he spots our dusters and eyes us sternly. 'Get back to work quickly now, or

I'll have to come up with a more suitable punishment for the two of you.'

'No need, sir,' says Colin, cheerfully, picking up the duster.

I don't let myself grin until Colin has chased me through the narrow spaces between the shelves with it and Mr Ringling has vanished again. Behind the taxidermy birds, we continue where we were interrupted.

COLIN

The moment Olive Garden looks at me, I'm thirteen again and full of embarrassing hormones that make my belly tingle. And she looks at me a lot. In class, in the dining room, on our afternoon work duty – although that's over now, and I'm actually missing it. She's really smitten, but the feeling's mutual, so who am I to talk?

Not that either of us would admit it. I'm sure that Olive Garden would rather die than confess it. And that's exactly why I like her so much. She's a woman of few words, at least when she's angry. And I can relate to that.

And I don't need many words from her to feel like I'm floating through the hallways of Dunbridge Academy on a silly little cloud. All it takes is to remember the night she got so drunk.

Of course I hate that she had the nightmare, but it's like I can still feel her body next to mine, even though it was quite a while ago now. Her lips on mine, and now, by daylight, I'm seriously asking myself how, now that I've started, I'm ever going to stop kissing her.

Apparently you can see in my face that something's changed, because once I've sought out my secret piano after study hour this afternoon, Cleo, who has a half-day today, won't let it go.

'No, there's something going on with you, Col,' my kid sister says, coming closer to the camera until her face fills the whole screen.

'There's nothing going on,' I insist, trying to sound fierce and not to let my lovesick grin give me away.

'Spill,' Cleo insists.

'What d'you want to hear next?' I try to distract her, but it's hopeless.

'Does it have to do with that Olive?'

Shit. How is this possible? How can she see through me so easily?

'I knew it,' my sister says flatly, and I have to fight against the urge to cut off the call right away. 'You like her, don't you?'

'She's irritating,' I say, feeling like a traitor.

'You like her,' Cleo repeats, hiding her mouth behind both hands. 'Does she like you too?'

'I don't think anyone here likes me.' But that's not true any more, I realize, as I say the words.

'Apart from Olive?'

I groan.

'Come on, tell me! I need to know, Col.'

'Yeah, OK. Maybe she isn't quite as irritating as she was at the start.'

Her smile broadens. 'I think that's the most romantic thing you've ever said.'

'Don't worry, it won't happen again.'

Cleo ignores me. 'But if you really like her – ' she falls silent and looks at me with her huge, brown doe-eyes – '. . . you'll still try to come home as soon as you can, won't you?'

'Yes, of course,' I promise hastily, but my voice sounds worried. Of course there's nothing I want more than to be out of here. The fact that Olive Garden is messing with my heart doesn't mean everything else here isn't grim. It's still a fucking strict boarding school in the wilderness of Scotland, and can't compare to my life in New York. But lately I get the feeling that part of me has given in and come to terms with it. And since then . . . it's somehow not so bad here.

Shit. I'm starting to like it. Not just Olive Garden, but . . . being a Dunbridge Academy pupil. Going to tennis with Kit and his guys, boxing, chatting at break time, sitting in the dining room, doing the morning run, going to midnight parties. Even rooming with Sinclair or strolling down to the hick village to buy a few things in the store.

And that's not good. I've got a big, fat problem here. And I can't hide it from Cleo: as I realize this, the smile dies on her face.

'Sure?' she asks quietly, voice wobbling. 'Colin, it sucks

here without you.' I swear, if she starts crying, I'll freak. But she's a Fantino: she's learned that showing emotions is a sign of weakness, so she does the only thing we freaking well know how: she hides them, to deal with them later, on her own. And seeing that hurts.

I've failed. I didn't want my kid sister to turn out like me, but I'm not there to stop it happening. There's nobody with her, and no way can I let that feeling get a hold of Cleo. Because once that happens, she'll never be rid of it. Never.

Shit. So what do I do now?

All I can do is calm her down and think about it in peace later.

'It sucks without you too, Cleo,' I say, an ocean and five hours' time difference between us. 'And there's no way I'm staying here.' I never thought I'd say that without feeling it. 'But it's not as easy to get expelled as I thought. I'll have to come up with something real bad, you know?'

Cleo's smile is strained and I'm not sure if it's real. 'You'll think of something.'

'You bet I will.' I smile at her. 'OK, now, tell me what to play.'

I can't stand the next two songs. Cleo's smile is fake, I can see that even as my fingers move mechanically over the keys and I'm tense because I've lied to her. I didn't mean to lie – of course I want to return to her – but every day at this school, I understand more and more that what I used to have didn't make me happy. My friends who ghost me and don't give a shit about how I'm doing. Maresa, who's moved on to the next sucker without batting an eyelid. I'd be such a goddamn loser if I went back now. Besides, I'm not even sure if I really want to. Even if everyone acts like nothing's changed, that's not true. It changed the second I got on that plane and flew to Europe. I wanted to close my eyes to it, didn't want to admit it, but that's impossible now.

I'm a different Colin from a few weeks ago. I'm a Colin who's in love with a Scottish girl who has green cat-eyes, and can't get enough of her insults.

I'm a guy who feels a pain in my chest when he notices how close the friendships are here, the way they all tell each other everything and know each other through and through. I'm sitting here among them all, playing my part, being jerkish and moody, until I'm lying in bed with Olive Garden, wanting to cry because it feels like something real. And at home in Manhattan, there's my kid sister sitting alone at her iPad, jumping if I play a wrong note but laughing it off, like she learned from me, and looking at me with eyes that tell me she knows. She's figured out what's going on with me and she's scared because I might not keep the promise I made to her. To come back. Not to leave her alone. Holy shit.

We say goodbye in a rush because Kirsten comes in to check that Cleo's doing her schoolwork. On the way back to my room, I feel ripped apart inside.

I know the way back to the east wing now. I recognize the people I see on the way. They say hi, I say hi back, and I feel like shit because I can't manage to hate everything any more. I've arrived here, it's true, but I can't let myself feel at home, I just can't, because I promised Cleo over and over again.

But that promise is at war with what Olive Garden is stirring up inside me, so much so that my hands are nervously looking for something to do.

When I get to the room, Sinclair isn't there. He must be out riding, which means he won't get back until just before dinner for a quick shower and to talk my ear off. So for now I'm alone. My heart is pounding – I can feel it in my throat as I pace uneasily around the room.

Fuck sake, don't be so dramatic. Nothing's happened, but something is happening inside me. I've faced up to something I've been denying for a while, and that was a mistake because now I have an unsolvable problem. All I can think of is Cleo, sitting alone at her desk at home, and then later on, having dinner with Mom and Dad. If Mom can even fit it in – on days she's filming, she usually eats at the studio, and Dad often works late in the office, where he can shut himself away and forget that he has a family: my thirteen-year-old sister, who no longer has anybody to teach her, as subtly as possible, that it's not *her* fault she's right at the bottom of her parents' list of priorities. Apparently, I'm now just as bad as them, because I'm prioritizing my own life over hers too now.

I clench my fists and stand by the window. God, this is impossible. I can't stay here and act like I'm different from my parents if I leave Cleo in the lurch. I swore to be there for her so that she wouldn't be as fucked up by our family as I am. And now I'm here and I'm part of the problem.

When I can't bear it any longer, I turn away and go over to the bed. Slowly, with as much control as I can manage, but it's hard to breathe. The lighter's well hidden between my insulin supplies, pumps and spare syringes, which I keep in a box under my bed. I'm pretty sure Sinclair wouldn't stick his nose into my stuff, but even if he did, he wouldn't look in here.

My fingers are shaking as I dig through the packets until I find the cool metal. I slam the box back under the bed and push up my sleeve because I'm not in the mood to find anywhere better. I need to move fast.

I notice again that it's good to take a break from time to time, because now that I've been strict with myself and gone without my lighter for a while, it's an unexpected relief when the flame meets my skin. I flinch after just a split second, because I've grown unaccustomed to it, but it's already helping to shift my mind from my crappy emotional pain to the physical.

Again now. Longer this time.

Don't be a fucking weakling, Fantino. This is what you deserve, so hang in there.

And then it happens, like it always does: the pressure eases, the relief floods in to take its place, my heartbeat settles down, everything's good, for this moment at least, until it's followed by the shame and self-hatred.

Fucking wuss, this is so lame. Why not go boxing like Kit showed you? Why do you keep doing this? Why haven't you learned from what happened in New York?

Clearly I haven't, and it bugs me. I flick the lighter on again, shut my eyes and dig my teeth into my bottom lip. Not long . . .

Five.

Four.

Three.

T—

There's a knock, my eyes fly open, and at this exact moment, the door opens wide.

23

COLIN

She saw, I know it, and I can't move as Olive stands there, frozen in the doorway. Her eyes are on me. On the lighter in my hand. The flame dies.

The whole thing happens in a fraction of a second, but it feels like an eternity. And then it all goes very fast.

Her face turns white, then red, and she hurls herself at me.

'Put that out! Put that out! Are you insane? You can't, not in here! You – you can't light fires in here!'

I immediately hide the lighter in my sleeve, but there's no point. My heart's racing again. I jump up.

She saw.

And I can only pray that she didn't have time to put two and two together. I should have been prepared for this. It was obviously going to happen at some point. And now I have no explanation. I just wanted to ... light a candle. OK, but where's the fucking candle? Why don't I smoke? If I did, Olive Garden would presumably not ask questions. But it looks like she'd still freak out that I wanted to light up in my bedroom.

Her eyes are wide with shock. For God's sake, she's totally overreacting again. Nothing even happened. It isn't the first time I've done it here.

Her eyes dart restlessly around the room, like she's scanning it for potential fires, and suddenly, her whole body is trembling.

'Hey.' I slip the lighter unobtrusively in my pants pocket and walk towards her, arms outstretched. Olive flinches back in such panic that she crashes loudly into the wardrobe. Pain twinges through her face, as does fear.

'No, Colin. No, no, no. I get it! You'll do anything to get expelled. Cool, go ahead, break every rule in this place for all I care, every single one, whatever, but for God's sake, not this one!'

'Chill,' I snap at her. 'It was only a lighter. I didn't do anything.'

'Aye, right, and those fuckers in the Dungeon last summer only had a lighter, Colin! It was only a lighter and a cigarette end that was still alight when they dropped it on one of the sofas, or wherever the fuck it was, nobody knows. Nobody knows, there's no answer, no fucking answer.' Her voice is shaking, she's breathing fast. Too fast. What's she talking about? She's well on her way to a full-on panic attack.

I go over to her without a word and take her shoulders. Olive tries to pull away but I won't let her. 'You're over-thinking this,' I say slowly.

She won't stop shaking her head. 'Oh, am I, Colin? You know what? Yeah. Yeah, maybe I am. I'm over-thinking this, OK? Would you still say that if you were the one who woke up in the middle of the night because you could smell something burning and you looked out and you saw the flames and your knees gave way even though you should run down the stairs, and when you finally did, there wasn't enough fucking oxygen and then you're lying there and you can't move and a fucking burning beam hits the floor right next to your head, and if the fire brigade hadn't got to your floor at that exact moment you'd have fucking died? Would you say that then?'

I feel how tense her shoulders are beneath my hands, and I go slowly numb.

'What are you talking about?' I ask gruffly. I've let her go.

Tears shine in Olive's eyes as she grabs the hem of her sweater and pulls it over her head. I can't think about the fact that she's facing me in a black lace bra, all I can do is stare at her upper arm, which is covered with red, scarred skin from her shoulder to her collarbone.

'Will you say that now?' she repeats. The tears are muffling her voice.

Rushing in my head.

Emptiness.

'Wait, you mean . . . there was a fire? That's what the repair work is all about? There was a fire here?' With every question, it's like part of me dies.

Darkness, cold.

My racing heart, the nausea creeping up my throat.

Tears run down Olive's cheeks. She's standing in front of me, half undressed, and suddenly everything clicks. Her panic as we walked past that closed-off building, and I wanted to go inside. Her rage as she stood by that trophy cabinet, her despair because the accident took everything from her. The accident was a fire. A fire that wasn't my fault, but I was to blame for a different one. A fire where somebody lost her life.

I stumble back slightly as dizziness washes over me. Olive wraps both arms around her upper body, I stare at her scars. The pain she must be in.

And then everything goes wrong.

I know that I should stay and calm her down, hold her. But I can't. I just can't.

'I'm sorry,' I croak. I don't look at her once as I push past her and leave the room.

I don't take in anything around me. Don't look to see whether there's anyone in the corridor who might have overheard us, doesn't matter any more. There's only a whirlpool of panic and desperation, which is sucking me in, and there's nothing I can do about it.

Would you still say that if you woke up and saw the flames . . .

I catch sight of the west wing as the stairway spits me out at the bottom. The tarps hiding the fire-blackened façade.

That can't be true.

I can hardly look, but I find myself walking towards it. It's Friday evening, and the workmen went home hours ago. The entrance to the west wing is no longer barricaded off these days.

I can't think straight as I duck under the flimsy tape with its *Building Site No Entry* sign.

It's presumably all in my imagination, but I can smell it. The stink of burned wood. The moment I leave the ground-floor arcades behind me, everything is dark. There are no motion sensors to make the lights come on. The electricity is shut off. And it must have been just this dark when Olive tried to walk down the stairs. Until the flames cut her off.

Her eyes wide with panic, her body frozen. The way she stared at me. *Me.* The guy she kissed, in whose arms she fell asleep without knowing who I am. And what I did.

I spin around and my fist connects with the wall. Again. And again. It doesn't help. Not in any way.

Mom's words on the phone as she spoke to Mrs Sinclair before she spotted me in her office doorway.

It's not ideal, Nora, I know that. But Colin is devastated. Nothing like that will ever happen again.

I sink back onto my heels and feel for my lighter.

Back then, I thought this principal just didn't want to have an arsonist at her fancy school. That made sense. But someone ought to have told me that she had a very different reason for her concerns. A reason that shocks me to my bones now that I know about it.

There was a fire here. I guess it was only a couple of weeks before the gym at Ainslee went up in flames in New York. How could they let this happen? How can I even be here? What made my mom think this was a good idea? How could I get close to Olive? How did I dare? If I'd known, if I'd had even the slightest hint of an idea of what had happened to her, I'd never have let things get this far between us. And neither would she. Obviously. Because I'm a fucking monster.

My throat tightens further with every passing second as I take in what all this means. Olive doesn't have a clue what I did. Does anyone at this goddamn school know that, or did my mother make sure the head was the only person who did? That must be it, because otherwise, how could anyone look me in the eye?

I have to get away from here. I have to get the fuck out. It's the only way.

I pull my phone from my pocket and I don't give a damn if Ava Fantino's in the studio, if she's filming, if she's having important conversations. She rejects the call, I try again. And again, so often that, in the end, she has to answer.

'Colin, this really isn't a good—'

'How could you not tell me?' I cut her off without any kind of greeting. It goes quiet at the other end. 'How could you send me here despite . . . How? How the hell?'

'Colin,' she says slowly, and now I'm madder than I've ever been.

'There was a fire here!' I yell. 'There was a fire! People got hurt! Just tell me who the fuck you think you're kidding!'

'That may well be, but it was an accident and nothing to do with you, Colin,' she says coolly.

I laugh mirthlessly. 'Did you think nobody here would ever find out what I did? Did you really think that?'

'What does it have to do with anyone else?'

'God, Mom!' I don't know what to do with myself.

'And the incident in New York was also an accident for which you are not to blame.'

'That's not true and you know it!'

'Colin, you're going to calm down and listen to me –'

'No, *you're* going to listen to *me*,' I interrupt. 'I'm not staying here. I can't, for Christ's sake. Send me somewhere else, to Switzerland, to France, I don't care, but I'm not staying here at this school waiting for everyone to find out what I did.'

'Dunbridge Academy is the right place for you – the head and I are in agreement on that. She will handle everything with the utmost discretion. You don't need to worry that anyone will hear about it.'

I shut my eyes as I pace restlessly up and down. 'I was there, Mom.' I hear the pleading in my voice and I despise myself. 'It's the truth, I was there, it was –'

'Then you'll learn from it,' she says sharply. 'Our family is too important to let one little mistake destroy your future.'

'Did you ever ask yourself, even once, how I'm meant to live with this?'

'Stop being so melodramatic and move on.'

'She had kids, Mom,' I croak. 'Four kids who've lost their mom because she wanted to *help*.'

It's pointless. I remember my mother's face as I sat opposite her the day after the fire. I don't think she's often seen me cry but I was desperate. I was scared, didn't know what to do. And I made the wrong choice – I went to her.

I understand, Colin. I'll take care of it. Don't speak to anyone until I've seen our lawyers.

But how was I supposed to know that meant she'd stop me telling the truth? I thought she wanted to get me the best legal defence there was, someone who'd help me know what to say, but that wasn't what she had in mind at all. Her plan was to cover up what I did, and I was too cowardly to fight against it.

'If you want to speak to a therapist, I'll send you some numbers,' she says calmly.

I shake my head, pulling at my hair. 'You don't get it. You don't want to get it. How can you want to cover up a thing like this?'

'How can you want your sister to have her brother publicly shamed even when there are *alternatives*?'

I grind my teeth, so hard that my jaw cracks. 'Leave Cleo out of this.'

'Think about your family. You're a Fantino and that comes with responsibilities. Now you have the chance to prove that you're capable of acting like an adult.'

'Do you ever listen to yourself?'

'Colin, you think you're so smart, but the truth is that you still have a lot to learn in life. This is your first challenge – take it with dignity. Anyone else would be grateful that their family supported them like this.'

'This isn't supporting me,' I manage. 'This is emotional blackmail.'

'You will stay at that school and not say another word about it,' Mom declares. 'Think about your sister. Think about your future. And I don't want to hear another word about this subject.'

I bite my bottom lip because there's so much I want to say. To ask my mother how she can seriously believe she's doing the right thing. How she can look at herself in the mirror, how she thinks I can look at myself in the mirror. Whether truth and justice aren't more important than our family's goddamn appearances. But I know the answers to all those questions. There's no need to ask them. Tears sting in my eyes. I'm weak and I don't want her to hear me like this.

'I hate you,' I whisper, and I mean it. But I hate myself too, more than anything, and I can't see any way out except taking action myself. Even if it means getting in touch with the police from here, confessing to what I did. She can't stop me. And I have to do it. Even though the thought of it sends me into a blind panic. I have to call them. And today, not tomorrow. Except that I should think about what to say. And how to explain why I've kept quiet this long.

'One day you'll thank me,' Mom says.

I end the call – I can't take any more. I hurl my lighter onto the floor and the sound makes me jump. I instantly regret it, but I prick my ears and listen, there in the dark, for a few seconds, and nothing happens, so I take a shivery breath. There's nobody here, nobody to have heard me. If I really want to go through with this, I have to prepare myself. In peace.

OK.

I stare up at the ceiling, I gulp hard. I bend down for the shitty lighter, which obviously didn't break. And then I lose the last of my self-respect as I flick back the lid and hold the flame to my skin.

OLIVE

He walks past me without once looking me in the face and, for a moment, I don't know how to keep breathing. There's just this pressure in my chest and the buzzing in my head.

He's walking away.

I told him what happened and *he's walking away.*

I don't care but apparently my body does, because when Colin goes, I feel sick. The door shuts, I stand in his room wearing nothing but my leggings and a bra, asking myself what just happened. A dry sob bursts from my throat as it sinks in.

How could he do that? How could he just walk out?

I don't know how long I stand there before I hear voices and laughter outside the door.

I have just enough time to pull my top back on before I spin round to face Tori and Sinclair. Sinclair frowns in confusion, and Tori's eyes fill with concern.

'Er . . . hi, Olive?' Sinclair says, as Tori comes over to me. 'You're in my room.'

'What happened?' I don't ask myself how she knows that something must have happened. Apparently, the sight of me is enough. 'Fantino?'

I nod with compressed lips and feel the tears well up again.

'Can you give us a moment?' Tori asks Sinclair, not taking her eyes off me.

'Hey, this is my room. Can't you two—'

'Out,' says Tori curtly, and Sinclair groans.

'Am I being thrown out of my own room yet again? What am I doing wrong here?'

I wrap my arms around my upper body and as the tears run down my cheeks, Sinclair seems to twig. He backs out of the room without another word, and shuts the door quietly.

'Spill,' Tori insists, but I can't get the words out. All I can do is shrug. My throat laces up tighter than ever as she hugs me.

'Livy, you're scaring me,' she whispers.

'We had a fight,' I manage. 'He . . .' I pause. *He had a lighter in his hand and I had a panic attack.* That's what I should tell Tori but, for some reason, I can't. All I can think of is Colin's wrist and the flame on his skin. It was only for a split second but I saw it. And there's only one explanation for what I saw. 'God knows. We argued and he walked out.'

I can't tell her. That I told Colin about the fire. That he saw my scars, that he let go of me and ran away. I'm not naïve enough to think he wasn't fazed. I saw his face, which froze into a mask as his eyes rested on me. He couldn't stand the sight of me. Fuck knows what it reminded him of, what emotions it stirred up in him, why he didn't fucking stay, to help me, to console me.

Because it's not his bloody problem. Because the guy clearly has enough issues of his own and doesn't need someone who freaks out the whole time. But part of me, a tiny wee utterly pathetic part of me, remembers the night he slept in my room. Colin's arms around my body as he held me tight. I thought we'd made progress. I thought things were serious.

'Really?' Tori asks. I can hear that she's cross and I know I could fool her. 'What kind of arsehole is he?'

But I don't defend him. It hurt too much to see Colin go. Why did he just walk out? Why does he sit around in his room with a lighter, and why does thinking about it give me bellyache? I don't want all this. I want to get back to when he was lying in my bed and we were kissing and it felt like the rules of this game we're playing might actually be a bit simpler than I thought. But clearly I was wrong. Nothing is simple, nothing.

'Forget him, Livy, seriously, he's not worth it,' Tori tells me, because she's trying to be a good best friend, but the truth is, she has no idea. She doesn't know that that's not an option any more, hasn't been for ages. OK, at first, I wanted to tell him 'Fuck you', but I'm afraid that too many people in his life have said that to him already. I can't explain why I get that feeling, not to myself, not to Tori. Maybe she's right, maybe I really should finish it with this guy – after all, he clearly can't wait to get kicked out of the school. Because what will I do if he achieves that? There was a time when I'd have been fine with it, but things have changed. I'd miss him. More than that. I don't know what I'd do if Colin suddenly wasn't here. This is the moment I realize I've got a major problem.

My phone buzzes in my hoodie pocket. I free myself from Tori's arms and pull it out. It's Dad, asking if I'm ready. What's he talking about? Then I remember. I'm meant to be going home this weekend because it's been ages since he and Mum and me were all together, just the three of us. I haven't spent a weekend with my parents since I got back to school. It's not like I used to be over there all the time, but since Mum and her affair, the idea of sitting around the dinner table with her and Dad, playing at happy families, makes me want to boak. Even now, the thought of it ties my stomach in knots. But I don't want to be a bad daughter either and, to be honest, what is there for me here? A choice between not sleeping for fear of nightmares and bumping into Colin in the corridors. I don't want either. I want some peace and quiet. Maybe a weekend at home *is* actually what I need.

'Dad,' I say, looking up. Tori frowns at me. 'He's waiting for me. I'm going home for the weekend.'

'OK,' she says, after a wee while. 'Maybe that's not such a bad thing.'

I force myself to smile. 'We'll see.'

24

OLIVE

It's not going to be good. I realize that when Dad asks me three times on the drive to Edinburgh if everything's OK. I say, 'Yeah,' three times, and stare out of the window to stop him seeing I'm close to tears. I manage not to cry. By the time we get home, I'm more or less in control. Or so I think. Mum's not here, she's working, which means she could be back any time, or not until the wee hours. A birth takes as long as it takes, she always says, and I believe her, but for some time now, I've found myself thinking that her work as a community midwife is excellent cover for spending nights away from home. It makes me want to boak.

She isn't back by the time we sit down to dinner, and she still isn't back when we move to the couch, ostensibly to watch a film, but then Dad asks how things are going and, in the end, I talk to him. Reluctantly at first, but after a while I see that it's doing me good. And then I tell him about Colin, which I really didn't plan to do.

'That's nice, Olive,' he says, his voice deliberately nonchalant. 'I'm sure it wasn't easy for him to start at a new school either.'

'Presumably not.' I shrug. 'But he isn't planning to stay long.'

'Really?'

'Well, that's what he says.'

'Hm.' Dad leans back slightly. 'That would be a shame.'

'Yeah,' I say, hardly recognizing myself. If anyone had told me a couple of weeks ago that I'd ever think that, I'd have laughed at them. But here we are. 'And what I said earlier wasn't true. Nothing's all right.'

'What's wrong, pet?'

'I told him about the fire. And Colin . . .' I falter. 'I don't know, he reacted really weirdly.'

'Uh-huh?'

'Maybe I shouldn't have told him.'

Dad looks at me, a funny expression on his face. 'It's never wrong to tell the truth, Olive. Don't let anyone tell you it is.'

I gulp hard and nod, because my throat's gone dry. 'You think?'

Dad nods. 'Absolutely.'

God, if he knew . . . I can't imagine Dad would still say that if he had any idea of the truth I'm lugging around. But with him sitting here with me now, giving me the feeling that I can tell him anything, I don't know how I can keep it from him even one day longer.

'So, do you think that the truth is better even if it could hurt someone?' I ask hesitantly.

'I think the truth is the most important thing of all, love,' Dad declares, giving me a brief smile. 'You know that.'

Apparently I don't. I'd forgotten, not just briefly but for way too long. Until now.

'If that's so, then there's something you should know.' No. *Don't do it, don't do it, don't do it.* But I have to. I can't bear not telling him any longer. I always used to think not knowing stuff was bad. Now I think I was wrong. Knowing things you're not meant to know is way worse. I shut my eyes for a moment, then carry on. 'Mum's . . . she had . . .' God, get on with it. Spit it out. There's no going back now. 'I saw her kissing another man.'

I shut my eyes once I've said the words. Why did I tell him? What good does it do Dad to know? It was just egocentric and selfish of me, to stop me feeling like a traitor. But his feelings should be way more important to me.

Dad says nothing, and that might be the worst silence I've ever experienced. When I look at him, he's pale but together.

'I wanted to tell you sooner, Dad, truly,' I say. 'I saw her in Ebrington, ages ago, and she convinced me not to say anything to you. Dad, I thought I was doing the right thing, I didn't want to . . .'

'I know, Olive.'

'I'm so sorry I didn't tell you sooner . . .'

'Olive,' he repeats. 'I know about it.' Dad stresses every syllable, and the world stops spinning. 'Your mother told me. A few weeks ago. We had . . . several long conversations.' He clears his throat and I want to jump up. To run away. 'Sadly, we haven't had a genuine relationship for a long time now. And I recently met someone too.'

Two sentences that shatter my world.

I feel numb. Dizzy. Empty.

'What?' I whisper. The expression on Dad's face as he leans forward slightly and I flinch back is one of pure pain, which matches the feeling in my chest.

'We wanted to tell you together. Calmly. When we were totally certain.'

'So you're getting divorced?'

Dad says nothing. Then he nods slowly.

I don't know what changes at that moment, but I can't remember how to cry. I don't yell. I don't create a drama. I just stand up.

'And now you're totally certain,' I suggest.

'We're still your parents. It won't change anything there.' Dad has stood up too. 'Olive, I'm sorry you're only finding it out this way. I had no idea that you knew about your mother and Alexis.'

'So she *is* still with him?' My voice has never sounded so empty. 'She said it was over. When I got out of hospital, she . . . I thought . . .'

'Your mother spoke to me not long after that.' Dad sounds serious, but he doesn't seem half as hurt as I always thought he'd be.

'And you ... you've already met someone new?' It takes every bit of my self-control to ask that. But I can't freak out now, I just can't.

Dad looks so sad that it makes me angry. What was he expecting? What? 'Nathalie,' he says, after a while. 'I haven't known her long. But she's really looking forward to meeting you.'

'You've told her about me?' My voice breaks.

'She has two grown-up sons, students – one's at Oxford and the other's at Cambridge. I'm sure you'll get along and . . .'

Dad keeps speaking but I don't hear the rest. I wait till he's finished. I nod when he asks questions. I feel like a shell filled with nothing.

Mum's back with Alexis then. It's official. Even though she and Dad only ended things a few weeks ago, he's ready for a new relationship, which can only mean one thing: he was expecting it. He knew it; he guessed it; he had time to come to terms with it. He knew it while the thought that I was letting him down was causing me sleepless nights. Now I know I'm not doing that. But what I feel now is no better. Now I'm the one who's been let down.

'Nothing will change between us, pet,' Dad insists again, and I wonder how people can flat-out lie like that.

'So are the two of them moving in here like one big, happy commune?' I burst out, because I'm only human and I can't

293

hold it in much longer. Not when my dad's making me promises he can't keep.

There's an embarrassed silence. 'We haven't quite come to an agreement about the house yet.'

'Well, I'm at boarding school anyway. And after that I'll be at uni.'

'Olive, this will always be your home.'

It's hard not to laugh. 'Right, Dad.'

'Darling, we weren't deliberately keeping secrets from you. We just had to work out what it all means and the best way to go from here. But we love you. We're your parents. We'll always love you.'

I try not to cry. I spent over a year beating myself up every day because I knew something that I thought would destroy my family when, in truth, it was already long broken. My dad isn't some knight in shining armour who goes out to work and comes home innocently, with no idea of what's going on. He was just slogging on, the same as Mum. And I was sat there between them, desperately trying to figure out how to save something that couldn't be saved. What an absolute idiot.

COLIN

I feel cut off. From myself, from reality. Nothing gets through to me, and I know myself well enough to be aware that that's dangerous.

My first impulse, after I was done with the lighter, was to go to Mrs Sinclair. I'd lost all sense of time, but it must have been later than I thought because her office was shut and Mr Harper was nowhere to be seen either. Maybe that's for the best, because I don't want to put myself through the humiliation of begging her to throw me out of the school and convince my mother that this is the last place on earth I should be.

The rest of the weekend blurs into a collection of moments. I'm such a loser that I can't even bring myself to call the police in Manhattan. I psych myself up to do it a bunch of times but always fail. I've never felt so ashamed.

I don't see Olive – she seems to be away, and I hear from her friends that she's gone home. Which is better for her, but it's stressing me out. I have to speak to her. I have to apologize to her, explain everything. Only then can I do what needs to be done.

But at the same time, I feel as if I can never again go anywhere near her. She doesn't have a goddamn clue what I'm responsible for. What a monster I am. But however I twist and turn, it's not an option to keep the truth from her. She'll hate me, if not for what I did, then for not accepting the consequences. Because if I understood her correctly, even now nobody knows who's to blame for the fire in which Olive nearly died. The buildings are old and so are the gas pipes. It could have been an accident. Not that it would change anything for Olive – I'm just wondering if it would help to know somebody was responsible for it. If it helps to be able to hate a specific person. Or if ignorance is bliss.

All I know is that I can't take any more. I didn't want to come here and start again: I wanted to stay in New York and take the rap for my actions. My own mother wouldn't let me – and what kind of lame excuse does that sound like? Why didn't I go to the cops the same night I realized what she was planning and turn myself in? Why did I convince myself that she'd do the right thing, at least until I knew what she actually had in mind? How could I have known that taking responsibility was the last thing on her mind? Because if your name's Fantino, there's no such thing as taking responsibility. All you have is your name, which has to be kept clean, whatever the cost. And in this case, the cost is my peace of mind.

But if there's one thing I'm sure of, it's that my name is the only thing connecting me to my mother. I'm not like her, even if she keeps trying, again and again, to convince me that I am. I wouldn't do *anything* for money and power; I don't let people slip under the bus if I can help it, let alone throw them under. I tell the truth if the truth needs to be told and, for fuck's sake, this is the time to prove it.

But I don't want to. I just don't want to, because it'll mean Olive finding out who I really am. And whatever it is that's grown between us in the last couple weeks, I'm not sure it would survive that. Or if I'd survive that.

I tried to fight it, but now Olive Garden, with the furious green eyes, is the person I look at and feel that my heart wants to be with. She got under my skin, she drove me crazy, and then she lay in my arms, crying, while I couldn't breathe. Nobody can expect to have an experience like that and not be affected by it. Olive Henderson has done something to me. And every time I think about the next few months, I'm thinking about her. I'm not thinking about New York any more, I'm thinking about everything here, even though I still hate it, but also kind of don't. It's stressing me out, especially when I realize I'll lose all this once the truth gets out. The fire in the west wing must have changed this school – I know that even though I haven't been here long. Maybe it used to be more chilled. No furtive glances and hushed voices when Olive walked down a corridor or sat out a competition. She must have been part of everything and wiped the floor with everyone. Back when she could swim, and wasn't so mad. Though I bet she was always getting mad. I haven't known her long, but I'm pretty sure that's a genuine personality trait. Hey, I'm talking from experience.

Shit, I don't want anyone to hurt her, and I hate myself for being the guy who'll do that when I tell her the truth. I shut my eyes for a moment, then walk back to the school from my favourite bench by this lake. It's gotten cold, but this is one of the few places I can be alone. I actually managed not to pick up the lighter for the entire weekend. I can feel the pressure building, but then I flash back to the panic in Olive's face when she burst into my room and screamed *What are you doing?* at me. Hopefully she didn't figure it out. Or, worse still, tell anyone. God, I'm a monster, but maybe I ought to tell her the truth and make clear to her that she can't give me away. Ava Fantino thinks she knows it all, but she doesn't have a fucking clue how much of a problem I have here. Let alone Dad – he'd have to show up at home for that. And I've always been careful around Cleo, obviously. Nobody has any idea and it has to stay that way. It's ironic that part of me still thinks I do this fucked-up shit to get attention when I never tell a soul. I know that's not healthy. But I can't face dealing with it. Not now. Sometime . . . But not now.

And now it's Monday again and I see Olive at the morning assembly. I can tell immediately that she's been crying, and I fight the urge to stand up and go to her. Olive keeps her head down and walks quickly past the groups of kids still hanging around the auditorium. She heads straight for the lower-sixth row and doesn't deign to look at me, which hurts like hell.

She doesn't look up until she's taken a seat, as far from me as possible, which makes me clench my fists. And it's like our eyes have no choice but to meet instantly. There's no other option.

She looks at me and I recognize so much that I gasp. Disappointment, pain, longing.

Damn it.

Over the last two days, I've had plenty of time to think about what my behaviour made her feel, but in this second, it hits me like a knock-out punch. I walked away. She told me what happened to her and I turned around and left her alone. She trusted me, she started to tell me things, and I gave her the feeling that her secrets were safe with me. And they are, nothing's changed there, but I'm dead certain she'd never have done it if she knew who I was.

Before I know what I'm doing, I give an almost imperceptible shake of my head.

My lips form the words 'I'm sorry', and Olive's face freezes. She turns away and I want to die. Seriously. I feel sick as she puts on a smile and others in our form fill the seats between us. Olive doesn't look at me again. She chats to Elain, laughs, and I get the feeling I'm supposed to see that she's not fazed. That she had a good weekend, doesn't give a shit what I do, and that I can't hurt her. Nobody can hurt her, not after what she's been through.

The doors to the auditorium shut, and I feel totally helpless.

It's Monday, so full uniform is compulsory. I find that as ridiculous as ever, but even I get goosebumps when we all stand up and Mrs Sinclair steps up to the lectern. She nods and we all sit down again.

'Good morning, everyone. I hope you've had a good weekend and that you're ready for the week ahead.' Her eyes roam over the lines of seats. 'It's a long way off yet, but I would like to use this assembly to tell you about the plans for our school's centenary celebrations. You all know, of course, that they had to be postponed until next year and now I'm happy to be able to give you more details. The whole of June will be focused on the anniversary, culminating with the official festivities just before the summer holidays.'

The others start to whisper and murmur, but I feel numb. I don't have to ask why the celebrations were delayed. How ironic that the school nearly burned down on its hundredth birthday. Everyone goes quiet as Mrs Sinclair continues.

'I am happy and proud that, after the awful events of the summer, I can now lead Dunbridge Academy into this special occasion at full strength. The centenary committee has been working hard on the plans for weeks now, and I would very much like to thank them all, on behalf of the whole staff, for their dedication. It's lovely to see you getting involved in the life of our school and all the effort you're putting into making this an unforgettable event. And, let's face it, a hundred-and-first birthday is an even more special occasion, isn't it?'

I sit motionless as the others laugh and nod. What's more special about that? It would have been nicer if there hadn't been a fire here and if Olive hadn't gotten hurt. I don't dare look in her direction.

I don't get up the courage until Mrs Sinclair starts talking about minor details of the week ahead. Olive's braid falls over her shoulder, giving me a glimpse of her slender neck, and now I can't stop thinking about her collarbone. The scars on her shoulder. I don't want to make a big deal of that because obsessing over perfect bodies and dumb beauty ideals and all that is total bullshit, but the story behind the scars won't let go of me. That, and the fact that she hides them. OK, it's fall, and I'm not one to talk. I always pull my cuffs way down over my wrists to cover everything. It's totally fucked up. At this moment, Olive looks at me like she felt my eyes on her. And her face is softer. I stop hearing what the principal says, I forget that there's even anyone else here. I sit in my seat and can't stop looking at her. She swallows, her jaw muscles working, and all I want is to go to her, to apologize for everything. She deserves the truth, even if it'll break her. I can't stand it any longer. Lying all the goddamn time. And even if I know I ought to keep my distance from her, I can't fight the attraction I still feel. A thing like that can't just vanish overnight. I want to be close to her. I want to be the guy who makes sure she's doing fine – not the one who does the opposite. But I can't. I can never be that guy, not after everything that's happened.

I feel sick as the others stream out of the hall after assembly.

Olive stands up right away and disappears into the crowd. I push my way through, muttering, 'Excuse me,' as I go, then start to run. I don't find her until I get outside.

'Hey.' I'm sure she hears me because I see her jump, then pick up speed. 'Olive!'

'What?' she snarls, spinning around. There's a suspicious glitter in her huge catlike eyes, and I stop abruptly. Too close to her, but she doesn't step back. She juts her chin like she always does, but today she can't hide how she's feeling. And I suddenly lose the ability to speak.

I can only face her, fighting the need to take a step closer to her. And to hug her. Like I ought to have done Friday.

'I'm sorry,' I say. My voice is no more than a croak.

'Stop it,' she replies. 'Just stop it.'

'No. This is truly important so let me speak.' The pain in her face makes my breath catch. 'I'm sorry that I walked away,' I repeat.

'So you should be,' she whispers.

'And I . . . I'd take it back if I could.'

'But you can't.'

'I know, I . . .'

'No, you don't get it.' There are tears in her eyes now. 'I can't bloody deal with this. I just need to be left alone. I just want a bit of peace. Is that really too much to ask?'

'What's happened?' I ask, because I'm suddenly certain that something must have. I definitely hurt her on Friday, but Olive is too strong for it to have knocked her sideways like this.

I'm sure I'm right when she chews her bottom lip and goes to turn away. Before I know what I'm doing, I reach for her. It's her right shoulder and seeing her flinch is like a punch in the guts. I let go at once.

'They're splitting up,' she blurts, before I can start apologizing again. 'No, that's not true. They split up ages ago. They just kept playing at happy family so that I wouldn't notice.' Her voice breaks and it's obvious who she means. But I ask anyway. God knows why.

'Your parents?'

'They're getting a divorce,' she says, so stiffly that it frightens me. 'We discussed everything over the weekend. It was dire, Colin.'

I put my arms around her. I don't just hear her sobs, I feel them. The pain shaking her body. I hold her tight and all I can think is: Fuck.

Her parents are splitting up, her family isn't a family any more, and I'm the one she wants to tell. Me. After everything that's happened. And how the fuck am I supposed to tell her what I did now? That I'm not the guy she thinks I am. That she'd never want me to hold her if she knew the truth. I should let go of her and tell her. It's the right thing to do, because the longer I leave it, the harder it'll be. I've learned that much in the last few weeks. But I can't.

'You told your dad?'

'Yeah. I couldn't help it.' She sniffs. 'But he already knew. He . . . he wasn't fazed, and I've spent months feeling like crap because I've been keeping secrets from him.' I flinch slightly, and pray she doesn't notice. 'He's met another woman.'

'Wow,' I say quietly, because I have to respond somehow. So this whole business is way more fucked up than I thought. I can see why it's sucker-punched her. Her father isn't the innocent she took him to be. Which could actually be a good thing – nobody has to get hurt, they're even – but obviously nobody would see it that way when it's their own parents. Least of all Olive, who was so tortured about not telling her dad.

I should say something, something comforting, but all I can think is how not good this all is. That if I just stand here now and tell her the truth, the way I planned, I'll tip her over the edge.

Shit, that sucks. But, Olive, there's something else . . . Yeah, I set my school in New York on fire, and, oh, yeah, somebody died. Thought you might wanna know before you tell me anything else about your life.

So I don't speak. I'm the world's biggest coward, and I just can't do it. I want to be the one she comes to when the ground crumbles beneath her. It's fucking selfish, but I can't help it. I shut my eyes, I hold her tight. And then, despite knowing I'm seriously going to regret this, I make my choice.

I say nothing.

25

OLIVE

I wanted to be angry with him, I really did, but the second I turned around and saw Colin, who'd followed me out of the hall, every ounce of my self-respect disappeared into thin air.

I'm still raging, but I'm exhausted by the weekend with my parents, after two days when I couldn't show any emotion. The time was mostly made up of conversations with Mum and Dad, who both cried and kept reassuring me that they loved me. I didn't cry. It's as though finding out that I've been fooling myself has flicked some switch inside me.

All these months, all these sleepless nights where I was wondering what to do, were for nothing. I seriously believed my family would get through this. That Mum would come back and everything would be the same as ever. But I never dreamed that Dad had moved on too. The woman, Nathalie, is also a doctor – he met her a couple of weeks ago at a conference in London. Maybe I should be happy for them but I'm just scared, and I don't even know what of.

It sounds like a cliché whenever they promise that nothing will change, but it's not that far from the truth: I'll still be at this school. Eventually, there'll be a few awkward dinners when I get to know Alexis and Nathalie; I might hate them, but I might find them surprisingly nice – after all, if my parents like them, they must basically be good people, right? But I don't want to. I don't want any of it. I want to stick my fingers in my ears when Mum and Dad talk about *options*, when they say stuff that sounds like they read it in clever online articles. *Ten Top Tips for Telling Your Kids You're Getting a Divorce as Painlessly as Possible.*

It's not painless. It's the exact opposite. And I'm asking myself more and more often if this isn't just some weird fever dream, especially since I've been back at school and finding it so hard to get myself together.

Luckily for me, I haven't seen Tori and the others. They'd have known right away that something was up. It was naïve of me to think Colin wouldn't notice. I realize that the moment I see him again in assembly.

He doesn't say a word, just sits on his seat, but when a muscle tenses in his jaw, I know he guesses something. He looks as if he wants to get up, maybe to run away again – he's got form for that – but he can't while Mrs Sinclair is talking about the school centenary. Even now, I'm dreading the over-emotional speeches about how this place can survive anything. Storms, natural disasters, the fire. Colin, standing in front of me and going pale at the sight of my scars. I'd never have dreamed anything could hurt as much as the moment he broke eye contact and left. It feels like that was weeks ago, yet the memory is way too intense.

But now he's standing here in the uniform that makes a new Colin of him, messed-up hair, breathless, and I can see on his face that his weekend must have been just as dire as mine.

I didn't want to tell him about the shit with my parents, but obviously I do. And then I weep in his arms, and this time, he stays.

He holds me tight, like he did that awful night when I saw the person he hides so skilfully behind his cynicism and don't-give-a-shit persona. The person I need, and today, I have him.

'Come on,' he says quietly, as voices and laughter move closer. Colin takes my hand in his and pulls me gently along with him. We walk fast. He keeps his head down. His hand is warm, the wind chilly on my wet cheeks. I wipe my tears away as we walk through the arcades and across the inner courtyard. He doesn't take his eyes off me over breakfast or in class. I can't concentrate on anything, and breathe a sigh of relief at an unexpected free period this afternoon, when my physio is cancelled. After lunch with the others, we head straight from the dining room to the east wing.

'To your room?' Colin glances at me as we reach the stairs. I nod without a second's hesitation. It's ages till study hour, but even that wouldn't stop me staying with him. Part of me wants to fight this, but I have to be close to him. I can't sit alone in my room just now, and I doubt that I've got the mental strength to knock on Tori's door and tell her about my parents either. Or even to speak at all.

Colin seems to feel something similar because, once we've made it to the corridor and he's shut my bedroom door behind us, we face each other wordlessly. His eyes take me in, then rest on my face. I want to say so much to him, but I don't. All I feel is the longing that makes me forget how disappointed I am in him. He needs to make it up to me, and he can do it this way for all I care. Whatever. And he does.

He shakes his head gently, taking a step towards me, which makes my stomach flip. His hands find my face and he presses his lips to mine, then presses me against the wall. I melt into his touch and his hot tongue as it parts my lips while he sets his fingers under my chin. My eyelids close automatically, my hands find him. I dig my fingers into the fabric of his blazer and pull him closer by the lapels.

There's something between us, a magnetism that's more than just attraction. The feeling that I'll lose my mind if Colin stops pressing against me now, his hips against my belly. His mouth swallows my slight gasp as I feel him.

I push my hands under his blazer, and now he lets go of me to pull it off and drop it heedlessly to the floor. Our kisses are hungry and fast, mouths wrestling with each other, but the gentleness of his touch is out of step. His fingers are warm, his muscles hard. I'm kissing Colin Fantino in my room and I know where this is going.

But then I think about what happened last time we were together in a room. It was his room, and the images are suddenly so vivid in my mind's eye that my blood runs cold again.

Colin must feel it because he stops at once.

I hesitate, but decide it's better to get this over with before I weaken again.

He shudders as I glide my hands from the back of his neck, across his shoulders and down his arms.

Colin understands. I grab his wrists before he can pull them away from me. He jerks up his head and looks at me, and I see the panic in his brown eyes. I hate that I'm doing this, but I'd hate myself even more if I ignored it.

'Colin,' I plead, in a whisper. He shuts his eyes. His jaw grinds as I undo his cuff buttons and push up his sleeves. The part of me that kept kidding that I'd misinterpreted everything breaks soundlessly as I see the burns on his forearms.

When I raise my head, he avoids my eyes. He tenses his shoulders and snatches away his hands. He turns his head and pulls his sleeves down.

'Colin,' I repeat, as he still won't look at me.

'Stop saying my name like that,' he growls, and here we are again, three steps back, just a few seconds after we were kissing.

'Saying it like what?'

'So sympathetic.' His voice sounds sharp but as he looks up I see the fear peeping through his protective walls.

'Why?' I ask.

'Why what?'

'Why do you do it?'

'I don't know what you mean.'

'God, do you think I'm stupid? I saw what you were doing in your room on Friday.'

'Nice, so what else do you want to know about me?' he snaps.

I shake my head. 'Have you got help?'

He rolls his eyes.

'Does anyone know? For fuck's sake, Colin, have you got anyone to talk to when you—'

'I don't need anyone to talk to.'

'Yes, you do.'

He laughs quietly, then bends down to pick up his blazer and turns away. He's already at the door before I twig.

'No.' My voice cuts through and he actually stops. 'If you do that . . . if you go, then . . .'

I can't see his face but I see the way his posture shifts. Only millimetres, but they tell me how much he must despise himself for what he did on Friday.

'Olive,' he says, his voice hoarse, and he slowly turns back.

'No, seriously. I'm here, I'm listening, I'm bloody telling you we can do this together, somehow, but if you just walk out again, because it's getting complicated, then don't bother coming back. Got that?'

I don't know why it has to be this way between us. Why we only want to yell at each other or to kiss. Why there's no middle ground. I should stay calm and collected, but I'm Olive Henderson, I'm all kinds of things, but I'm not that.

And that's why it works. I see Colin fighting with himself, but I also see that he gets it. That he knows I'm fucking serious. That I forgive him, but I notice it when he hurts me. And that I'm through with him if he does it a second time. It's not easy, but I have to stay hard. Out of respect for myself and my emotions.

His hand rests on the door handle, but then his shoulders droop.

'How long has it been?' I ask.

He doesn't answer right away. 'Does that matter?'

'Yes, it does.'

He grinds his teeth. 'A while. A couple of years, I guess.'

My stomach clenches. 'So, who else knows?'

'Nobody,' he says curtly.

'What do you mean, nobody?'

'Christ, what part of that is so hard to understand?'

'Your parents?'

He laughs. 'Are you kidding me?'

'You don't think they notice?'

'Olive, they don't notice anything. Not a thing.' He takes a step towards me and his voice starts to shake. 'They have this image of how I have to be, and since they discovered I don't match it, they've stopped even bothering to pretend that they're interested in me.'

I want to contradict him – I don't want that to be true – but I don't know Colin's parents. I only know him and, to be honest, I don't find it hard to believe. 'Would it help if I said I hate them on your behalf?'

For a second, I actually see the hint of a smile on his face. 'Doubtful.'

'And I guess it wouldn't help if I asked you not to do it any more?'

Colin's sigh sounds desperately tired. 'I don't think it's that easy.'

'Has anyone had a look at it?'

He shakes his head.

'Colin, you should at least see my dad . . .'

'I know how deep I can–' He breaks off. 'This here is all superficial, OK?'

'Here?' I repeat. 'So there are other places?'

He shuts his eyes.

'Colin,' I plead.

'I don't want to talk about it.'

I don't know if I can bring myself to accept that. But then I remember Colin in my bed and my floods of tears after that nightmare. When I said the exact same thing, not expecting him to accept it, but he did, so now I have to do the same.

'OK.' I bite my bottom lip gently. 'On one condition.'

He groans. 'Olive . . .'

'No, seriously. I want you to tell me if you do it again. And if it's bad, for you to come with me to see my dad. Or Ms Vail. You choose.'

'How generous of you,' he says, but I'm not in the mood for his sarcasm.

'Promise me,' I insist.

Colin glares at me, but in the end he nods. 'You're so annoying, Olive Garden,' he says quietly.

I glare back, then take a step towards him. 'Get tae fuck, Fantino,' I whisper, then wrap my arms around him.

COLIN

I slept in her room again when we got back from dinner, and everything about that is wrong – I can't bring myself to be honest with her, and I find myself constantly going over how she'd react if she knew the truth, and all the while, her head is resting on my chest.

She doesn't dream this time, luckily for me, but I still feel stressed. I'm a traitor, but it's surprisingly easy to forget that as I get drawn back into the everyday life of classes, study hour, duties and midnight parties.

More than that, it feels good with Olive.

I don't know if we're a couple, I only know that we're close. Her friends seem to suspect something, even though we're not exactly all over each other in front of them. Probably the mere fact that we no longer keep snapping at each other at every opportunity is enough. But I don't care what they think or don't think. I'm fine with everything so long as I don't have to spend every second remembering I'm keeping a secret from her. I know this isn't going to turn out well in the long term, though, so as the days pass, my plan takes shape.

I hardly dare believe it, but Olive has actually seen Ms Vail. And not to tell her that I'm self-harming. To talk to her about herself. At first, I wondered why she'd changed her mind, but I get it really. The shit with her parents has rocked her, and I'm so proud that she's decided to accept help. It shows, yet again, that she's way stronger than me. We don't talk about it much because I sense that her chats with the psychologist are exhausting and churn her up, but I hope they're helping.

I'm not surprised that things are tense with her dad, but at least I can listen to her, and she can talk about him to me without crying now. I don't want that to stop, which it would if I confessed everything to her at this point. I have to give us a bit of time – or that's what I tell myself, even as I know I'm only making things worse for when she finally does find out about it. But it's so fucking hard to hurt someone when they're the last person in the world you want to hurt.

Mom says I have to come home to New York for the half-term break, which is soon. Not because she misses me, obviously, but because it's her annual charity gala and the whole family has to put in a unified appearance for the look of things. Oh, joy. But when I try to refuse, she threatens yet again to cut off the fucking trust fund.

So I'm pretty pissed, but this could be my chance. Half-term in New York, and while Ava Fantino spends the morning after her crappy fundraiser scouring the papers for flattering headlines about the event, I'll have all the time in the world to make my way to the NYPD and finally confess. A couple of guys from my old class told me who's investigating, and that they haven't made any progress. Well, that's about to change.

It's the only thought keeping me going. I don't know if I'll come back to Dunbridge after that. In the worst-case scenario, I'm cuffed and locked up in a cell, but I try not to be over-dramatic. I was a minor at the time, I'm rich, white, and I didn't do it deliberately. I never intended to set fire to the gym, so I'm hoping for a lenient enough punishment that I can explain everything to Olive. Or for some miracle where I find the guts to tell her first.

Either way, I'm going to face the consequences of my actions, and once I've been to the cops, even Ava Fantino won't be able to prevent that. I might get a couple of years in jail; I might get lucky and only have to do community service. I don't know enough about the law to be certain, so I'll have to take what comes. If I can't go back to Dunbridge, I'll find another way to graduate high school. I doubt they'll let me study psychology with this on my record. And the thought of not fulfilling my dream is painful, but I can't change that now. I can only hope to try to hang in there that long.

They'll ask why I even had a lighter in the bathroom and I spend more time considering the idea of coming totally clean. If I'm gonna do this, then I'm gonna do it right. Not because it might look better for me. But because I'm scared I might really need help. It's bad right now, even though I'm in love, but lying to Olive Garden doesn't exactly ease the pressure. Kit seems to notice that something's weighing me down – he keeps making the time to go boxing with me in the gym. He once asked me what was wrong but I can't talk to him. I can't risk it getting back to Olive. If I decide to tell the truth, she has to hear it from me first. I owe her that much after everything she's done for me.

This evening, I get in from training and see a missed video call from Cleo. It's the second this week, and I realize with hot shame that I didn't get back to her after the last one.

I take a hurried shower. Then I creep down to the room with the piano and call Cleo. 'Hey.' She looks genuinely surprised to see me, which hurts. 'You're still alive, then.'

'Sorry, Peanut. I plain forgot – there's so much going on here.'

'So I saw in Olive's story,' she says, immediately lowering her eyes like she's let something slip that she didn't want me to know.

She's looking at Olive's stories. Presumably because I tagged her in a photo the other day. Nothing much, but I ought to have known that Cleo would analyse it.

'Sorry, but, hey, I'm here now.' I try to smile, but even I can see how fake it looks. 'And I'll see you soon.'

'So, you're still coming home for your fall break?'

'Why wouldn't I be?'

'I don't know, Colin,' she says. It's always serious if my kid sister calls me by my full name, but even without that I'd be able to hear that she's on the edge of tears.

'What's wrong, Cleo?' I ask.

'Nothing.' She swallows hard. 'You don't care anyway.'

'I do care. Really.' I have to force myself to sound calm.

'You hardly ever call me.' Her voice is muffled. 'Mom and Dad said you must be settling in at last.'

'They don't know shit,' I blurt.

'But are they right?' Cleo stares through the phone and right into my soul. 'Are you settling in, Colin? Are you going to stay in Scotland? Cos right now it looks that way.'

'Cleo.' I shut my eyes briefly. 'Can we just take one thing at a time? I'll be home soon and then . . .'

'And then you'll leave again?'

'No, I—'

'You know what? I gotta go too.' Cleo's voice sounds choked.

'Cleo,' I say, more firmly.

'Bye, Colin.'

She just hangs up. I clench my fist and call her right back. But she doesn't answer.

Shit. I could see she was nearly in tears, and the idea of her crying on her own in her room is driving me crazy. But I can't do a thing. I didn't even play her a song. I've totally failed her. Cleo gets what's going on here. She's not dumb, she can read people – she had to learn that growing up with Ava and Eric Fantino. In a family where nothing is said out loud. Cleo Fantino can see through people. Especially me. And I don't know what I can say to her when I see her during the fall break.

I lower my head and force myself to breathe.

I don't know what to do.

26

OLIVE

It doesn't take long for the others to get wind of the fact that Colin and I . . . Well, that we don't hate each other as much as we used to. There are a few days when the stuff with my parents is enough of a distraction, but then Tori starts asking questions. I deny it all, but constantly acting like I don't care about Colin at midnight parties and in the dining room is no fun. Especially not when Tori and Sinclair are winching, and Emma and Henry are happy together. I want to be happy too. With Colin.

But I'm not happy. It wasn't easy to face that, but Mum and Dad splitting up was the last straw. One afternoon, after a physio session when I constantly felt on the verge of tears, I found myself – on the spur of the moment – outside Ms Vail's office. It's a long time since my heart's pounded as fast as it was doing while I wrestled with myself over whether to knock or walk away. But I did it in the end, and since then, one thing's just followed another.

Ms Vail is nice, I knew that. What I didn't know was that there was no need for me to spend time before our first conversation coming up with explanations for why I need help or what my problems are. She has a bottomless supply of skilful questions. She always succeeds in finding out what I want to say, even when I don't know myself. And it actually helps to speak to her. She's impartial, she untangles the threads of thought in my head and she doesn't make me feel guilty. I wish Colin could bring himself to go to her too, because I've been worrying about him since finding out what he gets up to with his lighter. But it would feel wrong to tell Ms Vail about him. He needs to do that for himself. When he's ready. I only hope that's soon.

The same goes for Grace – she's seemed more cheerful lately, but I'm still anxious about her. I don't think she's lost any more weight. That might be down to Gideon, who watches her like a hawk in the dining room, to make sure she's eating. I can see that, even from a distance.

There's another thing I don't like and that's being set back a year. I wish I hadn't mentioned it to Ms Vail, but maybe it's for the best. She immediately switched tack to helping me figure out why I'm so desperate to rejoin my friends. Whether it isn't more about a general fear of change and of not being in control. And, sadly, I have to admit that going back up simply wouldn't make sense. I've already let the tutoring from Henry slide because it's hard enough just to keep up in the lower sixth now. It feels like failure, seeing that I've already done all this work once, but Ms Vail helps me get my head around the idea that measuring myself against other people isn't helpful. The fire was a trauma and I have to admit to that fact. And while the others get to focus fully on their schoolwork, *my* mind and body are mainly preoccupied with surviving and getting through the day. Everyone else has an advantage over me. Accepting that isn't half as straightforward as it sounds, but maybe I'm at least moving towards it.

These are crazy days. Lots of classes, lots of prep, creeping out after wing time for walks with Colin. It's become a habit. We never know where we're heading. We just know that we'll find out together.

Tonight, we end up in that room near the theatre, far enough away from all the dorm rooms that Colin can play the dusty old piano, while I remember what he told me the first time I saw him there. That he wants to study psychology and be a music therapist. I can really see it for him, but all the same, I think he needs some therapy of his own first. Not that I say so, or not in that room at least. Later on, in my room, I start to tell him about my sessions with Ms Vail.

'So, you're going regularly now?' Colin asks, lying beside me. He isn't looking at me because he's too busy winding my hair around his fingers.

'Yeah.'

'So, what's it like?' He glances up. 'Does she ask annoying questions?'

'Constantly,' I say, straight-faced. Colin is taken aback. 'But I think that's what you see her for.'

'Sounds stressful.'

'Hey, you want to be the one asking questions and analysing things, don't you?'

'Yeah, I prefer that perspective to the patient's.'

'Maybe they're both important.'

He doesn't answer straight away. 'Maybe,' he says in the end, looking away again.

'And you really won't even give it a try?'

'Olive . . .'

'No, I know. You said you don't want to talk about it, but I want to talk about it, OK?'

'Why would you want to talk about it?'

'Because I'm worried about you.'

He laughs quietly. 'Nobody needs to worry about me.'

'I'm not so sure of that, Colin.'

He doesn't speak for a while. Then: 'I haven't used the lighter for a week, OK?'

'For a week?' I repeat.

He nods, and he knows as well as I do that it's longer than a week since I caught him in his room. Much longer. I feel the urge to ask him why he didn't say anything. But I know that won't do any good. He's telling me now, and I should take that.

So instead, I ask: 'Where?'

He's fighting himself. 'Ankle.'

'Show me.'

'No.'

'OK, is it bad?'

'No, it . . . it's almost gone.'

'So you're going to need to do it again soon, then?' I guess.

He says nothing, caught out.

'Colin . . .'

'I'm trying to quit. I really am.' He looks up. 'It's just . . . My kid sister knows about us. But I promised her I'd be home soon so now I'm scared she's freaking out.'

I gulp, but my throat is dry. 'Do you still want to go back to New York as soon as possible?' I ask.

Colin sighs quietly. 'I want to be with you, OK? That's no secret. But Cleo . . . My parents are never there, all she has is school, and sometimes going to her friend's. But friendships at Ainslee, I dunno . . . it's not like what you guys have here. It's all surface-level, and Cleo doesn't know any different. What kind of life is that? I wanted to be there, to take care of her, to make sure things work out better for her than for me, you know?'

I nod, because I get that. 'What if you asked her about starting here too?'

Colin's eyebrows contract. 'At Dunbridge?'

'Yeah, why not? Then you *could* be together and . . . I'm sure she'd have a great time.'

Colin's hesitation speaks volumes. And I feel hurt because I'm suddenly not so sure how much he really wants to be with me. He's from New York: he wants to go back there. He's only in Scotland because he can't get away. I can't think about what he'd do if he had a choice.

'It's not that easy,' he says, and his voice sounds knackered. 'You don't understand – nobody understands. It's . . . Everything's kind of fucked-up right now.'

For a while I lie next to him in silence. He glances at me, then looks away again hastily. I want to know what he's thinking. Or maybe I don't, because I'm afraid inside his head is a pretty dark place.

'But, Colin, you know that things will get better again,' I say in the end. 'Don't you?'

He doesn't answer, just breathes heavily, which means that all this is getting too much for him so he's covering that up by being irritable.

'Fantino . . .'

'Things aren't going to get better again, Olive Garden. Not when you're me.'

'You can't know that.'

'You neither.'

I don't speak for a while. This conversation is heavy and I don't like where it's going. 'Colin, you . . . you sound kind of bleak.'

He laughs quietly. 'That's probably because I am kind of bleak.'

'How bleak?'

'A bit.'

'Colin, you should see Ms Vail.'

'That won't help.'

'Please.' I put my hand on his face and turn it so that he has to look at me. 'I know it feels hopeless, but things will get better. There'll be good times ahead. I promise.'

'You shouldn't promise things you don't know for certain, Olive.'

'Right,' I say. Nothing more.

He exhales slowly.

'You don't need to tell me I'm annoying. I know that already.'

His face is hard, because this is a hard conversation, but I can see in his eyes that it was right.

'Thanks for not stopping being annoying,' he says, to my surprise.

'I do my best.'

'I know.' It always does something to me when Colin Fantino takes my hand, but today it's special. I get goosebumps but, luckily, I'm wearing one of his jumpers so he can't see. I turn my head until my brow is resting on his shoulder and then we fall silent. I know him well enough that, even though it feels like I didn't try hard enough, I'm certain I won't get anywhere with him by forcing him. I can't make Colin go to Ms Vail. He has to want it for himself.

I really think psyching yourself up the first time is the

hardest part. I basically look forward to my sessions with her now, however tiring they are. Not physically, but emotionally, and not just the time in her office. The real work begins afterwards, when I'm sitting in my room, staring into space as I think about what she said. Not that Ms Vail actually says much. She mainly asks questions, which is irritating, but still better than being told what to do.

Later this afternoon, I spend my whole appointment with her wondering how I can talk to her about something that's not really anything to do with me. I don't pluck up the courage until I've stood up and got my hand on the door handle.

Ms Vail looks up as I turn back to her. 'Is there something else, Olive?'

'Yes, I . . .' I hesitate. 'There is one more thing.'

'I'm listening.' Ms Vail smiles.

I take a deep breath. 'If you knew someone who's . . . under a lot of stress . . . and you were worried about them, what would you do?'

Nothing at all changes in Ms Vail's face but I'm sure she's running her mind over the list of people I've mentioned in our conversation. I hope she doesn't think of Colin, because I already feel as if I've betrayed him by talking about him when I know he doesn't want me to.

'I'd speak to the person,' she says, 'and ask them if they want any help.'

'He doesn't. Er, that is, they don't.'

'I see,' Ms Vail says. 'Sometimes people are under so much

pressure that they're not able to take responsibility for themselves any more. Do you think this person still can?'

OK. I should have expected her to ask something like that. And I know that what I say now matters. If I say no, she'll want a name, and then Colin will be sat here against his will sooner than he can blink. But I'm not going to lie. Not about something this important.

I pause, listen to my heart and think about the last few weeks. And then I say, 'Yes, I think so.'

'Good. You don't have to hit rock bottom before you can get help. If this person has forgotten that, I'd just remind them of it.'

'What if they don't want to hear it?'

'Then I'd try to be there for them, and listen to them.'

I nod.

'And if the person ever changes their mind, I'd offer to come with them to talk to somebody, if it would help.'

'OK, I . . . Thank you, Ms Vail.'

'Not a problem.'

I give a brief smile and turn back to the door, but she hasn't finished. 'Olive, if you're worried that anything's going to happen, you can always call me.' She sounds serious. 'Any time, day or night. We'll always find a solution, and you're welcome to tell your person that, if you like.'

27

OLIVE

I feel like a traitor because 'my person' still hasn't the least idea that I've mentioned him to Ms Vail. It was only a few words, and I named no names, but I still get the feeling Colin wouldn't be happy if he knew. But I'm not happy that he's not doing well just now.

I can feel how torn he is, especially on his birthday, and I guess he'd suggested to Cleo that he'd be back in New York by now, at the latest. But he's not back in New York. He's here at Dunbridge Academy, and even though he claimed not to want to celebrate, the others organized a midnight party for him. Tori took charge and is calling it the Two Scorpios Party, because my birthday is the day after Colin's.

She wouldn't let me help with the plans, so I spend the afternoon at the school newspaper editorial meeting.

'Olive, this is great!' Theresa says for the fourth time, after I've presented the interviews I've done so far. 'You can really see how much you're enjoying this.'

In the old days, I'd have knocked back that idea right away, but I have to admit that it's true. 'I'm glad you like it,' I mumble, lowering my eyes.

'More than like it,' Theresa says. 'We totally have to keep you on the team. I'm not letting you go now.'

That actually makes me smile. 'If you insist.'

'I do. Maybe we could add a sports section to the regular editions. I'd never have thought I'd be interested in the rugby boys' matches, but you make it sound really exciting.' Theresa grins at me.

'You think . . . Really?' The almost total absence of sports news was the main reason I'd rarely bothered to read the school paper before.

'Definitely. That would be a real win for us.'

'I'd be happy to,' I say.

For the rest of the meeting, I just listen as the others discuss various articles. Afterwards, I head to the dining room, where my friends are clearly up to something. In the end, they invite me and Colin to come to the old greenhouse just after wing time.

I don't normally make much of a fuss about birthdays, but

there's something special about turning eighteen. And not just that I'm now officially an adult. After all, it's the date I've been longing for since the summer. But now I don't know what I want any more.

I'm sure Tori's thinking that too, later on, when she glances at me and points outside. The others are deep in a game of truth or dare, and don't even notice us slipping out. I follow Tori through the door and breathe in the cool air.

'Now you're grown up too,' Tori says, putting her arms around me with a sigh. 'The baby of the group.'

'Come on, you're not even six months older than me.'

Tori shrugs. 'Six months can make a big difference, Livy.'

'Yeah, I noticed,' I mumble, thinking about the others in the lower sixth. Although I have to admit that I feel surprisingly good around them now. Which isn't just down to how well the newspaper meeting went today. Classes are OK and my job helping to coach the swimming team means I'm no longer feeling so lost without my upper-sixth pals.

'Staying down a year, you mean?' Tori asks. She lets go of me.

'Aye. Dunno. I don't belong there,' I say, even so, because part of me still believes that.

'True,' she says sadly. 'I'd never have dreamed we wouldn't leave school together.'

'What can I say?' I mutter.

'I know.' Tori sighs. 'It's ages away yet, but I really don't feel up to making plans for after A levels. If you're not with us, I don't want to.'

'Yes, you do.' I don't say it to guilt her, just because it's true. 'You want to go to university with Sinclair and that's fine.'

'I want to go to uni with you *and* Sinclair,' she corrects me. 'OK, no, that's not true. Uni will be exciting – all that freedom! – but, actually, I wish I could stay here for ever. I'm not ready to say goodbye to Dunbridge yet.'

'You have to quit while you're ahead,' I say. 'But lucky me – I get an extra year here.'

Tori pulls a face. 'So you're not coming up to us?'

I shrug. 'No idea.'

'I mean, that was your plan, wasn't it? Sit out your time in the lower sixth until you turn eighteen and your parents don't have any say in the matter.'

'Yeah, it was,' I say. But that was before so much happened. Colin Fantino, for example. And realizing that my friends' lives go on without me. I wish I could be in the upper sixth with them, but I haven't come close to keeping up with their work in the last few weeks. I've been too busy living. And, to be honest, I don't hate that. That's how things are meant to be, right?

A twig cracks behind us and we whirl around. I stare into the darkness, and shiver as I see someone standing in the greenhouse door. I can make out his silhouette, which ducks back as we look in his direction.

'Colin?' I ask, even though I'm certain it's him. 'Wait.'

I leave Tori standing there as he turns away. Did he hear all that?

'I'd better go back to the others,' my best friend says guiltily, as she squeezes past us through the door.

'You're going up into the upper sixth?' he asks.

'No,' I say instinctively.

'Really? I thought that was your plan?' He sounds mocking, but I know him well enough by now to hear that he's hurt. 'You only wanted to sit out your time in the lower sixth until you were eighteen. I'm glad to have made that a bit more entertaining for you.'

'Don't be an idiot,' I snap.

'Fine, good, no problems. I'd want to rejoin my friends too. I should have known.'

'You have no idea,' I snarl. 'They're my family, have been since the juniors. Even if I did still want to be with them again, I'd have every right. Anyway, you're one to talk, with your plan to get back to New York as soon as possible.'

'Maybe that would be wiser.'

His words shoot straight to my heart, even though I know he's only saying them to hurt me. And two can play at that game. He should watch his back. 'Run away, then. You're good at that.'

Even in the dim light falling through the greenhouse glass, I see his eyes narrow.

'Bite me, Henderson,' he snaps.

What are we doing here? This is ridiculous. We both know it, but I have to say that we're pretty convincing. And suddenly I get scared. We don't mean any of this, right? He knows

I'm staying with him. And he doesn't actually want to go back to America any more. That's true, isn't it?

I'm not so sure of that as Colin shakes his head. His eyes rake over me, his face turns to stone. He digs his hands into his hoodie pocket and walks past me.

'Nice work, Olive. Amazing.' He laughs bitterly. 'Well, happy birthday, then. Have a nice time with your buddies.'

COLIN

OK, so we're fighting. I hate it, but not as much as I hate the feeling that came over me when I heard what Olive and Tori were talking about. I don't want to be irritating and controlling, but I also don't want to get my heart broken again. But I'm slowly starting to feel scared that you can't get close to anyone without taking that risk. It's a dilemma that I haven't found a solution to. Because staying cold and unfriendly is exhausting.

But so is this back and forth with Olive Garden.

I stomp through the cold, and somehow I'm hoping she follows me. But she doesn't and that makes me madder still.

What do I even want here? Why am I beating myself up with all this crap, keeping secrets from her, then getting mad when she does the same to me? I hoped to put some distance between us, but I'm closer to her now than ever. I can't believe how I keep forgetting that this isn't going to work out between us. That I have to tell her the truth instead of falling for her more deeply every day.

My phone buzzes in my pocket, telling me there's a comment on an Insta story that I'm tagged in. It's one of Tori's – like most of Olive's friends, she's now following my private account – and I thought it was cute. She videoed us while I put a silly paper crown on Olive's head at midnight. I wanted to kiss her. You can see that in my face. And in hers.

Tori's put *Happy Birthday to my Favourite Scorpios* at the top. I don't know what got into me, why I reposted it. We could put it down to the booze, or me wanting certain other people to see it. Seems to have worked, but not the way I hoped. Paxton's only answer is the pass–ag crying–laughing emoji. I feel a stab in my chest, followed by anger.

'Fuck you,' I mutter, blocking him from my story. As I click to see who else has seen the thing, my blood runs cold. There's a slightly cringy fan account that Cleo's been running for a while, to post about those British boy-bands she adores. She thinks I don't know it's her, but she made the rookie error of sharing a video of one of my piano covers that I sent her a while ago. I didn't mention it, because you can't tell it's me. And I get that she wants something that's just for her. There's no freedom on our official socials because Mom is constantly checking how we present ourselves in public. Parties and booze are absolutely out, along with any kind of thirst trap – Mom's target audience are seriously prudish and she doesn't want them seeing anything like that. Mid-level hot gym selfies and photos from important events are all that's allowed. So I haven't posted anything on @colinfantino for months. I prefer my secret account that just my friends know about, where I only show my face in stories that disappear after twenty-four hours.

Or sooner than that. My finger hovers over the delete button on the video of Olive and me. But I don't tap it. I'm fucked off with her, but if I trash it now, she'll know she hurt my feelings. God, I can't stand this.

'Hey, man, you're going the wrong way!'

I look up as Kit comes towards me. He's got a fresh supply of bottles in his hands and his arms open wide.

'Don't tell me you're leaving already?' he asks. 'It's your birthday.'

Wrong. It was my birthday. Now it's Olive's birthday. And there's really nothing I want less than to go back to that party. But I also know what would happen if I was on my own in my bedroom now. I've gone ten days without a lighter incident – a new record – and however much I'm longing for relief, I don't want to break my streak. So I need something else to do.

I snatch a bottle and do the thing that always worked in New York. I drink like there's no tomorrow.

Which works perfectly, better than I expected, even, because I've been drinking so little here compared to New York. I've gotten unused to it and it's not long before I realize I'm drunk.

The greenhouse is so crowded now that it's easy to dodge

Olive. When she sees I'm still here, she gives me a disdainful look, but I can also tell she's already regretting what she said to me.

I don't regret it. I keep drinking.

The music gets louder and the party gets good. Respect, seriously. I'd never have believed it, but these Scots really know how to party. And they can hold their drink in a way that makes my buddies in New York look like amateurs. Me too, but I only notice that too late. Maybe I took too much insulin at dinner. I'd better have another slice of the birthday cake that Sinclair baked for Olive and me – I have to admit it's seriously delicious. But I don't get that far. I'm standing in the greenhouse, loud music, dancing bodies, and a few yards away there's Olive, sitting in an armchair, looking at her phone. No, that's not right. She's staring at the screen, and she looks as though she's seen something terrifying.

I freeze. She lifts her head. She's gone pale. She finds me amid all these people. Her expression is blank and hunted. I can't move. And I know. I know.

This is it.

28

OLIVE

'Are you two OK?' Tori asks, as I get back to the greenhouse after the 'conversation' with Colin.

'Yeah, fabulous,' I say, reaching for my jacket.

'Livy, what's going on?' Tori insists. She's holding my wrist.

'I'm leaving.'

'It's your birthday.'

'I'm tired.'

'It's. Your. Birthday,' she repeats, stressing every word. 'Have you been fighting again?'

'He's an arsehole,' I hiss.

Tori sighs. I know I have two options. One, tell her everything or, two, stay here and bottle it up. I choose the latter, and regret it not long afterwards when Colin actually has the nerve to walk back in with Kit. OK, so it's his party too, but . . . I just don't want to look at him.

Luckily, I don't have to, because it's now so crowded that I lose sight of him.

It's my birthday, I'm celebrating with my friends, this is important, and Colin Fantino isn't going to mess it up for me. I just won't let him. End of.

For a while, I succeed in forgetting everything. When I start feeling tired, I've lost all sense of time. I've barely been drinking, to save myself a repeat of the humiliation of a couple of weeks back, when Colin Fantino had to hold my hair while I boaked. I wish I could wipe that unpleasant memory from my brain – and from his. Where even is he? I haven't seen him for a while, but it doesn't take me long to spot him with Kit and his pals. They're doing shots. My stomach lurches as I realize how drunk Colin is, but I ignore it. He can hold way more than me – he's proved that. He can look after himself and, anyway, this really isn't my problem.

I glance hastily away as he looks over. I hate him. I hate myself. I hate everything.

I want to look busy, so I pull my phone from my pocket and scroll through all the notifications I've had in the last couple of hours. Most of them are 'Happy Birthday' snaps or party emojis on my Insta story. I didn't repost the one Tori tagged me in. I'm all about understatement and it would have been too much, especially now that I've seen it in Colin's story too. Although the fact that he shared it gave me a pathetic warm glow in my belly. It's silly, but this video goes beyond the private-but-not-secret snapshots we've posted now and then in the last wee while. Colin's hands, my shoulder, our shoes, his back, never from the front, no faces, never any hint that there's really anything between us. Today he's broken his rule of only posting low-key stuff about us, and where's the evening ended? We've had another row, everything's gone to shite and I want to cry, but no way am I going to find him and apologize. Nobody has to tell me I'm being childish: I'm perfectly well aware of that, thank you very much. So I really should head out of here before things get any more complicated. It's one forty-eight, which seems plenty late enough. This is the kind of time our midnight parties generally break up, but everyone else has gone wild tonight. Not that I mean they're smashing the place up – they're just having a really fab time, and that's great. But the loud music is buzzing in my head, my eyes so tired they sting.

I'm about to click out of Instagram and say goodbye when I see a dot on message requests. It's an account I don't follow and not one I've ever noticed before. I can see that whoever it is has sent me photos.

I open the message cautiously, expecting dick pics or some creepy guy wanting to get in touch. That would be nothing new – my profile is public, I'm a woman, and I used to upload heaps of swimming photos. The sad fact is, I'm no longer shocked by that kind of thing. But this is different.

The first message is a comment on the photo I shared at the start of the party, back when everything was OK and Colin had just put his arm around me. You can't tell who we are, at least if you don't already know us well. I can't fit the account to any of my friends, but it seems to be someone who knows Colin at least.

Sometimes, you read a thing and the very first words tell you it would be better if you didn't. This is one of those times. But I can't stop myself.

Did you ever ask yourself why he had to change schools in such a hurry?

This is followed by screenshots of various online news sites. From New York . . .

Several injured after fire on 91st, including FDNY firefighters.

I don't understand.

Breaking News – Female firefighter, 42, killed in flames. Mother of four children.

My blood runs cold.

Accident or Arson? Investigations continue.

What the . . .? Now I feel sick.

Who's the firebug at Ainslee School?

It's like my chest has been laced up, and there's a crackling in my ears.

I look up because I feel like I can't breathe.

I see the others dancing, I see them laughing and, among all my partying friends, I see Colin, and he sees me. Dark eyes, empty gaze. Looking straight into my soul.

And something inside me dies.

No. No, that . . . that's impossible.

He'd never . . .

But, Olive, you saw him.

Colin with the lighter in his room. His shock as I came in, the way he tried to hide it. Me screaming at him. Him walking out when I undressed in front of him.

And suddenly everything makes sense. Colin staring at the scars the fire left on my skin. The despair in his face.

I stand up. My heart is racing as I see him coming over. He can feel that something's wrong. I can't hear the music now. I find myself in a whirlpool of panic, sucking me under, drowning everything around me.

Then Colin's facing me and I hold my phone out to him.

'What's this?' I don't know how my voice is still working. 'What is it, Colin?'

All the colour drains from his face and he doesn't need to speak – that's answer enough. But I can't believe it. I just can't.

'Where did you get that?' he snaps, but I ignore him.

'Is it true?' I croak.

He snatches my phone. I want to cry.

'Where the fuck . . .' he begins, but falls silent as he reads. His tongue is heavy with booze and I don't want this really to be happening.

'Tell me it's not true.'

He lifts his head, slowly, and he knows everything is lost, that there's no point in denying it. That I know. That soon everyone here will know.

'Olive, I . . .' he begins, but I shake my head.

'Who are you?' I whisper, as a hurricane is unleashed inside me. I grab back my phone. 'Who the fuck are you?'

He opens his mouth, pain, horror and remorse flickering in his dark eyes.

Remorse . . .

I'm falling. Or that's how it feels. Like the floor's disappeared under my feet, pulled away with a jerk, no chance to hold on to anything. No fucking chance. I was just getting somewhere. I wanted to get better.

'How can you live with a thing like that?' My voice breaks. He flinches like I've slapped his face. 'You should never have come here, Colin Fantino.'

He opens his mouth. He doesn't speak.

I feel dizzy.

I turn. I walk away. I run.

29

COLIN

I know this feeling. Numbing fear, paralysing shock. The world has suddenly gone into slow motion in front of me, while I can't move a muscle.

Who are you?

Who the fuck are you?

Even if my tongue was working, I wouldn't have been able to answer her question.

A monster.

A guy who doesn't deserve to live. Not with this guilt. Not with the certainty that it was my fault someone died.

I can't stay here. It's all too loud, too much. The others, by some miracle, have no idea what just happened between me and Olive. She didn't yell, she didn't cry, she was calm. I was calm. But now I have the feeling that it could go off course at any moment.

Her holding out her phone to me, and me seeing what it said. The pictures, the headlines. I didn't have to read them. I know every word by heart.

The firebug at Ainslee.

My legs move by themselves towards the exit. In passing, I grab a bottle – I'm in luck: it's heavy – and lift it to my lips the minute I'm through the door. Darkness, the uneven stone path outside the old greenhouse, with weeds growing between the slabs. We stood here earlier, yelling at each other, and I thought that was bad. I was wrong. It's nothing compared to what just happened.

The shock on her face as she looked at me. The horror in her eyes. She *truly* saw me for the first time.

Why did I let her find out this way? Why did I think it was a good idea to put off telling her? Why didn't I tell her myself? Not that it would have changed anything, although maybe it could have. Given me a chance to explain. I could have worked out what to say in advance, made excuses. But the truth is, there's no excuse for what happened. There never will be. I made a mistake and I ran. I turned away and shut my eyes to what happened. I let someone get killed. I let Mom take control and send me away, and I have no way of explaining that. All I have is my fear.

I swig the gin straight from the bottle. The glass hits my

teeth. The alcohol burns in my throat and eats its way down to my belly.

I should stop but I don't let myself. It has to hurt. That's all I deserve. Nausea rises in me, and dizziness, so I stand still, propping myself up on one of the school walls, which I've now reached. I crouch, gagging, and grip the bottle tighter.

You should never have come here, Colin Fantino.

I know. I didn't want to. I so didn't want to, but nobody asked me. I kid myself that I had no choice, but the truth is that you always have a choice. I could have gone to the cops, even after Mom had made all the boarding-school arrangements. I should have listened to my doubts – I could have done the right thing just one fucking time. But I took the easy route.

I should never have come to Dunbridge Academy, and I never would have if I'd known what had happened here. That there had been a fire, that a girl was injured, that I'd meet her a few weeks later, smash a display case for her, hate her, curse her, and fall in love with her. That I'd learn the truth and make the wrong choice yet again, before my lies blew up in my face. That I'd hit rock bottom. Everything's lost, it's dark, and I can't see a way out. I truly can't. I hate myself for the whimper of despair that crawls from my throat, the fucking pain, the self-pity I'm not entitled to.

I crouch, wanting to punch something, but I'm all out of strength. I'm eighteen years old and my life's a mess. Which is my own fault, so I have no right to feel sorry for myself. My actions caused someone to die.

The bottle shatters as I smash it into the wall.

How can you live with a thing like that?

I can't, Olive. I can't.

The shards of glass on the gravel path blur in front of me. I shut my eyes and sway. The taste of blood fills my mouth as I bite my bottom lip so hard it must have broken the skin, but I don't feel a thing.

I feel across the floor, I find some glass, I don't move. My heart is racing, but I can't. I wrap my hand around it. I squeeze. I feel the pain in my palm and I let go again.

The world spins as I stand up. It's still spinning.

Nobody taught me to do the right thing. Nobody took the trouble. Nobody but her. Nobody, goddamnit, except Olive Henderson.

OLIVE

This has to be a dream. One of the bad sort, the kind I wake from with my heart pounding and my T-shirt soaked with sweat, where it's all so real that I can't stay in bed.

This is real. And walking through the night doesn't help. As I walk further and further from the old greenhouse, it gets harder and harder to hold back the tears. I walk on. I don't stop when I start to cry.

Because Colin isn't who I thought he was. Because he lied to me. Because he let me tell him my deepest fears and worst experiences. He let me. He lay next to me, listened, nodded and comforted me. He just accepted it all.

Maybe it's not true. There's this pathetic wee voice in my head, which still has some kind of hope. Maybe it's all just a massive misunderstanding. Maybe it was someone who's out to get him.

But if that was true, why didn't he say so? Anyone who wasn't guilty would defend themselves when faced with something like that. But Colin didn't stand up for himself. He just stood there and I could see in his face that he'd been waiting for that moment. The moment when I learned the truth.

I walk faster. I feel the cool air on my wet cheeks.

His contradictory behaviour, his horror when he saw my scars. Back then, I thought the whole situation had been too much for him when in truth there was maybe still some kind of humanity in him. A conscience he'd been successfully ignoring. Once he finally knew what had happened in the west wing last summer, he kept absently glancing at it.

I can't bear to look as I walk through the hallways. My steps echo in the dark arcades and I don't know where to go.

My friends are partying in the greenhouse. My parents are living their own lives with their new partners. I'm just as alone as I was in the summer. The only one who left the Ebrington festival early, the only one on our floor in the west wing. Still the only one, and I'm fucking tired of it.

Why me? Why was I the one whose life went up in flames? Who had to give up her swimming, and let her friends go on ahead of her, and – like that wasn't enough – now even my parents are getting a divorce. I want to rewind time; I want a second chance. I want to stay with my friends, choose fun over self-discipline. I just wanted to do the right thing.

But I did everything wrong. I let Colin Fantino toy with me and pretend to understand me. His betrayal hurts, but it hurts more to feel that I let him take me in. That I was naïve and wanted to see the good in him.

I slept in the same bed as him.

I kissed him.

I told him everything, and thought he was doing the same for me.

I was wrong.

I'm a million miles from sleep, but I feel overwhelmed when someone knocks on my door. Must be Tori, who's noticed that I left and wants to talk. But I don't want to talk. Not to anyone. Ever.

I pull my duvet over my head. There's another knock. Louder this time.

God, is she nuts? If she keeps on like this, we'll have Ms Barnett out here any minute.

I throw off the duvet and stand up.

'Are you ins –' I fling open the door and the rest of the question dies on my lips.

It's not Tori outside my door.

It's Colin.

No. No way.

Shut the door, turn away. That's what I should do. Instead I make the mistake of looking into his face.

He's drunk. Really steaming. Worse than earlier, when he could at least stand up.

Now he has to lean on my door frame, his face pale.

'I didn't mean to,' he slurs. Too loud. Way too loud. I glance over my shoulder in panic. I want to tell him to piss off before Ms Barnett hears him. But Colin lurches towards me. I can smell booze. I can see blood dripping from his hand.

Fuck, is he out of his mind?

'Piss off,' I whisper, because I can't deal with this.

'I truly didn't mean to, do you understand?' He's crying – when I see that, all the blood drains from my legs. 'I didn't mean to. It was an accident. I . . .'

He stumbles, and before I know what I'm doing, I grab his sleeve and tow him into my room. Colin staggers into the wall and I hastily shut the door.

'It was the Homecoming Ball and I was angry at my parents, we'd had a fight, and I . . . I was burning myself with my lighter. Some guys walked in, some toilet tissue caught on fire, but it was out. D'you hear me? It was out. It was on the floor, and I stomped it out, but it can't have been out, not really, and I . . . I didn't mean to. And I don't know. I truly don't know how to live with that, Livy. I truly don't know.'

Colin's voice breaks and it's like an ice-cold shower down

my spine. There's pure pain in his sobs. He's so drunk he can hardly stand. I've never seen him like this and I don't think I can bear it even a minute longer.

I don't want to hear his explanations because they don't change the fact that he lied to me and ripped the heart out of my chest. But that's the same heart that every one of his stupid wisecracks and pathetic jokes has been healing, bit by bit, over these last few weeks. It belongs to him. It will always belong to him, whatever he's done, and no matter how much I hate that, I can't deny it while he's standing here, clearly a broken man.

I realize that, and I shiver. I feel a switch flick inside me and I make the choice to function. Just for tonight.

I turn around, grab a box of tissues and say, 'Stop that,' without looking at him. It's only a wee cut in his palm, but I still don't want to know how he did it. And while I despise myself for it, I'm glad he's here. In this state – pissed out of his skull and in total despair. I don't know whether I regret what I said to him.

How can you live with a thing like that? It's a genuine question. But maybe I shouldn't have asked him that today.

I move like a machine – I can't allow any closeness, any warmth between us. I ignore Colin's apologies. I want him to shut the fuck up, but that's getting harder with every minute.

God knows what he's been drinking. He lets me press him down onto my bed as I force myself to say it's OK. It's not OK. Nothing's OK. But we're not getting anywhere tonight, so I might just as well pull myself together and do for him what he did for me not so long ago. I owe this guy nothing, but I love him, so I have no choice.

'I never wanted to hurt you,' he manages, once he's sitting on the bed in front of me, and I hate him for how dark his eyes are. Brown and desperate.

'But you did.'

'I know.' *Stop looking at me like that. Stop doing this to me. Stop making me want to forgive you when I can't.* 'I didn't mean to. I didn't want to feel all this again. I wanted to do something right for once, Livy.'

I have to shut my eyes because it hurts too much. Because I suddenly want to say stuff I shouldn't. *It's not your fault. You did nothing wrong.* I don't know enough about the situation and I'm too hurt.

Instead, I say, 'Go to sleep.' I don't manage to sound harsh. Colin is sitting there, broken, drunk. I'm worried, I'm bloody worried about him, and even though I want to hurt him as much as he hurt me, I also want him to be OK. It's so tiring.

The booze has knocked him out, and so have the tears – that's probably why he lets me lean him back. Now he's in my bed and I don't know where to go.

'Olive,' he says. My name always sounds so hard from his lips, but loving too. I hate it when he does that. And now I hate it more than ever.

'No.'

'Please.'

'No,' I whisper, but now my eyes are burning again because even I don't believe that.

It feels like I'm letting myself down as I lie beside him. I don't want this, but I need it. My heart is racing. I'm not crying any more. We have to talk tomorrow, calmly, once he's slept and sobered up. I have to listen to everything and decide what it all means. Whether I can keep on loving him, or whether it's too awful for that. But I know the answer. Even if it is too awful, I won't be able to stop, and that scares me. It fucking scares me.

I don't want to touch him, but the bed is too narrow. So I lie beside him and feel him fall asleep. My thoughts are noisy; my head is throbbing with overwhelm. Every heartbeat is like a stabbing in my temples.

This has to stop. This all has to stop.

I screw my eyes shut.

30

I wake up and my first thought is Colin.

My second thought is that none of this can be true. But it wasn't a dream. He's really here in my room, and I must have fallen asleep. At least for a while.

I blink – it's pitch dark, so still the middle of the night.

I turn over and see him stirring. And then I notice how shaky his breath is.

I jolt upright. 'What's wrong? Are you about to whitey? Wait, I'll get . . .'

'No, I . . .' His voice trembles. 'I have to . . . I think I'm having a hypo.' It takes me a moment to get what he's talking about. His blood sugar. I'd pushed that issue way down in my mind.

'Have you checked?'

353

Colin just nods.

'So?' I ask. 'Wait, I'll put the light on.'

I lean over and switch on my bedside lamp, squinting because it's so bright. My head aches, but never mind that. Now I can see. Colin's even paler, and there's sweat on his forehead. I grab his phone and the number jumps out at me off the screen. Two digits. Low. Seriously low.

'Have you eaten?'

'I was just going to.'

'Should I fetch something?'

'No, it's fine.' He doesn't look at me, just digs in his jeans pocket and pulls out some dextrose tablets. His fingers shake as he tries to get the wrappers off. I don't know if that's because he's still drunk, or already too low. Probably a bit of both. I remember the website I was reading after I found out about his diabetes. *Alcohol can make your blood-sugar level drop quickly. Always be extra careful if you have been drinking.*

'Let me.' He doesn't reply as I take the sweets from him. 'Got any more of these?'

'No, I . . . I thought I did, but those are all there are. I already had to eat a couple, back in the greenhouse. Alcohol always makes things tricky.' He swallows. 'Do you have anything else? Cookies, a soda, anything like that?'

He's really struggling to form coherent sentences, and that sets my heart racing.

'Wait here.' I stand up. My mind is blank.

I bought that bloody tablet yonks ago at Irvine's, only to be unable to find it now. This can't be happening. I dig through my schoolbag, until I remember giving it to Gideon when Grace was feeling rough. I open my desk drawer, but my emergency chocolate stash hasn't magically refilled itself since my bout of eating my feelings last week. There's nothing left.

'I'll go and look in the wing kitchen.'

Colin's leaning both elbows on his knees and only briefly raises his head. If possible, he looks even whiter than before. He doesn't speak, just nods and shuts his eyes.

This is the moment I start to panic. He doesn't argue. That can't be a good sign. I take a step towards him, hesitate, stop. Can I even leave him here? He doesn't look good, he really doesn't, but staying to hold his hand is definitely not going to help. His blood sugar is way too low, he's been drinking alcohol, and the only thing that'll help him now are carbs.

'I'll be right back,' I promise. He blinks. 'Or should I wake Ms Barnett?'

'No,' he murmurs. 'I'll be all right. Just . . . just be quick, OK?'

'OK.' I turn and open the door.

I don't know how I manage to repress everything that happened earlier as I flit through our dark wing. It doesn't matter now – this is way more important.

I open the fridge in the wing kitchen. Butter, a jar of pickled gherkins and chillis, a limp lettuce and a couple of carrots in the salad drawer. There's one sole pot of yoghurt – I reach for it then groan. Sugar-free diet stuff. God, this can't be true. Then I see the bottle of orange juice. I grab that and shut the door. I open the cupboard at top speed and find a bit of bread. There's a bunch of brown bananas in the fruit bowl on the table too. I break two off and run back to my room.

Colin's crouched on the bed. He's pulled up his knees and rested his back against the wall; he looks like he's about to boak. He glances up as I come in. His eyes wander over to the food in my hands, but I get the feeling he's not all there.

'Is any of this any use?' I ask, heading over to him.

'Yes.' His voice sounds miles off. He lifts a hand and points at the bottle. 'That's . . . Thanks.'

If I was in any doubt about how shit he's doing just now, the fact that he can't even break the seal on the bottle would have banished it.

'Wait.' I reach for it. 'Let me . . .' It's easier than I expected. Colin takes it, not looking at me. I want to help him, but all I can do is sit beside him as he drinks. Little sips. It looks knackering.

'Want a glass?' I ask, but he doesn't hear me. I shiver as he puts it down. He props his head on one hand.

'Colin.' I shake him by the shoulder. 'Keep drinking.'

For once he does as I say. Tiny sips, slowly, so slowly, as I pray that the sugar will hit his body fast. I wish I didn't have to force him, but I have no choice. If he doesn't get something inside him now, I'll be in real trouble here.

We don't speak. I just sit beside him in silence. Until Colin leans his head against the wall and shuts his eyes. His face has now taken on the colour of the white walls.

'Getting better?' I ask tentatively, but he doesn't respond. 'Colin?'

I budge closer. His head slumps to one side, my heart skips a beat.

Fuck . . . My stomach drops away – it really feels like that.

I grab for the bottle in his hand before it tips over as his grip loosens and he loses consciousness.

'Colin, shit . . . Stop it. Look at me, Fantino!'

He isn't hearing me, all the strength has faded from his body. I put the bottle down and kneel over him. Fuck, fuck, fuck . . . I try to hold on to him because he's slumping side-ways, but he's way too heavy.

I pull my pillow over, to stop him falling so far, and shake him by the shoulder. Gently at first, then harder, but it's no good. Colin's completely gone. For a few seconds, I crouch there, paralysed, before I manage to muster a clear thought.

Stay calm. I have to stay calm. This is the worst case, but if I freak out now, it won't help Colin or me. Should I check his app? To be certain that his blood-sugar levels didn't come up enough. That's only going to happen if he eats something. But he *can't* eat now because he's so low he's lost fucking consciousness.

OK. *Breathe. Calm.* One step at a time.

Dad . . . I have to call Dad.

I glance at my phone – it's an ungodly hour, but that's the least of my worries. I listen to it ring without taking my hand from Colin's face. I can feel the fine film of sweat on his cold skin. He's not shaking any more, and that's doing my head in.

My heart is pounding.

Pick up, pick up, pick up.

Wouldn't it be better to call nine nine nine? An ambulance might get here faster and they could—

'Olive?' It's the middle of the night, but Dad sounds wide awake. And alarmed. Like he'd just been waiting for the time when I called him like this. 'Are you OK?'

'Dad,' I gasp. 'You have to come. Please. Colin's not well. I—'

'What happened, Olive?' he asks, in his doctor voice.

'He was drinking. And his blood sugar's too low. I brought him food but he was already so low, and now . . . He just fainted, Dad!'

'I see,' he says. 'Are you with him?'

'Yes.'

'Is he breathing?' Dad asks, and my blood runs cold: I have no fucking clue. I stare at Colin's chest for several seconds until I'm finally certain that it's rising and falling.

'I think so.' My voice is wobbly.

'Where are you?'

'In my room,' I admit.

Dad doesn't waste breath on us breaking the rules, which brings it home all the more how serious this is. 'I'll tell Nurse Petra,' he says calmly. 'She has a glucagon pen for emergencies and she'll come right over. I'm on my way, Olive. Get dressed, open your door, and stay with Colin until Petra gets there, OK? Put him in the recovery position, love. You know what to do.'

'OK,' I say. 'Please hurry.'

'I will. Goodbye now. See you soon, kiddo.'

'See you soon,' I whisper, but he's already hung up. My heart is still pounding as I put down my phone. Colin's head is drooping and the silence is driving me crazy.

Everything in me fights against getting up and leaving him so that I can open the door.

For a moment, I consider going to get Ms Barnett, but then my eyes rest on Colin again. I can't leave him on his own. I just can't.

My stomach is a wee ball of fear as I crook his leg, push his arm under his head, then roll him towards me onto his side. Dad made me practise these things so often, but doing this now, for real, feels more than I can bear. My shoulder hurts. I never knew how heavy an unconscious person could be. Colin's hands are ice-cold, so I pull the duvet over him and crouch there, stroking his hair and whispering that help is on its way. That I'm sorry. That I'm sorry for everything I said earlier, and to hang the fuck on in there.

These might be the worst minutes of my life as I count Colin's every breath. So that I'll know if they just stop.

They don't. But he doesn't react when the light comes on out in the corridor and, just a few seconds later, Nurse Petra appears in the doorway. She doesn't ask questions, comes straight to the bed.

She speaks to Colin; he doesn't respond.

'Can you get Ms Barnett, please, to show the paramedics the way?'

I shiver. 'Paramedics?'

'Yes. Your dad is coming too, but he's already called for an ambulance.'

I stand up, feeling weak at the knees, and do what she says. It feels as wrong as can be to walk away from Colin, but I have to.

Ms Barnett is out on the corridor in her dressing-gown. Later, I can't remember what I said to her. Or what she says when the first doors open and the other girls look out to see what all the fuss is about.

Ms Barnett sends a couple of them down to find the paramedics. All I can think of is Colin, but my hope that he'll have woken up dies silently as we walk back into my room.

He clearly hasn't responded well enough to the glucagon pen, so Nurse Petra is now putting a drip into the back of his hand. She passes me the plastic bag containing a glucose infusion. I have to hold it up. I know how it works, and so what if my shoulder's throbbing and black spots are dancing in front of my eyes? Nurse Petra checks again but the glucose meter doesn't give a reading.

'Is it broken?' Ms Barnett asks, looking over her shoulder. 'I can send someone down to the sick bay to—'

'No need, Maxine. He's so severely hypoglycaemic that it's not registering.' She sounds anxious. 'The alcohol in his system is making the pen less effective. I'm concerned that his body can't release the sugar reserves on its own, hence the infusion.'

Colin's lips are white. I want him to wake up and call me Olive Garden, crack one of his stupid jokes and wind me up. I want to be certain that nothing and nobody can harm him. Not even this disease. I want to undo the events of tonight and I don't want to see him like this. I don't want to think about what's happening. If I left it too late. If I should have got help the minute he woke up. If I shouldn't have waited until he was so low he was totally out of it. If I should have acted earlier when he was so drunk but I hadn't taken in what that could mean.

The ambulance gets here before Dad, and nothing has ever felt worse than stepping away from Colin. I start to shake as I pass the drip bag to one of the paramedics. Ms Barnett turns to me as my knees give way and I stagger backwards into my wardrobe. There's concern in her eyes, but before she can speak, someone puts their arms around me.

Some muffled sound emerges from my throat as I see Tori. Behind her, on the corridor, is Sinclair with wild hair and a guilty expression, ready for a sermon from Ms Barnett. But that's not at the top of anybody's priority list.

'Sssh,' says Tori, hugging me tighter. 'It's going to be OK, Livy.'

You can't know that.

Just look at him!

But I say nothing. My lips don't make a sound, or not until I realize that the paramedics are getting ready to take Colin away. What was I expecting? Apparently not that they'd take him to hospital – but the realization that I won't know what's happening to him is doing my head in.

Dad arrives. They send us out. I hear nothing.

'Go back to your rooms – there's nothing to see here.' Ms Barnett shoos the others away. Whose room should I go to? The one they're carrying Colin out of? Dad follows the paramedics, then comes over to me. And then I see it.

'They've intubated him?' I ask, horrified.

'The journey will be safer for him that way, love.'

I lean against the wall. 'Why? I mean . . . Is it really that bad?'

'Colin is in a critical condition. He needs to be taken to intensive care so that they can intervene in case of acute metabolic complications.' This is serious then. It's always serious if Dad drops into medical jargon, forgetting I have no idea what he's talking about. 'We can't risk that happening here in the sick bay.'

I nod, struck numb. *In case of acute metabolic complications.* I don't know what that means but it doesn't sound good. It doesn't sound good at all.

'But he – ' I gulp – '. . . he is going to wake up, isn't he? He will, right?'

Dad hesitates. 'The paramedics are keeping an eye on his blood sugar and I'm sure he'll come round soon.'

I give a careful nod, then Dad squeezes in front of me as I go to follow them.

'Dad, I . . .'

'I'm sorry, pet, but no.'

'Dad!'

'I'll go with Colin to hospital and keep you posted. You don't need to worry.' Dad gives me a look that can't be argued with. I hate it. I just hate it. Then his face softens. He hugs me. 'Oh, and, happy birthday, love.'

31

OLIVE

My skull is buzzing and I've lost all sense of time as I stand in Ms Barnett's office. She and I are waiting for Mrs Sinclair so that I can explain to the two of them what Colin was doing in my bedroom and why he was blind drunk.

I decide on the truth. The truth about our shared birthday party, which went about as wrong as it could possibly go. And the other truth that I know now. Which Mrs Sinclair knows too.

I see it in the way she jumps when I mention the fire at Colin's school in New York. And then she has a lot to say. She says she's sorry, that she was trying to avoid a fuss, but felt that she had to give Colin a chance.

I don't have the energy to yell and scream, so I ask my questions quietly. Why nobody told me. Whether she knew anything more about the accident, about whether it was actually Colin's fault. But she doesn't, of course. In the end, she sends me back to bed.

I don't get a wink of sleep all night. And that's got nothing to do with Tori creeping in to join me, to make us cups of tea and listen in silence as I tell her everything. Absolutely everything. I don't know if I've ever cried so much in my life as I do the night I turn eighteen.

I check my phone a million times, but dawn is breaking by the time Dad finally messages to tell me that Colin's awake.

COLIN

I come round, my head aching, and the sounds tell me that I'm on an intensive care ward. Beeping and low voices.

Shit. Been a while since that happened. I blink and try to remember how I ended up here, but there's nothing. Just darkness.

There's a nurse by my bed, and he immediately bombards me with questions. I get it – they need to find out if I'm all there, and if I know what happened. It doesn't take long before I start to remember. The midnight party, Olive's birthday, fight number one, booze, fight number two, more booze, and then my memories get kind of hazy. They tell me I had such a bad hypo that I lost consciousness. This is the third time in my life I've woken up in hospital from one of those, but that doesn't make it any less scary. More so, in fact, because the last time was almost two years ago. I was sick that time, spent half the night throwing up, couldn't keep anything down. The first time was soon after my diagnosis, before I'd gotten a handle on insulin units.

And now I've been dumb enough to drink myself into a state where I couldn't keep track of my blood-sugar levels.

I know I have to watch out with alcohol. I never had problems partying with my buddies in New York, but there's a fast-food joint on every corner there, so I could always get a greasy burger or two to counteract the booze-induced hypo. It always worked – until it didn't.

The doctor who looks in a bit later tells me it was a close shave. She bugs me to make appointments with the diabetes team to optimize my insulin regime, and about shit like impaired awareness of hypoglycaemia, as if I couldn't already write a book on that. And then she tells me I'm lucky my girlfriend was with me and called an ambulance.

I was already feeling shit, but now I think I might die. Because I vaguely remember. Olive knows everything. I got drunk and went to her. She let me sleep in her bed, and she must have known what to do later when I was ill. The emotions are stressing me out because I can't remember exactly what happened and I don't want her fucking help. But I can't deny that it's also kind of good to know she was there. I'd really have been in the shit if I'd been alone. But it's not good. It doesn't matter. Nothing matters a damn, because now Olive knows what I did.

Thinking about what happened last night makes my head ache. Suddenly those headlines were there on her phone. Where the hell did they come from? I didn't think of that in the heat of the argument, but that's not important either. She knows. She looked at me, and I could see in her eyes that something inside her had shattered.

A pathetic part of me is focused solely on the fact that she isn't here. Real life obviously isn't some corny episode of *Grey's Anatomy*, where you wake up in the hospital and the love of your life is sitting at the bedside, holding your hand, but . . . God knows. I'm in a foreign hospital, I've seriously fucked up, and I'm scared. Yeah. I'm scared of what will happen next. Will I be allowed back to Dunbridge Academy? Will I be sent home? Or will I be kicked straight off to some other boarding school, like Mom threatened?

Mom's not here either. All I have from her are several missed calls and a text.

Mom: *Call me as soon as you're feeling better, I couldn't get through to you.*

Yeah, that's funny. Sorry I didn't answer while I was in intensive care being pumped full of God knows what electrolytes. My throat hurts, because they intubated me last night and put me on a ventilator. Someone must have told my parents – the school, I guess.

Call me. Not *How are you?* Not *Want us to fly over?* Of course not. I didn't seriously think they'd get on a plane to Europe just for this. Even if I'd been in a hospital in Manhattan, I can't be certain they'd have come to see me.

Maybe I'm being unfair to her, but there's not much trace of motherly kindness right now. And that doesn't change when I do as she asked and call her. I speak to my mother who asks questions, her voice hard, and says she'll make sure Dr Calder knows about 'this incident'.

Whatever. I'm tired, Mom doesn't ask what happened. She doesn't want to know how I'm doing, just lectures me on the irresponsibility of drinking that much.

She's on another continent, but she still sounds irritated that she's had to be concerned about me and my state of health. When she closes by reminding me that I have to get on a plane to New York next week, and to make sure I'm fit enough by then, I don't know whether to laugh or cry.

I'm about to choose the second option when the young doctor comes back. She takes a seat beside me, which tells me things are about to get awkward. Sure enough, she says she's seen the scars on my body. Obviously, I downplay it, but when she asks if I want her to arrange help for me, I burst into tears.

I'm tired, it's been a stressful few days, and everything is exhausting. I hate to admit it, but I think I'm all out of the strength to act like everything's fine. And while I'm still not sure there are meaningful solutions to my issues, I've been more and more scared lately of what could come next.

I remember Olive and her serious expression as she sat beside me and said she was worried. And that was before she knew the fucking truth. Although maybe nothing would have turned out so shit if I'd been more sensible from the start. If I'd gotten help back in New York. If I hadn't needed to hide in that gym bathroom to burn off the goddamn pressure. If I'd taken responsibility for myself – after all, life's shown me I can't expect anyone else to take care of me. Neither my parents nor the people I called my friends.

Not that it was their job. It's mine. Entirely mine. And it took a girl, one I badly hurt, to teach me that I can start anytime. That it just takes a bit of fucking courage, trust and confidence. So I nod.

This is kicking off a chain reaction, I know that, but I also know I can't go on like this. That it won't do any good to keep denying I have a problem I can't solve on my own. I tried that and failed. But I feel a spark of hope now that, with support, I can tackle it.

The doctor stands up and hands me a tissue. She doesn't say that everything will be fine – and I really appreciate that somehow – but she does promise to take care of things. I don't know how drastic she thinks my situation is, but before the end of the day, I spend forty-five minutes being asked uncomfortable questions by a shrink.

I hate it at first, but after a while I realize nothing shocks him, however brutally honest my replies. He just nods, looks at me, takes notes and asks his next question. In the end, he gives me the names and numbers of therapists in Edinburgh. I mention that there's a psychologist at our school I can go to, and he thinks that's a good starting point. I don't know that I entirely agree, but I don't get a chance to keep wondering because Olive's dad comes in to ask how I am. It's depressing that he seems to take more interest than my own father does, but he's probably just doing his job, sent by Mrs Sinclair. I don't have the guts to ask him about Olive, but the intense way he looks at me makes me think he has some idea of how tricky everything is.

She doesn't come, and she doesn't message me either. But I dream of her when I eventually fall asleep – my body is forcibly taking what it needs, after I spent the last twenty-four hours running it into the ground.

In my dreams, Olive cries but listens to me. Sometimes she forgives me, other times she yells at me and walks out. Sometimes I find myself trapped in a burning building, either alone, or with her. The only constant is my paralysing, boundless despair. And the longing to be able to turn back time, to make all of this not happen.

32

OLIVE

'But you said he's OK?'

Dad agrees at once, and I have to fight down the urge to jump up from the sick-bay bed I'm sitting on. Dad came over to the school to fill in Mrs Sinclair on how Colin's doing. And to tell me that he'll still be in hospital overnight.

'I did, and he is, pet.' I can hear how hard he's trying to sound reassuring, which is actually worrying.

'He can't be, though – otherwise, why won't they let him out?'

'He's in a stable condition, Olive, but such a bad case of hypoglycaemia is exhausting for the body. Colin was lucky that no complications set in, but it would be irresponsible not to keep an eye on him a bit longer.'

'But you can do that here,' I say.

'Not as thoroughly as they can in the ICU, though.'

'Is he still there?' My throat clenches.

'Just to be on the safe side,' Dad says promptly. 'I'm pretty sure he'll be able to come back to school tomorrow so long as he keeps on improving. There's no need to worry, love.'

I nod, my lips compressed. That's easy for him to say – he wasn't the one sat next to him when he just keeled over. I can't shake off the mental images. Or the feeling that I couldn't breathe once Colin stopped responding.

I want to ask Dad if Colin asked about me, but I don't dare. Why would he have? He can probably barely remember a thing. He was drunk out of his skull, so that on its own probably wiped his memory, never mind the hypo.

'It's just as well you were with him,' Dad says, to my surprise. After all, we were breaking the rules.

'I don't suppose Mrs Sinclair sees it that way.'

'Speaking purely as a doctor, you understand.' Dad raises an eyebrow with mock severity, then grows serious again. 'You did a very good job, darling. I'm proud of how calm you kept.'

Calm. Don't make me laugh. I was anything but calm. Whatever it looked like from the outside. Inside I was the total opposite. Not just because of the worry about Colin, but also because of everything else I found out last night. It was too much, and since then, I haven't had a minute's peace to think it all through.

'Would you like me to call Ms Vail?'

I slowly shake my head. I only recently told Dad I'd been

speaking to her. He was surprised at first, but I think he's mainly relieved that I'm taking up the offer of help. 'I'm seeing her tomorrow anyway,' I say.

'That's good . . . You can always come to me, Olive. You know that, don't you?'

I can't help swallowing. 'I do know, Dad. It's just . . . sometimes it's easier to talk to somebody neutral.'

'I can see that.'

After a struggle with myself, I ask, 'How's Nathalie?'

Dad's slightly taken aback, but I can tell from the way he answers that he's glad I asked. 'Fine, great. She says happy birthday from her, by the way.'

'Thanks.' I smile. 'That's nice of her.'

'Do you think you'd be up to having dinner with us the next time she's in Edinburgh?'

I knew that would come sometime. But something about the way Dad poses the question stops me instantly saying no. He hasn't said 'We'd like to take you out for dinner', he's left me the choice. 'Yeah . . . that would be nice.'

'Really? I'm sure Nathalie will be pleased. I certainly am.'

'I want you to be happy, Dad.' Sometimes it's better just to say straight out what you feel, without spending ages thinking about it. Dad pauses, and I realize I've caught a nerve. 'You weren't happy with Mum any more, were you?'

He shakes his head with a sad smile. 'Your mother and I were happy together for many years. And I wouldn't have missed those times for anything in the world.'

'But now you've grown apart,' I say quietly.

'Sometimes a thing can be amazing, but not last for ever,' he says.

'I know.' I glance down. 'I'm learning that just now.'

Dad lifts his eyebrows. 'With Colin?'

'No,' I say hastily. This thing with Colin is complicated, painful and intense, but it's only just beginning. Only God knows why, but I'm absolutely certain of that. 'With my friends . . . I was determined to switch up into the upper sixth as soon as I turned eighteen and you couldn't tell me what to do any more.'

Dad grins, as if he knew that all along. 'Well, it looks like we can't tell you what to do any more now. So, what are you going to do?'

I take a deep breath. 'I think I'm better off in the lower sixth.' It hurts to say the words. But anything else would be untrue. 'I miss my friends, and I'm still angry. Not with you, Dad, but with . . . the whole world. The fire, the way everything's changed.'

'And you have every right to be, love.'

There are tears in my eyes, but I blink them away. 'I know. But I've learned that it doesn't get me anywhere. That it only wrecks the stuff I do have . . . And that's a lot, Dad.'

It's hard not to cry when he hugs me. A while ago, getting so emotional would have really embarrassed me. But this is who I am now. Lots of stuff has happened to me, so I'm allowed to have big feelings. I'm OK with that and I feel a wee bit lighter and freer as I walk back to my room once Dad's driven away.

I try to work on the school paper to take my mind off things but my thoughts are everywhere except in this room. Mostly with Colin. It might be silly not to text him, but something inside me refuses.

Dad relieved my worst fears, but I can't truly believe Colin's doing OK until I see him again on Tuesday. He was discharged yesterday. I knew that, and I didn't go to see him, even though every fibre of my being longed to be close to him. But for the most part, I'm still just disappointed and incredulous about what I learned at the weekend.

I spent a long time thinking about how to act when I saw him again. I've got nothing to say to him, yet at the same time, I have a ton of questions.

I forget every one of them when I see him before breakfast this morning. The corridor outside the dining room is deserted – most people are already inside but I'm running late because it took me ages to plait my hair. I used to be the champion of complicated plaits, and it's OK that that's changed since I've been unable to lift my arm above shoulder height without pain. But today at least I've managed a respectable Danish braid.

I'm just coming around the corner when I see him. And Colin sees me, as I slam on the brakes.

He looks good. That's my first thought. Not amazing – the shadows under his eyes are too dark for that – but he's not as deathly pale as he was that night in my room. Fortunately . . .

He stands there, he looks at me, and although I can't be certain how much he can remember, I see from his face that he knows exactly what happened before he passed out. Before he came to me and begged me to believe him. I didn't want to think about it – it hurts too much – but the images are seared on my brain. Colin, distraught, and although he looks more together now, I can tell at a glance that his emotional state hasn't changed.

And neither has mine. I'm still shocked, hurt and over-whelmed, but I'm feeling something else just now, which eclipses all other emotions. Relief, which gives way to burn-ing desire, and steers me towards him.

COLIN

After two nights in hospital, they let me go back to school. It feels like an eternity. Olive's dad gives me a ride, and although I'd never have thought it possible, the only thing I feel when I get out of his car and see the tall brick buildings of Dunbridge Academy is relief. First of all, Mrs Sinclair is waiting for me, along with Ms Vail. The head is justifiably pissed, but I can see concern in her face. Dr Henderson must have filled her in on the contents of the discharge letter from the hospital, including the psychiatrist's notes and his recommendation that I get therapy. Anyway, after a long sermon from Mrs Sinclair on breaking the rules, Ms Vail takes me off to her office.

Even after talking to the psychologist, I'm not too sure what to make of it. I guess it was kind of a relief, but also really tiring. My mind is still swirling the next day, as I go in for breakfast after the morning run, during which I felt like the PE teacher was watching me very closely.

I haven't seen Olive yet. She doesn't do the run, of course, and I hadn't spotted her at dinner yesterday either. I'm just scanning through my schedule for the day, to work out when I'll next be in class with her, when she comes around the corner of the cloisters and sees me outside the dining room door.

She stops, rooted to the spot, and suddenly I can't move either. Her eyes roam over me and I find myself remembering what the doctor said.

You were very lucky that your girlfriend was with you and called an ambulance.

My girlfriend who isn't my girlfriend and who hates me. I was sure of that, but now I read all kinds of emotions in her pale face, which have me doubting myself. Olive looks like she's had a few sleepless nights, and I hate that I might be to blame for that.

Do I need to say anything? Apologize to her? I really should, but I suddenly can't remember how to speak. Or move. But I don't have to because Olive's already walking towards me.

She doesn't look at me, only gives me a fleeting glance once she's right in front of me. And then she hugs me. Harder than I expect.

I feel her fingers in my sweater and her head against my throat. I'm so overwhelmed that I don't put my arms around her, and by the time I'm considering changing that, she's let go of me again. She takes a step back and looks up at me. Her green eyes sparkle threateningly. 'Never fucking do that again,' she says, through gritted teeth, gazing so intently at me that a shiver runs down my spine. 'Got that?'

Loud and clear. It's impossible not to get it, given the way she's looking at me. I swallow hard, then salute. 'Yes, ma'am.'

It's a pathetic attempt to lighten the mood, and she doesn't seem to appreciate my sense of humour. She shakes her head gently, but then, eyes still sparkling, she whispers, 'Get tae fuck, Fantino,' which might just have taken on a different meaning, these days, then walks past me into the dining room.

It takes me a second or two to follow, because I need time to process what just happened. She hugged me, but I'm not naïve enough to think that makes everything fine between us again. No way.

Olive sits as far from me as she can at breakfast, but she keeps glancing at my plate. She only starts to look moderately reassured once I've eaten. After that, we ignore each other for another six hours. This is exhausting, and I'm through with it.

Olive is finding it exhausting too. I can see the tension in her face. She looks tired. And desperate. I hate being the reason for that. We sit in classrooms, sneak glances, immediately turning away when the other notices.

And then the last class is over. Everyone else hurries out of the room into the bit of free time before study hour, and Olive slowly packs her bag. It's probably presumptuous to interpret that as a sign she's ready for a conversation. But I have to speak to her. I can't bear this silence between us any longer.

She looks up as I shut the classroom door once the group has vanished through it. 'What's the matter, Colin?' She sounds tired and resigned. And she says 'Colin' because she's not in the mood for games. I know that much, these days.

I walk over to her. 'I have to talk to you.'

For a moment, I'm certain she'll laugh, throw her dark blue bag over her shoulder and walk past me, out of the room. But she doesn't. She just crosses her arms over her chest and perches on the edge of the desk behind her chair.

'Fine.' There are two desks between us, which apparently makes her feel safe enough to give me a challenging nod. 'Talk.'

Yes . . . talk. But that means knowing what I need to say to her. And beyond *I'm sorry*, there isn't much. 'Are we still fighting?' I ask instead.

Olive looks at me and I can't read her expression. 'We aren't fighting, Colin. This is worse.'

Ouch.

'I know.' I could cry. 'And I didn't want to keep secrets from

379

you. I wanted to put it all behind me. I didn't think it would matter here. I didn't know . . .'

'It doesn't matter here, because you're not to blame for what happened at this school,' she says, to my surprise. 'But what does matter is that you didn't tell me the truth.'

'I know,' I repeat. What else can I say?

'Why?' she asks. 'Why didn't you say anything? I told you everything. I undressed in front of you – I had a bloody panic attack, Colin. You didn't say anything. You just walked out. That would've been the time when you could've told me, wouldn't it?'

It's not like I didn't know all this only too well, but hearing again everything I've done wrong, from Olive this time, is painful.

'I was scared.' I keep talking. 'I didn't want all this. I didn't want to be at this school, and I certainly didn't want to fall in love. But you left me no choice, and by the time I realized that, I also knew that there was no way to be together with you and to tell you the truth without hurting you.'

'And keeping secrets from me seemed like a sensible solution?'

I can't look at her. 'No.'

'But you did it anyway?'

'Yes, I did, because it's clearly my fucking destiny in life to always get everything wrong.' I'd told myself I wouldn't shout, but I'm already failing at that.

'You could stop using that belief as an excuse for every situation where you wimp out and take the easy option.'

'Easy? You think this is easy for me?'

'I don't know, Colin! I really don't know, because I'm starting to get the feeling I don't know you one tiny bit.'

'That's bullshit and you know it.'

'I don't know anything. I don't know who you are. I don't know how much I can believe you about what really happened, how much of what you told me is true. I don't even know if I'd ever have found out if I hadn't got those messages.'

'Wait, who even sent you those?' I interrupt.

'Not a clue. And does it matter?'

'Not really, but I'd still like to know.'

'It was some weird account,' is all Olive says.

'What kind of *weird account*?'

She laughs. 'A One Direction fan page, them and this other band.'

My blood runs cold. 'What?'

Olive eyes me sceptically. 'I showed you.'

That may well be, but I wasn't exactly taking in the details when she shoved her phone in my face.

'What's the account called?' I ask tonelessly. I have an inkling, obviously, but I don't want it to be true. Olive pulls her phone from her pocket and shows me again. My thoughts narrow to one single plea: *No. No, no, no, no. That's impossible. She can't have done.*

'What's wrong?' Olive asked insistently. 'Colin?'

'Nothing. I . . .'

'Who is it?' She stresses every word.

And then I blurt it out: 'Cleo.'

'Your sister?' Olive's voice squeaks unexpectedly.

I shrug.

'But why would Cleo do a thing like that?'

Yeah, why would she? In a matter of seconds, dozens of scenarios shoot through my head. Someone's hacked Cleo's phone (come on), Mom told her stuff that made her want to hassle me (more likely), mistake (yeah, right) or, sadly, the most probable version. Cleo panicked because she picked up that I was falling in love with a girl on another continent. But even so, I can't for the life of me imagine my kid sister trying to split me and Olive up, so I shrug yet again.

'I don't know.'

'I thought it might be someone from your old school,' Olive says.

'Yeah.'

'I guess I should thank her. After all, unless I'm very much mistaken, I'd never have heard it from you.'

'You don't understand,' I snap at her.

'No, Colin.' She steps menacingly towards me. 'I really don't understand. I have no bloody idea how you could go through with a secret like that. But at least now I understand why you wanted to get expelled from Dunbridge as soon as possible.'

'I didn't know all that back then,' I say in self-defence. 'That there was a fire here. That you—' I stop.

'Aye, just say it.' Olive's eyes spray sparks. 'That I nearly died. But, hey, I got seriously lucky compared to that firefighter.'

I grind my teeth and feel the tears stinging my eyes. 'Stop it.'

'What? Stop what, Colin, huh? Telling the truth? Just because you're too chicken to admit to what happened? It's so much easier to act like it was nothing when you're thousands of miles away. It must be dead easy when not a single thing happened to you.'

'You think I wanted this? It wasn't my choice to come to this school.'

'But you don't seem to have fought back.'

'You don't have a fucking clue what it's like to make one mistake, something so awful you don't know how to go on living with it,' I blurt.

'No,' Olive hisses back. 'But I know what it's like to have no idea what caused an accident that almost killed you. What it's like when people only ever say they can't be certain how it happened. Who's responsible. How d'you think you can ever move on from a thing like that when you're left with thousands of questions?'

Her words are like daggers in my chest. 'I don't know. I only know that my life's gone down the shitter since I made a goddamn mistake. No, two mistakes, actually. The first was that I took my lighter out at school and got careless. But the second, which was maybe way worse, was then to go to my mother rather than straight to the cops. To let her persuade me not to do anything because she'd take care of it. I thought she'd call a lawyer, but she packed me off to Europe and kept my name out of the inquiry. And I was too shocked to stop her.' I shut my eyes in torment. 'And, yeah, maybe it was kind of a relief too, and I despise myself for it.'

Olive seems not to have been expecting that. 'Hold the bus,' she says. 'She – she did *what*?'

I just nod.

'But . . .'

'Yeah.'

'OK. Have I got this straight? She wanted to cover up the truth?' I nod mechanically. Olive stares hard at me. 'Do *you* want everyone to know what really happened?'

Part of me wants to say no. That's the part that's scared of what will happen. Scared that Mom's right and I should trust her. But a larger, more desperate, part of me knows I can no longer live with the knowledge that I made a mistake and have been keeping my game face on ever since. I can't keep it up. It's time to take responsibility. 'Yes.'

'Good.' Olive falls silent for a moment. 'Then I'll help you.'

33

COLIN

Getting Mom to spring for another ticket to New York is easier than I expected. All I have to do is utter the words 'girlfriend' and 'plus one for the gala'. Ava Fantino is thrilled once she's found out that Olive is a model student at Dunbridge Academy, on top of which her dad's a doctor. Such a cute story for her to tell all the right people in New York society.

I didn't want to drag Olive into this whole thing, but she wasn't about to be talked out of coming with me once I'd told her my plan. Which was to fly to New York, turn up to Mom's dumb event and then go to the police. Now that I'm sitting in an airplane somewhere over the Atlantic, I'm not so sure it's such a good idea.

I'd been surprised by the sense of excitement and anticipation earlier today, the first day of the half-term holiday at

Dunbridge. Suddenly, there were packed suitcases and bulging bags filling the hallways. The courtyard was crammed with fancy cars; students were running into their parents' arms. Olive and I got into her dad's car so that he could drive us to the airport. The whole way there, I felt like I should apologize that she was coming to New York with me instead of spending the break with her family, though I imagine she might have preferred it this way. We haven't spoken any further about her parents' split, but I can't help noticing that she's still shaken up. I hate being so preoccupied with my own shit that I'm not taking as much time as I'd like to talk to her about her stuff.

I'm tense for the whole flight and get even more nervous once the pilot informs us that she's beginning the descent into New York. My hands are sweaty – my fingers need something to do. I don't even let myself think about the way I'd have calmed myself not so long ago. In our first session, Ms Vail and I worked out a no-self-harming contract. At first, signing the piece of paper felt dumb, but to my surprise it actually helps me take responsibility for my own actions. It would be naïve to think this has solved all my problems – the last few days have been shit. So shit that I broke the agreement twice, but I was honest enough to tell Ms Vail. The result was that I had to fill out these behaviour-analysis questionnaires with her to help me understand why I fall back into old patterns and to work out alternative strategies. She approves of the boxing thing, and she suggested that, next time, I write down my feelings before and after.

But now I'm on a plane with no punching bag anywhere in sight.

An hour later, as we're sitting in the car Mom sent to pick us up, I suddenly feel Olive's hand on my arm. 'Feeling the pressure?' she asks.

Bullseye.

My first instinct is to shake my head, but I remind myself: *No, Colin. We're not doing this any more. We're honest with the people who care about us.* 'A bit.'

'What can I do?'

I have no idea. Get two tickets for the first plane back to Scotland? I know that running away won't solve my problems, but right now I don't feel like I have the strength to face them. Or to face my mom's expression when she meets us shortly.

I look up as Olive hands me the scrunchie she's been wearing around her wrist.

'What am I supposed to do with this?' I ask, staring at the fabric-wrapped hairband.

'It's a coping mechanism,' she says. She's using Ms Vail's language so I bet she asked her what she could do to help me.

'It won't relieve the pressure.'

'It's not meant to. But it might help you deal with it in a less harmful way.'

I suppress a sigh and start to snap the hairband around my own wrist. It doesn't seem to do much at first, but combined with the Manhattan skyline as it comes into view, I feel slightly calmer. I wait in vain for a feeling of coming home, though.

OLIVE

New York is just like I imagined it, but bigger. Wide streets, skyscrapers so high that, from the car that picked us up at the airport, I couldn't make out where they ended.

I've been raging with my parents so many times lately, but I'm sure nothing could have stopped them coming to meet me and my boyfriend at the airport after a transatlantic flight. Colin doesn't seem particularly surprised that neither his mum nor his dad is here to welcome us, and that makes me sad.

I truly become aware of how different his upbringing's been from mine as we walk into an apartment-block lobby in the middle of Manhattan. It's like a film. All the noise of hooting cars, sirens and building sites that enveloped us outside are suddenly cut off as a lift launches us up to the top floor. The doors glide open and reveal a hallway that seems to be part of the Fantinos' apartment. You can't get up here without a keycode, which Colin entered downstairs.

I glance at him, but he's looking down the corridor and, at that moment, a girl runs towards us.

Cleo looks like I remember her from the video call I crashed. That seems a lifetime ago, but it's only been a fortnight; even so, those two weeks were long enough to turn my world upside down. And Colin's sister is at least partly to blame for that.

He hasn't yet brought up the fact that he knows she sent me the messages, but her uncertain glance from Colin to me and back again tells me she's just waiting for him to mention it.

Apparently, he doesn't consider this the right moment, though.

'Don't you have a welcome-home hug for me?' he jokes, but his voice sounds strained. The way it always does when he's trying to hide that he's a lad with emotions.

I chew my bottom lip to stop my eyes welling as Cleo throws herself into his arms and bursts into tears. I'm an only child, so I probably can't come close to imagining what it's like to have your big brother leave and not to know when he's coming back.

This is the first time Colin and Cleo have seen each other since then. I knew that, but I didn't know what it would really mean. That doesn't sink in until Cleo digs her fingers into his jacket and can't stop crying. Colin's dropped his suitcase. His eyes are also glittering a bit too brightly when he finally lets go of her and looks to me. 'Cleo, this is Olive. Olive – Cleo.' I can feel that he's on the verge of saying something else. But he doesn't.

Cleo looks seriously stressed, but she smiles back at me. 'Pleased to meet you,' she mumbles, looking down.

'Likewise,' I reply.

'Where are Mom and Dad?' Colin asks.

'Dad's still at the office and Mom had to go into the studio early. There was some kind of issue.'

'Obviously.' There's a bitter undertone in Colin's voice. He laughs. 'Well, it looks like you won't get the pleasure of getting to know them until later,' he adds, turning to me. I'd be lying if I said I wasn't relieved.

But I do meet Kirsten – the nanny, Colin explains. She shows me the guest room that's been made up for me, and I notice Colin's expression as I thank her.

Guest room . . . I can imagine what he's thinking. Wing time at Dunbridge can't stop us spending the nights together, so his parents are hardly going to.

'Mom asked if you guys wanted to go into the studio,' Cleo says, as we head back to the living room. 'Hayes Chamberlain is there today.'

I raise my eyebrows in amazement, while Colin looks like he hasn't a clue who she's talking about.

'Is this his first interview since the band split up?' I ask.

Cleo nods enthusiastically. 'Yeah, so I'm totally going! Maybe he'll say something about when Temporary Fix are getting back together.'

I just nod, because from everything I've heard about the boy-band lately, it doesn't exactly look like they'll be ending their self-imposed break any time soon. Tori's been keeping me up to date on all the gossip. She'd die if she knew that one of the band will be on Colin's mother's talk show this evening. I glance hastily at Colin.

'Up to you,' he says. 'We can stay here if you're tired.'

'Are *you* tired?' I ask, by which I really mean is he feeling up to it. I know that the long journey and jetlag will have messed up his blood sugar. But he shakes his head.

We have time to eat dinner with Cleo before we leave. There's a large neon sign that reads *Late Night with Ava Fantino*, in elegant script, adorning the building where the show is produced. The minute we walk in, I feel as though I've stepped into a world that couldn't be more different from mine.

Colin and Cleo seem to know the place like the backs of their hands – same as everyone who works here. I can instantly tell that we're going to meet his mother because Colin tenses more and more with every step. Cleo turns a corner and stops outside a door with Ava Fantino's name on it in discreet letters. And then I see her.

Ava Fantino is smaller than I imagined, but no less intimidating.

She looks up from her phone, her eyes rest on Colin. I don't know what I was expecting. Her features to soften at the sight of him, maybe. An emotional reunion with his mother. But there's no sign of any such thing.

'How nice that you both could come.'

Surely that's not how you greet a son when you haven't seen him for weeks.

'Did you have a good trip?'

'Yeah, amazing.' And, *bam*, my chilly, sarcastic Colin is back. Now I know where he comes from. His jaw muscles are working as he hugs his mum. She radiates an incredible presence, yet her eyes are like ice as she looks at him.

Then she turns to me. 'You must be Olive,' she says, holding out her hand.

I shake it. 'Thank you for the invitation, Ms Fantino.'

'Colin insisted on it,' is all she says in reply, and I decide not to like this woman. 'Please call me Ava. I'm afraid I have to ask you all to excuse me now. If you want a thing done properly around here, you have to take care of it yourself, same as ever. Debra will show you to your seats – we're going on air in a few minutes.'

Wow, that was a quick introduction. I seem to be the only person here who's surprised. Colin glances at me, and we follow a tall woman with waist-length black curls through the maze of corridors to the studio. And now we're in the part I recognize from TV: the set with the famous couch in front of a screen displaying the show's logo. It looks much smaller in real life. So does the packed-out audience area.

We're shown to seats on the back row. Soon the lights go out and a loudspeaker instructs us to applaud. Colin's arms are crossed over his chest and he makes no move to clap as his mother walks on stage.

Ava Fantino is an ice-cold woman with the impressive skill of seeming like a completely different person on camera. She sits there on the sofa with a beaming smile, ready to welcome her first guest, totally unlike the woman I just met.

Colin watches the show, apparently entirely unimpressed. Cleo, on the other hand, squeals in excitement twenty minutes in, when her mother introduces the British singer.

Hayes Chamberlain looks just as stunning as he does in glossy magazines and on the album covers I recognize him from. Seriously tall, seriously thin, dark hair with a hint of a curl, which is – to put it mildly – pure perfection. The audience goes wild, only quieting down when Colin's mother starts to speak to him. I'm aware of the direct way she asks questions, and even before today, I found it pretty outspoken, but she excels herself this time. It's clear that Hayes has no intention of giving a straight answer to what's going to happen with Temporary Fix. I'm not surprised by that because, thanks to Tori, I know that he was the one who – to the horror of all their fans – left the band out of the blue and disappeared from public view. After that, the three other band members decided to take a break too. Only they know the real reasons for it, yet Ava Fantino wheels out the big guns in an attempt to get answers from him. He's clearly had a lot of media training – I'm amazed by the way he always manages to keep his replies innocuous yet charming. At least until Colin's mum brings the conversation round to the other band members. She seems determined to goad him into saying something negative about them, and that leaves a bitter taste in my mouth. I'm starting to see how the media operates and to understand why Colin hates it all so much. He gives a barely perceptible shake of his head and, when I glance over, he nods towards the exit.

I hesitate, then nod back, and stand up. We leave Cleo, who has eyes only for the singer, and ignore the hand signals of horrified assistant producers as we slip through the door.

'She really went out of her way to be insensitive and cross the line tonight,' Colin mutters, as we walk down a corridor.

'Didn't seem like it was much of a stretch for her,' I say. 'She really grilled that poor lad.'

'Her specialty.' Colin shrugs. Then he looks at me. 'Want to get out of here?'

I nod without hesitation.

'Scared?' I ask, once we've retrieved our coats and got out into the street. By night, New York is even more overwhelming than by day, and I have no idea where we are. Colin seems to know where he's going, though.

He doesn't answer me straight away. 'Yeah,' he says in the end, like he's just remembered the plan. Which is to show up at Ava Fantino's charity gala the day after tomorrow but leave early, and go to the police the day after that. I'm glad Colin's decided to give evidence at last, but I can tell how afraid he is of reliving the evening of the fire. 'But I'll be glad to get it over with.'

I'm sure I would be too – in my eyes, there's no other option. I might have forgiven him, but only because I believe in the good in him. That he didn't mean anyone any harm.

Sometimes, when I suddenly remember that someone died in the fire, that's hard. A firefighter, a mother, a wife. Every time, it's like I can't breathe for a moment. It wouldn't be right to blame Colin for that because nobody can be certain that the fire really started because of him. He was in despair: he never meant to start a fire – but neither did the upper-sixth crowd in the Dungeon. None of that can change what happened, though.

Colin's actions don't define him, any more than mine define me.

He's a good person; he deserves to be loved, and I'm *allowed* to love him, despite the things that happened. We'll do this together. And some day, sometime, there'll be a day when everything gets easier again.

34

COLIN

It was a mistake to visit Mom at the studio; I should have
known that before we set off. I didn't exactly expect her to do
cartwheels at the sight of me, but I'm hurt by how cold she
was. I can never change Ava Fantino, though. I can only
change the way I deal with her behaviour.

In the past, I'd have been furious and disappointed. And
then, so I didn't have to feel that, I'd have done things that
haven't proved particularly constructive. Changing a mindset
like that takes time, and right now I'm still furious and disappointed, but I'm choosing a different consequence. I talk to
Olive on the way home. We walk, even though it's almost
two miles and the night is cold, but it's helping me to clear
my head.

There's nothing but silence to welcome us to the apartment.

Kirsten has left, Dad's still at the office and I'm tired. I'm so tired of this shit.

Olive takes a shower and I wait for her in the guest room. My head is heavy. I shut my eyes and I feel as though the bed moves beneath me, floats up, sinks down, like the plane only a few hours ago. God, I'm tired. I could fall asleep, I really could just . . .

I startle out of my doze as Olive creeps into the bed beside me and cuddles up to me.

'Go back to sleep,' she whispers. Her voice is gentle. She smells of rose shampoo and vanilla. With my last ounce of strength, I roll over and nestle into her body. Her back is against my chest, she takes my arm as I wrap it around her, and starts to stroke my wrist.

'Have you eaten?' she asks, turning her head slightly towards me as I don't answer right away. 'Colin?'

'Yeah,' I murmur, and feel her nod.

'Good.'

Good . . . Yes, it is good. And warm, she's so endlessly soft and warm. The tension drains from my muscles, everything grows heavy and I give in. I'm holding her in my arms. Nothing can happen. I'm sure of that.

OLIVE

Colin's nodded off by the time I get out of the shower and lie down beside him. He blinks, opens his eyes a crack, rolls over towards me, and then he's asleep again.

He's not moving now.

He sighs gently and a throbbing starts between my thighs. The weight of his sleeping body settles over me, like a warm blanket. His chest rises and falls against my back, slowly and evenly. I don't need to see his face to know that it's relaxed. Must be thanks to the jetlag, because earlier he was so tense that I was sure he wouldn't sleep a wink tonight. Mind you, now I'm scared that that fate will befall me instead.

The journey was exhausting. It's now three in the morning in Scotland and I'm tired, but I'm nervous too. I'm lying in Colin's arms in a strange bed. In a strange apartment. In a strange city.

We were all alone here earlier; he showed me his room, then came to mine while I had a shower, but after a while I hear Colin's mother and sister get in. The guest-room door is closed, it's late and nobody disturbs us, but I still feel like an unwelcome visitor. Colin's mother wasn't unfriendly to me, but she wasn't exactly gushing either. I hate the idea that Colin and Cleo grew up like this. That nobody ever gave them a hug just because. That nobody tells them how amazing they are. I know Colin tells Cleo, to make up for it, but he's human too, and he deserves affection.

I interlace my fingers with his and hold tight to his hand. I'm glad that he's joined us at Dunbridge. At a place where people are nice to each other and can feel welcome. He belongs there and I really hope he'll manage to convince his parents to send Cleo to our school too. God knows what will happen after what he's planning to do.

I barely know Colin's parents so I can't tell how they'll react to him going to the police. They might threaten not to pay his school fees any more, but if they do, we'll find a way. Colin is – surprisingly – a bright lad. I could hardly believe it, but his grades are on a Henryesque level, and that's saying something. If push comes to shove, we can ask Mrs Sinclair about a scholarship. And Colin's an adult now. He'll be able to live his own life. Once he's without the people who have never shown him what love is, they'll never be able to hurt him again. Never.

35

OLIVE

I must have fallen asleep eventually because, after a while, I wake up. I'm lying on my front and no longer in Colin's arms. He's propped himself on his elbows beside me and is doodling little patterns on my back. So gently that that can't have been what woke me.

All the same, he stops when I move, and lays his hand on my head. But I'm awake. Properly refreshed, even.

And so's he – I can see that as I squint over to him.

'Good morning,' I whisper, my voice rough with sleep.

'Hello.' His smile is tense, which I can understand. He must have been thinking about what lies ahead of him.

'What's the time?'

'Guess,' he says.

'Ten?'

Colin laughs quietly. 'It's four o'clock.'

I sit up. 'In the afternoon?'

'No, four in the morning.'

'No way.' I feel wide awake and fully rested. It can't be true, but Colin shrugs.

'You've got jetlag to thank for that one. Your head thinks it's nine a.m.'

'How long have you been awake?' I ask.

'Dunno. Half an hour, maybe,' he mutters evasively. Definitely longer than that, then. So much for me being glad he was able to sleep.

'How are you doing?'

The question still stresses him, that's no secret, but I won't stop asking it. Especially not now that Colin's genuinely trying to answer honestly.

'I'm scared.'

'That makes sense.'

Colin shuts his eyes. 'I wish I could just go to the cops right now and get it over with.'

'Let's go, then.'

'What?' He opens his eyes. 'You mean . . . now?'

'Yeah.' It's my turn to shrug. 'If you wish you could get it done right now, then that's what we'll do.'

'It's the middle of the night.'

'There must be someone at the police station round the clock.'

I can feel that this is too much for Colin. But then he seems to consider it seriously. Maybe I'm rushing him, but this way he doesn't have to spend two whole days torturing himself, and hiding his plan from his family.

Colin looks over to the window. I follow his gaze and see the lights of the skyscrapers against the night sky.

And then he nods.

COLIN

We have to be quiet, but this isn't the first time I've crept out at an ungodly hour without waking my parents. I've practised this, even though the reason we're now taking an Uber across the city is way less fun than when I snuck out in the past.

It's shortly after five. The streets are pretty quiet, but One Police Plaza is not.

I feel like I might throw up as I go to the desk and ask for the officer whose name I saw in the news reports. He's not here at this time of day, but the receptionist promises to get someone to call him. Olive lets go of my hand and gives me a kiss, then takes a seat in the waiting area, while I explain that I'm here to make a statement about the Ainslee fire, after which I'm led to an interview room, which is every bit as bare and charmless as they look in the movies.

They take my details, don't bat an eyelid as I say my name, and after a while Detective King walks into the room. And then I tell him everything. Mechanically, like a robot.

About the Homecoming night, my lighter, the toilet tissue in the gym bathroom, and the moment the paper caught fire.

'Why were you hanging around in a bathroom with a lighter?' the cop asks.

So I could have a smoke. It's the answer I've given so often, so that nobody finds out what I'm really doing. But I'm through with that now.

'I was self-harming.' My voice sounds alien. 'I was stressed out, had a bunch of issues, couldn't deal with them any more. I went into the bathroom to distract myself from the emotional pain.'

'Had you often done that?'

'Yes.'

He makes a note. 'And then what happened?'

I take a deep breath. 'I heard people coming and accidentally dropped the lighter. It landed on a couple squares of toilet tissue that were on the floor, and they caught fire. I stomped the burning paper out right away. The floor was kind of damp, and I was certain the fire was out. Then I walked out of the stall and into the washroom where a few guys from my class were hanging around.'

'Can you give me their names?'

I pause, then just blurt them out. 'Trent Barlow, Isaac Hawk and Jeremy Westwood.'

'Are they your friends, Colin?'

'Not exactly. We had kind of a tense relationship.' I take a breath, then tell him about my mom spreading stories about

Trent's influencer sister. That he'd sworn to get revenge and fucked with me any chance he got. I tell him everything I know, and then I carry on with what happened when I was out in the schoolyard and saw the flames.

'You dialled nine one one but didn't give your name?' the detective confirms. I nod and he asks his next question. 'And you left the site before the emergency services arrived?'

I nod again. My throat tightens more with every answer, but I force myself to keep talking. 'I panicked and was afraid of getting caught. So I ran away. At that moment I didn't see any other way out but . . . I regret that. Running away was the wrong thing to do – I should have gone to the police. I was in shock. And I kept asking myself how the fire could have started. I was sure the toilet tissue was out, you know? I would never have started a fire intentionally, but I was afraid Trent and the others would figure out what I was doing in the bathroom. That stressed me out, and I worried that maybe I'd been careless, that I hadn't extinguished the paper after all. I don't remember exactly any more.' My voice is shaking, but I try to hold my nerve. 'I'd never have believed the fire could spread like that or that a firefighter could die. It's no excuse, but I'm truly remorseful. I'd do everything differently if I could. I didn't mean any of it to happen, least of all for someone to die.'

I don't know when exactly I start crying again. The detective's face shows no emotion. He just pushes a box of tissues across the table to me. They're next to the voice recorder that's taking down my statement.

'Why didn't you come here right away?'

'I went to my mother. I was afraid and thought she'd help me. She convinced me not to say anything. I thought she meant just until she'd arranged for lawyers to advise me, but then my parents sent me to boarding school in Scotland. It all happened so fast, I was overwhelmed and didn't know what was happening to me. And then I was on another continent and I . . . didn't do a thing.'

'So how come you're here now?'

I swallow. And I think of Olive. 'I can't live with the guilt. I lied to everyone who matters to me. I couldn't go on like that. And I'm still scared, but I have to tell the truth.'

The detective makes more notes. 'That's a wise decision,' he says, after a while. 'Thank you for your testimony, Colin.'

I wait for the door to open and his fellow cops to come in, cuff me and take me away. 'That will be a great deal of help in our investigations. The names you gave me are particularly interesting.'

I immediately start to feel guilty. Should I have kept quiet about who exactly I saw in the bathroom? However much I hate Trent and his buddies, I don't want to get them into trouble.

'You did the right thing, Colin,' Detective King says, like he's reading my mind. 'It's always right to tell the truth, don't forget that.'

I gulp, then nod.

'Is there anything you want to add to your statement?'

I think for a minute, then shake my head. 'No, that's all, sir.'

'Good, well, you're free to go. We'll get back to you if we have any more questions.'

'What?' I hesitate. 'I don't have to . . . stay here?'

The detective eyes me. 'No, no. You've given us your contact info, and you've made a statement. That's all we need right now.'

Is this a trap? I'm not sure of anything. 'Do I have to stay in the US? I mean . . . I'm supposed to fly back to Scotland at the end of the week.'

'We'll be able to contact you there. You can travel as planned.'

'Good, then . . .' I glance at the door. 'Thank you?'

'Thank *you*, Colin. Have a nice day.'

'You too,' I reply, as I stand up. All through the long corridors back to the waiting area I'm expecting the other shoe to drop. Cops, armed to the teeth, to pop around the corner, wrestle me to the ground and lead me off in cuffs. But nobody pays me any attention.

I don't know if I'm innocent. I only know that the detective didn't consider it necessary to arrest me. And that's . . . a good sign? I can't think straight.

Olive jumps up from her chair in the waiting room as soon as she sees me. The concern in her face makes me go weak in the knees. I haven't eaten. I really need to do something about that, but I can't.

'So?' she asks, walking towards me.

'I told them. They're still investigating and . . . they'll be in touch.'

'OK. And how do we feel?'

We. Don't ask me why, but that tiny word makes me want to cry. She doesn't have to be, but she's with me. Even though I lied to her and hurt her. She's still with me.

'I don't know,' I manage. 'Overwhelmed. Empty.'

'But a wee bit relieved?'

That's it. I feel it the second she says the words. The pressure in my chest has eased, and so has the buzzing in my head. 'Yeah, that too.'

Olive's eyes rest on me. She's seen all of me. Every single version. Furious, unfair, broken, desperate. And now she's seeing one that I could almost call brave, and that's not something I ever expected to think about myself.

'And you're free to go?'

'So Detective King said.'

'OK.' She takes my hand. 'Then let's go.'

Dawn is breaking between the skyscrapers. It's rush-hour traffic now so we don't call an Uber. We walk back.

The air is fresh and clear and it helps me get my head together. Once we're finally in the elevator, heading up to our apartment, I suddenly feel a total exhaustion. It's not physical tiredness, it's more emotional. Because I've done all I can. It's out of my hands now.

'Where have you two been?' asks Mom, as we run into her in the living room. Seems like she's already been out jogging – an early-morning run in Central Park is a fixed part of Ava Fantino's day. She sticks fast to her morning routine, regardless of weather or the day of the week.

The newspaper and empty espresso cup on the breakfast bar show that Dad's already left for work.

'To the police station,' I say, watching calmly as my mother's face changes. She hesitates, as though she thinks she's misheard, and then it slowly seems to dawn on her what it might mean. I help her out anyway, though. 'I made a statement.'

The mask slips. 'You did *what*?'

'Made a statement,' I repeat, as if she were hard of hearing. 'To the police.'

'Colin Fantino, you cannot be serious?'

Olive gives me a tiny glance but stands, arms folded, by the breakfast bar as I take a step towards Mom.

'I am. Deadly serious.'

'What did you tell them?'

'The truth.'

'What truth?'

'What I was doing in the bathroom.' I feel my throat constrict. 'I wasn't smoking – that part was a lie. I was burning myself with a lighter.'

'What the hell?' Mom's voice gets shrill. 'Why in God's name would you . . .'

'I've been doing it for a couple years,' I say. My voice trembles, but I carry on. 'It was the only way I could deal with my emotions.'

'Colin.' I've shocked her, there's no mistaking that.

'I'm not doing it any more,' I say, although that's not entirely true. It will be soon. 'I've been seeing Ms Vail for the last few weeks – the school psychologist, you remember?'

Mom's gone pale. 'Is that helping?'

'Yeah,' is all I say.

'OK.' She holds a hand to her forehead. 'Good, that . . . I can't believe you did that, Colin.' I don't reply so she continues. 'But it was still a mistake, right?'

'In the school bathroom?' I ask. 'Yeah. I was careless. A piece of toilet tissue caught fire but I thought I'd stomped it out when I left.'

'So why go to the police, for God's sake?'

'To tell the truth, Mom!' I'm raising my voice but it's no good. She doesn't get it. Not even now. I told her the one thing I never wanted to admit, and she hasn't followed up. She now knows I'm speaking to a therapist, so as far as she's concerned, that box has been checked. I shouldn't be surprised, but it still hurts.

She keeps looking at me like I've lost my mind, and I'm expecting her to start shouting too. But she doesn't. Not in front of Olive. She gives me a death-stare, then picks up her phone.

'You must be insane. I'll let your father know – he might be able to intervene and keep your statement off the files.'

'He can try, but if he does, I'll testify again.'

That's the moment my mom seems to grasp that we're not on the same page any more. If we ever had been.

'Colin, are you out of your mind? Do you know what this means? For you and for our family? For your sister?'

I'm about to answer when I hear a little voice. 'What about me?'

Cleo's standing in the doorway in her favourite purple pyjamas, staring at us. I don't know how much she's heard, but it doesn't matter now. I've got a bone to pick with her too.

'Yeah, what about you, Cleo?' I turn towards her. 'I've been asking myself that since you sent Olive those screenshots of the headlines.'

The colour drains from my kid sister's face, and I hate having to do this. But I can't keep acting like it never happened.

She looks at me in shock and, before I can say another word, her eyes well up.

'Maybe you should ask your daughter what it means for her and this family if she goes behind my back to send my boarding-school friends news about the fire.'

'You did *what*?' Mom turns on Cleo, who bursts into tears.

This is painful, but I'm not going to take it any more. I turn to Olive, who looks stressed but composed, and point towards the elevator. She nods. We don't need words. Looks are enough. One look.

Let's get out of here.

As the doors close behind us, I exhale – I hadn't known I'd been holding my breath.

36

OLIVE

A little later, we're walking through Manhattan. I don't ask Colin where he's headed because I've sensed for a while that we have no destination. He just couldn't stand arguing with his family any longer, or justifying himself for finally doing the right thing. I hate his mother for trying to convince him he made the wrong choice. And for being so cold when he told her about his self-harming. There was emotion on her face for a split second, but it wasn't long before she was accusing him of stuff again.

I found it hard to believe that she'd really be so determined to hush up the truth, but now that I've met Ava Fantino in person, I'm no longer surprised. Her name and her family's reputation seem to matter more to her than Colin's peace of mind.

'I have to talk to Cleo,' says Colin, suddenly, as we wait at a red light. He looks at me. 'That was mean of me earlier.'

'It was right to confront her with it, though,' I argue.

Colin doesn't seem particularly convinced. 'I ought to have done it some other time. Calmly.'

I say nothing immediately. 'You'll have time to talk to her later,' I suggest, and the light changes to green. We cross a multi-lane road with dozens of other people. It feels so weird that I'm actually in New York. With Colin. And no matter how stressful this time is, I'm thrilled to get to know the place he's from. This loud, hectic city, the complete opposite of Dunbridge Academy. 'Now I understand why you hate Scotland so much,' I say.

Colin glances at me in surprise. 'I don't hate Scotland.'

I'm taken aback. 'You don't?'

'It's . . . quiet. But kind of OK.'

'You didn't talk like that a couple of weeks ago.'

'A couple weeks ago, everything was different.'

I nod. 'But I get that you'd miss this. Big-city life, so much going on.'

'Right now, I'm mostly missing the peace at Dunbridge,' he says, to my astonishment. Colin doesn't look at me. 'Apparently, you get used to that very quickly.'

'Is it good or bad?'

'Good, I think.' He darts a look at me. 'Isn't it?'

'Course.' I have to smile. 'Very good, even.'

We keep walking, and we can finally catch our breath after

the events of this morning, which came thick and fast. We still haven't eaten. At this very moment, we pass an Italian restaurant, and I stop. 'Oh, so this is why you've been calling me that all this time?'

He frowns, then catches on. He laughs. For the first time today. 'Yep, Olive Garden, this is why.'

I shake my head. 'You're unbelievable.'

'Want to go in? I'll pay.'

'Maybe we really should. Do you want to check first?' He hesitates, but I continue. 'If you're being this arsy, it can only mean one thing.'

'I'm not arsy,' he replies, in a pretty arsy way.

I just raise a speaking eyebrow. Colin snorts disdainfully, but pulls out his phone and opens the blood-sugar app.

'Ha!' I exclaim in triumph, glancing at the screen. 'OK, in we go, Fantino.'

'It's too early,' he says. 'They don't open till noon.'

'Oh.' Bummer.

'To be honest, I hate the place,' he admits.

'Oh, so that's why you called me after it?'

'Totally.'

'Thought as much,' I say.

'That's not actually true,' he starts.

I sigh. 'God, Colin, stop being so cheesy.'

He has to smile. 'Can't help it.'

'Go on, hurl insults at me. I know how to deal with that.'

'Is that one of your kinks?'

'Apparently,' I say. 'Come on, pick a place where we can get something to eat before you bloody well pass out.'

'Oh, please.'

'Yes, please do.' I glare at him.

'Fine. There's a great breakfast place around the corner. Might not be such a bad idea after all the excitement.'

COLIN

We spend most of the day exploring New York. I show Olive around Central Park and take her to my favourite burger joint, and then we just stroll around seeing the sights.

Late in the afternoon, the lack of sleep and jetlag take their revenge. Olive falls asleep in her seat on the subway back home. Her head slumps onto my shoulder, awakening an overwhelming desire in me to lie in bed with her, shut out the world and do nothing more than kiss her, fall asleep and . . . well, maybe try some other things after that.

When we get back to the apartment, I think at first we're alone. But then Cleo appears, her eyes red with crying, and my stomach cramps again. 'Where are Mom and Dad?' I ask coolly, taking off my jacket.

'Work.' She sniffs. I hate her because I know this isn't fake. I can't stand seeing her cry. Especially not because of me. 'Colin, I . . . I'm so sorry.'

I glance at Olive, who's stopped a few steps behind me. She

still looks totally exhausted. 'I think I'll have a bit of a lie-down,' she says.

'OK.' That will give me a chance to talk to Cleo. I pull Olive to me and give her a kiss. She says nothing, but her hand glides gently over my cheek, then she pulls away and vanishes into the guest room.

And then I'm alone with Cleo.

'Colin,' she says, her voice pleading.

'Yeah, what?' I turn away and walk into the kitchen, not that I need anything. But I won't be able to stand firm if I look at her. 'Why did you do it?' I ask.

Cleo doesn't reply. All I hear is a muffled sound, and I count the seconds before I turn back to her. 'I asked you a question.' My voice sounds cutting and I despise myself for it.

'I . . . I don't know.'

'You did it, so you must know why.'

Her eyes fill with tears again. 'I . . . I wanted . . .'

'Yeah, what? To split me and Olive up? To make everyone at my school hate me? Congratulations, you nearly succeeded.'

'No, Colin. I didn't want that.'

'Oh, no? So what did you want then?'

'I wanted to help you,' she blurts out. 'You kept saying you wanted to get away from that school and come home. And you promised, Colin! Every time we spoke. But then you said it less and less and . . . I thought if I didn't do anything, you might just forget about me.'

I want to keep cool, but I don't have a chance in hell as the tears stream down Cleo's cheeks. She buries her face in her hands and sobs her heart out.

My eyes well as I look at her, as I put my arms around her. 'How could you think anything as dumb as that?'

Cleo says nothing, but her sobs are answer enough. She digs her fingers into my sweater. I just keep holding her.

'You can't be angry with me. Please, Colin. What I did was wrong. It was really mean. I just thought if Olive knew everything and . . .'

'Dumped me, I'd come back?' I suggest.

Cleo's shoulders start to shake again.

'It was a big success, I'll give you that. Worked so well that everything got out of hand and I landed up in the goddamn hospital.'

Cleo's head jerks up at that. 'That was my fault?'

'Well, mainly mine, to be honest, but after Olive saw the screenshots, I started drinking.' Cleo opens her mouth but I cut her off. 'Now, listen here,' I say firmly. 'Sending her that stuff was a crappy thing to do, and I'm seriously pissed. Mainly because you can't seriously think I'd suddenly stop caring about you. That's not true. You're my sister. You're more important to me than anything. Got that?'

My voice catches, but only briefly. Then I've got it under control again. And I say it: 'I'm not coming back. I'm going to stay at Dunbridge Academy. It's the first place I've ever learned what friendship and love really mean. And I'd like you to experience that too.'

Cleo doesn't move. 'You mean . . .?'

'It was Olive's idea. She suggested that you could enrol too. I'll speak to Mom and Dad if you like the idea.'

'Going to boarding school in Scotland?' Cleo asks, and I hear the panic starting to build in her voice.

'Yeah, to Dunbridge Academy, with me.' It sounds way less scary that way. But apparently she disagrees, because her face stays sceptical. 'It's beautiful there and the people are really nice. I'd always be close by. You could see the out-of-tune piano for yourself, and I could play you your songs. No time difference, no FaceTime.'

It's too much for her. I can see it in her eyes, and I get that. 'Think about it, OK? How about that?'

Cleo nods, her lips pressed tightly together.

I keep looking at her. Then she shakes her head slightly and I pull her into my arms again. 'You're impossible, Cleo Fantino.'

She presses her head into my chest.

I shut my eyes. Maybe there is hope.

Maybe there's something better for her than life here. I'd never have believed it either until I went to Scotland.

Cleo seems a bit calmer when I eventually tell her I'm going to check on Olive. I want to ask her if she's in the mood to watch a movie with me and Cleo, but as I open the guest-room door, I see there's no point.

She's fallen asleep. Obviously. Olive's curled up on the bed and her face is relaxed.

She groans reluctantly as I lie down beside her.

'You look cute when you're asleep,' I whisper.

'Take that back,' she murmurs.

'No chance.' I have to smile. 'Olive, you have to wake up.'

'Can't . . .'

'If you go to sleep now, you'll be up at four in the morning again, babe.'

'Babe?' she repeats slowly, in her rough, sleepy voice. 'You're such a Yank.'

And she's such a Scot.

'Would "darling" be better?' I ask.

'Oh, my God.' She groans. 'Say it again.'

'No chance, Olive Garden,' I whisper into her ear.

She turns towards me. 'Please, Colin.'

'I want a nickname too.'

'You've got one, Cowboy.'

'I don't identify with that.'

'Your problem.'

'Come on.'

'Darling,' she says, shutting her eyes again. 'You can have that one.'

Darling . . . Darling, in that soft Scottish accent I'd die for.

I run my lips over the skin on the back of her neck. Olive's suppressed moan shoots straight between my legs. I'm so hard it hurts. I want to finally do it with her, but we're at my parents' place, besides which I'm scared I have too many complexes. I only have to think about what happened last time she undressed in front of me. And one thing's for sure, I can't lose my nerve at the sight of her naked again. Possibly she'd understand now, but I can't do that to her.

She's the woman of my dreams, I don't have to tell her so, but she's also a person with feelings, however much she likes to pretend that isn't true.

As she rolls towards me, my head stops thinking. I lean down to kiss her.

She puts her hand on my face and presses herself into my body. I wrap my arms around her waist and pull her onto me. Her breath catches, and then she starts to move. Rhythmically but tantalizingly slow. I feel like I could explode any second.

It takes a huge amount of self-control to twist back onto our sides. I press her gently onto her back, and then I'm over her.

Her dark hair is crazy, her lips are red and gorgeous. I kiss them, to make them more beautiful still. And then I run my mouth down her throat.

Olive leans her head back and turns slightly as I let my hips sink down onto her. She shuts her eyes and gasps my name. I feel dizzy.

She wraps her legs around my hips and lifts herself towards me. Her belly is warm as I slip my hand under her T-shirt. Just a tiny bit, to find out how she likes it. When the hand doesn't move, she opens her eyes.

'Don't grin like that,' she hisses, but her voice is shaking.

'Like what?' I ask, pushing my hand a little higher.

Whatever answer had been on the tip of her tongue, she seems to forget it as I reach her left breast. It's almost ridiculous how perfectly it fits into the palm of my hand.

My stomach muscles contract slightly as Olive stretches her back and pulls me closer by my T-shirt. There's too much fabric. Much too much. But before I can spin out that thought any further, I hear them. Voices – my mom's and then Cleo's – through the closed door. I feel like someone's tipped a bucket of icy water over me.

Olive looks like she's similarly sobered up when I meet her eyes. She lies motionless beneath me, listens, then shoves me off her.

I laugh quietly as she hastily pulls the covers over herself and lies on her side. 'Don't worry, they won't come in.'

'I'm glad you're so sure of that, Colin,' she mutters. She's still breathing hard. It's good to know that it was at least as unsatisfying for her as for me. Which isn't to say that it was bad. Just . . . too short.

We fall silent again, the voices fade. Then I hear the TV.

Olive sighs, half with frustration and half with tiredness. In my mind, I agree with her. I could never have imagined I'd be looking forward to getting back to boarding school this much. It's just as possible that we'd get caught there, but anything is better than risking it at home while my parents are sitting on the couch in the room next door.

Olive seems to feel the same.

'Hey,' I say hoarsely – she's shut her eyes again.

'What?' she mumbles. 'I'm still tired.'

'I thought I'd woken you up.'

'You wish, Fantino.'

'You might as well admit you didn't find it so bad yourself.'

'Hm,' she says, and no more.

'Livy . . .'

'Tori would have your head on a platter if she heard that name on your lips.'

'I'd like to see her try. And stay awake now. It's too early.'

'Just five minutes,' she mutters.

I can tell that she's really tired and I'd be lying if I said I wasn't feeling the same. This day has been too much. I mean, I've been to the police, had a fight with Mom and then with Cleo. My eyes rest on Olive's face and see it relax – she's beat.

You'll never adjust to the time here if you give in to the jetlag, I want to tell her, but then it occurs to me that we have no reason to adjust to New York time. Seriously, none at all. We'll be flying back to Edinburgh in a few days.

Olive sighs with relief as I put my arm around her and pull her close. Her head is resting in the crook of my arm – exactly where it belongs – and growing heavy.

'Tell me how you're doing,' she says, to my surprise.

I study her face and don't have to think long about it. 'Fine, now.'

'What did Cleo say?'

'She mainly cried and apologized.'

Olive blinks. 'So it was her?'

I nod but don't reply.

'Was she scared you wouldn't come back?'

I nod again. 'But we talked. She knows I'm staying. In Scotland,' I add hastily, as Olive opens her eyes again. She tries to play it cool, but then a blissful smile creeps over her face. She buries it in my neck.

'You're staying,' she repeats, sounding so happy.

Where else would I go? There's no point to a place if Olive isn't there. Obviously, I'd never tell her that. But I don't have to – I figure she's known for ages now.

'And I'll speak to my parents, ask if Cleo can come too.'

'Would she like that?' Olive puts her hand on my chest. She always does that. Her little hand with the delicate fingers that she runs an inch or so over my body. I'm lost. My heart beats faster.

'It was too much for her,' I say. 'Let's see what she says when she's had a while to think about it.'

'I like her. She's like you – like a cute version of you.'

'Hey,' I say.

'You're cute too, obviously. Not that you want to be, right?' she replies.

'Depends.'

'On what?' She's the devil and she's slowly running her hand from my chest to my belly. Below the bellybutton, things get critical. I have to stop myself taking her hand and leading it lower. Until I feel her around me, so that she can squeeze and whisper 'darling' until I explode.

'Are you hungry?' she asks.

Yeah, for you. I'd love to say that. But, of course, she really means do I feel low and need to eat. Since that whole hospital incident, I can feel her concern, and I hate that.

'No, you?'

Olive gives a tiny shake of her head. 'God, I'm tired.'

'Try to get some sleep,' I say, in a hoarse voice that betrays how much I want her. But she's too sleepy to notice, so I force myself to get a grip.

'Babe,' she whispers, imitating my accent. She giggles quietly to herself.

'Shut it, darling.'

She grins, and then I see the smile slowly fade from her face as she falls asleep.

37

OLIVE

It feels like we were in New York for way longer than a week when we leave the plane in Edinburgh. It's early morning, Dad's picking us up, and Colin's not entirely with it. If I hadn't known before, the weight that fell from his shoulders after his confession and conversation with his sister becomes clear when he fell asleep beside me within half an hour of take-off and didn't come round until our landing in Edinburgh. Colin still seems knackered, but relieved too.

We didn't go to his mum's gala, which created a fuss, obviously, but his dad pointed out that Colin is an adult now and can make his own decisions. Although I somehow doubt that he was including speaking to the police in that. On the other hand, he didn't tell him off when we finally saw him on my third day in New York. He seems much nicer than Ava

Fantino, but that doesn't change the fact that he also seems to live entirely for work, and isn't there for Cleo, or Colin. The day before our flight back, Colin had a chat with his parents about the idea of Cleo coming to Dunbridge too. To his surprise, it doesn't seem to have been a total disaster, but they haven't made up their minds yet.

I didn't wake Colin during the flight to remind him to check his blood sugar because I know the PIN to his phone so I did it for him. I still can't shake off the images of Colin and the paramedics in my room, which is possibly making me paranoid – after all, he wakes up by himself if he gets low and his body lets him know that he needs to eat. Better safe than sorry, though, in my opinion – I never want to go through a thing like that again.

Sometimes the fact that he's easily six foot two makes it hard to believe that anything could ever harm him. As he heaves our suitcases easily off the luggage carousel, or lugs them up the stairs in the east wing when we get back to school, I really can't imagine it. Obviously, I insisted I could carry my own stuff, but he just ignored me and walked off with both cases.

After a week of spending every night in the same bed, it seems positively silly to go our separate ways once we get to my floor.

It's less than half an hour before there's a knock on my door and Colin comes in. His hair is damp so, like me, he's had a shower, and as he pulls me close and kisses me, he smells like Heaven.

'How is it possible to create so much chaos in only thirty

minutes?' he asks in disbelief, as we step over the clothes and shoes covering the floor.

'*And* I had a shower too,' I point out, tapping the towel turban on my head. 'I bet you didn't achieve half as much in the time.' I'm very good at showering quickly. A remnant of my time as a swimmer. Which reminds me that I promised to help Ms Cox out with training again from tomorrow. I've had lots of conversations with Ms Vail about that. It's still painful that I can't swim yet, but it's doing me good to be in my familiar surroundings and to help the others improve. It's possible that I'm even looking forward to tomorrow's session. And as soon as it's been six months since the skin graft and I don't have to avoid chlorinated water any more, I'll get back into swimming. To be honest, I can hardly wait.

Colin tugs at the towel, which makes it come loose and slip off my head. 'Yeah, I can't compete with you there.' He catches the towel and strokes the wet hair back from my face.

'Want me to trash your room too?' I offer, batting my eyelashes at him.

'If you want to face Sinclair afterwards, be my guest.'

I roll my eyes as he hangs the damp towel neatly over the back of the chair. 'Ah, come on, he's total carnage.'

'Not compared to you, babe.'

Warmth floods my body because he's called me that again. I can't let on how much I like it, no way am I letting him know, but it's hard not to give the game away. Everything's hard when Colin is standing there. My breathing, for example, and a heavy heat fills my belly as he kisses me again. Possessive and urgent, with his tongue, which is driving me out of my mind.

'Is he back?' I gasp.

'Who?' Colin sounds kind of distracted. I love that.

'Sinclair.'

'Don't think so.'

'Tori's not either,' I remark.

Not many people are back yet. That's usually how it goes at the end of a short half-term holiday. Everyone wants to make the most of their free time. The school is deserted and quiet, and that won't change until everyone's around this evening.

So now we're alone. I know it. And Colin knows it too.

He makes a reluctant sound as I turn slightly away from him and look towards the door. It's unlikely that anyone will come in, but . . . should I lock it? Do I need to, for what we're going to do? Are we even going to do anything, or am I imagining the spark between us just now?

I must be imagining it. Hey, we only just got back from a very tiring trip. We should rest. But I don't want to rest. I want to touch Colin and be touched by him. And not gently.

God, I want to sleep with him. Not beside him, not in his arms. I want to feel him. I've wanted that for so long. I'm addicted to his company and his touch, and if I don't get more of it soon, I'm in danger of going insane.

But I'm not going to be the one to force anything. This thing between us will happen when he's ready.

And Colin's ready. He lets me feel that as he steps up behind me. Close behind me. So close that my bum is touching his crotch. He presses against me. Hard and unyielding, and I don't care that those two words mean much the same. My brain stopped functioning in the second that I realized he has a hard-on. Because of me. I feel kind of dizzy.

I want to turn around to him, but Colin's hands hold me tight. Then they stroke my hair over my shoulder and he presses his lips to my skin. I feel their heat on the back of my neck. As I rub myself slightly against him, he groans aloud. Colin leans my head back a wee bit.

This isn't a friendly or a fleeting touch. It's an exploration, tender but possessive. My knees soften, and I have to shut my eyes as he caresses my neck. His tongue slides over my hot skin and I burn up.

His voice in my ear is rough but strong. 'Want me to stop?'

'No.' It's hard, but I manage to keep my voice firm as I answer. 'I want . . . more. I want you.'

'And I want *you*,' he says, turning me to face him in one quick movement. 'You, Olive.' His hands hold faster to my hair, but when his lips find mine, they're gentle, only brushing against me.

I expected something different, and the softness of his kisses overwhelms me. My stomach clenches and I let my head sink back slightly. I melt in his hands. Colin sighs as if this is what he's been waiting for. My pulse is racing, my skin burning, as he slowly explores me with his mouth.

He presses me onto the chair, reaches into my hair again, rougher now. Only a wee bit, but I like it. The sweet pain as he pulls my head aside to make more room for himself. His hot breath on my sensitive skin, his large hand gliding over my collarbone to my breast. I whimper with longing as he takes it in his hand and strokes his thumb over it.

'Harder,' I breathe, and Colin obliges. He's doing it all at once. He's touching my body, he's kissing my neck, my jaw, my temples. The speed makes me dizzy; although I'm sitting down it feels more like I'm floating.

I lean into him, but Colin presses me against the chair back and steps in front of me.

'Shut your eyes,' he demands.

I don't want to at first, but when I do, the intensity of his touch hits me with an unexpected force. I can't see him, can't touch him. I can only squirm and hope he won't stop.

His kisses grow hungrier, more urgent, wetter. He runs his lips over my jaw and down my throat, where he finds a spot that makes everything within me contract.

I lift my chin and arch towards him because I need more of it. I get it when Colin's hand slips under my top. I'm not wearing a bra because I only just got out of the shower, and I feel his warmth directly on my skin.

'Undress me,' I whisper, my voice trembling.

I only realize what I just said when Colin hesitates. And I know what he's thinking about. What happened the first time I undressed in front of him.

Shit. I've fucked up. He's standing behind me, I can't see his face, but I feel his hand twitch on my breast. I hold it tight and turn towards him.

His perfect lips are slightly swollen, his sharp cheeks flushed. The lust hasn't disappeared from his eyes, but there's a hint of panic now too.

My knees are weak as I stand up.

'Undress me, Colin,' I repeat, not breaking eye contact with him. 'Please.'

He doesn't move. He's gone, the dominant male who presses me onto the chair and holds me there where he wants me, to kiss me. And I need him back, so I take a step towards him.

I lay my hand on his flat stomach. Colin's eyes darken, so I move it lower. Colin takes a deep breath and his abs tense. Then I pull the hand back and reach for the waistband of my leggings.

'Or would you rather we did it together?'

He pauses a moment. He gets it.

And then he nods.

COLIN

Stay calm.

Everything's fine.

You're not going to panic when she takes off her top. You're not going to mess up this time.

Kissing Olive is so good that I've forgotten everything. But now it's back. The feeling of paralysis that starts in my chest and works its way up through my tight throat into my head, but I'm not going to let it. I focus on Olive as she stands in front of me, looking me in the eyes as she slips off her leggings.

Her legs are long and slim. I want to know what it feels like when she wraps them around me to draw me closer, and then spreads them for me.

I've reached for my jeans without thinking about it. It just happens, and once I've unzipped the fly and pushed them down so that there's nothing but my black boxers, which can't contend with how hard I am, I feel vulnerable and powerful at the same time.

Why is it that wearing nothing but an outsized T-shirt makes women look so hot? By contrast, in my white T-shirt and underwear, I feel like an elementary-school kid at a slumber party. Olive begs to differ, though – she seems anything but amused by the sight of me.

'Come here,' she orders, and her voice trembles slightly. I do as she wants, no longer thinking. 'Sit on the bed,' she says, and my brain switches off completely. I had no idea that her bossing me around would turn me on. 'Now, look me in the eyes.'

For a brief moment, I'm scared she'll take off her T-shirt, and I feel like a failure. But she steps between my legs and forces me to lift my chin. Her thigh is only an inch from my erection and I fight back the urge to scooch forward and rub against her. And then I forget everything as she runs her cool hands over my forearms and under my sleeves. She's kissing me, more gently than before, almost soothingly.

My hands reach for her, I find her, hold her, pull her closer. We groan together as her hips meet my hard-on. There's much less annoying clothing between us than only a short while ago, and the idea that it could soon be gone entirely makes me feel nothing but a thrill of anticipation.

'Oh, shit.' She digs her fingers into my hair and moves her hips against me. 'Shit, Colin.'

Yeah, shit. I feel my balls clench and breathe in her sweet scent. Deeply. I need to taste her. Her mouth, her breasts, her belly, and the throbbing core that she's pressing against me. I have to, right now, or I'll die.

I lay my hands on her hips, ready to pull her to me, but Olive acts first. She leans over me with a hunger that makes me gasp as she kisses me.

She kisses me. She sets the pace, she knows what she wants, and I'd do anything to give it to her.

As she puts her hand around me, I get so hard it hurts. She's gentle, and then she isn't – a perfect mix that drives me insane. There are still these useless boxers between my skin and her skilful fingers, but I almost forget that as some kind of animal instinct comes over me and I thrust into her palm.

Olive smiles her impish smile, the one I'd die for. 'Patience, darling.'

She's got a nerve. And I'm all out of patience. I mean, all out.

'Olive.' I groan, and she moves back. I want to grab her and pull her to me, but she's already lowering herself onto me. And it's better than in my wildest dreams.

I have to throw back my head. Bite my lips and put my hands on her hips to guide her, as if the beat with which she's rubbing her pounding heat against me wasn't pure perfection already.

Her legs are left and right of me, her knees are bent, her thighs spread. I push up, against her, and Olive groans my name.

Enough is enough. I need her naked and beautiful beneath me. I shut my eyes as Olive runs both hands over my belly to my groin. Her hair's almost dry and tumbling in soft waves over her shoulders. And, God, she's the most beautiful person in the world. She's a work of art with challenging green eyes and a mouth that's red from kissing.

She slides her hands back up over my chest and leans over my face until her hair falls onto the pillow beside my head, like a curtain of black silk.

'Hi,' she whispers, as her face moves right over mine.

'Hi, Livy.'

'I'm going to undress now,' she says in her honey voice. 'Is that OK or will you freak out again?'

'I don't think so.' My voice is raw. 'But if I feel like it might happen, I'll let you know.'

'I'd be most grateful.'

I nod, because my mouth is suddenly too dry to speak. I lie under her and force myself to keep breathing normally as

Olive straightens up. And then she pulls the T-shirt over her head. One single, fluid movement, her curved hips, her soft skin. Her perfect breasts, which fit into my large hands and . . . I look at her. The scars that cross her shoulder are part of her, just like her little nose and her dark brown hair. My heart is beating fast, but it was doing that already.

Olive stays poised over me. I know that she's waiting for a reaction from me. The right reaction. I could say something, some dumb cliché, something that nobody needs to tell her. *You're beautiful*. Yes, she is, but right now it wouldn't be a compliment, just a desperate attempt to act like her body isn't marked. *You're beautiful even with those scars*. I'd never say that to her. I have to show her in my own way. So I get started.

She gets goosebumps as I lay both hands on her bare thighs and run them upwards. Until I can put them around her hips. A surprised squeak escapes her as I hurriedly turn on my side, pulling her with me. Until she's under me.

She's breathing hard, her chest rises, her lips are slightly parted. She looks at me and breathes faster still as I bring my lips down to her bare skin. She sighs and digs her fingers into my shoulders, so I keep going. I kiss her, lick her, with no hurry. I want her to enjoy it, and she does, as I explore my way from her belly button to her breast. Her legs tremble as I get there.

'Colin.' She sighs. I feel dizzy at the pleading note in her voice. I'm so hard as she writhes beneath me, making sounds that could bring me to a climax on their own. But I have to get myself together a bit.

I slow down as I run my tongue over her right breast. Up to her collarbone. And then I feel her tense, almost imperceptibly.

I lift my head and catch her eyes, scan her face, searching for the tiniest hint that this could be too much for her right now, but all I see are her widened pupils and the delicate flush to her cheeks. 'Tell me if I should stop.'

'Don't stop.' Her voice almost overwhelms me. 'Don't stop, Colin.'

She tightens her grip on my sides, so I don't stop. I close my eyes as I run my mouth over her shoulder. Not because I don't want to see it, but to feel her. Her scars, which are a bit smoother and firmer than the rest of her skin. I kiss every inch of her body and I take my time over it.

The sounds she's making are a mix of sobs and whimpers. They meet something deep down inside me, make me want to tell her things. Things that are true.

'Livy,' I whisper. Her hands feel for me. I look up.

'Please, Colin.' Her voice trembles, and whatever was holding me back, it now breaks.

I bend over her and kiss her. I press her into the mattress with my whole weight, carefully enough not to hurt her, but still letting her feel my body. She digs her hands into my hair and pulls me closer.

'Have sex with me, Livy,' I whisper to her. The shiver that runs through her body transfers to mine. She pauses to look at me, then one thing leads to another.

She rolls onto her side to fetch a condom, while I take off my boxer shorts. I feel her gaze as I hastily lower my basal rate.

'I'm just getting ready,' I explain. 'For the next hour, you can do whatever you want to me.'

Her eyes darken slightly. 'You always were too big for your boots, Colin Fantino.'

'Please.' I give an offended huff that she doesn't trust me to last very long, but I'm already fighting myself as she kneels over me and presses herself to me, almost before I've slipped on the condom.

'God, Livy . . .' My voice shakes, my balls contract as she sinks down onto me. And then I'm inside her. We're both holding our breath, then she inhales, I exhale, and then she tilts her hips and lets herself sink slightly deeper onto me. I can't hold out any longer and, at the same moment, I'm thrusting, not gently and carefully, but for real. She throws her head back, arches her spine and, Lord, it hits me. This isn't just sex, it's more than that. It's real, it's Livy's stunning body over mine, trembling and shaking, her perfect face, her closed eyes, her open cherry lips, and I have no chance. I'm lost as she runs both hands down my chest, throws back her hair and gasps with a sound that kills me.

My abs tense, I groan – I never normally groan, but with Livy everything's different. It's perfect. We speed up, harder, greedy and desperate. One thrust, one last thrust, her name, leaving my lips, and then I feel her twitch as she contracts around me.

Her body slumps onto mine and relaxes, just as mine does. She falls into my arms, I pull her to me, feel her heat, her breath, which is coming in gasps, and I'm proud that I did that. Me alone. And I want to do it for her countless more times.

'God, Colin,' she breathes, her cheek lying on my chest, once I've pulled out of her. 'Stop grinning like that.'

'Why?'

She lifts her head, but I've fucked all the strength out of her, so she has to sink down again right away.

'Didn't you like it?'

I feel the soft laugh that runs through her. 'I'm not answering that question.'

'No problem. Your body did it for you.'

She lifts her chin, and I lower mine, so that we can look at each other.

'There's no one like you.' Her voice is serious now. 'No one.'

And I understand. It's her version of *I love you*. I stroke her temple with my lips.

'Just don't say anything naff.'

I can't help grinning. 'Never, babe.'

She loves these nicknames, though she'd never admit it. Olive Garden, Livy, Henderson. I'll come up with more, no problem. Because we have time. We have so much time.

38

OLIVE

The scaffolding on the west wing comes down before the Christmas holidays. The first snowflakes are falling as we sixth-form girls pack our things and form little processions carrying them from the east back to the west. You can see our footprints back and forth across the snow-covered courtyard.

The west-wing staircase still smells of paint and fresh starts. I'd be lying if I said there was nothing nightmarish about climbing the stairs I last ran down in a panic, almost not making it out alive. But, fortunately, I don't have to do it on my own.

Colin's behind me, carrying a huge box full of my school stuff; he says nothing but doesn't take his eyes off me for a second. He'd notice if this was getting too much for me, I'm sure of that.

I'm waiting for it to happen, but even as we get closer to the lower sixth's floor, my heart doesn't start racing wildly. Not much has changed here, and it looks fundamentally the same as the boys' corridor in the east wing. The only difference is that we all have more space now that each year group has a floor of its own.

I got my old room back, because I asked if I could have it. It's a room full of memories, but no more than that. I'm no longer going to let my life be driven by fear.

Colin follows me in silence as I walk in, and I'm sure he knows what I'm thinking just now.

Here we are then, I should say. *Welcome!* But I can't speak. I put my bag of clothes on the floor and stop in the middle of the room.

Does it smell of smoke or am I only imagining it? Is my heart beating faster, or am I just out of breath from having heaved my stuff up three flights of stairs? I listen to my senses for a while, until I have no choice but to stop. Colin puts the box on my desk, turns to face me and takes me in his arms. Just like that.

He says nothing, just holds me tight. And I shut my eyes because I feel safe. I feel his heart beating against my cheek. I smell the scent of him. In my mind's eye, I see Colin Fantino standing in the semi-darkness by that trophy cabinet, raising his arm and saying, 'You need to break something or the anger's gonna break you,' before he put me back together again, piece by piece. Like I did for him.

'You OK?' he asks quietly, not looking at me.

I nod instinctively, because everything is OK when it's him asking me. He puts his hand on the back of my head and gently strokes my hair.

'The view from the east wing is way better.'

I laugh. 'Nope.'

'Whatever. Not that I care – I'm not usually interested in the view when I'm in a room with you.'

'Are we being naff again, Fantino?'

He nibbles gently on my good shoulder. 'No, just honest.'

'Stop it.' I giggle.

Colin raises his eyebrows. 'Was that a giggle? Did badass Olive Garden just giggle?'

'No, it was not.'

'Oh, it so was. Can you do it again?'

'No,' I say firmly.

Colin sighs. 'Fine, you asked for this.' And then he goes on the attack.

'Stop it,' I cry, gasping for breath, as the bastard actually tickles me.

'Not till you giggle again.'

'I'm . . . not . . . gonna . . . giggle.'

'Then I'm afraid I won't be able to stop.' He throws me onto the bed, and then he's on top of me. 'Just once,' he begs.

'No.'

'You're so boring, Livy.'

'And you're so *annoying*.'

He beams and then we freeze as the door flies open.

'Oh, no, I think I've gone blind!' Tori covers her eyes with her hands and stumbles backwards out onto the corridor.

'What's up?' Sinclair shoves past her. 'God, Victoria, you'd better just shut it.'

'Yeah, Victoria,' I repeat her name severely, trying to look unfazed as I sit up. 'D'you think it's fun for me to crash the two of you winching?'

'Yeah, so I get that now.' Tori grins. 'But, seriously, who even are you?' She turns to Sinclair. 'Can you see this too? They're smiling at each other and look besotted. Where are Olive and Colin, and what have you done with them?'

I roll my eyes at Colin.

'Your friends are seriously weird,' he remarks.

'They're your friends now too,' I point out.

'I didn't choose them,' he says.

'Bad luck.' Sinclair strolls into my room. 'Emma and Henry were talking about going into Edinburgh to the cinema. Want to join us?'

'Now?'

'Aye, there's a bus in half an hour. Grace and Gideon are coming too.'

I glance at Colin who just shrugs.

'OK, see you downstairs, then?' I ask.

Tori and Sinclair nod. 'I'm never walking in without knocking ever again,' I hear Tori say, as she shuts the door.

I have to smile.

COLIN

I don't remember much of the movie because I spent most of the time holding hands with Olive Henderson. Yeah, it's every bit as embarrassing as it sounds, but I stand by it. Besides, it's better than constantly thinking about whether I'll ever hear anything back from the police in New York. It bugs me, but all I can do is wait.

After the movie, we go for something to eat. All the Christmas lights are up as we walk back to the station through the old town of Edinburgh. I love it here. It feels like a giant version of Disneyworld, but no way can I say that aloud if I don't want Olive to call me Cowboy or refer to me as 'such a Yank' again.

It's true, though. There are these narrow, cobblestoned streets and tall, thin buildings, which are kind of magical. I wish I could show Cleo around here. She'd love it. I'd take her to London so she could see the phone box on her British boyband's album cover for real. The thought makes me smile.

I drop back slightly when my cell phone rings. Olive glances at me, but I gesture to her to go on with the others as I take the call. It's an unknown number.

'Hello?' I dig my free hand into my coat pocket and watch Olive link arms with Grace and Emma.

'Am I speaking with Colin Fantino?'

I stop. 'Yes, that's me,' I say.

442

'My name is Detective King. We spoke when you came to One Police Plaza in New York.'

'I remember.' It's amazing how calm I sound, even as my heart is pounding. Are these my last seconds of freedom? I'm suddenly not so sure that I really want to hear what he has to say.

'I'd like to bring you up to date with the investigation as it currently stands. We had another talk to the students you mentioned and confronted them with your statement. Two of them decided to correct their original statements and gave us a sequence of events that fits with your version, Colin.'

'What does that mean?'

'Trent Barlow is our current number-one suspect. The other students' statements suggest that he started the fire. He is choosing to remain silent.'

Olive has stopped and is walking back towards me. 'What's up?' she asks quietly, but I shake my head.

'OK,' I manage, though it sounds like a question.

'We would like to summon you for the trial so that you can repeat your statement under oath.'

I hesitate. 'OK, it's only . . . I don't know if you remember, but I go to school in Scotland.'

'It would be important for you to come back to New York for this,' says Detective King.

'When will the trial be?'

'Probably early in the new year. You'll receive an official

summons in the post. I just wanted to let you know in person first. It's very important that you testify in court, Colin.'

'I'm sure that can be arranged, Detective.'

'Thank you, Colin. The letter will tell you everything else you need to know. Thank you for your help.'

'No problem,' I mumble, before I say goodbye. Then I lower my phone.

'Who was that?' Olive looks at me. 'Colin?'

'Detective King, from the NYPD.'

'And?' Her eyes scan my face, searching for any sign of what this means for me.

'They think it was Trent.'

Olive hesitates. 'The guy with the sister . . . the one your mum . . .?'

'Yeah.' I force myself to breathe deeply. 'Sounds like Isaac and Jeremy testified against him. Maybe they panicked.'

'OK. That's good. That *is* good, right?'

'I think so.'

Olive nods encouragingly.

'I have to fly to New York to testify again. In court.'

'Will I come?' she asks, and I'm touched that that's her first thought. But I shake my head.

'I don't know when the trial will be yet. Detective King said probably early next year. I'll have to ask Mrs Sinclair if I can go as it's likely to be during school time.'

'OK. I'll ask too,' she says, right away. I have to smile. She's as stubborn as ever, which is why I love this woman.

'I can manage without you.'

She looks like she wants to argue, but then she just takes my hands. 'I know. But you don't have to manage on your own any more.'

It still feels risky to believe that, but I have hope these days. I have genuine hope.

'Are you guys coming or what?' Sinclair calls.

'Don't you start,' Olive yells back, and he laughs and sticks his middle finger up at her.

'Behave yourself,' Tori tells him. I can't help smiling.

'So the trial will be after the Christmas holidays,' Olive says, as we follow the others.

'Sounds like it.' Christmas holidays. It's hard to believe, but it won't be long now before the break, when I'll fly back to New York again. To my family. I don't know how to feel about that, but I'm ready to find out. 'And I'll be able to bring Cleo right back with me.'

'So that's settled?'

'Yeah.' I grin. 'She's starting in the second form in January.'

'Lucky thing. She's got so many Dunbridge years ahead of her.'

I can't help noticing Olive's eyes turn thoughtfully to her friends, who are a few paces ahead of us. Next summer they'll do their A levels and leave Dunbridge Academy.

'I wish I did too.' She smiles at me, equal parts sad and serene.

'We still have eighteen months,' I say.

'You've changed your tune, Fantino,' she teases.

'Oh, shut it, Ms I-Belong-in-the-Upper-Sixth-Really.'

'Gutting that my plan failed,' she says, not taking her eyes off me.

'Nightmare.'

'Well, you can't always get what you want, but whatever you get instead, you get it by the bucket.'

I laugh quietly. 'I'm exactly what you wanted. You were just too proud to admit it.'

'True.' She shrugs. 'And you know what you're talking about there, don't you?'

'I love your smart-ass mouth, Livy.'

'Hey, since when has he called her that?' Tori exclaims.

'Since he fell for me,' Olive replies, with an impish grin and a warning note in her voice. 'And he's never going to stop.'

'I obviously never stood a chance against the pair of you Scorpios,' she says, with a sigh.

'Don't be sad, Victoria,' I say, which makes Olive giggle. I don't need to mention how much that pleases me, do I?

'We have to hurry,' Henry says. 'If we miss the bus, we won't be back for wing time.'

'That would be a disaster, Henry,' says Grace. Their eyes meet, then Grace looks at the ground. I'm well aware there's a complicated history between them.

Olive told me that they were together for ages, before Henry fell in love with Emma. That must have been miserable for all three, but Grace seems to have found someone in

Gideon who gives her what Henry couldn't. But Olive is still worried about her friend.

I don't know exactly where things stand between Grace and Gideon, but I hope the two of them can have a fairytale ending too. Not that this is a happy ending between Olive and me. Happy, definitely, but this is not the end. Anything but.

Other things will come to an end, though. The time we still have with Olive's friends at Dunbridge. I'm sure she's thinking about that as we sprint for the bus, barely catching it, and all pile into seats at the back. Olive's gaze wanders from Emma and Henry to Tori and Sinclair, to Gideon and Grace. I don't like how expressionless her face is.

She doesn't look at me until I put my arm around her and give her a squeeze. 'How do you feel about them leaving soon?' I ask quietly. The others are deep in conversation and don't hear us.

Olive chews gently on her bottom lip before she answers. 'I'm trying not to think about it. But it's not exactly nice when I do.'

'I get that. Then you'll be stuck here with just me.'

'Shut it, Fantino,' she murmurs affectionately. I have to grin. 'It won't be just us anyway. Will and Kit will still be here, Elain, Theresa, the rest of the swimming squad. And your sister too soon.' She leans her head against the seat, then looks back at me. 'And I'm sick of fighting the whole time. I'm going to take things as they come.'

I merely nod in reply. In the past, I'd have rolled my eyes at

447

pearls of wisdom like that, but I really feel them now. Because I'm sick of it too. The world has proved that what's meant to be will be. Olive and me, for instance. I fought against it but had no chance, and now the thought of everyday life without her is unimaginable. I never thought I'd find anything like this when I got on that plane to Europe a few months ago. I thought my life had ended. But it turned out to be just the beginning.

Five Months Later

COLIN

The hundred-and-first anniversary of Dunbridge Academy is a month-long party. I'm glad it's taking place in June because it means Cleo can now be part of it all too.

Her first weeks of boarding school were hard. I can't count the number of times I comforted her because she was homesick and afraid of not making friends, but she's well settled in now. I feel proud seeing my kid sister in a bunch of second-formers, darting across the lawn or the inner courtyard, where tables, chairs and marquees have been set up.

She's a Dunbrigonian now, and looks sweet in her little uniform. That makes me proud too.

My parents as well. Yes, they're here. It's hard to believe, huh? But apparently even Ava Fantino considers the centenary enough reason to fly across the Pond and treat herself to a few days in Scotland. If I was bitter, I could think she's only made the trip for Cleo's sake. But I don't want to be bitter any more. Life's too short. I want to be happy, regardless of the actions of the people who brought me into this world. I'm still learning, but I'm putting in the effort. And that plays out in my moods, which are the most stable they've ever been.

Especially since the trial in New York, where Trent Barlow eventually confessed and was sentenced. I'm sorry for him, although I shouldn't be, seeing he started that fire. He put me through hell – almost six months of thinking I was to blame for someone's death. But I'm not. I wasn't mistaken when I thought the burning toilet tissue was out before I left the bathroom. It was Trent, who set the wastebasket on fire with the end of the cigarette that I lit for him.

He cried like a baby in court, so he clearly did feel some remorse. And luckily he was still a minor at the time, so he got off lightly. Even so, he still glared at me when I gave my evidence.

Meanwhile, Isaac and Jeremy came up after the trial and apologized to me. I had no trouble believing that Trent had pressured them into not saying anything. Which they didn't, not until they were questioned again after I went to the cops. I get that. But nobody has to live with a lie any more. I chose the truth, which feels liberating. I did the right thing. It was a hard road, but I walked it on my own.

No, that's not true. I walked it with Olive Henderson. The girl I've fallen madly in love with, even against my will.

She's beaming as she walks towards me, proudly waving a copy of the school newspaper. The centenary edition is a real bulky tome, full of class photos, interesting articles and anecdotes about people's time at Dunbridge. I've never seen Olive work as hard on anything as she has on her profiles of members of the various sports teams at the school. Her perfectionism made it a pretty stressful process, but I get that it's important to her. Now her name is there on several articles and photos. She picked Kit to interview from the tennis team, and I feel proud to be in the team photo that Olive took.

I belong here now. Seriously. And I don't want to change a thing. I've arrived here, and although the way time flies by sometimes makes me sad, I'm happy I got the chance to experience boarding-school life and the sense of community at this school.

It all goes so fast. The cricket match in the morning, the evening events at which Henry and Mrs Sinclair make touching speeches, the gala dinner, the performance by the school band, while everyone dances and parties in the courtyard, and the music echoes off the walls.

The first parents start to say their goodbyes as the younger forms are packed off to bed. Olive and I sat at the lower-sixth table at first, but once the formal part was over, we joined her buddies in the year above.

I know that Olive wants to make the most of what little time she has left with her friends. The upper sixth have been doing their A-level exams, and I can see that it's all a struggle for Olive. No wonder – she's spent several years thinking she was going to leave this school with Tori, Sinclair and the rest.

I'm sad they won't be around much longer too. After the girls moved back to the west wing, it felt weird not to have to share a room with Sinclair any longer. I'd never have thought I'd end up missing him, but here we are.

I've moved down a floor too, along with Will, Kit and the other lower-sixth boys. Otherwise, life goes on pretty much the same. I go to class, tennis practice, box with Kit and talk to Ms Vail. I'm doing well enough that our sessions are only every two weeks now. There came a point when I couldn't remember the last time I'd used the lighter. I know I'll have relapses, and I shouldn't get cocky, but the thought doesn't make me panic any more.

There's a peace within me that surprises even me. Peace of mind. Most of the time, anyway. It would be naïve to think all the bad times are in the past, but they're the exception now, not the rule.

I only laughed when my parents suggested that, now my name was clear, I could come back to New York. Nothing has changed in my relationship with them, but I realized that my anger wasn't doing any good. It just made me feel worse, so now I focus on the future and what I want to do next. I think about studying music therapy in England, especially now that Olive is talking about a journalism degree in London – I can genuinely picture us there.

Olive is emotional this evening, which I'm putting down to the general vibe. There's a relaxed, celebratory atmosphere, which must have been what it was like last summer, the day the fire broke out at the school.

Her friends seem to sense that too – soon after dinner, they suggest leaving the party and borrowing bikes from Mr Carpenter so we can cycle towards the coast. It's only a few miles and the country road that winds over the rolling hills from here to the sea is deserted at this time of the evening.

This is still Scotland after all, so I'm not surprised when it starts to drizzle soon after we reach the beach, but nobody cares. The sun set a few minutes ago, bathing the scene in an unreal light.

I have to smile as Tori spreads her arms and runs through the rain over the sand. Sinclair chases her, to catch her. In the past, I'd have thought running around on an empty beach with my friends was dumb, but somehow it suits the way I feel right now. Young, free, upbeat.

Emma and Henry sprint away too, but I have eyes only for Olive, whose dark hair is curling in the rain. Like it does when she's been swimming, which she recently started again. We'll all be soaked in a few minutes. But she's laughing. She takes my hand and pulls me along.

And I follow.

I'd follow her anywhere, anytime. There's no question of that.

I don't know what's going to happen, but I'm not afraid.

I look at her, I watch Olive, and I have one thought. A single word. I think *home*.

OLIVE

The Dunbridge centenary celebrations feel like a fever dream. More than once during the jam-packed day, my thoughts stray back to the Ebrington festival last year. It's no secret that that's making me tense. I know it's irrational because this evening has nothing to do with last summer. But I can't stop my eyes roaming over to the west wing. Even so, I don't freak out.

That's not least down to my friends, who are keeping an eye on me today. It's a nice feeling, but it's making me sentimental too, because I just can't forget that we've only got a few weeks until they leave. Henry has an offer from St Andrews to study English, and Emma's planning to do sports science there too in the autumn. So they're not going to be a million miles away. Unlike Tori and Sinclair, who are heading off to London. Seriously. It might not be what they were originally planning but, to nobody's surprise, they got places at RADA. They are reprising last year's roles in the school play. I can hardly wait to see them on stage as Romeo and Juliet again. And eventually on the biggest stages in the country.

Tori cried when she told me she's not going to St Andrews with Emma and Henry. And I cried too, because London is over five hours away by train, which makes it hard to pop down for a visit. Hard, but not impossible, and Tori and Sinclair insist that their doors will always be open.

There's no denying I'll miss them. Gideon and Grace are going to Cambridge. Or so I thought. During the cricket match this morning – a friendly between the current senior team and one made up of old Dunbrigonians and staff – I can't help noticing that Grace keeps glancing my way. After victory for the senior team, she doesn't run down the stand to hug Gideon, she comes over and asks if we can talk.

Despite the spring weather, Grace is wearing her school jumper with her pleated skirt, as if the clothes could hide that, with impending A levels, she's lost even more weight.

'I have to tell you something,' she says, once we've put the pitch behind us, breaking a silence I couldn't bear. 'I'm not going to Cambridge right away.'

'What?' I only realize I've stood still when Grace does too. 'Seriously?'

She nods.

'But . . . why? You've put so much work into getting the grades for law.'

'I know.' She swallows hard. 'But I'm going to a clinic first. I'm on a waiting list and I'm hoping for a place in the summer.' Her voice shakes, and Grace isn't meeting my eyes.

'To a clinic?' I repeat. 'An eating disorder . . .?'

Grace nods and I feel pure relief. 'That's good. That *is* good, right?'

She's scared. I can see it in her eyes. 'I hope so.'

'It's definitely good,' I insist.

'It kind of just happened,' she says. 'Henry suddenly turned up on our doorstep, for the first time in ages. He said he couldn't stand by and watch what was going on any longer and he offered to make an appointment with Ms Vail for me, to get in touch with clinics, and to get Gideon on board if I didn't want to go to things alone. I was raging at first, with him interfering like that, but then . . . we both cried, and he helped me write some emails and phone people. And you know how persuasive he can be.'

I also know that Henry Bennington wouldn't stick his nose into other people's business lightly. Just like I know that he never wanted to hurt Grace, and that he still loves her even though his heart belongs to Emma now. And what he's done for Grace proves that it's in the right place.

'So, what's the thinking on all this?' I ask cautiously.

Grace tries to smile but fails miserably. 'I think I'm scared,' she says in the end. 'But it's probably the right thing.'

When I hug her, I can't help but agree – I feel her bony shoulders under my hands, despite all the clothing. 'You're so important to me, Gracie,' I whisper, and I hear the muffled sob that escapes her. 'To all of us. And my wish for you is that you'll matter enough to yourself to be able to stop this.'

I know perfectly well that it's not as easy as all that, but this is a first step in the right direction after so many months when I've been – to put it mildly – at my wit's end with

Grace. Growing up is painful in so many ways and realizing that you can't save people is hard. But if there's one thing I've learned in the last few years, it's that Grace has the strength to save herself. And we'll be there to support her if she wants us to.

'Hey!' We whirl around as we hear Gideon's voice, calling us from the sports ground. He's wearing a grass-stained cricket jumper and a beaming smile that's all for her. 'We won!'

'Of course you did.' Grace squeals in surprise as he puts his arms around her and lifts her off her feet. 'I said you would from the start.'

Once I've congratulated Gideon on the victory, I follow them back, and find Colin in the stands with Kit and Will as the whole school cheers the cricket team.

Colin immediately twigs that something's wrong, so I whisper to him some of what Grace told me. I'm glad she's finally ready to get help, but it doesn't change the fact that she'll soon be gone, like the rest of my friends. However much that hurts, I feel sure it'll be good for Grace to get a fresh start in a new place. Or I hope it will.

After dinner, the others suggest ditching the party and cycling to the beach. I look around for Dad. He's here with Nathalie, and I'm OK with that. They asked me if I'd mind. And I didn't, because I have to admit that Nathalie's pretty nice. We've met a few times since our first dinner together back in the winter. She makes my dad happy, that's obvious, even now as she stands beside him in a little group of staff, chatting with Mrs Sinclair.

Mum didn't come, and that's OK too. She and Alexis moved in together to a flat in Edinburgh a couple of weeks ago. I haven't been there yet, but I think I'll be up to it soon. I met him over a meal in the new year, and I was surprised by how much I liked him.

'Are you OK?' Colin asks, as we slip away with the others and walk through the arcades. We'd already changed out of our uniform into more comfortable clothes after the official celebrations were over.

'Yes,' I say. And it's true, even though today also showed me that everything's changed – or is about to change. 'Are you?'

He smiles. 'I'm in love with you, Olive.'

'That doesn't answer my question.'

'Don't you think?'

'No.'

'Shame.' He grins and presses a kiss on my nose, then pulls me on.

Not so long ago, I'd never have believed it. That Colin Fantino would be walking cheerily through the school with me and my pals. But I wouldn't have believed a lot of things. That I could have forgiven him for keeping such a major secret from me, even though I now get why he did that. I'm relieved that the trial in New York really did clear his name. You could see what a weight it was off Colin's shoulders not to be to blame for the accident. There's still nobody to blame for the fire at Dunbridge either, but I've learned I don't need that to heal. I only need myself. And Colin.

He's with me as we reach the sea in the last of the evening light, and he's with me when it starts to rain. Tori shrieks as she runs over the sand and Sinclair puts his arms around her from behind. He picks her up and whirls around, spinning one-eighty with her, which is kind of cute. Colin would never do such a thing. Or so I thought when he started here as such an incredible arsehole. He's not that guy any more. He's broken down his protective walls. Now he's soft and vulnerable, but still the strongest person I've ever met. I can't stop watching him, and I don't have to.

I'm still watching him when we gather wood for a little fire in the sand, once the shower has stopped.

'Promise me you'll be back,' I say, as the wood crackles and we sit around the fire. I can do this. I can feel the warmth of the flames and I don't want to run away. I'm here. This is OK. 'At least to visit.'

'Of course we'll be back,' Tori says. Sinclair nods in agreement.

'Dunbridge Academy will always be home,' Henry whispers. I can hear in his voice how hard he'll find it to leave this place soon. But I know he'll be back. I'm more certain of him than anyone else. And he'll be the best bloody teacher this place ever had.

'I never imagined that I'd experience anything like this

with you all,' Emma says thoughtfully. I feel for Colin's hand as Henry pulls Emma close.

And I'd never have thought we'd be sitting in this combination. Just now, it feels like the only possible outcome of everything this school year has thrown at us. Nothing was the way I expected, and I guess that's life, but it doesn't scare me any more.

Sinclair throws more wood on the fire; I watch the sparks dancing up into the dark sky and feel Colin's eyes on me. He nods enquiringly at me, as I look at him. And I smile, then rest my head on his shoulder.

It's one of the first mild nights of the year and I'm looking forward to these last days of term with him and my friends. But I'm looking forward to the autumn too. To next year. To the upper sixth, to everything that comes after that.

There's something inside me again, I can feel it. A spark that went out all those months ago. I'm me again, even though the old Olive doesn't exist any more. I like the new version, maybe even more, because she can be both strong and weak at the same time. That isn't a contradiction in terms any more: it's something urgent and necessary. Colin taught me that with every day he challenged me and drove me mad, before he was there to hold me together when I was convinced everything was breaking apart. With every day, all the time. And every time I look at him, I know it. I've come home.

Thanks

To my team at the erzähl:perspective literary agency, Michaela and Klaus Gröner for your support, it's wonderful working with you, and not just on this project; and thank you, of course, for my new favourite cheese! Thank you for always having a solution to every problem, and for always being there for me.

My thanks to the whole team at LYX, especially my new editor Alexandra, who has been there for me through thick and thin on my travels to Dunbridge Academy. I've never felt as free yet secure in my writing as with you. Thank you for taking such good care of me and always being on the spot when I need you. I'm very proud of what we've created.

Many thanks to Susanne George for her eagle eyes on *Anytime* and for bringing the best out of the text.

Thank you, Stephanie Bubley, Ruza Kelava and Simon Decot for letting me tell the stories I always wanted to tell. Your trust means the world to me.

I would like to thank my beta- and sensitivity readers, Julia, Jule, Evi and Anni, for their feedback, which is always valuable and constructive, and always makes my books better. This time, I'd particularly like to thank Annika S and Eva J for their help and for talking about *Anytime* with me. You are so strong and I thank you with all my heart for trusting me.

My friends Gaby, Rebekka, Anni, Leo, Anna, Lena and Merit for moral support when writing books, and in life in general.

My family, who always remind me to take pride in myself.

To all the booksellers and trainees who championed *Dunbridge Academy* – I'm still speechless.

To my readers: I thank you from the bottom of my heart for making Dunbridge a place where everyone can feel at home – that will always be true, whatever happens next. There were days from the initial idea to the final sentence when the doubts were deafening. Thank you for your messages – they all helped remove those doubts and encourage me to keep going. Writing books for you will always be my favourite thing in the whole world. It means everything to me that I can carry on doing that on your behalf.

Translator's Thanks

Huge thanks go to Chloe Mitchell and Ciara Bowen for their invaluable help, yet again, in keeping the Scottish characters sounding Scottish. In this visit to Dunbridge, I also needed a New York correspondent so my thanks here are due to Tim Mohr, and to Katy Derbyshire for putting us in touch.

I've learned a lot about type 1 diabetes through Colin's story and I'm very grateful to Tina and Molly, Susan and Nate for answering my questions about living with and managing the condition and helping me get my head around its jargon.

Thank you again to Stef Bierwerth and everyone at Quercus for all their hard work making these books look and sound their best in English.

And finally the hugest of thanks and love to Dave, Ben and Simon for everything.

Rachel Ward, MA, MITI, lives in Wymondham, near Norwich, UK, and has been working as a freelance literary and creative translator from German and French to English since gaining her MA in Literary Translation from the University of East Anglia in 2002. She specialises in translation for children and young adults, as well as in crime fiction and other contemporary literature. She can be found on social media as variations on @FwdTranslations and @racheltranslates.

Trigger Warnings

(And spoiler warning!)

This book contains potentially triggering content.

This includes:

Self-harming behaviour, post-traumatic stress disorder,
divorce, eating disorders and chronic illness.

Please read this book only if you currently feel emotionally
able to. If you are struggling with these (or other) issues,
free and anonymous help is always available from MIND
(www.mind.org.uk) and Samaritans (www.samaritans.org).